HERE'S SOME OF WHAT IS BEING SAID ABOUT "…FAKE NEWS!"

"The best way to lie is to tell the truth . . . carefully edited truth." – *Anonymous*

"This is the best book I have ever read!" – *William Shakespeare*

"There is nothing to fear but fear itself and some of the Fake News that is floating around, ask Eleanor." – *Former President Franklin Delano Roosevelt*

"Fake News? Who Knew!" – *Sen. Chuck Schumer*

"Bible, move over. Now there's Absolutely, Positively, Genuine, Real Fake News!" – *Karl Marx*

"Change means movement. Movement means friction. Only in the frictionless vacuum of a nonexistent abstract world can movement or change occur without that abrasive friction of conflict. Since I've read I Fake News I now see that my ideas in 'Rules for Radicals' are bullsh*t – *Saul Alinsky*

"This book is so good I feel like crying" – *Harvey Weinstein*

"The rumor that I am Trump's love child is Fake News...I look nothing like Trump!" – *Vladimir Putin*

"I can't believe how many people lie! Finally, a book that puts undisputed truth above personal bias...I applaud Fake News" – *Peter Strzok*

"I love that you can email the Fake News book to me and I can read it on my computer. This is very convenient as it is difficult for me to stay awake." – *Hillary Clinton*

"I've been to all 57 states including Guam and Puerto Rico on the Intercontinental Railroad and as far as I can see; there is very little Fake News except for what is in this book." – *Former President Barack Hussein Obama*

"We admit that men menstruate too, especially us. Now, that's Fake News!!!" – *Bill Maher, Alec Baldwin and Stephen Colbert*

"The truth is that Fake News has been the bulwark of our case against Trump. Russia is only a ploy to take us off our game. I will continue to use Fake News without fear of retribution. By the way I need another 56 attorneys to look into this." – *Robert Mueller, Special Counsel*

"Fake News! Ha, these guys don't know what real fake news is! I practically invented it!" – *Former Senator Harry Reid*

ABSOLUTELY POSITIVELY GENUINE REAL FAKE NEWS

FIRST EDITION

A Jaunty Romp through the Deep State, Media-Industrial Complex and the Progressive Mind

CONSIDERED, EXPERIENCED AND ELUCIDATED BY

SIR TELSUNN MARGRAVES

AS TOLD BY MICHAEL MEDICO

ISBN-13: 978-0-692-16209-5

DEDICATION

To President Donald J. Trump

And

To all the reporters, editors, newswomen, newsmen, anchors,

commentators, actors, actresses,

News media support staff, numerous radio, TV, podcast hosts and

hostesses, Rush Limbaugh, Barack Obama,

Nancy Pelosi, Maxine Watters, late night liberal talk-show hosts, Sean

Hannity, all conservative talk-radio, the DNC, politicians, Russians, Special

Counsel Mueller and 13 Democrats on the Special Investigators team,

And

Chuck Schumer, Maxine Waters, Nancy Pelosi, citizens of all political

stripes, academics, snowflakes, protestors, Henny Youngman, orphans,

former FBI Directors, Associate Supreme Court Justices, swimsuit models,

hip-hop artists, gansta' rappers, Kim Jong Un, pseudo-intellectuals and

anyone and everyone who makes Fake News what it is today!

CONTENTS

INTRODUCTION

You may say to yourself, "Who the hell is Telsunn Margraves?" and that would be a good question. "Who the hell is Telsunn Margraves?" Well I'm he and I've enjoyed being me for quite some time. My life's experience is what formed my perspective and thoughts on the many happenings that I've been able to discover since leaving the United Kingdom and settling in the colonies more than thirty years prior.

I must say to all of you readers out there, this is quite a remarkable country you have. When I arrived from the UK my first impression was the sheer magnitude of so many things in America: billionaires-per-capita, super highways, Beanie Babies, buildings, cars, food portions and much more. It is a veritable wonderland where you are able to procure anything you want at any time you want it; from Ethiopian food to stores that sell only buttons...just remarkable!

When I undertook the challenge of considering fake news, I discovered that "Fake News" is actually a wonderful thing in that it allows for so many appealing possibilities to contemplate. All fake news needs to have is some element of truth in order for it to reverberate with viewers and readers in any format consumers consume news. For example, there *is* a James Comey, he *is* a former director of the FBI; there *is* a Justice Ruth Bader Ginsburg, she *is* a current justice of the United States Supreme Court; both persons work out of Washington, DC; sexual harassment exists and used cars are sold via classified ads all the time. That seems pretty ordinary when considered as separate items, but when you combine them in a single news item you get *"Former FBI Director Comey Accuses Justice Ruth Bader Ginsburg of Sexual Harassment!"* See...simple, quick, easy, hard-to-prove and hard-to-disprove and the prospect that it could be true makes the possibility even more compelling; even scintillating.

Another question you may ask yourself, "How the hell does he get into all these places?" and that is also a good question! "How the hell do I get into all these places?" Well, to tell the truth, there are many times I am just part of the audience, large or small, that gather at these events. Take the presser where the Clooney's came back to the US and are met by adoring throngs. The power couple came back to the United States to ostensibly announce the opening of the *George and Amal Clooney Beverly Hills Muslim Outreach Center.* I use opportunities like these to expand on my ruminations so that you may consider my experiences as your own. Another of my favorite episodes is when *Chelsea Handler launches the*

"I Hate Trump Fan Club" and a stellar event it was. The "I Hate Trump Fan Club" Advisory Board is comprised of so many women who have such little regard for the President that it makes for an excellent example of what you Americans may call a study in cohesive and collective thought.

There are, however, times that I need to be surreptitious in observing certain news worthy events. You need not go any further than when I witnessed the ceremony at which North Korean Supreme Leader *Kim Jong Un and actress Madeleine LeBeau Wed.* It was a super-secret ceremony that was held in Pyongyang, NK and I was joined by more than one million guests. I was compelled to disguise myself as a leper and I must admit this was a creative way to attend the wedding and have enough room around me so that I was comfortable.

I was also able to follow John Oliver as he taped his soon-to-be-released HBO documentary *The Snowflake Lounge.* In compiling my astute observations, I was able to go unnoticed by merely dressing up like one of the many students that occupy the 60,000 square feet of safe space that can be found on the campus of the University of California at Berkeley. It is comforting to note that a new additional 150,000 square foot wing of safe space will soon to be added. This surreptitious observation is a sobering look at a situation that evokes a kind of perverse need to understand the way the snowflake mind works.

I even used my credentials to be one of two reporters at a hastily called press conference at which time Bill Nye, *The Science Guy Blames Man-made Global Warming for drastic drop of UFO Sightings.*

There is so much to consider that it virtually boggles the mind; Google discovering that men menstruate, a shadow government being formed in Barack Obama's basement, Colin Kaepernick signing with the NFL, European Union campaign for wearing a burka to work, a startling comparison of President Trump to various diseases, banning bananas and their peels on college campus', how Democrats hope to market the 'Better Deal' to the voting public, the very sinister Trump-Limbaugh Barbeque and so much more!

Absolutely, Positively, Genuine, Real Fake News is a jaunty romp through the absurdity of the Deep State, Media-Industrial Complex and the Progressive Mind. It is written as my tribute to America. I marvel at the fact that even when the various media sources report fake news they do it in a truly magnificent style. The mainstream of news networks, entertainment venues, online blogs, prestigious newspapers and other media have seemingly turned a blind eye toward the curiosity for truth that had been purported to be their hallmark. Now it seems that lock step uniformity and common purpose, guides so much of what is thought, written, reported and accepted by the fifth estate. Whether there is a story about destroyed emails or Russian collusion, real or imagined, sourced or unsourced, founded or unfounded, that does not deter the ever powerful cannons of the major mainstream news outlets from using the American media consumers as fodder...truly magnificent. *TM*

SAMANTHA BEE INTERVIEWS THE CLINTONS

As, Sir Telsunn sat in the audience, he pondered what a Hillary Clinton presidency would be like. Sir Telsunn is always cautious in keeping his identity cleverly hidden so no one will know that he is chronicling these many fake news events. This occasion was especially revealing as Ms. Samantha Bee was brave enough to confront Mrs. Clinton with hard-hitting and probing questions. As you might have guessed, former President Bill Clinton does not disappoint, so please enjoy your front row seat at this informative interview.

Las Vegas NV – The auditorium is filled to capacity and everyone in attendance is excited and can't wait to hear the former President, William Jefferson Clinton, and the former Secretary of State and Presidential candidate Hillary Rodham Clinton expound on many things including the 2016 Election.

This will be only the 43rd interview that the Clinton's have done since Secretary Clinton's tragic defeat at the polls on Tuesday November 8th 2016. Enormous disappointment and suicidal tendencies still run deep among aggrieved loyalists in what is defined as the greatest loss this country has experienced since the death of Teddy Kennedy and the cancellation of "West Wing." The lights slowly dim as the audience takes their seats in eager anticipation of what is yet to come. The stage is sparsely set with three comfortable looking chairs, each lit in a dramatic way with spotlights, kind of like the ones that they featured at the end of the old Jimmy Durante show.

Somewhere off stage a voice booms as the crowd is hushed and silence finally reigns. The announcer makes the introduction to the crowd, "Ladies and gentlemen, we are pleased to announce the latest in the series of in-depth interviews with the best and brightest political minds in America today. Our host presenter is Samantha Bee. Ms. Bee is a senior Fellow at the Chelsea Handler Progressive School of Holding Your Breath Until Your Face Turns Blue. This exclusive interview is being taped for Samantha Bee's popular late-night television show "Full Frontal" which is seen on cable in over 50,000 homes across New York City and San Francisco. And now, here is the moment we've all been waiting for; here is Samantha!!!!!"

The audience bursts into unrestrained cheers, raucous cat-calls and the clapping of hands and feet. Samantha is reveling in the crowd's adoration as she tries to shout above the thunderous applause, "Thank you ladies and gentlemen, thank you so much!" but the crowd will not be mollified. "Thank you, thank you so much!" Finally the crowd settles down in eager anticipation of what is to come.

"Ladies, gentlemen, Hindus, Muslims, Buddhists, Jews, Christians, Pagans, Agnostics, Atheists, Secular Humanists, African-Americans, Latinos, Multi-Racial, Native-Americans, members of the LBGTQIA communities, those questioning, Androgynists, Eunuchs, Transvestites, Pan-Attractional, people with Nazi hair, white descendants of slave owners...let me see, have I forgotten anyone?" Someone from the audience angrily yells out, "What about the Otherkin community?" Samantha realizes her major faux pas and apologizes. "I am so sorry that I forgot to include the very special souls who identify as Otherkin. Please accept my heartfelt apology." The audience seems to be in a forgiving mood and responds with a smattering of polite applause.

"Before we start, and in honor of Colin Kaepernick, I want to encourage you to sit down as we don't sing the Star Spangled Banner and don't say the Pledge of Allegiance." Dutifully, the entire audience sits in silence until the requisite time has passed. Samantha has been checking her notes during the non-playing of the National Anthem and non-recital of the Pledge of Allegiance and looks up when it's over.

"Tonight is a very special night. Tonight we are privileged to be able to conduct an in-depth, one-on-one discussion with former Secretary of State, Hillary Rodham Clinton and former President, William Jefferson Clinton. Now I am enormously proud to introduce to you, here tonight, the afore-mentioned HILLARY AND BILL CLINTON!" The crowd erupts in a deafening cacophony of noises to express their adoration for the pair. The couple waves to the audience as they walk hand in hand onto the stage. It takes at least three minutes for the auditorium to settle down and both President and Mrs. Clinton stop waving to the crowd as they take their seats.

"Mr. President and Madam Secretary I can't begin to tell you what an honor... that I am completely, I mean, wow, what an honor", Samantha is gushing with praise.

Bill Clinton, to make her feel more comfortable says, "Hey Samantha, you're looking pretty good yourself."

"Well, thank you Mr. President." Turning to Hillary, Samantha continues gushing, "Mrs. Clinton I am thrilled to have you here tonight. You have long been a hero of mine and to have this opportunity to speak with you is a life-long dream fulfilled!" Hillary is glaring at Bill who is smiling at Samantha. She turns to face her interviewer and icily replies, "The honor is all mine."

"If you don't mind, I would like to begin with a question for you, Mrs. Clinton. I am a known for my hard hitting questions, so I want this to be a no-holds barred, give and take session."

Hillary nervously responds, "Go ahead, I'm ready."

Samantha begins, "As secretary of State you expertly dealt with so many life and death situations like the attack by peace loving Muslims in Benghazi and all because of a racist movie. You have said that both you and President Obama took this so seriously that golf games were cancelled, dinners postponed; you even missed your Pilates class. Tell me, and you can be frank, do they serve popcorn or Milk Duds® at these types of briefings or is it all business?"

"Well, as much as President Obama loves Milk Dud® at all of his meetings, we did manage to serve both popcorn and Skittles® along with the Milk Duds®. The president is a very thoughtful man and he understands the need to satisfy the many diverse tastes that abound in his administration."

You can tell that Samantha is having a tough time being objective, but there seems to be some skepticism on her part so she continues, "Thank you for that frank and honest answer but I need to ask a follow up, Mrs. Clinton. You are known for having logged the most miles of any Secretary of State having continuously visiting countries around the world with the commitment of finding ways for all humanity to exist in peace. I need to ask, what is your favorite food among all the countries you have visited?"

Hillary relaxes a bit and answers, "Well Samantha, you can imagine how difficult it must be for me to choose one food among the many regional and national cuisines I have eaten over the years so may I give you my top three?"

Samantha quickly interjects, "We don't mean for you to betray any confidence but the audience is anxious for the truthful answers behind these questions."

"Well, here are my top three favorite foods. When I dined with Vlad, I enjoyed the traditional Russian favorite; stuffed Kalduny dumplings. At a state dinner with the now deceased but lovable Abdullah bin Abdulaziz Al Saud, I ate a delicious Quzi also called Qoozi or Ghozi. Another of my very favorite foods is an Indonesian favorite that I had when I met with the Putera Sampoerna called Bebek Goreng...spicy but nicey!" Now the audience laughs uproariously at the play on words and that makes Hillary smile.

Samantha joins in the laughter and then turns to Bill Clinton, "Mr. President, I don't mean to ignore you but I am fascinated by the insights into your wife's storied career."

"Oh Samantha, don't worry about that. I'm sure we can find a way for you to make it up to me", and he and Samantha seem to have a moment. Bill Clinton continues saying, "You know, I'd love to give you a personal tour of the Clinton Library…" Samantha and Bill Clinton stop when they realize that they are in front of a thousand people.

Hillary is now becoming incensed and demands, "Don't you have better things to discuss than this Bill?"

The former President Clinton smiles at Hillary and says, "Of course I do" and he winks at Samantha.

Samantha is a bit confused and she wants to get the interview back on track so she asks Hillary her next question. "Mrs. Clinton, we all know of the awful treatment you have had to endure over your career: the failed Hillary-care program during your husband's administration, the unsubstantiated, never proven, well, except for one or four incidents of so-called sexual abuse committed by your husband, plus the deleted emails, the investigations, and unfounded accusations of a poorly run campaign and your personal lack of any likable qualities. I could go on and on, but through it all you still are able to maintain that air of dignified ignorance. My question is, were you ever able to get over the fact Sir Edmund Hillary used your name and never once thanked you?"

"Samantha, honestly that is too painful for me to even talk about it but I will say that is the one thing that has left a permanent stain on my soul." Hillary seems to have aged 20 years and just slumps back in her chair.

Samantha is at a loss as what to say next when she notices that Mrs. Clinton seems unresponsive. She reaches over and gently pats her hand, "Mrs. Clinton? Mrs. Clinton? Are you alright?" Not knowing what to do next she turns to Bill Clinton in bewilderment. "Mr. President, something seems very wrong with Mrs. Clinton."

Bill Clinton just smiles and knowingly shakes his head and turns to Samantha and tells her she's doing it all wrong and explains, "Don't worry, this happens all the time; this is how you do it." He gets up from his chair and grabs his wife by the shoulders and violently shakes her saying, "Hillary, wake up! Come on honey, wake up." He feels he owes Samantha an explanation so he says, "She's still trying to catch up on her sleep since the campaign." He turns back to Hillary and says, "Come on honey bunny, open those baby blues."

Slowly but surely Hillary opens her eyes and sits up straight in the chair. She looks around not seeming to know where she is but suddenly realizes that there is a large audience that has become strangely silent. Feeling that she needs to explain, Hillary says, "I am so sorry for that momentary blackout. Bill and I were up late planning Aidan's Bar Mitzvah and I didn't get to sleep until almost 7:30PM."

Samantha breathes a sigh of relief and asks, "How are your adorable grandkids?" Bill Clinton jumps in and answers, "You know they are just the most beautiful things in the world. I can't stop talking about them, I can go on for hours, just ask Loretta Lynch. I remember that we talked and talked and the time just flew by. We could have spoken even longer but her plane had to take off."

Samantha Bee is mesmerized by Bill's devotion to his grandkids and the twinkle in his eye. She is just staring at him and he seems to notice and winks at her. Samantha Bee's face turns red as she snaps out of her spellbound state and stammers, "Well ladies and gentlemen and all the other groups mentioned earlier, let's keep the excitement going. Mrs. Clinton, I'd like to change the subject from world affairs to domestic politics, if that's alright with you?"

"Of course it is, go ahead." Mrs. Clinton has become used to having to deal with her defeat at the polls on Election Day, so she is prepared for any and all questions. Samantha thinks to herself, "What a brave woman she is!"

Samantha asks, "Mrs. Clinton, it has been reported that you practiced and practiced for the three debates you had with your opponents. Key staff like Huma, Robbie, John and your whole team spent countless hours coaching and preparing you for what was the most viewed series of debates for the presidency in history. Tell me, did they also choose the lovely clothes and pantsuits you wore or did you choose them yourself?"

Hillary wants to appear thoughtful in her response so she tells Samantha, "Well, when I attended Wellesley College I took an elective course in home-making. Part of the course curriculum taught the basics on how to make your own clothes and..." but Samantha is incredulous at this revelation and interrupts,

"Don't tell me you made your own clothes for the debates?!"

"Hillary smiles, "Yes I did!"

Now Samantha can hardly contain her outright adoration of the woman who was robbed of the presidency. "Madam President, uh I mean Madam Secretary; you are a modern day wonder. You travel the world, you meet with foreign leaders, you are responsible for keeping America safe and now we learn you make your own clothing. I am truly stunned and amazed."

A collective gasp and sigh can be heard from the audience and that turns into a sustained burst of cheering and applause. Mrs. Clinton simply smiles and acknowledges the tribute her fans are paying her. Once the cheers turn to a quiet murmurs, Hillary tells her fans, "It was really nothing much."

Samantha is slack jawed at the disclosure knowing that it would be a major above the fold article on tomorrow's New York Times front page. "Nothing much? Nothing much? Mrs. Clinton, you are a miracle. I would love to continue probing you on this stunning revelation but I need to ask you other important questions about the campaign. There were many questions regarding the DNC and the alleged collusion to keep Sen. Sanders from getting the nomination. After all was said and done, Bernie Sanders gave you quite a run for your money didn't he?"

Hillary simply says, "Yes he did."

"I need to ask you something and I hope you don't take it in the wrong way but do you think that Larry David did a good imitation of Senator Sanders?"

"Well he was a hell of a lot better than Baldwin's imitation of Trump." Hillary, Bill and even Samantha laugh at her comment.

"That's very funny, but on a serious note, I do want to ask you about the many reports during the campaign about your health. You had a few episodes where you seemed to be stumbling and falling and your enemies who shall remain nameless..." Samantha whispers aside to the audience, "Trump, the Republicans and Fox News." Samantha continues, "They made it seem like it somehow precluded you from becoming President. Your spokespersons mentioned that it was a simple case of pneumonia and you were taking medications to return to your renowned vitality and strong good health. Please tell the audience, were you able to get the liquid medicine in your favorite flavor, cherry?"

Bill interrupts again, "Samantha, let me tell you something that Hillary is too humble to say. Not only did the medicine *not* come in cherry flavor but she never complained once…well maybe twice or three times…about having to take that disgusting tasting medicine. I would personally give a full tablespoon to my brave little girl and she was a real trooper."

"What a wonderful husband you are and all Americans are grateful that you were there when Mrs. Clinton needed you most. Mrs. Clinton, I do have one last question before I turn to President Clinton for some added insights. If you had been elected, what would you have done first to make sure that our country remains strong and prosperous?" Samantha is proud of the way she formulated the hard-hitting question and is looking forward to Hillary Clinton's response.

Hillary stands up and faces the audience. It is like she is in campaign mode and addressing an adoring crowd. "Thank you for this opportunity to expound on what I feel is the imperatives facing America and how I propose these issues would be solved. First and foremost, we need to end the awful practice of not allowing non-profit organizations from taking money from foreign countries. We give a lot of money to foreign countries so why not get some if it back? Huh! Why not! Second, stop the persecutions of Otherkin and I do mean right now!"

The audience erupts in applause at the mere mention of Otherkin and Hillary sees this as a moment to consolidate support among the Otherkin community, "Are there any Otherkin in the audience?" There is a very small smattering of claps from at least three people in attendance and Hillary takes note. "I don't care if there are only 316 Otherkin in the United States; they all deserve equal access and opportunity. I would set up separate schools for them; I would make sure they have their own lairs, I would also make the government cheese program available from surpluses now rotting in mid-west warehouses!"

Again the audience erupts in applause. "Third, I would make sure that we establish an entitlement program to subsidize Hollywood and reward them for the great work they do. In a Hillary Clinton Administration, I will, I mean would proposed The Harvey Weinstein/Brent Ratner Memorial Bill to make sure that each and every American would be given $30 subsidy for each movie they go to. This way movie producers and theatres can up the ticket price to $60 and they can have enough money to create memorable entertainment such as "Dumb and Dumber 2", "Jonah Hex", "Valentine's Day", "Saving Mr. Banks", "A Little Bit of Heaven"; didn't you just cry at that one, and the classic movie based on the comic book hero 'Green Lantern' and the edgy, 'Sin City; A Dame to Kill For' and so many more classics. Not only will you be able to view movies of this caliber, but you will also make a political statement. I understand that Harvey, Brent, Al Franken, John Conyers, Charlie Rose, Matt Lauer, Oliver Stone, Louis CK, Glenn Thrush and my husband, along with countless others of our friends are under investigation." Hillary screams into the mic, "BUT THIS IS STILL AMERICA AND WE ARE ALL INNOCENT UNTIL PROVEN GUILTY!!!" The audience is a bit confused, even Bill Clinton and Samantha Bee are a bit confused; what is the political statement being made.

Hillary takes a moment to explain. "We can get rid of Citizens United so large greedy capitalist corporations and billionaires like the Koch brothers will not be able to fund corrupt campaigns. By subsidizing Hollywood, this allows regular ordinary corporations and citizens like Amazon, Miramax, Netflix, New Line Cinema, Castle Rock and individual Americans like Tom Steyer, George Soros, Haim Sabin, Oprah Winfrey and Warren Buffet along with wonderful stars like Barbara Streisand, Ashley Judd and Rosie O'Donnell, are allowed to contribute to campaigns such as mine and get the money out of politics!"

It is like a light has gone off in the minds of each member of the audience, and they finally understand what Hillary Clinton is talking about. There is a collective nod from everyone and a loud cheer along with a standing ovation for Mrs. Clinton.

"Thank you so much! I also want to mention other initiatives that I would have instituted if I wasn't cheated by Donald Trump and the Russians out of the presidency. I would have redesigned special uniforms for the US Military to include transgender and Otherkin persons and things. I would turn over border control to the United Nations, so that we can free up the funds that we've allocated for that function to service my newly formed committee to be named The Special Fund for Mainstream Media Relevancy. I would make sure that I appoint Oswalt Patton to head this newly formed commission in order to determine if there is any possibility that the Constitution is a big fat lie.

I would also create a "Stop Snowflake Suicides" hotline and I would make a law to provide payment of all college tuition for all people under the age of 35 years, no matter how old they are. I will, I mean would, grant citizenship to all hotel workers, maids and gardeners, including my housekeeper and gardener Juanita and Carlos. All these initiatives would have been done in my first 100 days in office. Alas, however we may have to wait until 2020 to find out if all of this is not just another campaign promise." Hillary knowingly smiles; Samantha Bee seems to be having a heart attack, and Bill Clinton's reaction can't be determined because he has his hands over his face.

Samantha tries to regain her composure, but she can only stammer, "Ar...er, *am* you, I mean *is* you...I mean, *are* she is saying?" She is so flustered that she can't get the words out of her mouth.

Mrs. Clinton tries to help and says, "Samantha, let me make this announcement for the first time right here during this interview. I have formed a super-secret committee to review the prospect of developing another committee to examine the potential of forming a sub-committee to raise the necessary funds, to continue to explore the possibility of creating an advisory board to help in writing commercials, for a decision to decide for a possible presidential run."

A single tear runs down Samantha's cheek and the audience can hear an audible sigh coming from the host of the event. You can tell that the entire audience feels the exact same way; the prospect that Hillary Clinton will be around far longer than they can ever imagine is mind-numbing!

"Mrs. Clinton, I can't begin to tell you what you have given to me, given to us all; hope for the future, hope for the Earth and the various alien civilizations that could be populating the Universe. You are a wonder, a treasure, and you make me proud to be a woman but even if I were a member of the LGBTQIA community, an androgynist, a eunuch, a transvestite, a pan-attractional, even if I was an Otherkin, I would be just as proud."

Hillary tries to blush, but she can't, so she says, "Thank you."

"I would love to take more time to speak with you, but I have been handed a note that says we only have the auditorium for another half-hour, and I am anxious to question President Bill Clinton about his tenure and duties as President and Commander-in-Chief."

Bill Clinton smiles, "Samantha, I would love to answer any questions you have."

"Thank you Mr. President. I've asked the audience to send me questions they would love to ask of you about the rigors of the office and how you managed to survive under such extreme, hysterical rantings of your Republican enemies. The first question is from Emily Tramsillit. Emily writes that former Time magazine White House correspondent, Nina Burleigh says, and I quote, *'I'd be happy to give him oral sex just to thank him for keeping abortion legal.'* Were you proud of her for exercising such strength of character?"

President Clinton responds, "Thank you for that question Emily, I can't tell you how much that quote means to me. I've cut the article out and I carry it around in my wallet in case Ms. Burleigh and I ever meet again."

Samantha reads the next question submitted by Cameron 'Felicity' Shift, "I am a transgender female and I am looking for your advice on a delicate subject. What do you wear; boxers or briefs?"

Thoughtful as ever, the president responds, "Well Cameron, I tell you that having reached the age of 70, I feel gravity is settling in, so where boxers have worked in the past, I've had to switch to briefs. I am happier now that my junk is being held in place, and not so 'free- wheeling', if you know what I mean."

"Mr. President, I am sorry to say that we have run out of time and the maintenance staff is anxious to put the chairs away and sweep the place but I hope to have the chance to meet with you again and get answers to this stack of questions." Samantha Bee holds up a large stack of index cards to show the president and she smiles, "I have a few questions of my own!"

"Well Samantha, I would be happy to spend time with you. Wait I have a great idea! Why don't you fly down to Arkansas and I'll give you a personal tour of the Clinton Library. There are many interesting rooms and I even have an apartment there, imagine that."

Samantha considers the prospect and says, "Will Mrs. Clinton be there too?"

Bill Clinton and Samantha Bee turn to look over at Hillary and she has fallen asleep again. He answers, "I don't know, but it doesn't matter anyway."

Samantha closes by saying. "Ladies, gentlemen, Hindus, Muslims, Buddhists, Jews, Christians, Pagans, Agnostics, Atheists, Secular Humanists, African-Americans, Latinos, Multi-Racial, Native-Americans, members of the LBGTQIA communities, those questioning, Androgynists, Eunuchs, Transvestites, Pan-Attractional, people with Nazi hair, white descendants of slave owners and Otherkin, the evening has just sped by and I want to thank former President William Jefferson Clinton and former Secretary of State Hillary Rodham Clinton for their time and candor in participating in this special in-depth interview. We hope you enjoyed yourselves and forgive me for the tough, hard-hitting questions. I look forward to continuing this give and take with President Clinton when I fly down to the Clinton Library very soon. In closing, I want to leave you with this thought, remember no matter how difficult the rigors of holding high-office may seem, it is easy just to blame someone else. Goodnight and drive carefully!"

GEORGE AND AMAL CLOONEY OPEN MUSLIM OUTREACH CENTER IN BEVERLY HILLS

London, England's loss is Beverly Hills, California's gain as the "A List" billionaire power couple relocates to Los Angeles. Sir Telsunn Margraves was able to blend into the crowd as the dynamic duo arrives at the airport to announce the opening of the "George and Amal Clooney Muslim Outreach Center in Beverly Hills." Eric Garcetti, Mayor of Los Angeles, Jerry Brown, the Governor of California and Weldon Blunt, Airport Public Waste Technician are all there to greet George, Amal and their children.

Beverly Hills, CA – The crowd assembled on the tarmac is eagerly anticipating the arrival of superstar George Clooney, his wife Amal and their children Alexander and Ella. As Clooney's Bombardier Global 7000 private jet lands a loud cheer could be heard from the many fans there to greet their idol.

A number of dignitaries are present including Governor Jerry Brown, Los Angeles Mayor Eric Garcetti and Airport Public Waste Technician, Weldon Blunt among others. There is also an expansive cadre of representatives from the national media who have set up cameras surrounding the stage where Mr. Clooney and others will speak. The plane taxis to the hanger and the hatch opens to deafening cheers for George and Amal Clooney. They appear at the top of the stairway along with their children and they all wave to the crowd. The couple is greeted by the dignitaries who line up to shake hands with the Hollywood power couple. All the celebrities on hand are escorted onto the stage so that they may say a few words in honor of the Clooney's. The emcee of the event is Los Angeles Mayor Garcetti's press secretary and out of work actor, Tennyson 'Funky' Yablonski who will make the introductions, the first of which is Governor Jerry Brown.

A smiling Governor Brown is first to take to the podium as he eagerly addresses all those assembled. "What an honor to welcome George and Amal Clooney and their adorable children Anderson and Emma. When George called me last month and told me that he was coming back to California to live, and to establish The Beverly Hills Muslim Outreach Center, I became his very first supporter. I had a deep and meaningful discussion with George and Amal and asked a number of pointed questions; how will this help to solidify relations with Muslims, how will this assuage the fears that many Americans have toward radical Islamic terror, will the meeting hall have air conditioning, how much tax revenue will be generated for California and if I attend a meeting will I have to take off my shoes? I have a foot odor problem and I don't want to offend my Muslim brothers but that's another story." Governor Brown turns to George and Amal and they express assurance to him that he could keep his shoes on.

Governor Brown continues, "I have to gratefully acknowledge that George and Amal took the time to listen to my concerns and assured me that my fears were baseless and I believe these fine people. Now I know there are a lot of unfounded rumors that the Clooney's moved from London in fear for their lives due to increased terror attacks and sharia courts popping up all over but I want to state to all that it is simply not true. They chose to leave London so that they may do their outreach in Beverly Hills because the climate is similar to that of Syria, Iraq and Iran without the bombs blowing up all around and people being beheaded. In closing I want to thank you all for being here to welcome California's newest, former citizens, George and Amal Clooney and little Alasdair and Edda." Governor Brown joins in the clapping and the audience cheers at the mere mention of the Clooney's names and after a moment they settle back to hear the next speaker.

The emcee stands at the mic and says, "Thank you Governor Brown, now please welcome my boss, and all-around great guy, Los Angeles Mayor, Eric Garcetti who would like to say a few words." Mayor Garcetti acknowledges the applause and approaches the podium. He shakes hands with the Clooney's and Governor Brown who takes his seat as the mayor faces the audience. "What a thrill it is to be here to welcome again, George and Amal to our fair city. Given that Los Angeles is the home to Hollywood and Hollywood is home to many stars, we are delighted that George and Amal have decided to settle back here in Los Angeles to begin their good works. The mission of the Clooney's Beverly Hills Center for Muslim Outreach is to foster an unbreakable bond between Americans and Muslims and examine the cultural and ethnic influences that make us all children of the world. In Los Angeles we are proud to have a robust and settled Muslim population and we are hoping that they will continue to assimilate and accept our ways and traditions or not; it's up to them. We do have a few minor and very, very small problems to resolve however before we can claim victory over the Islamophobia that is overwhelming any meaningful dialogue. There is a trivial issue of homosexuality that seems to be at odds with our view and that of Muslim faith and traditions. We are trying diligently to keep certain Muslims from practicing their religious tradition of throwing gays and lesbians from rooftops or cutting off their private parts and I think we are making great strides, after all something worth doing is worth doing well. The next issue that we here in city government are determined to resolve is honor killings. Now, to all those Muslims in the audience who believe in this practice, please don't take this personally, but you really need to stop. I know that women covering their body, legs, face, hands, feet, including toes, arms, wrists, hair and foreheads as well as not driving cars or going to school are wonderful traditions. I think it is instructive to remind all Muslim women that speaking with men you don't know or driving, or wearing western clothing and make-up seems, in some significant way, disrespectful to Islamic religious culture. So, hey, is it worth it to get yourself killed? I say 'No', just keep yourself hidden and stay out of the way of all men not part of your family and things will be fine.

There are many other cultural differences that I am sure we can find some accommodation between us peoples of earth such as female genital mutilation, child sexual slavery, pedophilia, forced marriage, polygamy and other non-conformist behavioral traits and habits that could appear at odds with our norms. At the Clooney Center, George and Amal hope to foster a better understanding and make sure our differences are acceptable to each other. Again, welcome George and Amal and all our best wishes for your success." There was polite applause to Mayor Garcetti's speech and he took his seat.

The last of the dignitaries to speak is Weldon Blunt the airport's Public Waste Technician. Mr. Blunt seems genuinely thrilled at the honor of addressing the crowd. At first he appears a bit nervous, but he calms down as he speaks to the audience. "Hi everyone! I just want to say please be sure to pick up all the garbage that you may have made while waiting for the Mr. and Mrs. Clooney to arrive. There are wire metal baskets all over the place so please use them to drop any cups, tissues, napkins or other debris. I'll empty them when you all leave." Mr. Blunt turns to George and Amal and says, "I also want to say that, in honor of the Clooney's I will be more than happy to empty the garbage from your private jet. I'm sure after your long flight there is a lot of crap onboard and even though it's against the rules of my union contract, I'll do it anyway." The crowd seems very grateful for Weldon Blunt's generous offer and applauds loudly for him as he sits down.

Funky now rises and tells the audience, "Finally the moment you all have been waiting for! Ladies and gentlemen please welcome George and Amal Clooney!" George Clooney waves as he stands to address the crowd of his admirers and with Amal at his side he walks towards the podium. He gratefully accepts the adulations of the many fans present and speaks, "Thank you! Thank you so much!" The more

George Clooney says thank you the louder people clap but finally claps are exhausted and quiet reigns.

George beams his patented smile and says, "What a wonderful and much appreciated welcome that you have given to me, Amal and our children Alexander and Ella, and to all I say, we have come HOME!!!" and the throng goes crazy. "This means more to us than you can possibly know. If you will indulge Amal and I, we want to clear up a few misconceptions about moving to the United States. First, our home in the UK is not for sale unless you have about $20,000,000 US" and the crowd laughs. It is also a scandalous lie that the rising crime and the installation of more than 80 Sharia Courts in London was another reason that Amal and I moving to the US...not true! We only left London because there were so many Italian Restaurants that closed. Speaking of Italian, we also have an Italian villa on Lake Como, as you may have heard. We are thinking about selling that one but it's gonna cost a bit more...say $100,000,000." There is more applause and laughter from the crowd.

George goes silent for a moment and continues, "Islamophobia has taken over the residents of Como, where I have a home. A group of freedom loving refugees have set up camp near where Amal and I live adding much needed diversity to the area. The waterside town of Como on Lago Di Como overlooks one of the most beautiful lakes in the world. Now many of the locals said that these refugees trashed the town and their once-pristine streets are now littered with trash, human waste and overrun by homeless, unemployed refugees from various Muslim regions in the Middle East and Africa. You all need to realize that they have to sleep on mattresses in the town square because a hotel rooms costs $1,950 per night, service not included. I want to take this opportunity clarify what is the truth behind the story. Many of these refugees are part of a delegation sent from the UN to study the impact of garbage and filth on the streets of Italy. It is very important work as I am sure Mr. Blunt will attest."

Weldon Blunt yells to George, "You're damn right!"

Amal Clooney interrupts her husband to speak, "Excuse me George but I would like to say a few words." George looks lovingly at his wife and says, "Of course darling!"

"As some of you may know I am of Lebanese extraction born in Lebanon and raised as a Muslim in the United Kingdom. I am a Barrister with degrees from St.

Hugh's College, Oxford, and New York University. I work at Sullivan and Cromwell, a very small, insignificant international law firm with a mere 792 attorneys. Sullivan and Cromwell has offices all over the world and I am licensed in both the United Kingdom and in America. My father is a lowly MBA graduate from the American University of Beirut and struggled by starting his own lowly travel business. My mother, the poor soul, is a foreign editor of the Pan-Arab newspaper al-Hayat and a founder of the public relations company International Communication Experts, which is part of a larger company. I have a net worth of $10,000,000 but that's nothing compared to old money bags standing next to me." George and the audience convulse in laughter and Amal smiles as she gently touches her husband's cheek.

She continues, "From these humble beginnings I developed a passion for helping people and I believe that I can do more good in Beverly Hills than anywhere else providing that a bomb does not go off. I will not be stopped until each and every Muslim settling in the United States has the right to follow Sharia law or the US Constitution, which ever they want, in this country where freedom reigns!" George beams with pride as he says, "Darling, I am so proud of you." He then turns to the crowd and shouts, "Can we please hear it for Amal?" and the audience erupts in sustained cheers and applause.

George and Amal stand side-by-side, united in their struggle. George is passionate as he speaks, "It is our desire, Amal and I, to have all refugees accepted by every community in America regardless of any objections of the locals. All refugees should be able to settle wherever they want, worship whatever or whomever they want, eat whatever they want, defecate wherever they want and be allowed to follow the traditions and values that have made headlines around the world. When Amal and I were flying from London to California we both had a wonderful idea and the amazing part is we both came up with the same idea at the same exact moment and I am here to announce it for the first time."

George waits until he has the complete attention of the audience before he makes his announcement. "We are actively considering opening the George and Amal Clooney Beverly Hills Muslim Outreach Center in Fargo, North Dakota!" The audience, mostly comprised of California residents, erupts in a crescendo of sustained and unrelenting cheers and applause. George continues to explain the rationale behind their decision to consider Fargo. "There are many compelling reasons; first, Fargo is fast becoming a highly desirable place for an outreach to middle-east Muslims so they can get out of the heat. Second, there is a plethora of people who will work for a lot less than in Beverly Hills, third, the commute will be a lot easier, fourth, the second floor of the Masonic Hall in downtown Fargo is available at a very reasonable rent. Lastly, more ducks reproduce in North Dakota wetlands than anywhere in the nation so there is a consistent and plentiful source of food for refugees given that Duck a l'orange is a perennial favorite among Muslims. The final decision has not yet been made but I must admit the Fargo is a very favorable option. Amal and I will examine all factors and we will keep you informed."

George and Amal conclude their address to the crowd, "Now we must leave you to have the nannies put little Alexander and Ella to bed. We love our children but like most parents we are a bit over protective. In that regard we have secured the services of personal body-guards armed with Pfeifer-Zeliska .600 Nitro Express pistols to watch over the tots. Each bullet costs $40 and will blow a hole in someone's chest the size of a basketball regardless of their race, religion, gender, ethnic origin, sexual orientation, skin color or weight. But like I am reminded by Amal, what is money when it comes to our children after all Amal is worth $10,000,000!" The audience erupts in laughter and cheers for the couple as they wave to the crowd and are escorted off the stage.

The Clooney's say goodbye to the celebrities present and leave the airplane hangar in their bullet-proof limousine with their entourage. The crowd disburses and there is one lone figure left to survey what remains. "Motherf*****s left all this sh*t all over the place and now I have to clean it up. The mother******s should have stayed in Italy or England or wherever the fu*k they came from." Weldon Blunt knows he is speaking to himself but that doesn't make him any happier as he picks up his broom and starts to sweep.

FORMER FBI DIRECTOR JAMES COMEY ACCUSES JUSTICE RUTH BADER GINSBURG OF SEXUAL HARASSMENT

Progressive women in DC recently voted the former head of the FBI James Comey as the sexiest man in Washington. Allegedly this did not go unnoticed by Supreme Court Justice Ruth Bader Ginsberg. The entire lurid tale is told to the investigators in an interview at police headquarters. Sir Telsunn Margraves was fortunate to be secretly ensconced in a room viewing the interview through a two-way mirror. The former FBI Director Comey tells the interrogators of his attempt to buy Justice Ginsburg's Hummer. The outcome was truly upsetting and unnerving for Mr. Comey in light of all the sexual harassment claims that have become front page news!

Washington, DC – In recent days very disturbing articles have been published by certain news sources and reported in the New York Times and Los Angeles Times. Columnist Nicole Serratore and writer Robin Abcarian have hurled accusations of sexual harassment at President Donald Trump related to his interaction with former FBI Director, James Comey. The reports suggest that Director Comey experienced the same form of sexual harassment and molestation that many women experience every day in the workplace and elsewhere.

The authors of these articles reported that James Comey referenced an *"intimate dinner"* where the director was forced into *"awkward silence"* and the writers told of a *"disgusting hug"* that the president gave Comey during the dinner. Mr. Comey even said that President Trump tried to get him alone and that made the director squirm. He confided that he was forced to hide behind a curtain so that he could not be personally violated. Ms. Serratore and Ms. Abcarian both likened this outward display of affection by the president to the type of sexual harassment some women experience when they interact with strong and powerful men. Mr. Comey has also indicated that he felt frightened and violated by the mere fact that the President of the United States, Donald Trump, hugged him.

In a separate item, it has also been reported that among progressive and liberal women, former FBI Director James Comey is now considered the sexiest man in Washington DC. Both the NY Times and the LA Times are quick to point out that the facts reported are from unnamed sources.

In recent days Mr. James Comey has experienced another alleged episode of sexual harassment that he considered so vile and prurient that he was forced to file a police report in hopes of getting an order of protection. The following is a summary of various documents, police reports and interviews related to the alleged crime of sexual harassment as reported to the Washington DC Police Department by former FBI Director Comey.

Mr. Comey made the allegation after he had a private phone call and meeting with Supreme Court Justice Ruth Bader Ginsburg. The purpose of the meeting was to ostensibly discuss the terms and conditions for purchasing Justice Ginsburg's 2006 Hummer H3.

The following is a transcript of the initial interview that was recorded at 2:13AM, on June 2nd 2017 DC 2nd District Sector 10, PSA 2036. Those present at the interview were Lt. Ralph Feltonne, Officer Jason Marvex, Officer Silvia Thomas, and the accuser, Mr. James Comey.

Lt. Feltonne – Good evening Mr. Comey, my name is Ralph Feltonne, I am a Lieutenant with the Washington DC Metro Police Department. The others present are Officers Jason Marvex and Sylvia Thomas. I am here to ascertain certain facts related to the alleged crime of sexual harassment that you have filed with the department.

Mr. Comey - I understand.

Lt. Feltonne – Please state your full name for the record

Mr. Comey – James Brien Comey Jr. that's' B R I E N.

Lt. Feltonne – I thought Brian was spelled with an "a" and not an "e"

Mr. Comey – It can be but my parents spelled it with an "e"

Lt. Feltonne – Well, that does appear a bit strange but let's move on, are your married Mr. Comey?

Mr. Comey – Yes, happily married to my lovely wife Patrice and that's what makes this all the more tawdry, I...

Lt. Feltonne – Please Mr. Comey, we'll get to that in a little while but first I need to get some personal information.

Mr. Comey – I understand.

Lt. Feltonne – Do you have any children?

Mr. Comey – Yes I have five kids. I don't know how to tell them about all this... (At this juncture in the interview Mr. Comey' complexion appears to be turning a light shade of green)

Lt. Feltonne – Mr. Comey, are you feeling alright?

Mr. Comey – I...I don't feel so good. I'm feeling a little queasy. May I have a glass of water?

Lt. Feltonne – Of course, Officer Marvex, would you mind getting a glass of water for Mr. Comey?

Officer Marvex – No problem lieutenant. (Officer Marvex reaches into the refrigerator in the interview room and hands a bottle of water to Mr. Comey) Here you go Mr. Comey.

Mr. Comey – Thank you very much. (Mr. Comey takes a long drink from the bottle)

Lt. Feltonne – Mr. Comey would you like to take a break before we continue as there may be some difficult questions that we will need to ask?

Mr. Comey – No, I'd rather continue. I will try to be strong.

Lt. Feltonne – That's good now, how old are you Mr. Comey?

Mr. Comey – I am 56 years old

Lt. Feltonne – Where do you currently reside?

Mr. Comey – Washington DC (He asked that the actual address he provided is kept off the record due to a fear of continued harassment by person or persons unknown. The actual address is being placed on file and will be kept confidential except for those with the requisite clearance.)

Lt. Feltonne – What is your occupation?

Mr. Comey – I am currently unemployed.

Lt. Feltonne – What was your last job?

Mr. Comey – I was the Director of the Federal Bureau of Investigation.

Lt. Feltonne – Really?

Mr. Comey – Yes.

At this point I (Lt. Feltonne) change the focus of the interview to the events that took place earlier in the evening of June 1ˢᵗ 2017.

Lt. Feltonne – Mr. Comey, we will need to ascertain the chronological order of events that took place earlier this evening.

Mr. Comey – I understand.

Lt. Feltonne – Good, where do you allege the incident took place?

Mr. Comey – I don't allege it took place, it actually took place.

Lt. Feltonne – I know you believe that but before we have a chance to interview the other party and establish the facts we must assume that this is only an allegation. It is up to the courts to decide the truthfulness of the matter at hand.

Mr. Comey – I know, I know. I learned all this at FBI school but I never thought it would actually happen to me.

Lt. Feltonne – Now Mr. Comey, where do you allege the incident took place?

Mr. Comey – It all started with a call I placed to the offices of Justice Ruth Bader Ginsburg at Supreme Court of the United State Building, 1 First Street NE, Washington, DC.

Lt. Feltonne – You mean THE Justice Ruth Bader Ginsburg?

Mr. Comey – (Heaves a deep and profound sigh) Yes.

Lt. Feltonne – You say she sexually harassed you in her office in the Supreme Court Building?

Mr. Comey – No, not there.

Lt. Feltonne – You mean she sexually harassed you at some other place?

Mr. Comey – Yes, but I need to explain what happened.

Lt. Feltonne – Sorry to interrupt, please continue.

Mr. Comey – It all began when I started looking for a used car to be able to drive the kids around in, you know to soccer games or for ice cream. I wanted something safe and large enough to accommodate my family. I was reading the classified ads in the Federal Government Workers Daily when I spotted something I thought was perfect.

Lt. Feltonne – And what was that, Mr. Comey?

Mr. Comey – I saw an ad for a 2006 Hummer H3. It was metallic black, it was in great condition and it had less than 6,000 miles. Imagine only 6,000 miles and it was listed for just $12,995. Well you can imagine how excited I was...

Lt. Feltonne – Please Mr. Comey, can we get back to the issues at hand.

Mr. Comey – Oh, sorry. I became excited and I wanted to see the car and take it for a test drive, so I called the number listed in the ad.

Lt. Feltonne – Did the number belong to Justice Ruth Bader Ginsburg?

Mr. Comey – Yes, it was her office number.

Lt. Feltonne – And you dialed the number.

Mr. Comey – Yes, much to my regret.

Lt. Feltonne – Go ahead.

Mr. Comey – When I called, a Ms. Duncan picked up the phone and answered 'Justice Ginsburg's Office.' I told Ms. Duncan that I was interested in a Hummer I saw advertised and that I would like additional information. I told her that I didn't want to bother Justice Ginsburg and asked if there was some way I could get the information and a test drive. Ms. Duncan said "I cannot divulge this and Justice Ginsburg is adamant about speaking to any prospective buyer personally."

Lt. Feltonne – Personally?

Mr. Comey – Personally, much to my profound regret.

Lt. Feltonne – Go on.

Mr. Comey – Ms. Duncan put me through to Justice Ginsburg and she picked up the phone. I introduced myself as James Comey, former FBI Director, and she gave me a strange reply.

Lt. Feltonne – Strange reply? What was the strange reply?

Mr. Comey – She said that she knew who I was and that she liked the comely photos of me that she saw on MSNBC, CNN® and in the New York Times, Washington Post and LA Times as well as other news sources.

Lt. Feltonne - Comely photos? What does comely mean?

Mr. Comey – You know, comely... pleasing and wholesome in appearance, attractive.

Lt. Feltonne – (I looked at Mr. Comey to see if Justice Ginsburg's assessment was correct and I determined after a brief evaluation that she was correct) Mr. Comey, it appears Justice Ginsburg's appraisal of you is correct, you are comely.

Mr. Comey – Excuse me Lieutenant, that isn't the point.

Lt. Feltonne – Maybe not but I am trying to determine if Justice Ginsburg is being truthful, please continue.

Mr. Comey – Well I didn't know how to respond, so I just thanked her and I let the comment go by. I wanted to turn the discussion back to the Hummer I wanted to buy from her. I asked if she could tell me a little more about the Hummer.

Lt. Feltonne – What did she tell you about the Hummer.

Mr. Comey – This is where our discussion took a very strange twist.

Lt. Feltonne – What do you mean, 'a strange twist'?

Mr. Comey – Well, I had a list of questions, but first she asked me if I ever had a Hummer before? I told here no, and she said, well you'll never have a Hummer like my Hummer.

Lt. Feltonne – What did she mean by that?

Mr. Comey – I really didn't understand at first, but I was hopeful that it would be a Hummer that I could enjoy, and you know what she said to me?

Lt. Feltonne – No

Mr. Comey – She said "Well, like I've said before, you've never had a Hummer like mine!" That comment made me hopeful, but I was somewhat confused by the enigmatic references to her Hummer.

Lt. Feltonne – It does seem puzzling to me too, please go on.

Mr. Comey – I tried to get the discussion back on track. I needed to know more about the Hummer, so I asked Justice Ginsburg if it was an automatic or a stick shift.

Mr. Comey stopped speaking and a far-away look seemed to come over him. I let the moment linger so that Mr. Comey could gather his thoughts. After it seemed to me that enough time had passed, I tried to get Mr. Comey's attention.

Lt. Feltonne – Mr. Comey? Mr. Comey!

Mr. Comey – Huh? What?

Lt. Feltonne – What happened next?

Mr. Comey – Uh, well she told me that she loves to hold a stick when she drives' or even when the car's in park. I was a bit confused.

Lt. Feltonne – What were you confused about Mr. Comey?

Mr. Comey – I can't see why you would hold a stick in park?

Officer Marvex – I think I know what she means!

Officer Thomas – So do I!

Lt. Feltonne – It isn't important what you think Officers Marvex and Thomas; it's only what Mr. Comey thinks that's important. Mr. Comey what do you think she meant?

Mr. Comey – I can't imagine. I used to drive a stick in some of my cars over the years but I usually work it only when I am moving. My wife also likes to use the stick in my car every now and then, but only in drive.

Lt. Feltonne – Was there anything else that you can remember about the conversation with Justice Ginsburg that could be significant in this alleged sexual harassment incident?

Mr. Comey – Yes.

Lt. Feltonne – What was it Mr. Comey?

Mr. Comey – I don't know how significant you would consider this but Justice Ginsburg continually mentioned that there are reclining front seats, and that she was sure that I would like this feature of her Hummer.

Lt. Feltonne – Reclining seats, huh.

Mr. Comey – Yes. I told her that I probably would enjoy the Hummer more knowing the seats recline.

Lt. Feltonne – Good point. Anything else?

Mr. Comey – Yes, and that's when things turned ugly!

Mr. Comey appears to get very agitated at this point and I suggest to him that we take a break, and he agrees. I offer Mr. Comey some more water and he politely declines and asks to use the men's room. Officer Marvex escorts Mr. Comey to the restroom while Officer Thomas and I wait. After a half-hour, Officer Thomas and I became worried. We left the interview room to go find Officer Marvex, to determine what is taking so long. We walk down the hall to see Officer Marvex standing by the men's room door. He tells us that he is waiting for Mr. Comey to finish whatever he is doing. Officer Marvex notices that Mr. Comey is taking much longer than usual even for No. 2, so he opens the door slightly to make sure all was well. When he does he could hear Mr. Comey whimpering in his stall. Officer Marvex was unsure as what to do, so he speaks through the stall door and asks, "Is everything alright?" Mr. Comey replies, "Yes, but can you just give me a moment longer." Officer Marvex answers, "Of course" and he leaves Mr. Comey alone.

I am just about to go into the restroom to see if Mr. Comey needs assistance but just at that moment I hear the toilet flush and the water running in the sink. Mr.

Comey comes out of the restroom wiping his face with a wet paper towel, looking pale and nauseous. I express my concern to him and ask if he would like to postpone the interview until the morning. He thinks about it for a moment and decides that he wants to continue. We walk back to the interview room and take our seats.

Mr. Comey – Lieutenant Feltonne and Officers Marvex and Thomas I want to apologize for the excessive time I spent in the men's room. I experienced a sudden bout of nausea as a result of what happened this evening and I'm afraid that it took me a long time to recover.

Lt. Feltonne – That is quite alright and understandable given the alleged trauma you had to endure. Shall we continue?

Mr. Comey – Yes

Lt. Feltonne – Prior to our break you said, wait, I'll read my notes; "...that's when things got ugly." What did you mean when you said that?

Mr. Comey – Justice Ginsburg and I spoke for a few minutes more and I asked her if I could take the Hummer for a test drive, you know, to see how it feels behind the wheel.

Lt. Feltonne – Sounds like that was the proper thing to do.

Mr. Comey – Let me tell you this right now, it was anything but proper.

Lt. Feltonne – What do you mean by that?

Mr. Comey – I suggested that I come to her home, or to wherever she wants over the weekend to experience the Hummer first hand but Justice Ginsburg had a different suggestion. She said that we could meet later in the evening at a place that is a little friendlier. Justice Ginsburg also implied that there might be someone else interested in her Hummer and that if I wanted to be the first to get the Hummer that I must act quickly,

Lt. Feltonne – A little friendlier? What did she mean friendlier?

Mr. Comey – She suggested that we go someplace quiet where we could talk and I could get the complete Hummer experience. At first I was a bit taken aback but I really wanted a Hummer so I told her that I would meet her at 7PM.

Lt. Feltonne – Where did you go to meet her?

Mr. Comey – Felix's Dew Drop Inn.

Lt. Feltonne – I know that place, it's the one on "Maple and 12th St NW.

Officers Marvex and Thomas – (said in unison) I know that place too!

Lt. Feltonne – So what happened next?

Mr. Comey – I called my wife and told her about going to look at the Hummer and that I would not be home for dinner. I told her that the car belonged to Justice Ruth Bader Ginsburg and Patrice was very impressed.

Lt. Feltonne – So let me get this straight, you agreed to meet Justice Ginsburg at Felix's Dew Drop Inn at 7PM that evening. You call your wife and tell her that you're going to see the car and you won't be home for dinner. Is that essentially correct?

Mr. Comey – Yes, except for one thing.

Lt. Feltonne – What was the one thing?

Mr. Comey – I memorialized the essence of my phone conversation in a private memo to myself. I didn't mention it to Patrice but I wanted this available in case anything sinister happens to me.

Lt. Feltonne – Sinister?

Mr. Comey – Well, you can't blame me for wanting to protect myself in case the worst happens.

Lt. Feltonne – Worst happens? What did you suspect might happen?

Mr. Comey – That's just it, I couldn't even imagine what might happen so I wanted to be sure I was protected.

Lt. Feltonne – Ah, well if you couldn't imagine what might happen then why did you agree to meet Justice Ginsburg

Mr. Comey – Because the opportunity to get the Hummer from her was worth the risk.

Lt. Feltonne – I guess...go on.

Mr. Comey – It was only 5PM when I hung up from my call. As I wouldn't be home for dinner, I went to Stavros' 24 Hour Greek Diner across the street from my office and had something to eat. I wanted to eat light so I just had a cheese sandwich with organic mustard on gluten-free bread, a small kale and quinoa salad with no dressing and Nik-L-Nips for dessert.

Lt. Feltonne – Nik-L-Nips? What are Nik-L-Nips?

Mr. Comey – You know, those little wax bottles that are filled with flavored syrup. You suck the syrup out of the bottle. Sometimes I even chew the wax especially if there is still some syrup that won't come out. There was this one time...

Lt. Feltonne – Please Mr. Comey, let's get back to your account of the incident

Mr. Comey – Oh, sorry. Well, as Felix's Dew Drop Inn is about a 30 minute drive, I left the diner about 6:30PM in order to be there to meet Justice Ginsburg at 7PM. I felt that the traffic would be light at that time, so I didn't think it was necessary to allot for additional time.

Lt. Feltonne – Go on, please.

Mr. Comey – I had never been to this particular lounge before. I was a bit taken aback by the overall appearance of the place. After all, I was meeting with an Associate Justice of the Supreme Court of the United States of America.

Lt. Feltonne – Why were you taken aback? What was the appearance that didn't seem to meet with your expectations?

Mr. Comey – The first thing I noticed was the neon sign that was prominently displayed on the roof over the door. There were a number of letters not lit, so it just read "F...IXS ...EW DR...P INN." In addition there was an outline of a buxom woman, also lit in neon, and it appeared the lights were out on one of her breasts. As you can imagine, this was a bit surprising to me.

Lt. Feltonne – Of course.

Officers Marvex and Thomas – Of course.

Mr. Comey – It was not very late and as I understand it, Felix's doesn't really get crowded until much later in the evening, so I was able to park my car in one of the spaces near the front door. I would later lament that this was the only lucky thing I would encounter for the rest of the evening.

Lt. Feltonne – Did you go inside, or did you meet Justice Ginsburg outside in the parking lot?

Mr. Comey – I met her inside. The bar is very dark as if the lighting was meant to convey a certain mood.

Lt. Feltonne – Mood? What do you mean certain mood?

Mr. Comey – It looked as if Felix wanted to create a seductive atmosphere. I looked around and although it was hard to see, I spotted Justice Ginsburg sitting in a booth located in a dark corner of an already dark bar. I walked over to her and introduced myself, and quite frankly I was shocked by what I saw.

Lt. Feltonne – What, what did you see that so shocked you?

Mr. Comey – Justice Ginsburg was sitting, alluringly, on one side of the wooden booth. She was wearing an extremely low cut dress that, much to my chagrin, nearly exposing one of her breasts. Unlike her official Supreme Court photo, she was wearing her long, wavy hair down and she had chosen a ruby red lipstick and dark eyeliner. My face turned red, but I am sure that Justice Ginsburg couldn't tell because it was so dark. She gave me a smile and asked me to sit down. When I moved to sit opposite her in the booth, she suggested something very disturbing.

Lt. Feltonne – Disturbing?

Mr. Comey – Yes, she said, and I quote, 'Why don't you sit next to me?' I was dumbfounded and didn't know how to react. There were no curtains in the place and I guess that Justice Ginsburg saw my dismay and she clarified.

Lt. Feltonne – Clarified?

Mr. Comey – She told me that she had the complete servicing records and some of the original brochures of the car. Even though I was somewhat reticent, I agreed and sat down beside her to be able to review the documents.

Lt. Feltonne – What happened then?

Mr. Comey – Just as I sat down a waitress came over to the table and asked us what we wanted to drink. Justice Ginsburg ordered a vodka martini, very dry with 4 olives. I ordered a plain ice tea with sugar substitute on the side. Sometimes pure cane sugar doesn't dissolve quickly...

Lt Feltonne – Please Mr. Comey, just the pertinent details.

Mr. Comey – Oh, sorry. Justice Ginsburg did ask me if I wanted something stronger but I thought that I needed to keep my wits about me so I declined. The waitress returned with our drinks and Justice Ginsburg suggested we toast.

Lt. Feltonne – Who gave the toast?

Mr. Comey – She did.

Lt. Feltonne – What was the toast?

Mr. Comey – She said "Here's to the best damned Hummer you could ever have!" We clinked glasses and took sips from our drink. It was what happened next that disgusted me to no end.

Lt. Feltonne – What was that Mr. Comey?

Mr. Comey – I was about to ask to see the documents when she reached under the table. I assumed that she was going for the list records of oil changes but it was then I felt a hand glide along the top of my leg. I gulped and looked at Justice Ginsburg and she just smiled at me.

At this time I think that it is important to note that Mr. Comey's accusation was quite shocking to me as well as Officers Marvex and Thomas. As officers of the law we constantly confront the most despicable of crimes and aberrant behavior but this was among the vilest any of us have had the misfortune to investigate. Mr. Comey seemed to recognize our dismay and continued to speak.

Mr. Comey – Lt. Feltonne and Officers Marvex and Thomas, I detect your complete and utter revulsion at what I've had to experienced and I thank you for your sympathy and understanding.

Lt. Feltonne – Mr. Comey I think it would be best if we continued. What happened next?

Mr. Comey – I got a hold of myself and gave Justice Ginsburg the benefit of the doubt.

I said to her "Can I see the oil change history?" She just looked alluringly at me and said, "Oil keeps the rods real slick! That's why I made sure all my rods are always oiled and slick. Know what I mean?" and she winked at me. I really didn't know what she meant, but I said that I like it when my rods are slick.

Lt. Feltonne – She winked at you?

Mr. Comey – Yes and smiled!

Lt. Feltonne – and smiled?

Mr. Comey – (Mr. Comey's chest heaves as he says) I'm so ashamed.

Lt. Feltonne - Mr. Comey, please take time to come to grips with your emotions, and when you are ready, please continue.

Mr. Comey – Thank you, but I want to continue now. I want the world to know what I've gone through.

Lt. Feltonne – That's very brave of you, please tell us what happened next.

Mr. Comey – Justice Ginsburg then took the opportunity to move closer to me under the pretext of showing me a dealer invoice that indicated the motor mounts had been changed.   She also suggested that we go outside and take a look at the car and take a test drive. Well, against my own better judgement, I agreed and we left Felix's Dew Drop Inn and exited the front door.

Lt. Feltonne – Where was the car parked?

Mr. Comey – It was parked in a dark corner of the lot under a river birch. Those are the trees that have the white bark that peels and it looks like it's dying but...

Lt. Feltonne – Please Mr. Comey, just stick to the details of the alleged incident.

Mr. Comey – Oh, sorry. Well I walked with Justice Ginsburg to the car and joked, telling her I that I wanted to see if her Hummer was all it was cracked up to be. I mentioned to her that it was awfully dark and that I don't know if I could see any scratches on her rear end. Justice Ginsburg assured me that her rear end was in great condition, and I could have all the time I wanted to check out her rear end.

Lt. Feltonne – Well that seems reasonable to me.

Mr. Comey – It seems reasonable to me too, however, that was the myth...now here is the reality!

Lt. Feltonne – Reality?

Mr. Comey – Yes, it was all a clever ruse to get me into the car.

Lt. Feltonne – What happened when she got you into the car?

Mr. Comey – (Mr. Comey's chest heaves again. He appears very uncomfortable at having to tell us what happened) I...I don't know how to say this.

Lt. Feltonne - Mr. Comey I know that this is very difficult for you, but I need to know what happened or I can't take action to determine guilt or innocence among the parties involved.

Mr. Comey – She insisted that I take the driver's seat, and it immediately became apparent to me that her obsession with the reclining bucket seats had a very sinister purpose. The moment I sat down the driver's seat it careened backwards, and I found myself in a horizontal position staring at the Hummer's tufted ceiling. I didn't realize that this model of Hummer had the deluxe ceiling...

Lt. Feltonne - Please Mr. Comey, stay with the pertinent facts and details...

Mr. Comey – I became very unnerved and started to shake when I heard Justice Ginsburg whisper, 'Ready for the full Hummer experience!' I didn't know what to do, so I started to grab for the door knob and planned my escape from this den of iniquity.

Lt. Feltonne – Iniquity? What's iniquity?

Mr. Comey – You know, immorality, heinousness, evil, sinful.

Lt. Feltonne – Ok, got it.

Mr. Comey – It was dark, but I could sense Justice Ginsburg's leering eyes looking over my body, as if I was some piece of meat. I felt so violated. I was unable to open the car door, as it seemed that Justice Ginsburg's depravity knew no bounds. She had automatically locked the doors, and I was like the Prisoner of the Zenda, except I wasn't in Ruritania and I wasn't a King and I didn't have a body double and...

Lt. Feltonne – Please Mr. Comey, I must ask you to stick with the facts related to the incident

Mr. Comey – Sorry...I finally was able to push the unlock button and I heard the click that was like music to my ears. I estimated that I was 30 yards from my car. Given my height, 6 feet 8 inches and a stride greater than most, I estimated I could make the run in 20 steps or less. Justice Ginsburg appeared to be barely 5 feet tall, so it would take her at least 35 to 40 steps to catch me. I also thought that I would take my car keys out on the way and use this opportunity to escape.

Lt. Feltonne - Mr. Comey, did Justice Ginsburg follow you?

Mr. Comey - I didn't bother to check to see if she was following me I just ran and ran and got into my car. Unfortunately, I hit the gas very hard and the rear wheels of the car spun out. Felix's Dew Drop Inn parking lot had pebbles instead of asphalt and the pebbles scratched the fenders of my car. I never looked back, and I decided to come here to report this immediately.

Lt. Feltonne – Well you've had quite some evening and I want to commend you for your bravery and intestinal fortitude at having to endure such a violation of your body and personal space. I will have this interview transcribed and ask you to sign it, and we will issue a warrant to question Justice Ginsburg and get to the bottom of this.

Mr. Comey – Thank you Lieutenant, I would like to have an order of protection so that Justice Ginsburg will never darken my doorsteps again. Perhaps my actions taken will stop this from happening to some poor unsuspecting person looking for a Hummer from this woman.

Lt. Feltonne – Well, we'll see Mr. Comey, we'll see.

Update: Fake News has learned from and unnamed source that Justice Ginsberg categorically denies any involvement in the accusation of the alleged incident related to the yet to be proven and heretofore undocumented assertion that she has even contemplated the clandestine meeting with the former FBI director.

An unnamed source is also quoted as saying that Justice Ginsberg has never been to Felix's Dew Drop Inn and has never even known it existed. She may have driven by the lounge but she never got out of her car and never had a drink there. The source is also quoted as saying the Justice Ginsberg hates dry martini's especially with four olives.

THE TRUMP-LIMBAUGH BARBEQUE

In his years of covering fake news, Sir Telsunn Margraves has learned that when the media hears either the name Trump or the name Limbaugh, they descend into the depths of anger, grief and despair. Put both notables in the same sentence, however, Democrats and the media descend to the depths of hysteria. The New York Times, CNN, Associated Press, The View and all the mainstream news outlets have allocated resources to what they see as a blatant attempt by the White House to savage the orphan children community, or as they have become known as, 'no parent persons'. One report builds upon another until a horrific crescendo is reached.

New York, NY – **"Fox and Friends"** – The reporter announces, "President Trump has invited a group of orphan children over to the White House for an outdoor barbeque. The president is anxious to have them be an important part of a dinner that promises to be a total surprise to the young tikes. The entire Trump family and many from his administration will be there to enjoy the festivities, and given all those that will be in attendance, there are sure to be a lot of hungry mouths to feed.

All the children coming to the event are from the "Rush Limbaugh Home for Children." This is a charity that Rush formed many years ago to allow orphan children to go into the world prepared to assimilate and succeed in society, knowing the sacrifices that they must make without the past intruding on them. Limbaugh said, "I just love children; they are truly God's gift to the world. I also love to educate them about the truth behind the founding of America, and all that it represents to its people and to the world at large."

The reporter continues, "Rush Limbaugh is the best-selling author of the children's book series "Rush Revere Time Travel Adventures with Exceptional Americans." Rush Limbaugh has already sold millions of the books and has been named the 2014 Children's Choice Book Award for author of the year. Limbaugh is also a long-time friend and supporter of President Trump and he has offered to fund the event so that the kids can experience what it is like to be near the seat of power in America and be inspired to achieve all that they can.

● ● ●

May 3rd 2017, New York, NY, "New York Times" – **Excerpts from the article "No Democrats invited to Lunch with Orphans" By Thomas Friedman** – The irony of this latest Trump mishap is that there are just as many Democrat orphans as there are Republican orphans, but you wouldn't know that from the latest selfish, cowardly failure to invite Democrats to the White House for the Trump - Limbaugh Barbeque of Orphan Children. Genghis Khan, or is it Attila the Hun, a moniker that Limbaugh proudly wears, seems to be in charge and he will likely serve as chair for the event.

President Trump took out time from his daily routine of manipulating the rack room rates at all of his hotels, to announce the festivities by saying, "There are far too many beautiful orphans in America and we need to do something to increase adoptions." Come to think of it, I never liked the word orphan. I find it demeaning and connoting a condition that can brand a person something negative, so I choose to call them "no-parent persons." How can Trump be so inclined to think this way when he was never, ever a no-parent person? He grew up in privilege and it would seem the only way he ever could relate to how a no-parent person feels, is by giving up every dime he made to go live in a cold, miserable hovel like so many no-parent persons.

It is difficult to imagine how the President of the United States and the self-appointed "America's Anchorman" can perpetuate such horror on a group of innocent children by creating an event for them that is a short sighted, one sided attempt to make little Herbert Hoover acolytes out of these innocent no-parent persons.

The article goes on to explain that Thomas Friedman theorizes "The only way we can ever stop the proliferation of no-parent persons is to end man-made global warming."

● ● ●

May 3rd, 2017, New York, NY, "Associated Press", Staff Reporters, Exclusive Late News Item – The Associated Press has released the following item to major mainstream media outlets including ABC, CBS and NBC, MSNBC, CNBC, NPR, PBS, The NY Times, Washington Post as well as the Farm Radio Network. "The Associated Press has learned that the President of the United States is now planning what has been termed a 'major shift' in how we care for no-parent persons. He, and incendiary, right wing radio talk show host, Rush Limbaugh, have teamed up to usher young children into a secret area of the White House Gardens out of the view of ,what has been cited by unnamed sources as, 'prying eyes.'"

The White House Press Corp is already in an uproar demanding that the President and Limbaugh come clean as to the purpose of the event, and what is likely to become a major incident in the first term of the Trump Administration.

When asked to respond, a White House spokesman said, and we quote, "It's just a barbeque for orphan children." At this time the Associate Press cannot confirm or deny the statement, but now the burden of proof will rest on Trump and Limbaugh. Hopefully they will find the courage to come clean.

● ● ●

May 3rd, 2017, Atlanta, GA - New York, NY, "CNN® Tonight with Don Lemon" – The following is a transcript of an interview with host Don Lemon and actor and political activist, Alec Baldwin:

Don Lemon – "Tonight we have a very special guest. Alec Baldwin, the world renowned actor and political activist, a long-time Donald Trump critic and a good friend of this show. Good evening Alec, thanks so much for coming."

Alec Baldwin – "No problem Don, it's always a pleasure to be here."

Don Lemon – "Well Alec, I guess you've heard about the latest embarrassment and controversy of the Trump Administration."

Alec Baldwin – "Which one?"

(Both Don and Alec start laughing)

Don Lemon (wiping away tears of laughter) – Well, Alec, the one I'm talking about is the latest travesty relating to the so-called barbeque of no-parent persons at the White House."

Alec Baldwin – "Don, would you mind if I vented to your audience?"

Don Lemon – "Of course not Alec."

Alec Baldwin – "Where does this piece of sh*t get off doing such a thing to poor orphans."

Don Lemon - "You mean no-parent persons."

Alec Baldwin – Oh yeah, no-parent persons. Where does he get off doing such a thing? Haven't these young kids gone through enough in their lives? Do they need to be dragged, kicking and screaming I'm sure, to be held up as some sort of trophy so that Trump and Limbaugh can get off on these kids?"

Don Lemon – "Now Alec, we don't know that for sure."

Alec Baldwin – "Let me tell you something Don, I have heard rumors coming from someone, shall we say, that is about as high as you can get in Democrat circles in the Senate. He took me aside on the Senate floor and told me that it is plausible these orphans, oh I mean no-parent persons, will likely be in danger at the White House barbeque."

Don Lemon (looking incredulous) – "Come on Alec, please don't leave us hanging, our viewers have the right to know."

Alec Baldwin (looking smug) – "Don, you may want to ask your viewers to have all young children to leave the room. What I have to say may shock some people in your vast audience."

Don Lemon (looking very nervous) – "Um...ah...To all CNN® viewers, please take the time to escort all young children from the room."

Alec Baldwin (waits patiently as children leave their parents rooms) – "Parents, you've had your chance. What I am about to tell you is about as gruesome as you can imagine. The White House Head Chef, known for his special sauces, is preparing something totally new and original and some of the Trump cabinet members have been overheard saying that their mouths are already watering."

Don Lemon (staring wide-eyed) – "My God! (pause for effect) Ladies and gentlemen, we must caution you to consider that CNN® has not received definitive proof of this horror that I am aware of. CNN® is a major news organization so we may have the proof lying on someone's desk right now, but for the moment we will treat this revelation as a story to watch."

Alec Baldwin – "We don't have definitive proof at the moment but you know and I know the potential is very real especially with these people."

Don Lemon (visibly shocked) – Th-thank you Alec and to our viewers, hold your children tight in your arms tonight. Good night and God bless, or whoever you believe in, from all of us at CNN®."

● ● ●

May 4th 2017, New York, NY, "ABC Television Studios", Recent roundtable discussion on "The View", Participants; Whoppi Goldberg, Joy Behar, guest Rose Perez and some others who never have a chance to speak. The following is a transcript of a discussion that took place today on "The View". We join the discussion in progress;

Whoppi Goldberg – "Well he can kiss my ass!" (**Laughter can be heard coming from the audience**)

Joy Behar – "Can you believe this? I told you, I told you, we should have elected Hillary. She doesn't even like kids!" (**Audience bursts into thunderous applause**)

Rosie Perez – "Now ladies, tsk...tsk...tsk...please don't use vulgarity when you talk about that piece of sh*t." (**Peals of laughter can be heard coming from the audience**)

Joy Behar – Seriously, how can any American just stand by and allow this to happen to poor no-parent persons." (**Joy wipes a tear from her eye**)

Whoppi Goldberg – "I'm telling you this, you in the audience and you at home; if you have a vagina you should be outraged." (**Thunderous applause from the audience**)

Rosie Perez – "You know I'm from the hood and even if we were starving, we wouldn't ever contemplate what it seems the Republican President is doing." (**Members of audience shout "yeah!"**)

Joy Behar – "And don't forget Rush Limbaugh, he calls me 'Maude' as if it were some kind of derogatory. I am proud to look like Bea Arthur and remember when he said that no one wants to watch Hillary grow old in the White House. Remember when I suggested that Hillary could have apologized to the tramps that were screwing, I mean allegedly screwing, her husband Bill. Wasn't that a magnanimous thing she could have done? Huh Rush, Wasn't that magnanimous?"

Whoppi Goldberg – "Well he can kiss my ass!" (**Audience convulses in laughter**)

Rosie Perez – "LADIES, LADIES WE SEEM TO BE GETTING OFF THE SUBJECT (**screaming above the others at the table**). What about those poor no-parent persons? What about the reported rumors that the White House is planning some damned fool thing they want to do to kids?"

Joy Behar – "Well you know Rosie, I'm not one to spread rumors or insults without proof but if these rumors are correct we need to bring an exorcist into the White House to drive Satan from Donald Trump. I'm not sure about Rush Limbaugh, an exorcism might not work." (**Some more convulsive laughter from the audience**)

● ● ●

May 5ᵗʰ 2017, New York, NY, "Huffington Post", Alec Mohajer, Political Writer and Commentator – Alec Mohajer recently wrote, *"Congress, the only governing body with the constitutional authority to impeach an American president, should initiate proceedings against Donald Trump as early as Inauguration Day."*

"This is my latest expansion on the expression of political dissent I feel honor bound to communicate; I must tell you how prophetic my plea to Congress is. I have been following the recent stories related to the "Trump-Limbaugh Barbeque" that has now come to be known as "No-parent Persons-gate."

My investigation of this event has literally taken me to the bowels of the White House, directly into the kitchen of the White House, where I was able to interview some of the staff who asked for anonymity in fear of their lives. I spoke to someone I will call 'Jose' who is the person in charge of vegetables. I asked Jose what he knew of the event that is taking place next week. He told me, and I quote, "I don't know nothing!"

This obvious double negative is an admission of what we could only speculate about in the last two days. After more careful digging, I found someone who was willing to speak, again under the conditions of anonymity. She said, "The barbeque sauce Chef created is a secret blend of spices with a not-so-subtle hint of tomato, vinegar and molasses. He cooks the combination for at least an hour, stirring constantly so that the mixture melds into a mélange of flavors that would make any meat taste much, much better." I was nearly floored when I heard this, 'any meat taste much, much better'.

Under normal circumstances, I would not make such a provocative statement, but as of this moment I am asking that a special session of congress be convened to investigate this horrendous attempt that could very well imperil the existence of these no-parent persons!

● ● ●

May 6th 2017, Washington DC, "Media Matters for America" – Blog post, Tyler Cherry "Children with Good Taste or Children that Taste Good" –

To paraphrase Michelle Obama, "This is the fiftieth time I am ashamed to be American." You may ask why and I will tell you, it is all about the appalling events connected with No-parent Person-gate. According to articles written by respected journalists and commentators and interviews with luminaries from the worlds of entertainment, acting, theatre, stage, screen, television and music there are events shaping up that will become known as America's greatest shame.

Media Matters for America has been carefully investigating rumors surrounding the White House and a right-wing cabal headed by none other than Rush Limbaugh and the secret barbeque that is being held on May 8th. According to unnamed sources close to the Trump Administration, the event hosted by the president himself, and right wing bomb-thrower Rush Limbaugh, is being heralded as a special day for orphans, better known as no-parent persons. What has been rumored is that these small innocent children will fall prey to the highest echelons of evil US businessmen, Republican Trilateralists, a secret organization of ex-communicated Roman Catholic Jesuits, The Illuminati, Mail Order Meats 'R Us and Charcoal Makers of America among other sinister groups.

Ladies and gentlemen, you must believe me when I say that what I am about to tell you literally breaks my heart. At this event these innocents will be lured to a place out of earshot and where no cameras can see and they will be treated to a barbeque where they are purported to be the main course! You cannot ever know the pain and anguish I feel at this moment.

• • •

May 6th 2017, Washington DC, "The Washington Post" – Headline: "Democrats Unite for 'Make May 8th No Meat Day' Go Fund Me Fundraiser" By Michael Kranish –

"With great fanfare, senior Democrat officials announced the launch of a "Go Fund Me" campaign to help expose the contemptable practice of eating no-parent persons.

Harry Reid, the former Senate Democrat Leader told the Post, "How can these people eat children? What kind of savages are they? If they are so hungry I'll buy them dinner." Nancy Pelosi, who barely retained her position as Minority Leader of the House after crushing defeats of the Democrats over prior election cycles was visibly angry. "This is what you might expect from Trump, the Republicans and a reprobate like Limbaugh. As Democrats we must unite to fight this evil in any way we can. The best way I can think of is to send us money." Harry Reid, Chuck Schumer and Barack Obama can be heard agreeing in the background.

• • •

May 7th 2017, "Twitter" Post, by Chelsea Handler "Those c**ks*****g piece of s**t better not try to eat my housekeeper's kid. I'll bury those m****rf****r and cut off their b***s and feed it to the f****s."

• • •

May 7th, 2017, San Francisco, CA, "Mother Jones Magazine" Jointly with "Rolling Stone Magazine" – Headline: "Eating No-parent Persons to become the New Normal…America! Wake Up!" The entire editorial staffs of Mother Jones Magazine and Rolling Stone Magazine, has combined to contribute to this editorial:

"Shame on US! How is it possible that in this day and age there is still such a thing called "cannibalism?" Mother Jones Magazine, in cooperation with Rolling Stone Magazine has done extensive research into the heinous act of cannibalism and we can find no incidence of cannibalism in America with the exception of those guys who ate each other at Donner Pass. We can, however, excuse that because they were snowed in and there wasn't a single thing to eat so they needed to improvise and that's what they did.

But what excuse can the Trump White House give...huh...what can they say? Well we'll tell you what they can say, nothing, that's what they can say, nothing. What possible excuse can they have to lure unsuspecting no-parent persons under the guise of an invitation to a wholesome traditional American barbeque and then... *The editorial staffs of both Mother Jones and Rolling Stone must ask your indulgence at this time. The details of what we suspect will happen to these children are far too horrible, too gruesome to convey to our readers. However we pledge you this, we will pursue this story, leaving no stone unturned, no truth undisclosed, no child left behind, no ways tired, no surrender, no time like the present to rid our nation...this greatest land on earth that continues to oppress African-Americans, Hispanic-Americans, Transgender-Americans, Otherkin, among so many others. Our pledge will remain sacred because Trump is President, and a true believer in the potential benefits of cannibalism against no-parent persons!*

In closing, we can hear the echoes of plaintiff cries coming from our readers right now saying, "What can we do? How can we save these loving, adorable no-parent persons? How can we help?" The editorial board of Mother Jones Magazine and Rolling Stone Magazine strongly suggest that all Americans contribute to the Democrats Go Fund Me, "May 8th - No Meat Day." As a sign of our appreciation, to all who contribute, we will give a 5% discount on subscriptions to either Mother Jones Magazine® or Rolling Stone Magazine®. It is also our sincere hope you decide to order both magazines and when you do, you will have your choice of a men's, women's or transgender T-Shirt boldly printed with the slogan "Hands Up! Don't Eat!"

● ● ●

May 9th, 2017, New York, NY, "The New York Times" from an AP News Item, Section D, Page 26, Item (5 lines) lower bottom, left hand side –

The New York Times is reporting that the Trump-Limbaugh Barbeque took place as scheduled. The no-parent persons arrived and all got to meet President and Mrs. Trump who both made it a point to speak to each child. They received a tour of the White House and were treated to a barbeque, played games of skill and were entertained by a number of performers. When the event ended, the children were taken to see a movie, and they also spent time at a go-cart track as part of what could have been a tragic day.   The excited but exhausted group of children then went back to the "Rush Limbaugh Home for Children." It could not be ascertained at the time of publication if a wonderful time was had by all there, but we at the Times reserve the right to update the story if it becomes necessary." **Note: Same AP news item appeared in The Washington Post, in the Late News on cable networks CNN®, MSNBC, CNBC as well as ABC, CBS and NBC and other news outlets.**

● ● ●

May 10th 2017, Corporate Headquarters of "The Drudge Report", "Breitbart News", "Newsmax" "Fox News" and "Rush 24/7" – The following is a news item posted to various websites, but could not be readily found on any mainstream media news sources

"It has been reported that, based on the news coverage of the Trump-Limbaugh Barbeque, there has been a huge influx of people calling to inquire about the orphans who attended the event.

Among the thousands of people who called, most expressed great interest in adoption. Millicent and Jeffrey Di Carlo of Somerset New Jersey said, "When we saw those beautiful faces on TV, Jeff and I said we had to try and give a good home to one of the orphans. We have gone on Rush's site and downloaded the documents necessary to begin the process. We are very hopeful that we can have a child to brighten our lives and complete our family."

KIM JONG UN AND ACTRESS MADELEINE LEBEAU WED

England has William and Kate, Harry and Meghan and now North Korea joins the community of nations as the country celebrates the marriage of supreme leader Kim Jong Un to the lovely and talented actress Madeline LeBeau. An intimate gathering of 1,297,618 guests and press from around the world are there for the joyous celebration. There were so many people in attendance that Sir Telsunn Margraves was forced to disguise himself as a leper in order to have enough room to witness this stellar event and report his observations to you, the reader.

Pyongyang, NK, August 12th 2017 – The glorious and supreme leader of North Korea, Kim Jong Un, married actress Madeleine LeBeau today in a resplendent outdoor ceremony. The groom wore a military style Chairman Mao tuxedo designed by noted fashion icon Vera Wang, and he had his trademark hair trimmed especially for the occasion. The bride was hidden behind a curtain but the news media was assured by the North Korean army that she looks lovely.

The groom, Kim Jong Un, the beloved, supreme dictator seemed a bit nervous but very happy at the prospect of marrying the woman who he calls, "the love of my life." He further states that the first time he saw Madeleine LeBeau was when she starred in the classic romance drama, *Casablanca*. Kim is proud to tell anyone who would listen, and everyone does listen, that Madeleine LeBeau played the jilted mistress of Humphrey Bogart's character, Rick. Kim Jong Un appears giddy as he recounts the accolades she received for her role in the movie and other roles she played in her long, storied career. Kim Jong Un says proudly, "She makes me tingle every time I see her!"

Kim Jong Un appears in an uncharacteristically jovial mood when he agrees to take questions from the news media that have gathered in full force to cover this event. One AP reporter asked, "Can you tell us what happened to you wife and girlfriend when they heard the news of your marriage?" Kim smiles and says, "They both cannot be found, and may have left the city, but we discovered handwritten notes they left behind to wish Madeleine and I much love and happiness in the years ahead." The soldiers then drag the reporter to the rear of a building where a volley of gunfire can be heard.

Murmurs and quiet whispers among the crowd can barely be heard as it well-known to most attending the wedding that Madeleine LeBeau had died months ago at age 92. This prompted a CNN® reporter to ask Kim Jong Un about the obvious dilemma the supreme leader faced. Supreme leader Kim Jong Un thought for a moment, but he declined to answer, and ordered the reporter immediately be shot.

Over 1,297,618 guests were invited and everyone responded they would attend. Each guest was asked to bring their own food, and a gift of $1,000 per person (not couple) was strongly demanded.

CHELSEA HANDLER LAUNCHES THE "I HATE TRUMP FAN CLUB"

Late night host, Chelsea Handler takes charge as Chairperson, with Madonna as Music Director, Rosie O'Donnell as the Head of The Food Committee, and many more notables on the Advisory Board who meet in a gathering that will boggle the mind. Hear Maxine Waters, Nancy Pelosi, Ashley Judd and so many others speak their minds as they address the packed auditorium. The insights they provide on the philosophical direction of this new grass roots organization is both fascinating and very enlightening. With so many notables and media present, there was no need for Sir Telsunn Margraves to be surreptitious, all that was required was to sit there and enjoy...hope you will too!

Washington DC – The grand ballroom of the five star hotel, spa and casino in the nation's capital is filled to capacity. All are there to witness Chelsea Handler, the author, stand-up comedian and star of television and film, happily announce the launching of the *"The Women's Collective Initiative to Emotionally and Physically Join the I Hate Trump Fan Club."*

Chelsea steps center stage to cheers and applause and begins, "Welcome! I am so pleased to see so many from the news media here today for this truly important event. I am so proud to announce the launch of *'The Women's Collective Initiative to Emotionally and Physically Join the I Hate Trump Fan Club'* or the sake of brevity, the *'TWCITEAPJTIHTFC'* as we have come to call it. The *TWCITEAPJTIHTFC* was founded to provide women of all stripes; as long as they are of the leftist, progressive, liberal, socialist, communist stripes as well as any resident of San Francisco and Manhattan's West Side with a forum to vent against the piece of sh*t that was elected as President of the United States. Originally I thought of inviting men to join our group but then we'd need to change the name of the organization to *"The Women's and Men's Collective Initiative to Emotionally and Physically Join the I Hate Trump Fan Club* or the *'TWAMCIEAPJTIHTFC'* but we thought that would be too long and difficult to remember."

The gathering of main stream media reporters immediately burst into raucous and sustained cheering, and applause and Chelsea is deeply moved but appeals for quiet so she can finish her speech. "Thank you so much for your acknowledgement and support and now I would like to introduce you to the persons of renown that have agreed to become lifetime members of our organization and sit on our advisory board. The curtain opens to reveal some of the most famous people who have made it well know that they are virulently anti-Trump. Chelsea introduces the luminaries by joking, "From left to extreme left..." The audience bursts into laughter, and Chelsea smiles that her joke is appreciated by the audience, and continues, "Let me introduce to you our first mega-star, the hilarious comic and boundless Trump hater, Kathy Griffin. She has made us proud with the hilarious photo of her harmless, innocent fun-loving spoof where she is holding the decapitated, bloody head of Donald Trump. Even ISIS could not have done a better job." The audience goes into thunderous applause for Kathy Griffin and she stands up and blows a kiss of thanks to all and walks to center stage.

"Thanks to all of you here at this rally for that wonderful welcome. Well it's certainly been an eventful time for me!" The audience bursts into laughter at the thinly veiled reference to the photo of her holding President Trumps bloodied head. "I was just trying to be funny and the right wing cabal of commentators took this totally out of context. What I was trying to illustrate was my hypothesis that a head, when detached from the body, doesn't breathe anymore; this was an innocent scientific experiment to prove a hypothesis that needed to be validated. I wanted to use Trump's head in order to stop this despicable man from cutting federal government funding of such worthwhile scientific projects like *"How Monkeys Gamble"*, *"Swedish Massages for Bunnies"*, *"Whether 'Angry' Spouses Are More Likely To Stab Voodoo Dolls"*, *"Synchronized Swimming For Sea Monkeys"*, *"A Video Game About Food Fights"* plus many more real important studies that will have a lasting impact on so many Americans and monkeys."

The audience gives Kathy Griffin a standing ovation. Chelsea, realizing that they are already behind, asks the audience to calm down, and suggests that they hold all applause until all notables have been announced. There are a few moans of disappointment but those in the audience reluctantly agree to hold the applause.

Chelsea now feels she in in complete control as she continues. "Next we are proud to have on-stage, the international music miracle, the woman who has graciously accepted the official title of the *TWCITEAPJTIHTFC* Director of Music, Madonna! She has honored us by composing the official *TWCITEAPJTIHTFC* anthem that is sung to the tune of the Star Spangled Banner. We encourage all here to sing along and the lyrics will be projected by the big karaoke machine onto the screen above my head."

Madonna waves to all the attendees, as she stands and approaches the mic. The brightness of the stage lights is dimmed, and all in the crowd stand with hands in their pockets. The music rises, and Madonna begins to sing as the audience accompanies her,

Oh, say can you see
All the way to DC
Where so proudly we nag
At the Trump and his hag!
If it's dark or it's light
We will stay through the night
And if we get too hungry,
There's always Chinese delivery!
You must tear down the fences
And send us money for expenses
So we can look to do more
For Hollywood and the poor!
Oh say, does the *TWCITEAPJTIHTFC*
Bring joy to you and me
From the yachts that we sail
To the our time spent in jail!

Chelsea is awe struck and Madonna is nearly moved to tears, "I can't believe the great voices that there are in the audience. You make me proud to be a British citizen after I changed my US citizen status, so I'm signing you all to recording contracts!" The audience cheers in approval and Madonna waves and then takes her seat. Chelsea is thrilled at the outpouring of love and adoration for Madonna, and tells the people, "There is so much more to do at this event, and we asked Madonna to sing just one of the stanzas, however, you can go on our website www.*TWCITEAPJTIHTFC*.org/*TWCITEAPJTIHTFC.anthem*, and see the complete lyrics as written by our own Music Director, Madonna!"

Chelsea grudgingly knows she must allow the applause, so she hastily introduces the next person. "To the 'left' of Madonna is the star of film and television, and a visionary Trump hater, Rosie O'Donnell! Rosie has agreed to be in charge of planning all of the meals at our meetings, and we are sure to be inspired by her love of food."

Rosie rises and makes a funny face to the audience, and everyone bursts into peals of laughter as she playfully waddles to center stage.

Rosie gets in the spirit of the event and yells, "Is this f**kin' great or what!?" The audience agrees, and yells their approval. "When I read about the club, and spoke with Chelsea about its charter and mission, I immediately said, where do I sign up?" More cheers for those present and Rosie continues, "I thought about what role I could play, and how I could have the greatest impact on the mandates of the *TWCITEAPJTIHTF,* so I decided to become the head of the food service committee. It is an awesome responsibility that I take very seriously. For instance, take the meal that I planned just prior to the event. The first course was yummy fried shrimp from Long John Silvers®. I just love the way the juices flow down my chin as I suck the meat from the tail. Next we had the fried chicken fingers from Kentucky Fried Chicken™. I love the way the Colonel's secret crunchy coating of the chicken explodes with juices from the chicken thighs as it runs down my chin...and the fries, oh the fries..." A glazed look comes over Rosie's eyes as she seems to be in a trance-like state. Chelsea Handler sees that Rosie has lost the ability to continue to speak so she walks over and guides Rosie back to her seat. Those people seated in the front rows heard her mumble "Dairy Queen Blizzard®...Dairy Queen Blizzard®..."

Not knowing what to make of what's happened to Rosie O'Donnell, the audience shrugs it off and starts applauding. At first, Chelsea feels that she should admonish the onlookers as she has previous told them to save all reactions until the end. Chelsea thinks to herself; don't these idiots know to save their applause, but she recognizes these are members of the media, and many of them are clueless therefore blameless.

Chelsea tries to brush off this insult to her rules and regulations, and speaks, "Wasn't that wonderful? Thank you again Rosie!" More mumbling can be heard but Chelsea moves on, "Now going from left-to-further left, the next person needs no introduction. She has been a driving force; a stalwart in the fight against racism, the fight against injustice and the fight against all that is Trump, here is Congresswoman Maxine Waters."

The audience wants to burst into a massive show of raucous cheering and screaming, but Chelsea Handler is staring them down and that seems to drown any enthusiasm that may erupt. Rep. Maxine Waters hobbles to the center of the stage and begins, "I feel like the only black woman here." Then she suddenly realizes that she is the only black woman there and says, "Why the hell aren't there more black women here?" Chelsea is flummoxed as she nervously tells Rep. Waters that some of the invitations must have been lost in the mail, and assures Maxine that she will follow up as soon as possible.

This seems to somewhat mollify Maxine Waters so she begins again, "First I would like to apologize for hobbling to the center of the stage. I bought a new pair of shoes for this event and for some reason they don't fit properly. I don't know why, they seemed to fit fine in the store but now..." Maxine can't stand the pain any longer so she reaches down, and takes off her shoes. When she does take off her shoes, a metal shoe horn falls from inside the right shoe and clanks on the floor. Maxine looks puzzled at first, but then it becomes apparent to her, and she grows angrier and angrier and screams at the audience, "Can you believe this? The shoe store purposely put a shoe horn in my right shoe, and it almost killed me. I am going to sue the bastards back to the Stone Age. I will also sponsor a new anti-shoe horn Federal legislation that will stop this assault on the feet of American citizens forever!"

Maxine still looks angry, and she wants to let the audience know exactly what's on her mind. "My time is limited and there are so many things that I want to say, I became the advocate for women, protesting and marching against the all evils that Trump and white people represent." Maxine then looks around and corrects herself, "...of course, present company excluded." Maxine looks at the women on the stage and she smiles and continues to speak, "*I am a woman and it started with my mother. I have to march because my mother could not have an abortion. I only wish she could have had an abortion,* then maybe I wouldn't have to march. *Guess what this liberal would be all about? I am a liberal and this liberal will be about socializing...uh, um...Would be about, basically, taking over, and the government running all of your companies. I think that when you saw Donald Trump absolutely calling Hillary Clinton 'crooked', the 'lock her up, lock her up,' all of that was developed. I think that was developed strategically with people from the Kremlin, with Vladimir Putin. I just think the American people had better under-stand what's going on. This is a bunch of scumbags. That's what [Russians] are!* Maxine stops speaking and reaches for a glass of water on the podium and takes a drink, and she concludes with her take on issues of the economy and jobs, *"I do not necessarily support the president's decision. If* [Donald Trump] *wants to do good things, let's see it. Let him do it. I can't stop him from doing good things.* But if Trump allows *sequestration, more than 170 million Americans could lose their jobs!* Considering only 134 Million peo-ple have jobs that would mean nearly 40 million people who don't have jobs would become even more unemployed according to the Bureau of Labor Statistics."

Chelsea walks over to Rep. Maxine Waters, and she gives her a big hug. "Repre-sentative Waters, Maxine, I have never heard such a powerful, eloquent and cogent speech in my life. You are an inspiration to all *TWCITEAPJTIHTFC* members. Max-ine smiles at Chelsea, waves to the crowd, and limps back to her seat.

Chelsea claps, and she says, "Isn't she brilliant! Moving on, I am very proud, and pleased to introduce our next member of the *TWCITEAPJTIHTFC* Advisory Board, Minority Speaker of the US House of Representatives, Nancy Pelosi!" Before Chelsea can continue with her introduction the audience jumps out of their seats screaming and chanting PEL-O-SI, PEL-O-SI! No one seems to care about Chelsea's admonition for quiet until all on the stage are introduced so she just stands on stage embittered by the rebuke. When all finally calms down, Chelsea Handler turns her back to the crowd and thinks to herself, 'these a**holes can just go f*ck themselves', and she continues, "Nancy Pelosi has become an inspiration to all women from all walks of life except perhaps from some who may need to work. She has been single handedly responsible for the flawless implementation of Obamacare in spite of the fact she never read the 2,700 plus page law. Now that Donald Trump has rescinded the individual mandate, she remains strident in her belief that Obamacare is lower-ing costs, and the deficit, and personally I believe her!"

Rep. Nancy Pelosi takes her turn at the podium, and she begins to speak, "Thank you Chelsea for the marvelous and much deserved introduction. Ladies and gen-tlemen I am afraid, very afraid for the American people. Do you want to know why I'm afraid for the American people?" The audience screams, "Yes, we want to know why you're afraid for the American people!" Rep. Pelosi continues, "I hate to have to contradict my beloved colleague and fellow Democrat, Maxine Waters, but I believe her statistic is wrong. *Every month that we do not have an economic recovery package 500 million Americans lose their jobs!* You hear the Republicans say that our deficit is out of control, and that we are spending too much. Well I say *it's almost a false argument to say we have a spending problem,* but we do have a problem, NOT ENOUGH TAXES!" The audience now goes wild, they are in rapture. Nancy acknowledges the cheers, and she says, "They also try to tell us that our beloved President Obama, and our beloved Democrat party is doing all this for political reasons, well let me tell you *Obama has never done anything for political reasons.* Remember who told you this about Republicans and remember it well; *Civilization as we know it today would be in jeopardy if the Republicans win the Senate* and what happened? They won! How the hell did that happen?"

Nancy Pelosi needs to take a break as she seems out of breath, but when that passes she is able to continue. "...And to paraphrase *what our founders said in the Constitution of the United States: they said great social changes are impossible without feminine upheaval. Social progress can be measured exactly by the social position of the fair sex, the ugly ones included. As President Washington said during the Gettysburg Address, It takes a great deal of bravery to stand up to your enemies, but a great deal more to stand up to your friends. Don't underestimate your opponent, but don't overestimate them, either.*"

The audience seems dumbfounded. They are confused as to whether they should applaud or they should scratch their heads, but they all decide to applaud anyway and Nancy recognizes the devotion to her that seems to fill the room.

Chelsea Handler now turns to the people seated in the grand ballroom, and glowers at them to stop any thought of excess clapping against her express orders. The audience suddenly becomes silent so she continues, "The next woman is an activist beauty in her own right, a star of stage and screen and a national treasure, Ashley Judd. Ashley is a true champion, a voice for women all over the polo deprived areas of Beverly Hills, the no public restroom sections of Chevy Chase, the vegan restaurant free subdivisions of San Francisco, the over-priced coops along the East and West sides of Manhattan...I could go on and on, but you get the idea. It is my extreme pleasure to introduce the personification of what a Trump Hater should be, Ashley Judd!"

Ashley Judd, wearing her trademark pussy hat, gets up and playfully courtesies and goes to the podium to address the audience that is going crazy with adoration. After the applause dies down, she begins speaking, *My name is Ashley Judd and I am a feminist.*" The audience is rapt as Ashley begins to speak. "I didn't have time to actually write a speech, but I did a great job in Washington DC at the Women's March don't you think? Well, I thought that I would give you some of the highlights of that speech if that's okay?" There is a roar of approval, and Ashley smiles and continues, "*I am a nasty woman. I'm as nasty as a man who looks like he bathes in Cheetos dust. A man whose words are a distraction to America. I am not as nasty as your own daughter being your favorite sex symbol, like your wet dreams infused with your own genes.*" Judd continues to tell everyone how nasty she is and says, "*I am nasty like my bloodstains on my bed sheets. We don't actually choose if and when to have our periods. Believe me if we could some of us would. We do not like throwing away our favorite pair of underpant. Tell me, why are pads and tampons still taxed when Viagra and Rogaine are not?*" This quote seems to get the audience thinking, 'why don't you just wash your underpants?' This seems odd to the members of the audience but they shrug their shoulders and cheer! Ashley Judd continues, "*And our pussies ain't for grabbing. They're for reminding you that our walls are stronger than America's ever will be. Our pussies are for our pleasure. They are for birthing new generations of filthy, vulgar, nasty, proud, Christian, Muslim, Buddhist, Sikh, you name it, for new generations of nasty women. So if you're a nasty woman, or you love one who is, let me hear you say, hell yeah.*" The audience now erupts with one gigantic "HELL YEAH!"

Chelsea Handler is thrilled to hear Ashley's speech and is confident that her words define those women she anticipates will be joining *TWCITEAPJTIHTFC*. Even though Chelsea has admonished against cheering by those gathered in the grand ballroom, she will allow the adulation to exhaust itself...and it does. Chelsea wipes a tear from her eye, and she grabs Ashley and they embrace so hard that Ashley's pussy hat is knocked off her head. Chelsea gushes over her, and says, "Oh Ashley, sorry about that but I've said it before and I'll say it again, you are a national treasure you silver-tongued devil you. Thank you for the inspirational, clear, persuasive, eloquent, and lucid annunciation of what the *TWCITEAPJTIHTFC* is all about." Ashley blushes, waves at the audience, and takes her seat.

Chelsea looks at her wrist watch and tells the audience, "I just checked the time and it seems that we are running behind schedule so I would like the rest of the advisory board to introduce themselves, and say something about why they all joined the *TWCITEAPJTIHTFC.*"

Chelsea motions to Comedian Amy Schumer who stands up and walks to the center of the stage to the cheers of her many fans. Amy says, "I promised you all as a loyal American that *if Trump wins I am moving to Spain.* Unfortunately I found out that they speak a different language there so I promise that as soon as I learn Latino *I am moving to Spain!*" Someone from the audience yells out, it's Spanish. Amy looks a little taken about and asks "What's Spanish?" and the audience member yells back, "The language in Spain is Spanish." Amy stares at the mic, and says, "Oh", and she sits down.

The next Advisory Board member to speak is comedian Margaret Cho who rises to address the gathering. Margaret starts by telling the audience, "My name is Margaret Cho, and every time I think about Trump I'm in the crapper, and as I wipe my ass I look at the paper, and say this about Donald, *you're like no ply toilet paper. Just trash!* I want to close by saying those immortal words of the singer, actress, and all around modern-day philosopher Kristen Bell when she said of Trump's election, *'anyone else wanna puke?'"* A looks comes over Margaret as her face turns green, and she says, "OH SHIT, I actually do need to puke!" Almost on command, Margaret Cho projectile vomits her entire lunch including the Fried Shrimp, chicken strips and French fries all over the stage.

Chelsea doesn't know how to handle this as she makes her way next to Margaret and tries to avoid the vomit that is slowly spreading all over the stage floor. Chelsea yells loudly into the mic, "Is there a janitor nearby? Can you come up here and clean this mess?" She takes Margaret by the hand and slowly walks her back to her seat. By this time Ashley Judd and Amy Schumer have moved further left to give Margaret

Cho plenty of room. Chelsea is at a loss to know what to say so she just asks the next board member to introduce herself, and continue speaking.

Now at center stage stands Lena Dunham the actress, writer, producer and director. Lena Dunham steps up to the mic and says, "It really stinks up here" as she realizes that she is standing right next to Margaret Cho's vomit. Knowing it is impolite to mention Margaret's unfortunate accident, Lena tries to be more understanding, "Hey Margaret, here is something that I remember from reading Sylvia Plath, *'There is nothing like puking with somebody to make you into old friends'* even though I didn't puke I consider us good friends." Lena laughs and the audience follows. "You may have read in the news that I promised to move to Canada if Trump was elected, and unfortunately he was elected." The audience boos, and Lena asks them to calm down, "Please ladies and gentlemen, please! It is something that I must do. I have not settled on an exact timetable, but I am working on it. I did experience a problem in that I couldn't find my suitcase and I need it for my clothes and object d'art. I could have left it next to the cabstand when I visited Havana, Cuba or is it languishing in a CIA or FBI office. Regardless, I am moving as soon as I am able to sell my $4.8 million dollar townhouse in Brooklyn. Unfortunately no one wants to buy in Brooklyn anymore due to the small number of Starbucks® so I will be staying there for the immediate future. Please 'like' me on Facebook® and I'll keep you posted. I will let everyone know when I move and I'll give all of you my address, and perhaps we can exchange Holiday greeting cards." The audience is now wrestling with the logic but after all it is Lena Dunham so they applaud anyway. Lena bows and goes back to her seat, to the very, very left of Margaret Cho.

The last board member to stand and say some words of inspiration to the audience is Miley Cyrus. She is about to speak but goes strangely silent as a single tear rolls down her eye, *"Donald Trump is a fucking nightmare.* He has hypnotized women into becoming hunters and *this makes me so unbelievable scared and sad.* Let me show you this." Miley hits a button on the podium and an image projected by the karaoke's video component appears on an overhead screen. The image is of a woman hoisting up an animal that has been shot. Miley laments *"Not only for our country but for* *animals that I love more than anything in this world.... My heart is broken into a 100,000 pieces ...* With all due apologies to Margaret Cho, *'I think I may vomit ...' That picture on the right is so disturbing.... YOU are not destiny! It is not your job to decide when a living things life is over.... & YOU DT* [Donald Trump] *ARE NOT GOD NO MATTER HOW MUCH YOU THINK YOU ARE!!! (& if he doesn't think he is 'God' he thinks he is the f*cking chosen one or some sh*t! We're all just f*cking jam between his rich a** toes!"* Miley is wound up and she screams at the audience, *"Honestly,* like I said on Instagram, *f*ck this sh*t, I am moving if this is my president! I don't say things I don't mean!* Hey, maybe Lena and Amy and I can buy a house together and live off the grid or something."

Chelsea walks to center stage, embraces Miley, and they both start twerking to the new *TWCITEAPJTIHTFC* anthem. The audience gets up out of their seats and start twerking too. All seems to be going well until a twerk goes awry. A huge fight breaks out between Shia LaBeouf, Stephen Hawking, Jack Black, Bette Midler, Olivia Wilde, Kumail Nanjiani, Katie Couric, Lady Gaga, Mark Ruffalo, Stephen King, J.K. Rowling, Susan Sarandon, Samuel L. Jackson, Cher, George Clooney, Jennifer Lawrence, Johnny Depp and a number of other "A" listers as well as "B" and "C" list entertainers who are hoping to get some exposure.

Punches are being thrown and Chelsea is starting to get hysterical. She tries to get the advisory board to help calm things down by having them all yell in unison, "This is not the way progressives, liberals, left wing, antifa social activists and members of *TWCITEAPJTIHTFC* act. Think of Bernie..." but it's no use. Better Midler is kicking Lady Gaga in the shins; Shia LaBeouf is trying to drag Stephen Hawking from his wheelchair; Stephen King steps on J.K. Rowling's toes, and he screams '*Dark Tower* is better than *Harry Potter.*' Although Chelsea and the board members are appealing for calm, the frenzy shows no signs of abating; George Clooney tries to get Johnny Depp to swallow his necktie; Samuel L Jackson yells to Katie Couric, "come on bitch and show me what you got!"; Jack Black, Sarah Silverman and Kumail Nanjiani are throwing chairs and dinnerware at each other; and no-one seems to care about Cher and Mark Ruffalo so they just sit down and spit at each other.

Finally the former FBI Director James Comey, and an FBI team of former investigators who have been put in charge of security, come to the grand ballroom as they try getting everyone to stop fighting. They usher all notables out the door and into non-descript stretch limos. Given the stature of the advisory board and famous guests, it is deemed that the riot should be kept quiet and an explanation be offered to the news organizations.

The next day reports of the event were published in both the New York Times and Washington Post, and both articles said essentially said the same thing.

"It was the inaugural launch of Chelsea Handler's *"The Women's Collective Initiative to Emotionally and Physically Join the I Hate Trump Fan Club"* or *TWCITEAPJTIHTFC* as it has come to be known. There were many progressive, politically active women and men present, and a wonderful time was had by all. The comradery was evident as everyone was hugging and kissing each other and there was so much love in the room.

"Toward the end of the event there was a small ruckus caused by a group of right-wing fascists, Trump-loving white supremacists that infiltrated the meeting and damages were extensive, including broken chairs and dinnerware. The hooligans were brought down by the former FBI investigators under the strong leadership of former FBI Director James Comey. As readers may remember then FBI Director Comey exonerated Hillary Clinton from everything in connection with her private server, emailing of classified documents, lying and charges related to Russia and alleged collusion and coercion.

Ms. Handler was quoted as saying 'After the launch I was able to reflect on the importance of the *TWCITEAPJTIHTFC,* and the nature of responsibilities in such an organization as ours. Given the scope of work, and my extensive commitment to the mission of the *TWCITEAPJTIHTFC,* I feel it best that I enter a rehab facility to come to terms with this awesome undertaking. In the interim, I have asked my dear friend and comrade in arms, Sarah Silverman to take the mantle of leadership until I am released under my own recognizance."

Apologies to the readers, I know that I promised absolutely positive, genuine, real, fake news but I also included a series of actual quotes from a number of the famous personages referenced in this story. You will note these quotes are in "italics" as it sometimes is tough to compete with reality-TM

THE SNOWFLAKE LOUNGE

Sir Telsunn Margraves felt duty-bound to fly to California to see, firsthand, how their University system accommodates its students in light of Donald Trump's ascension to the presidency. HBO® commentator John Oliver and his crew perform research and provide probing insights that went into the documentary, "The Snow-flake Lounge." Disguised as part of the maintenance crew, Sir Telsunn, was able to explore the newly built 60,000 S/F facility, soon to be enlarged to 210,000 square feet, located on the campus of UC Berkeley. The lounge was built to accommodate a growing segment of their students in constant need comfort and succor. It's an opportunity to meet the students affectionately known as 'snowflakes' and to find out what goes on in their minds.

Berkeley, CA – In the wake of the disastrous election of Donald Trump, John Oliver, the host of HBO's® "Last Week Tonight with John Oliver", has decided to do an up-close, personal examination of the effect this political upheaval is having on college students. For this feature John Oliver has selected one college campus that will serve as a microcosm in examining the recent phenomenon emerging on campuses across America. This phenomenon is affectionately referred to as "The Snowflake Lounges."

Some critics in progressive circles have taken exception to the term 'snowflake' as they see it as derogatory toward those who have been traumatized by the recent election of President Trump. Mr. Oliver, however, sees it in a different way, "Think of what a snowflake represents! Each is different and unique, each is frosty cold and immediately melts when you touch it, get enough of them you can totally stop traffic thereby lowering carbon emissions so as to put an end to global-warming. An ancillary benefit is that when combined with other snowflakes you can build a snowperson."

To create this examination of "The Snowflake Lounge", Mr. Oliver has selected The University of California, Berkeley. When asked why by the powers at HBO®, John Oliver said, "It's kind of like the Independence Hall for Snowflakes where safe-space and tolerance reign triumphant. It is where all LGBTQIA, pro-progressive, pro-antifa, pro-Democrat, pro-politically correct Halloween costumes, anti-White, anti-Conservative, anti-Trump, anti-wrong thinking people can be safe to express individual opinions based on collective thought and where group thought becomes victorious." Mr. Oliver voiced the entire explanation without breathing.

John Oliver completed the necessary forms and was given permission by the University of California at Berkeley administration to begin production. Unfortunately the Chancellor had to resign because in adopting this policy he failed to include groups that supported the Otherkin community. Undeterred Oliver and his companions made the arduous journey by flying first class to Berkeley, California where they explored the campus with a sharp focus on how to capture all the excitement in his special report. It took very little time for the crew to find the 60,000 square foot safe-space Snowflake Lounge. They had to navigate through the hard-hat area as the administration has approved the construction of an extra 150,000 square feet of space to meet the demand for additional safe-spaces. The new building complex will be dedicated as *The Sarah Silverman/Samantha Bee/Kathy Griffin Building for Building Self-Esteem to Find a Way to Better Communicate with All Those People We Like but Not Those We Don't Like.*

John Oliver and the crew enter the lounge area and are surprised when they see the building, and rooms are nearly filled with students participating in various discussions. They were puzzled at first but it was explained to them by the receptionist that classes have become optional for all those who cannot cope with the excessive rigors of studies as well as those traumatized by the presidential election. Expecting to hear about silly courses like Physics or Biology or Business Management, John was gratified when the receptionist confided that some of the courses like *"The Joy of Garbage"*, plus new additions like *"Getting Dressed"*, *"Oh, Look, a Chicken!"*, *"Interrogating Gender: Centuries of Dramatic Cross-Dressing"*, *"What If Harry Potter Is Real?"* are among many curriculum courses that require time for the subject matter to congeal.

Each safe space is crowded with young people who have taken the opportunity to discover anodyne and solace in simple practices and where they can find succor. In one of the first places the crew notices is a safe space where a lone young woman is holding and petting a gerbil. Her face is stained with the remnants of dried tears and she appears to be in a trance-like state as she keeps mumbling the name "Steve Bannon...Steve Bannon...Steve Bannon."

John decides that this student would be perfect for the opening segment so he sits on the floor next to the student and asks her name.

She looks up in bewilderment, "My name?"

Ever sympathetic John says, "Yes, dear, your name."

The young woman pauses and begins the thinking process to be sure she gets it right, "Willow Tree Feinstein."

"Willow Tree, what a lovely name."

"Actually I just go by the name Willow, Tree is my middle name."

"Oh, okay then Willow it is. How are you today Willow?"

Willow then bursts into tears as she clutches the gerbil and screams, "Suuu-suusteeveee Bbbaannonnn!!!!"

John is now becoming frightened, "I don't mean to upset you Ms. Feinstein but what about Steve Bannon?"

Willow now screams even louder, "SUUUSUUSTEEVEEE BBBAANNONNN!!!" Now the gerbil is starting to lose its fur as Willow is petting him harder and harder.

John Oliver doesn't know how to react but he wants to calm the hysterical woman. "Ms. Feinstein please you're disturbing the people over at the 'Bernie Sanders is the Living god' safe-space."

The gerbil is now turning blue as Willow is squeezing the poor animal harder and harder and the poor young woman continues to scream, "WHO IS SUUU-SUUSTEEVEEE BBBAANNONNN!!!"

John finally realizes that it would be better for everyone, including the gerbil, if they moved onto another safe space. He tells Willow, "Ms. Feinstein we'll go now but it was very nice speaking with you." Much to the relief of the gerbil, Willow has calmed down somewhat and her screams have turned to blubbering. She looks up at John Oliver and says, "Steve Bannon? Where is he? Who is he? What is he?"

John Oliver and the crew get up off the floor and walk down the main hallway on the first floor of the Sarah Silverman et al Building and walk through the "Chelsea Handler Wing" past the "Michelle Wolf Vomitorium." It is there they hear what seems to be an argument coming from one of the rooms. John looks through the doorway marked the "Ashley Judd Room" and he notices chairs that are placed in a circle. There are eight women and one man and they seem to be having a heated discussion about something. John Oliver knocks on the door and the group talking stops and those in the room look over to see the man standing in the doorway.

"Good morning, my name is John Oliver and I am here to do a special report on safe spaces for snowflakes here at Berkeley. Would you mind if we set up a camera and tape your conversations for airing on HBO®?"

The group just looks at each other and collectively shrugs their shoulders as one of the female students attending said, "Sure, why not."

Ever empathetic, John tells the group, "I apologize for barging in like this as it appears your group is discussing something very important."

A young woman who seems to be the leader of the group rises to address John. "Our group is contemplating the use of pussy hats in protests. There is some discussion of color given the many diverse groups that will participate as well as an in-depth analysis of appropriateness for men to wear a pussy hat."

The only man in the group jumps out of his seat and practically screams at the group leader, "Man! You call me a man! How could you even say such a thing? I am a questioning, intersex transgender person and I demand the right to wear a pussy hat just like the rest of you."

The leader tries to assuage any anxiety that the questioning, intersex transgender person may have. "Please Lacey, I know this is important but we must try to remain calm. These are significant points that must be covered, after all our next protest is only two days away."

John Oliver senses something important that is about to happen and asks what important issue is the focus of the next protest; "By the way, I never got your name."

The leader says, "My name is Franklina Roosevelt."

John smiles, "Oh, I see you were named after the president."

Franklina looks puzzled, "Who?"

"Never mind, what is it that you will be protesting? I am sure it is a very important cause."

Franklina becomes animated as she explains to John Oliver the nature of their protest. "We will march in our pussy hats, color to be determined, to the *'Free the Nipple'* protest being held Wednesday on campus. Throughout the modern world, women have been forced to cover their nipples by a society that abhors exhibition of brown or purple or red or pink nipples that are among the colors of these protuberances. We have been inspired by our sisters and brothers and others who began this protest at UC San Diego and we are hoping to expose this so it spreads to campuses around California and the country. You also may be interested in hearing about our next protest, the *'Sh*t In'* to encourage poop equity. This important cause began at

Cal Poly to protest the lack of access to gender neutral bathrooms. We are beginning with nipples and moving onto the assholes...a small joke."

Lacey shouts out, "I want my nipples to be freed! Free the Nipple! Free the Nipple!" Now everyone in the group is chanting "Free the Nipple! Free the Nipple!"

John feels that this is a good opportunity to leave the group and he thanks everyone for their time and exits into the hallway. There are many sessions where students have gathered to help alleviate the angst that permeates snowflake thinking since the election of Donald Trump. Signs have been posted on the doors to indicate what is happening inside and one reads "Relieving the Stress of the Elections and How You can Survive!"

John peaks into the room and sees a professor gently prodding the students while trying to tell them all the demonstrations have done to relieve the pressure they face daily on campus. The groups of students are all stone-faced as they stare at the man who is speaking to them. John decides to stand by the door and just listen until he is able to break into the discussion.

"As you all know, in the past four weeks our administration has taken unprecedented steps to make sure you are all safe. We have made the decision to cancel all testing as it degrades those of the student community who don't study." The class still remains expressionless but the professor continues. "We, your instructors, have demanded that the administration make permanent Taco Tuesdays in celebration of the large undocumented Mexican population that work as gardeners and kitchen staff at our university." There is a small smattering of polite applause from the audience so the professor assumes he is having the necessary impact to reach the group.

At this time, John Oliver interrupts the discussion and informs the professor and all those assembled why he is here in The Snowflake Lounge. He explains that he would like to tape the professor's speech and the student reaction for his upcoming HBO® special. This announcement seems to generate quite a bit of excitement and there is excitement among the students expressing anticipation that they could be seen on television. They all start to look at their reflections in the window to see if their hair is still a mess. Some students even smell their armpits to be sure they don't offend any of the TV viewers who will be watching.

The professor is pleased as he thinks it's an opportunity to showcase the university's accommodations to various segments of the student body. He is also anxious to showcase and how the administration is able to acquiesce to the snowflake demands and still maintain some semblance of humiliating dignity. The professor turns to the class and asks, "Are we all okay with this?"

The group answers in unison, "Sure!"

The professor tells John and his crew to set up wherever they want, but please do not disturb his discussion as it is important. "I know it is quite exciting to have a famous person here to record this discussion so let us continue. I want to be the first to make you aware of a very important initiative that is being instituted at UC Berkeley. We have done painstaking research to find the most advanced and appropriate steps to make it more comforting in these very trying times. First, we have adopted the policy of the University of California system to not use common phrases like *'America is the land of opportunity'* or *'I believe the most qualified person should get the job'* because even these clichés could be considered micro-aggressions. Next, we will allow all professors, administrators, janitorial staff, kitchen workers, parking lot attendants, grounds keepers etc. to beat and pummel all students who do not participate in protests and/or are members of Republican and Conservative groups. This was started at the University of Missouri and we will keep the revolution going." John looks around the class to see if there is any reaction from the students and all he can see are the same stone-faced looks along with some students still are smelling their armpits.

"Following a precedent set by Yale University, we will offer each and every student who does not want to pay for tuition, support to go on a hunger strike but they will be allowed to eat if they get hungry. Unlike Yale however, we will extend this policy to both graduate and under-graduate students!"

Now the professor is nervous that he is getting no reaction from the assembled mass so he decides the he will up the ante and with more announcements. "In addition, UC Berkeley will follow the lead of the University of Texas at Austin by holding a *'Cocks not Glocks'* protest against campus carry laws that are non-existent but eternal vigilance is still needed. The protest will be held next Friday and free dildos will be available through a generous donation from "Ralph's House of Passion and Pain." The professor looks around hoping to see some reaction to his announcement but still nothing but blank stares.

The professor is a little shaky, but remains undeterred as he continues, "We are also expressing solidarity with the University of Virginia and we will stop quoting Thomas Jefferson and start to quote only George Jefferson or the Jefferson Starship or both. UC Berkeley will also march in lock-step with Lebanon County College and demand that Lynch Memorial Hall be renamed." At this point a number of students jump out of their seats and begin to screaming at the professor, "Why do you want to change the name!"

The professor is feeling the heat and says, "Lynch is an offensive word to some..."

The students are now shouting, "We stand by LORETTA LYNCH! LORETTA LYNCH, LORETTA LYNCH..."

The professor is sweating profusely, "No, no you don't understand."

"Yes we do! You want to suppress Loretta Lynch...LORETTA LYNCH, LORETTA LYNCH, LORETTA LYNCH!"

"No...the hall's name connotes a term that is associated with racism! The building was named after Charles Lynch, the founder, and the word lynch implies awful crimes..."

The students look at each other and one among them stands up and faces the professor. "Well instead of naming the hall after a racist term we should advocate a hall be renamed Lynch Memorial Hall after Loretta Lynch." The professor considers this and says, "Good idea, we will suggest that Lynch Memorial Hall be renamed Lynch Memorial Hall. I'll draft a letter to UVA and read it at our next meeting."

For the first time the students appear to favorably respond and this gives the professor a reason to feel he is reaching the students on a deep and personal level. He says, "I have two more initiatives I would like to proclaim, first, the University has agreed to purchase, on behalf of the students here at UC Berkeley, 2,000 complete sets of Scobee Doo and Peppa Pig™ coloring books. Extensive research has found that many students find comfort and positive reinforcement when they color such characters as 'Velma', 'Shaggy' and of course 'Scobee' and there's 'Mr. Dinosaur',

'Mummy Pig', 'Suzy Sheep' and 'Pedro Pony' as well as 'Peppa Pig' himself. This is a very exciting step forward. Finally, there is a heated discussion among all the administration here at UC Berkeley, and we will institute daily *'Cry-Ins.'* Students can come to cry about everything from Trump being elected President to Trump failing to provide free tuition to Trump not paying for ethnically appropriate foods on campuses to Trump not disbanding the US Armed Forces and using the money to pay for your college tuition to Trump being responsible for not funding free Netflix and Hulu to Trump forgetting to mention Otherkin in his Inaugural Address and many more reasons for cry-ins. By the way parents are allowed to participate."

John Oliver is ecstatic as he realizes that he has just recorded a major segment for his upcoming documentary and he is anxious to see the reaction of the HBO® higher-ups. John compliments the students and the professor and thanks them for allowing him to tape this lively and provocative discussion and the snowflakes seem pleased.

As the crew is packing up there is a great out-cry from the group and the students begin to shout at the speaker, "How could you! How could you deny our rights?"

The professor is near the point of collapse and asks in as apologetic tone as he can muster, "What, what have I done? Please let me know and I will be sure to make things right."

A spokesperson among the students stands up and says, "Sure, you tell us we can protest but who will pay us? Huh, who will pay us for the time we spend protesting and not going to classes? Our brothers and sisters and members of the LGBTQIA community, Atheists, Socialists, Communists, Otherkin, and every group from Oberlin College are putting their lives on the line demanding that they be paid $8.20 an hour for protesting. Can you imagine the disgrace? Only $8.20 an hour! You've been preaching to us about all these things but you never mentioned paying us for our time and efforts protesting. We all agree that first, you should give us a minimum living wage of $15.00 per hour and second, you need to resign."

The color completely drains from the professor's face as he makes a feeble attempt at trying to protest the protestors protesting by saying, "But..."

John and the crew take this as their cue and leave the room looking for another example of how the Snowflake Lounges are creating a more comfortable, safer environment to explore feelings of anger, sexual questionings and Steve Bannon. As they begin to walk down the hallway to see if there are any other possible sectors of snowflake to include in the documentary, the sound of cheers and applause could be heard coming from an auditorium located nearby.

This sounds like the perfect closing feature for John Oliver's HBO® Special. He and his crew race down the hall past the "Patton Oswalt Transgender Bathroom" and enter the packed "Saul Alinsky Memorial Auditorium" and try to find space and set up the camera. At first you couldn't hear the speaker above the raucous screams and hysteria and given that everyone is up and jumping to see a person on stage. It's difficult but John Oliver works his way through the crowd and finds a vantage point to where he can see what the excitement is all about. A man is standing center stage behind a podium in front of a closed curtain. He is smiling as he steps from behind the podium and begins to pace back and forth and the crowd is enthralled.

"Now, ladies and gentlemen, here is what you've all been waiting for. The curtain parts and reveals the most amazing life-size statue of Barack Obama made completely out of LEGOS®. The student snowflakes now go into complete and utter rapture. "Ladies and gentlemen, through those difficult times in life you can find peace and comfort in creating anything you want to with LEGOS®. As you can see, I've built this statue of the former president using a rainbow of colors to symbolize the diversity and all-inclusiveness that was the hallmark of his administration. Now, please take your seats and I will demonstrate how to make one of your very own statues to keep and cherish. Remember, this will take commitment and patience and I have received permission from the UC Berkeley administration to offer this as a fully accredited college level course earning those of you who enroll four credits toward your degree. Of course it will be free to all those who do not want to pay!"

Now the entire group of students assembled in the "Saul Alinsky Memorial Auditorium" burst into unrestrained applause and cheering. John Oliver tries to overcome the flood of emotions he is feeling after observing this outpouring of excitement and love the snowflakes lavish on the speaker. He wants to cry as he grasps the full meaning of what he has observed on his visit to UC Berkeley. John fully understands the meaning of life and how it impacts these young men and women who will lead America in the years to come and nods as he mutters to himself, "LEGOS®…"

John Oliver is thrilled; he has taped what he believes will be the definitive documentary about these gentle souls that populate campus' across the country. He is anxious to get back to HBO® so that they can begin editing the footage for his HBO® special. The crew gathers the entire pile of equipment used in the production and they become very animated discussing their favorite interviews. They exit UC Berkeley's Snowflake Lounge when they confront a group of screaming, shouting protestors. More than a thousand protestors are carrying homemade signs that read "Oliver is an Asshole"…"Stop Premature Christmas Decorations"…"Boycott Oliver and HBO®"…"Oliver is an Elitist Pawn of the Military Industrial Complex" "I Am Insecure about my Masculinity and Afraid of Death" among hundreds of other invectives.

John and the crew are both puzzled and frightened by what they see as an unruly mob. They are desperate to speak with someone, anyone of the protestors to find out why there seems to be such hate and vitriol towards them. The horde surrounds them and their shrieks are so loud that John Oliver and his crew cannot be heard above the screams. Finally one of the protestors', a young man dressed in a panda suit, calls for the mob to quiet down. He demands Oliver and his crew explain why they have failed miserably at the single most important issue facing the students of UC Berkeley.

Panda man demands, "Well! Answer me! Answer all of us NOW!"

John Oliver feels his bowels growing weak as he begs, "What? What have we done?"

"WHAT HAVE YOU DONE?!" The crowd now chants "What have you done! What have you done! What have you done!" The self-appointed spokesperson grabs a megaphone from one of the students present and screams into John Oliver's ear "PANDA EXPRESS®!!! That's what you've done!"

John is beyond frantic as he sees no way out of this predicament. He is about to cry but he blubbers, "Panda Express®? What about Panda Express®?"

The panda man snorts and says in a menacing tone, "You'll soon find out" and a sub-group of 283 students approach John and the crew Each student protester is carrying a bowl of bamboo shoots and they hurl them at Mr. Oliver and his crew. Soon John and the crew are all covered in the Chinese delicacy with one of the crew asking for mercy and another asking if anyone has soy sauce.

That evening HBO® received a note from the snowflake lounge committee on behalf of the student body at UC Berkeley telling their board of directors that they will free Jon Oliver and his crew once Panda Express is removed from campus' student lounge.

Please note that the protests and college level courses referred to in this Fake News are in fact, real and offered at a number of colleges and universities referenced across the country. Makes you want to go back to school doesn't it? TM

SENATOR ELIZABETH WARREN TO BE FIRST GUEST ON MISTER ROGER'S NEIGHBORHOOD® REBOOT

Sir Telsunn Margraves' talents know no bounds as he was employed as a hydroponic expert on the new set, a marijuana growing facility in Denver. It's all part of the new PBS® children's program "Mr. Tarantino's Neighborhood." Quentin Tarantino brings his own unique style to the beloved children's program reboot as he welcomes his very first guest, Senator Elizabeth Warren. There are a series of new characters including Officer Poe Poe, Carlos Comeback, Queen Trunky Monkey and more. You will even hear Sen. Warren converse with these young viewers in her Native American tongue. It's a new spin on a PBS® classic that your kids will come to know and love.

Boston MA – With great fanfare, PBS announced today the relaunch of the beloved children's program, Mister Roger's Neighborhood®. The program was originally hosted by Fred Rogers, an American television personality, musician, puppeteer, writer, producer and Presbyterian minister. The preschool television series Mister Rogers' Neighborhood® featured his kind-hearted, gentle, soft-spoken personality and directness to his audiences ran on public television from 1968 until 2001. In May 1997, the series surpassed Captain Kangaroo as the longest-running children's television series, a record the series held until June 2003, when Sesame Street beat Mister Rogers' record. Fred Roger's passed away in February 2003.

When asked by various news outlets why Public Broadcasting chose to relaunch the show, they responded that the prospect of a newer, hipper version of the show had done very well in polling among PBS® viewer focus groups. PBS® management has also performed extensive research to find a replacement host that would offer children the same warm friendly welcome that Mr. Roger was known for and one name seems to eclipse all others; Quinten Tarantino. PBS® management is also excited to introduce a number of new characters including "Wass UP!" the questioning transsexual puppet, lovable "Mr. Willie Holdup" the neighborhood thug, "Officer Poe Poe" the local policeman, "Queen Trunky Monkey" the royalty of S&M, "Carlos Comeback" the hilarious illegal alien, "Abdullah IS I IS or IS I AIN'T ben Affleck" the very mysterious stranger as well as many others.

The media cadre present is being treated to a special 5 minute showing of excerpts from the first episode of Mister Tarantino's Neighborhood. Mister Tarantino's very special first guest is Elizabeth Warren the senior senator from Massachusetts. The set has changed quite a bit as the show takes place in a marijuana growing facility in Denver. The facility is fully set up with an automatic watering system and rows of lights overhead. This sets the table for a lot of antics that take place between Quentin, the guests and recurring characters. A new theme song has been written and performed by Mr. Tarantino himself titled "I Ain't Your Lawyer but You Ain't no Wangsta!"

(Opening: The music comes up as the camera moves in for a medium close-up of Mister Tarantino (QT) coming through the door. He smiles at the camera and walks down the steps and takes a deep breathe)

QT – "Wow, I love the smell, I shoulda slept here. Hey kids, it's me Mister Tarantino! **QT**(*pauses and asks*) "Can you say Tarantino? Anyway we have a great show planned for you. We are going to have a real Native American Indian as a special guest. She is the senior US Senator from the State of Massachusetts and her name is Elizabeth Warren. She is part Cherokee or Mohawk or something like that...can you say Cherokee, Mohawk or something like that?"

QT (*waits and says*) "Close enough for government work. I have another surprise for you...did you know that Mister Tarantino is also a Native American? That's right, I am a Native American and I am sure that Senator Warren will have many fun things to tell us and Mister Tarantino will be sure to ask her lots of questions but first I need to do this."

(QT walks to a screen set up in the corner of the marijuana facility and steps behind it so you can only see the upper half of his body)

QT – "Mister Tarantino needs to put on this jock strap to protect his balls from being broken by Officer Poe Poe."

(QT steps from behind the screen and grabs his testicles)

QT – "There, that's better! Now without any further ado, here is our special guest, Senator Elizabeth Warren!"

(SEW steps into the set and QT claps and welcomes her to the show.)

QT – "Welcome senator welcome! We are very excited to have you on Mr. Tarantino's Neighborhood."

SEW – "Yakohsatens Ohnekanos! I am so pleased to be here."

QT – What a special treat! I am thrilled to want to greet the children in your Native American tongue. I know what it means so please let the children know."

SEW – "Loosely translated 'Yakohsatens Ohnekanos' means my horse eats potatoes to stay awake."

QT – "Boys and girls can you say "YAK-OH-SAT-TENS OH-NEK-AN-OS?"

(*QT waits*) "Close enough. When did you learn the language?"

SEW – I have been a great student of Native American languages having lived among the tribes of a number of years. As we always say 'kohsera'kène atennàt-shera yothore tsikeren'tanhnyaks' which means 'in the winter buffalo frogs eat whole wheat toast' or something similar."

QT – Children can you say 'kohsera'kène atennàtshera yothore tsikeren'tanhnyaks', I'll wait until you finish." (*QT waits*) "Close enough. Well, Senator lets walk over to make-believe land so you can meet a very special someone!"

(*QT leads SEW to a special place in the middle of the facility surrounded by marijuana plants to reveal a magical place*)

QT – "Well senator, what do you think?"

SEW – "Ohsyehònta Wahyakeri!   (*Aside to camera*) To you children, that means 'the tee pee is eating tomato basil while listening'...My ancestors would marvel at what you have done here. Where did all this barbed wire, duffle bags, candles, earth-moving equipment and so much more come from?"

(*QT sees Carlos Comeback (CC) and they embrace and walk towards SEW*)

QT – "Well Senator Warren, here to tell us is our favorite undocumented alien, Senor Carlos Comeback! This is the 46th time he has made it across the border and we are so proud to have him here."

CC – "Gracias, Senor Quentin, much gusto Senora Warren."

QT – "Children, can you say 'mucho gusto?' Close enough!"

SEW – "Nihstenha tewahsen-tsyatak Carlos that means, 'the arrow gets stuffed onto the mosquito.' It is a pleasure to meet you too but I still want to know, where did you get all this stuff?"

CC – "Oh Senora Senator, I find in the dessert and Senor Quentin ask me to bring it here. There is much more but I cannot carry so heavy Una carga de esta mierda."

QT – "Children, can you say Una carga de esta mierda?" (*QT waits*) "Not so good, you need to stop shoving non-vegan crap into your mouth."

(*QT, SEW and CC walk all around make-believe land exploring all the wonderful items they find*)

SEW – "What is this Carlos? It looks like Senate Minority Leader Chuck Schumer?"
CC – "Si that is one of my costumes that I use when I cross the border. You would be surprised how little I used to get stopped. Now it is very different."
SEW – "Different? What do you mean different?"
CC – "Well now I need to use this one."

(*CC reaches under a pile of clothing and grabs another costume*)

SEW – "That looks like Hillary Clinton! Is it a costume of Hillary Clinton?"
CC – "Si! I figure nobody cares so who's going to stop her."

(*There is a knock on the door to the marijuana warehouse and there is a loud bang when the knock goes unanswered. There are shouts from person or persons unknown and all eyes focus on the path leading to make-believe land. Officer Poe Poe and his entire police unit appear and walk directly toward QT and CC and yell*)

PP – "Get on the floor you piece of no-good rat-muffin!"
QT – "Officer Poe Poe, what are you doing? This is America and we are entitled to our rights.
PP – "Well here are your rights...and my lefts!"

(*Officer Poe Poe now pummels QT with both of his memory foam stuffing-filled hands and QT is rolling around the floor laughing*)

SEW – "I am a United States Senator and I demand that you 'akaratsi sha'tekon hnekirha' atorats!' (*Aside to camera*) Children, that means 'sing manure to the corn stalk.' Do you hear me?!

(QT *still laughing, faces the camera and speaks*)

QT – Well boys and girls so many exciting things happen in Mister Tarantino's Neighborhood every day so that I know you can't wait to see tomorrows exciting episode. Will Carlos Comeback still be here in America or will he need to 'come-back' the next day? Get it, 'comeback'!

(QT *laughs again*)

QT – "Oh and on tomorrows show we will have some more fun with Wass-UP, Queen Trunky Monkey and Mr. Willie Hold-up plus a very special surprise guest. I want to take the opportunity to thank Senator Elizabeth Warren for speaking to us in Mohawk or Iroquois or whatever, and to her we say 'tsi yekhonnyàtha terinwayenhstha' ohstyen" which means 'chondroitin and telescopes make me vomit.' Can you say 'tsi yekhonnyàtha terinwayenhstha' ohstyen'?' Oh well, try practicing this over the next few hours and always remember this, you've got a friend in Mister Tarantino's Neighborhood!"

(*Music up and under*)

The producers of Mister Tarantino's Neighborhood want readers to know that they are very grateful to Senator Warren for appearing on the show. Her ability to communicate in her native Mohawk or Iroquois or whatever, is flawless and illustrates why she is lovingly referred to as Pocahontas or Fauxcohontas or whatever.-TM

THE SCIENCE GUY® BLAMES MAN-MADE GLOBAL WARMING FOR DRASTIC DROP OF UFO SIGHTINGS

As one of the two reporters present at a news conference recently, Sir Telsunn Margraves had a chance to probing questions and watch fake news history in the making. Appearing very anxious, Bill Nye the Science Guy, announced that in the year 2016, America and the world experienced a dramatic drop in visits by extraterrestrials. Through independent research by Paul's Astronomy Club and SETI (Sarah's Extra-large Telescopic Institute), he concludes that this precipitous drop can be directly attributed to man-made global warming. Former California Governor Arnold Schwarzenegger and current Governor Jerry Brown are both concerned as they lament the possible end of the world.

Los Angeles, CA – William Sanford Nye, better known as Bill Nye, The Science Guy® held a press conference today at world headquarters of the "Intergalactic Terrestrial Society of Alien Life Forms" or ITS ALF. The presser is being held to publicize Bill Nye's crusade against man-made global warming and to issue a dire warning to all concerned citizens of earth.

Mr. Nye welcomes the two reporters who are present as he addresses what he calls the greatest calamity to mankind since the end of the last ice age more than 100,000 years ago. Mr. Nye says, "I want to thank you all for being here. In my studies of man-made global warming I have performed many hours of research and I am very distressed at having to report my findings. Man-made global warming is a catastrophe that is waiting to happen and I have discovered another unintended consequence of the greenhouse gas effect on our fragile environment; aliens have stopped visiting the Earth. You heard correctly, alien life forms have stopped visiting earth and it is our fault."

"I have checked the records of various organizations that monitor visitors from other worlds and I am sad to report they have all recorded record low numbers of extraterrestrial UFO sightings in recent months. For example, in a recent study performed by Paul's Astronomy Club that's 'Waiting for ET' or PACWET, there is proof positive that the individual sightings recorded during the calendar year 2013 were 248,395 and during the same period in 2016 there were only 12. This precipitous drop in visitors is a very disturbing sign and one we should all take seriously. Although I have always counted on the members of Paul's Astronomy Club to validate my many conclusions about man-made global warming, I feel that I need to have corroboration of their findings so I contacted SETI which as you all know is "Sarah's Extra-large Telescopic Institute." I spoke to Sarah herself and she confirmed the findings but she also had a number of ominous warnings."

At this point one of the two people in the room asks, "What warnings?"

Bill Nye tells those present, "Sarah cautioned that it is very difficult to understand the language that many alien civilizations speak. Sarah said that alien languages do not use the tradition alphabet we know. In order to translate their language she needed to develop a method of conversion to be able to provide a rough translation.

Sarah indicated that it took her 34 years of study just to get to this point. Her latest communications revealed she had spoken to the *FBerrBel* (loosely translated: Senate Minority Leader) from planet *ALLTTv6v* (loosely translated: Mipdfrrom) in the *XcZiMToCGu* (loosely translated: Faldesparl) Constellation and was told that their *VeLMCaC* (loosely translated: Crenchielwbc) had many concerns. Their leader indicated that if man-made global warming does not stop there would be major consequences to the peoples of Earth.

The second reporter said, "Consequences? What consequences?"

Bill Nye considers whether he should tell the reporters of the consequences for fear it could start a panic among the inhabitants of earth. It was with a heavy heart that The Science Guy feels it best to remain true to his calling...science...that he reveal what he was told. He reluctantly tells his audience of two, "I am very saddened to report that if we do not stop man-made global warming one of two things will happen; either the earth will be annihilated by the powerful *D/dVINuGYEjYT* (there is no loose translation) Death Ray or texting capability will cease on all smart phones immediately.

There was a quiet moment where Bill Nye seems to gaze into the distance. Now he asks these rhetorical imponderables out loud; "Why can't people see what I see? Why is it that the Death Ray annihilation of planet earth or the loss of texting capabilities is not being taken seriously? How can we bring back the extraterrestrial tourist business to pre-2013 levels?" Bill Nye sighs because he doesn't have the answers to his own questions.

Later that day former California Governor Arnold Schwarzenegger and current Governor Jerry Brown held a joint press conference to tout California's man-made global warming initiatives. At the event they both took the time to endorse Bill Nye's premise on man-made global warming and the extraterrestrial response. Governor Jerry Brown is even more emphatic, "California has always welcomed other-worldly visitors who bring diversity and much needed tax dollars to our state. Many of these aliens have even settled in Los Angeles and San Francisco and have climbed to the highest echelons of state government and the world of entertainment. We cannot allow the free flow of those life-forms, especially from the rock-like orb 'Senagelcc' near the star array in the constellation Dxelicron, to abate. *If we don't do something about it (global warming), it is the end of the world.*

The actual quote from a speech on man-made global warming in italics was given by Governor Jerry Brown

CHRISSY TEIGEN'S MOMENT TO SHINE

One of the most glamorous swimsuit models ever to grace the cover of Sports Illustrated, Chrissy Teigen, and her musician/husband, John Legend, attend the Gala Fundraiser for "Black Lives Matter." The gala is a gathering of the elite of New York society with the top acts from the world of hip-hop and rap, local politicians and leaders of the Black Lives Matter movement looking to raise funds for the cause. Sir Telsunn Margraves, disguised as Ed Sheeran, was able to find a seat at the dais to record the event that he likes to refer to as his special tribute to Tom Wolfe.

New York, NY – The streets surrounding America's preeminent China owned hotel is closed to traffic. The streets instead are filled with protesters, onlookers and celebrity hounds looking to get a glimpse of their favorite politician, sports star, entertainer or radical.

Police have cordoned off a pathway into the hotel and the officers' line each side of the front entrance to be sure that no one, other than invited guests, could enter. You know it must have been disturbing for these police officers to have to protect all the luminaries there for the annual "Black Lives Matter" fundraiser. The police manage to keep their attention on the business at hand and remain stoic as they scan the crowd looking for anything unusual. It must have been very hard for them but it is their job and they try to do it in as professional a manner as the occasion will allow. It is especially hard for some of the attendees not to spit in the faces of the police. Many thought, however, it was a useless protest as the cops are wearing protective masks so the spit would just run off.

Screams from the crowd increase at least 100 decibels, as they look to see the "Mutha-F*****S" arrive in a stretch limo. The "Mutha-F*****S" have the number six recording on the hip-hop charts titled "Mutha- F*****S" by the album of the same name. Next to arrive is the San Francisco 49er's third string former quarterback, Colin Kaepernick. He's recently made headlines for refusing to stand during the national anthem. He was also accused by his detractors for allegedly defecating in underwear with the American Eagle imprinted on the front and rear. Limo after limo continues to arrive and discharge their passengers. There's Missy Miss Missy, the famous female gangsta rap star who has the number four single on the hip-hop charts, and Reverend Minister Waseem Tayyib Shamim Abdul-Muqaddim, aka Cameron, as well as many more luminaries from every industry imaginable. More screams explode from the crowds as the actor/director Fielding Pomeroy arrives with the star Trisha Pomeroy (no relation) of his latest epic documentary, "Journey to the Center of American Crimes and Racism against the Awful Stuff that has Plagued Humanity." The mayor of New York Bill Di Blasio is prepared to give the opening remarks and Reverend Minister Waseem Tayyib Shamim Abdul-Muqaddim will give the convocation. There is even a rumor that Hillary Rodham Clinton, the former Democrat candidate for president will be a surprise guest and Chrissy is beyond excited. Where else but New York City, the center of the world, could you ever assemble such a group of unique minded individuals that think so much alike; Chrissy is convinced that it couldn't happen anywhere else, well maybe except for Chicago, Hollywood, San Francisco, Washington DC, Boston, Santa Fe, Boulder, Portland, Seattle, Austin and perhaps a few other places.

The press is also there in full force shouting questions and hoping for answers but the guests just wave and are ushered into the lobby. Lastly George Soros, the billionaire currency manipulator and global financial titan, who is funding the event, makes a grand entrance. He has contributed tens of millions to the cause and is said to have been a victim of fake news. He has been falsely accused of saying he funds the Black Lives Matter movement because he wants to 'bring down the racist United States' and the leftist members of the African-American community are the easiest to manipulate.

The fundraiser is in full swing when Sports Illustrated swimsuits model Chrissy Teigen and her husband, the music star John Legend arrive. She and John like to make a grand entrance especially with something as important as this. Chrissy walks down the cordon of police and is saddened by their presence. She whispers to John, "Why can't the police be more like Ice Cube and Ice T?"

The organization has reserved the Grand Ballroom of the Waldorf Astoria and Chrissy is confident that all the people who attend the event will be pleased. Chrissy is sure that the guests will appreciate all the extra space set aside for speaking, drinking and eating. Chrissy also detects a whiff of an odor from smoke that seems pleasant enough and she immediately feels happy!

The board of directors has appointed Chrissy as the coordinator for decorations and music and she takes her job very seriously. There are black balloons all over the place; tied to chairs, hanging from the ceiling, all along the dais, even in the gender neutral bathrooms. She had hired one of those balloon people who make animals out of the long skinny balloons. Chrissy asked him to be sure to make life-like pigs out of pink balloons and police hand guns out of black balloons. It is just lovely... lovely and it is all because of her efforts. She worked tirelessly, well except for the two weeks she spent in Ibiza with John.

Chrissy feels naked without her husband John and refuses to go to any gala affair unless she can take him with her. Sure he's shorter than her, but what does it matter, he's John Legend!

As far as music goes, Chrissy has been listening to various urban music stations and popular segments on music networks. She has become familiar with the multitude of artists and entertainers that have become popular in the rap, gangsta-rap and hip-hop genre. Initially she searched for lyrics that would be relevant to the occasion...thankfully most of the lyrics were appropriate. Chrissy feels that it is of utmost importance to become intimate with the struggle, and what better way than to listen to rap and hip hop artists and, of course, John.

Chrissy takes a long, long look around the ballroom to see if she detects anything out of place. She is satisfied that all is in order, acknowledging to herself that she has done a fine job. While Chrissy is distracted, she detects something like a hand on her ass. She smiles, suspecting to see John but is surprised to find it's the Hip-hop Phenom "Suck my D**k" whose latest recording had reached number 14 on the hip-hop charts after just two weeks.

"My, oh my Suck, I didn't expect to feel, 'er see you until later. How are you doing?"

"How the f*ck does you think I'm doin, huh? Room full of white pieces of sh*t and black balloons, who the f*ck had the idea to use these black balloons? What the f*ck do they think we are full of hot air, mother f**ker?"

Chrissy is a bit nonplussed as to how to answer Suck but she comes to her senses and responds, "Oh, Suck, we are sorry you don't like the decorations, I will be sure to take it up with the board the next time we meet. I do hope you are enjoying the event though, we are hopeful to raise a lot of money for the cause."

"You f**kin' better raise a lot of money for the cause. If I have to spend another minute here I think I'm gonna puke all over that; what the f**k kinda dress is that?

Now Chrissy is flummoxed, "It's a Dolce and Gabbana."

Suck looks especially confused, "A what and what?"

"Umm, Dolce and Gabbana."

Now Suck is getting even more confused, "What kinda f**kin' name is that, some kind of f**kin' dago name?"

Chrissy is more than happy to enlightened Suck, so she tells him, "How clever of you to know that, YES! They are Italian designers and I am so impressed that you were able to discern that just from their names!"

"What! You tryin' to say I'm some kind of f**kin' idiot? Who the f**k do you think you are insultin' me like that, I ought to…"

But Chrissy stops him, "No Suck, I'm mean of course not Suck, I don't mean to demean you in any way, I was just trying to…" But Suck cuts her short, "Shut the f**k up bitch, I got to go on in a few but I'll be back."

Chrissy takes a few moments to regain her composure as she is determined not to let anything spoil the gala event. She takes a glass of champagne and walks through the crowd assembled in the ballroom. She looks to mingle and perhaps find some friends to help her get a grasp on reality, after all what do these people know of her life. How can they know of the hardships she has had to endure. Yes, she recognizes how African-Americans have had to endure slavery, hardships and how they have found it necessary to do whatever is needed to survive. But what do they know of her? What do they know of her sacrifices? She thinks of the summer of 2000, the summer of her 15th birthday, when she had planned a wonderful vacation with some of her closest, dearest friends. They were going to spend a glorious week at her parent's home in Hawaii. Fun, sun and sand would have been the order of the day but at the last minute, mom and dad had to cancel the trip. Dad had to work on a hedge or something and her birthday month was ruined.   Did she cry? NO! Well, maybe a little. Did she scream and have a tantrum? NO! Well, actually yes, but after a few days she apologized and told her parents she understood and she felt better. Her shrink told her to try and work things out in her mind before she overreacts to any situation, and that is what she did. Chrissy smiles, takes a deep breath and seems to smell some of that smoke and now she feels just marvelous.

The dais is filled with all the honored guests. Chrissy is getting more excited by the minute. She thinks to herself, "Can you just imagine, Suck my D*CK on the same stage with Fielding Pomeroy, the "Mutha F*****S" sitting next to George Soros and the hi-hop impresario Russell Simmons sitting with her husband John and Harvey Weinstein sitting all alone next to Brett Ratner. Chrissy whisper to no one, "Could this be more perfect?" and she answers herself, "No, it's perfect!"

Chrissy takes her seat at table 12. It seems to be adequate but she would have preferred to be on the dais next to John, but she's a brave girl and understands that her sacrifice is important to so many of the people who have suffered at the hands of the police. Actually, most of the guests here have never suffered at the hands of the police, but Chrissy takes comfort in knowing that the money raised will go to those folks who weren't invited to the gala fundraiser.

The Master of Ceremonies is Paulson W. Cronk, the famous newsman and award winning anchor. Cronk is 85 years old, semi-retired and he has been a long-time supporter of the cause and George Soros has made him head of his foundation. Paulson makes a salary of $4 million a year, not counting undisclosed perks and, as his detractors might say, spends most of his time on his knees kissing George's ass. Paulson introduces the first speaker, Reverend Minister Waseem Tayyib Shamim Abdul-Muqaddim who will make the convocation. The minister solemnly approaches the podium and lowers his head,

"To all assembled here, let us meet in unity and peace.

Let us not submit to violence and animus but rather appeal for calm

As we gather to support our cause, Black Lives Matter.

What else matters is that we get the money we need to fight injustice,

To fight inequality, to fight the good fight for more money to do what is needed.

Sure we have suffered but that is what we need to do in order to

raise the funds to eliminate suffering!

Good Lord, please fill our coffers with the money we need

And the blessings it will generate.

Amen"

Chrissy is practically in tears as she nudges the man sitting next to her. She says, "Wasn't that marvelous?" The man is in the process of swallowing a mouthful of salad and he mumbles, "Mffumph!" The next speaker is the leftist mayor of New York, Bill Di Blasio, a particular favorite among the many white leftist liberal throngs that have gathered tonight.

There is a smattering of applause as he gets up and walks to the mic to begin speaking. "Ladies and gentlemen, thank you so much for your generous applause and for coming to this very special event! I remember the first time I came across the organization, Black Lives Matter and I want to share…" but he needs to stop speaking in order to duck his head, so he won't get hit by a fifteen grain, seedless, organic, brick oven baked, gluten-free, and quinoa and kale scuffler. The mayor now pleads, "Please! Please, ladies and gentlemen…" but he didn't have enough time to duck the next scuffler. The scuffler bounces off the over-head banner that says www.Send-MoneytoBLM.org and onto the top of the mayor's head. Discretion being the better part of valor, the mayor thanks the audience for their kind applause, of which there is none, and he rushes back to his seat. Suck MY D**k and the lead of the "Mutha-F*****S", No F'n Way and Missy Miss Missy are all in hysterics and calling for the waiter to bring over more scufflers.

Chrissy is too enthralled to notice the flying scufflers as she scans the various tables for any signs of notables and finally she spots Professor Cecily Tessler-Stubbs. Chrissy had once attended many lectures given by the professor at Wellesley and she simply adores the woman. Her favorite lecture was titled "African-American Woman in the World of Anachronistic Happenstance Leading to a Cultural Shift in the Anthropomorphic Resilience of Literature Spanning the Early 19th Century." As Chrissy remembers the lecture was based on a lot of books and things and she simply idolized Professor Cecily Tessler-Stubbs who was always there to help her with what she didn't understand.

Chrissy waves frantically hoping to get the professor's attention, "Oh Professor! Professor! Over here professor!" The professor turns around pretending that she doesn't see Chrissy but it is too late and she acknowledges her greeting. "Hello, Ms. Teigen, it has been a long while since we've seen each other. What are you doing here?"

Chrissy is delighted, "Oh Professor, I'm so glad you remembered me. I am on the committee that is celebrating the Black Lives Matter anniversary gala fundraiser.

I am responsible for the balloons and decorations!" Chrissy is beaming with pride. "I still have so many fond memories of your lectures and the time we discussed the African American Women's version of Little Red Riding Hood, simply fascinating... fascinating."

Professor Cecily Tessler-Stubbs is already looking for an escape route when Chrissy asks, "You know professor there is one thing I still can't figure out; did the wolf really look like grandma? I can't understand how Red Riding Hood couldn't see that. What do you...?"

But the professor cuts Chrissy short and says, "Oh look, there is Councilmen Rahim Taylor-Billings, I must go say hello. It was great to see you Ms. Teigen, I like the balloons." She then makes a hasty retreat leaving Chrissy to contemplate possible answers to her question.

The preeminent Paulson W. Cronk takes the mic on the podium to make an announcement. "Ladies and Gentlemen, I have a very special surprise for you tonight. In celebration of the annual fundraiser for Black Lives Matter, and for the first time together on the same stage, "Suck-My-D**K", the "Mutha-F*****S" and "Missy Miss Missy" are going to perform the hip-hop platinum selling recording of "Yo Wigga I'm a F**k You Up." They will also perform a special anthem written especially for this event, "Pigs in Paradise." The three performers take center stage and the lights go down as the spotlight goes up. Suck My D**k and No F'n Way come out from different sides of the stage and Missy from the middle and they meet in the center. To Chrissy this is virtual nirvana and she can't believe she is about to witness this once-in-a-lifetime confluence of talents. The bass beat comes alive with the rest of the Mutha-F*****S" joining in with DJ Yo 4 Sho mixing it up. The performance has everyone in rapt attention after all this is what the entire crowd came for. This is what they believe the cause is all about, making people take note of the injustice in the country with the confluence of music and spontaneously planned riots.

Chrissy walks over to listen to a reporter who is interviewing Nobel Laureate Tyrese Bowen, the political activist. Mr. Bowen is fulminating to the reporter who is standing by him in eager anticipation. "Oppression! Oppression! What better way to express solidarity with the freedoms allotted all Americans in the Declaration of

Independence, or is it the Constitution, I forget, and sometimes you need to take matters into your own hand. As Saul Alinsky wrote in his masterwork, "Rules for Radicals", and I quote, *'The most unethical of all means is the non-use of any means. It is this species of man who so vehemently and militantly participated in that classically idealistic debate at the old League of Nations on the ethical differences between defensive and offensive weapons. Their fears of action drive them to refuge in an ethics so divorced from the politics of life that it can apply only to angels, not men.'* Now who can argue with that?!"

The reporter is feverishly writing down every word. He really doesn't understand anything that Tyrese Bowen said but he doesn't want to forget a thing. As they continue speaking, Chrissy stares, starry eyed, at Tyrese Bowen, trying to absorb the brilliance of the statement and the relevancy to the event. It has been several hours and the fundraiser now seems to be in full swing, people are dancing and drinking and there is the wonderful smell of smoke that continues wafting it way through the air and Chrissy is very happy.

The music stops and Chrissy Teigen turns her gaze to the stage as the lights go dim again and the spotlight shines center stage. Statesmen-like Paulson W. Cronk is at the podium as he addresses the crowd. "Ladies and gentlemen, wasn't that a marvelous rendition of the hip-hop classic. But now we must turn to more serious matters and this is, after all, a serious occasion. The gentleman I am about to introduce needs no introduction. After more than 20 years of struggle, 16 convictions for petty crimes, after 5 individual episodes whereby he endured unnecessary and unwarranted arrests for merely carrying concealed revolvers and that false accusation of robbing a Piggly Wiggly in Beaufort, North Carolina, I am proud and honored to present the conscience of Black Lives Matter, Melvin 'Zilabamuzale' Garfield!"

The crowd roars with approval when out of the shadows comes an unnaturally large man, not fat just tall and large. The conscience of the organization, Black Lives Matter, Melvin 'Zilabamuzale' Garfield, walks straight to the podium but stands there and does not acknowledge the crowd's applause. Chrissy is scrambling to get closer so that she can be near the legendary man who has made this all possible. Finally the assembled guests calm down and Mr. Garfield speaks,

"My African name is Zilabamuzale and you pasty faced white crackers probably don't know what it means, do you. Huh! Do you?" Melvin looks around the audience to see if anyone knows what Zilabamuzale means but no one raises their hands so he continues to speak, "It means 'sickly one' and you want to know why I'm sick? Huh, you want to know?"

Now the crowd goes totally silent, waiting to hear why Melvin is sick.

"I'm sick because all you crackers and whiteys make me want to puke, that's right, I wanna puke just from looking at you all. Has anyone here ever tried to buy something, maybe even a joint? I'm just sayin', at 3AM, huh, any of you crackers ever try?" There is a smattering of applause from the white people in the audience who actually have tried to buy a joint at 3AM. Melvin continues, "Well let me tell you, even if you can't find a single blunt you take your life into your hands. All the police tryin' to stop you from exercising your constitutionally protected rights to lead your life the way you want to ain't that right?"

In response to Melvin's question, the crowd cheers in unison, "YES!"

Melvin communicates the pent up passion he is feeling, "Damn straight! I also get sick when I see brothers and sisters, innocent of any crimes, being shot by the police. I get sick I tell you because if they wanted to get shot they could just stay home! In the comfort of their own homes in their own neighborhoods in places like Chicago, Baltimore and LA where they don't even have to go outside to get shot. This is why I'm sick, I tell you sick!" The passion can be felt by everyone in attendance and the significance of his words is not lost on Chrissy.

"Now we all here in this nice hotel, with all this beautiful furniture and decorations; there are some tasty notes from Suck, Missy and F'n, good food, booze up the ass, served to us hand-and-foot by some old white guys...by the way, where are the black waiters huh? Now do you know how I feel, huh? SICK! SICK to my stomach! Where the f**k do you get off having this much fun at our expense. Now I got one thing and one thing only to say. We are having some kind of a blind f**kin' auction for a bunch of sh*t that nobody wants, but I better see some good feddie, no funny money. I wanna see bricks goin' down and at the end of this f**kin' night we better have enough good cash to make this all worth it because just lookin' out on this crowd makes me sick and the only cure is money. Remember, I'm watchin'." With that, Melvin Garfield turns his back to the audience as they begin to cheer wildly! He walks past Paulson W. Cronk who is holding out his hand to shake Melvin's. Melvin stops, looks at Paulson, turns green and vomits all over him.

It is then that Chrissy snaps out of her euphoria and realizes that the board will want to announce the results of the silent auction. As part of her role at the fundraiser, she will be announcing the winners of the auction so she rushes to the stage and confers with the board. The bids have been submitted all evening long and now there will be winners of some fabulous prizes. Chrissy is reveling in it all! She is handed the list that has been compiled by the committee and she takes it to the podium. Normally Paulson W. Cronk would have introduced her but he's gone to the bathroom to try and wipe some of the vomit from his tuxedo. He prays that along with the vomit, the puke smell will also go away.

Chrissy stands at the podium thrilled to begin and she announces, "Ladies and gentlemen, it is now time to announce the winners of the silent auction!" Applause rings through the grand ballroom as people anxiously wait to see if they had the winning bid for one of the fabulous prizes. "There are so many truly unique and useful items that I know we will have a few happy folks and a lot of jealous ones." Now laughter can be heard coming from the audience and Chrissy begins.

She is reading the description of the gifts from index cards, "The first item is a special gift for the young at heart. A singular object of such beauty and amazing utility, it is sure to become a prized possession and heirloom for future generations to come." Chrissy holds up the prize as she beams over with pride and screams, "This amazing Louis Vuitton Skateboard complete with a Louis Vuitton carrying case. This item has a retail value of $8,250 and the winning bid is $19,000. The winner of this prize wishes to remain anonymous. Congratulations and bon chance!" Chrissy is using one of the few French phrases she can remember from the four years of French she took as the audience politely applauds.

"Never let it be said that the people in this room aren't in simpatico with our African-American brothers and sisters. To illustrate this we are so proud to offer a fashion item that screams, 'Yo homie I'm down wid dat!'." Her colloquial was impromptu and not included on the index card she was given, but Chrissy is thrilled that she got through improvisation. She looks over to the board of directors who have buried their faces in their hands. Chrissy is sure they are trying to hide their reaction, but she is also sure they love it. "We have this fabulous Diamond Studded Hoodie Worth $10,000. This piece of urban couture features over 4000 Swarovski crystals and a 3 carat diamond zipper pull and hand-painted designs. The winning bid is $35,000 and the winner of this prize wishes to remain anonymous."

Chrissy is on a roll! "The next prize is sure to make your housekeeper the envy of every other housekeeper who cleans the houses among all your friends. A Crystal Ergoripado Vacuum Cleaner that features 3,730 genuine Swarovski Crystals encrusted on the vacuum cleaner. I keep thinking, why hasn't someone thought of this sooner? This item has a retail value of $18,993 and the winning bid is $50,000 and the winner of this prize wishes to remain anonymous." Again there is a smattering of applause and a few guests are looking envious.

"Next we have a wonderful basket of gifts for the combination business executive and hi-tech junkie!" Chrissy considers her use of the word 'junkie' but continues anyway. "First of the items in the basket is a Diamond Encrusted Bluetooth Headset with a retail value of $50,000. The next item included is a Gokukawa Genuine Leather Keyboard with a retail value of $603. The third item in the grouping is Gold and Diamond Earbuds with a retail value of $5,175; I wish I could bid on those!" Chrissy is waiting for a reaction from the audience but the silence is deafening so she is forced to continue. "The final item in this very special gift basket is Gold Plated Staples packaged in a velvet jewelry box and they have a retail price of $175. All these items have a retail value of nearly $56,000 and the winning bid is $175,000 and the winner of this prize wishes to remain anonymous."

Finally we have what has to be considered the ultimate object for the sport fisherman in your life. A product that is so truly useful and unique everyone who sees it wants to have it. We are truly honored to be able to have this item in our silent auction and, I know firsthand, the bidding was fierce." Chrissy reaches down to the shelf below the top of the podium and lifts the small leather covered fitted jewel case. She opens the case and looks down at the item inside; it seems to catch all its luminance from the lights above the stage. She would love to look at it longer, but she knows that the crowd is waiting in eager anticipation so she holds it up for all to see, "This is, ladies and gentlemen, the grand prize and the final item of the silent auction." There is a lump in Chrissy's throat as she is practically on the verge of tears. "For those of you who have guessed, you are right, this is the both the Mac Daddy and the Daddy Mac of fishing lures, encrusted with over 4,000 diamonds and rubies, that's more than 100 carats. The fishing lure that is made from over three pounds of gold and platinum and that guarantees it will sink fast. The retail price is one million dollars and the winning bid is for $4,250,000!" The audience bursts into applause and cheers for the winning bid and Chrissy adds, "The winner of this prize wishes to remain anonymous!"

The silent auction was a resounding success and the crowning moment of a wonderful evening. "Thank you so much, ladies and gentleman, the money raised will go to fund the cause we all hold so dear. There will be a formal presentation of the check to Melvin 'Zilabamuzale' Garfield once we get the money deposited in the bank and the checks clear. Please enjoy the rest of the evening!"

Chrissy leaves the stage and checks her watch and it is 12:30AM and the grand ballroom was rented until 1AM. Some of the crowd has already left and others are saying their goodbyes as Chrissy starts to think about having the limo come to pick her and John up. She reaches for her phone when she feels a hand on her ass and she turns to see it's both Suck MY D**K and No F'n Way standing there with shit eating grins on their face. Chrissy is getting nervous as she asks them, "Ah, well, how did you enjoy the evening fellas?"

Suck says, "Hey bitch, the evening ain't over. What say we skip this bullshit and partay?!" No F'n Way totally concurs, "Yeah bitch, Suck is right, let's go party. Get us a magnum, blunt and room in this dump and we can get fucked up."

Now Chrissy is getting nervous so she is trying to gracefully get out of this situation. "I am so sorry gentlemen but I, uh, I'm going home with John. As a matter of fact he's waiting for me outside. I would have loved to party with you but..." She continues to speak but she is backing away looking for the door. "Let's try to get together sometime soon. I know, how about spending the weekend at our summer home in Newport!

Doesn't that sound like fun? I will be sure to write to you with dates so you can put it on your calendars. I promise it will be fun, don't forget to bring your bathing suits but don't worry, we have plenty of towels." Chrissy turns and walks very fast through the door leading to the lobby and Suck and No F'n Way, watch, shrug their shoulders and smile at each other as they yell, "Hey Missy! Let's partay!!"

Chrissy is exhausted and exits the hotel and waits patiently for John to arrive. As she's standing there she feels a hand on her ass and she turn and shouts, "Suck stop grabbing…" but she sees and smells that it's Paulson W. Cronk. He has a very leering smile and asks Chrissy, "Why don't we entertain each other at my flat…clothing optional!" Chrissy smiles coyly as the limo arrives and says, "Can John come along?"

Paulson gulps and decides that discretion is the better part of valor and opens the door of the limo to allow Chrissy to enter. Her last words to him are, "Goodbye Paulson, go home and take a shower, you stink!" as the car leaves to go north on Park Avenue.

This story is dedicated to the late, great author extraordinaire Tom Wolfe and his hilarious "Radical Chic and Mau-Mauing the Flak Catchers" TM

Please note that this event took place before the celebrity status of certain individuals have experienced dramatic reversals

ISIS TERRORIST CHECKS INTO SEATTLE CLINIC

Abu Bakr al-Baghdadi, the leader of the terror group ISIS recently checked himself into the Seattle's Happy House Center for the Treatment of Obsessive Compulsive Disorders. Sir Telsunn Margraves was able to tap into a conference call coordinated by Mr. al-Baghdadi's psychiatrist, Dr. Evan Tamper. In this impactful discussion the terrorist, who is now referred to as 'Chip' by his fellow residents, confronts his sickness and seeks the appropriate therapy to become a productive member of society.

Seattle, WA – Abu Bakr al-Baghdadi, the leader of the terror group ISIS has recently checked himself into the Seattle's Happy House Center for the Treatment of Obsessive Compulsive Disorders.

Readers may recall that Mr. al-Bagdadi had promised to rid the world of all non-believers and now he recognizes that all this stems from a condition called "Obsessive Compulsive Disorder" or OCD. In a brief written statement Mr. al-Bagdadi said he tried, but could not understand why he kept cutting off the heads of people but in the declaration he ended his statement with a hopeful; "...now I know." He said that he remembers incidents where he demanded his followers' line up his captives in perfect order before he commanded their heads be cut off. Mr. al-Bagdadi now laments, "What difference does it make?"

The head of Happy House, Dr. Evan Tamper said, "This need to have perfect order is a common symptom of OCD and, along with other compulsions, can make life truly difficult for people like Mr. al-Bagdadi to function." Dr. Tamper also listed other symptoms such as germ-o-phobia, aggression towards others and excessive handwashing as all contributing to the patient's inability to lead a normal life.

Mr. al-Bagdadi has adjusted to life in the clinic very well. Although the attendants have taken any sharp objects away from him, he is responding to the daily regimen of therapies including psychanalysis, family therapy, psychodrama, eclectic therapy, accelerated experiential dynamic psychotherapy, classical Adlerian psychotherapy, dance therapy or dance movement therapy, Gestalt therapy, transference focused psychotherapy, sexual identity therapy as well as crocheting and badminton. He is quoted as saying, "I love the various therapy sessions and I have crocheted scarfs and mittens for all the doctors who are treating me."

Dr. Tamper held a press conference by phone to provide the news media with information as to what life is like for Abu Bakr al-Baghdadi as he tries to find his inner self, get in touch with his feminine side and search for his inner child. Dr. Tamper explains to all those participants from the media how the process works. "Life at Happy House is very different from what Mr. al-Baghdadi had experienced in Raqqa. In Raqqa you had to walk around or over the many dead bodies that litter the streets. In Seattle our biggest problem is the increase of the minimum wage to

$15 an hour although you may have to walk around the homeless. In Raqqa there is no running water, no functioning sewer system, no food, no hospitals, no schools and no functioning government other than ISIS. At Happy House our pool heater is broken, it rains all the time, the food is salt-free, we don't take Obamacare, the toilets flush properly and we have Mr. al-Bagdadi' s favorite classes; crocheting and floral arrangement."

Dr. Tamper continues with background on their newest resident. "A number of reporters have also asked what the other patients at Happy House think of Mr. al-Bagdadi. I must admit I was concerned that he would not be accepted by the patients; however, I was pleasantly surprise at how warm and open they are about having a murderous, bloodthirsty terrorist among them. Mr. al-Bagdadi has proven himself to be quite a joiner and he seems to have a fondness for badminton. Recently after an intense game for the Happy House Badminton Championship, Mr. al-Bagda-di was made captain of the team. His teammates have also given him the nickname 'Chip' as a sign of acceptance."

Dr. Tamper is very open in discussing his latest celebrity patient and he wants to be forthcoming about the man and his daily regimen. "As you can imagine, there are accommodations that needed to be made; prayer rugs, Qurans, halal foods, eth-nically appropriate clothing, including underwear although Mr. al-Bagdadi indicated he doesn't wear underwear. There were also some rather unique requests including GPS systems to track troop movements back home, posters of Miley Cyrus and Ash-ley Judd, among others, recent issues of Sports Illustrated Swimsuit editions and a daily ration of Hostess Ding Dongs."

"There is one topic that I must address. When Mr. al-Bagdadi initially checked himself in, I was concerned that an immigration service such as ICE would not look at this in a kind way. We were visited by ICE agents, Navy Seal Unit 6 and a SWAT Team from Seattle PD. They insisted that we release Chip in their custody as they had a number of concerns. We needed to remind them that Seattle is a Sanctuary City and that we would look very unkindly at any attempt to keep him from com-pleting his therapy and resuming a normal productive life. Thanks goodness the 9th Circuit Court of Appeals upheld our position."

"There were a number of requests to speak to Mr. al-Bagdadi but I need to remind you that he speaks little English. This could cause some miscommunication among the various media as they report his quotes so he has asked me to read a statement that he has written." Dr. Tamper concluded his phone conference by reading the statement of Mr. Abu Bakr '*Chip*' al-Bagdadi.

"I, Abu Bakr al-Baghdadi also known as 'Chip' to my fellow residents, send greetings from Happy House Center for the Treatment of Obsessive Compulsive Disorders. There is an old saying among the ISIS warriors, 'Look to the sky for wisdom, look to the sky for enlightenment, look to the sky for awareness and look to the sky for drones before they blow you up.' These are words that I have lived by but no longer! I use to wake up to sounds of crying children, hungry for food, hungry for their loved ones, hungry for their safety. Now I wake up to posters of Cher and Bryan Cranston and I am able to begin the day with good thoughts. Through daily therapeutic sessions with the fine staff at Happy House I have tried to get in touch with my feminine side but I refuse to wear burkas, especially the ones that cover the face. I can also look toward my inner child and see that there are many reasons why I am the way I am. I was neglected by my parents and I was always told to clean my room. They would constantly nag and gripe, 'clean your room' they would say. After a few weeks of this I killed them and I thought that in order to solve problems I must take matters into my own hands. I now realize I was wrong."

"I Abu Bakr "Chip" al-Baghdadi note that before I came to Happy House I developed a facial tic. These tics came on very suddenly and the ISIS medical team told me to take aspirin and see them in the morning. When I awoke, the tic was still there so I had them killed...again, I was wrong. Then there were bouts with eye blinking, facial grimacing, shoulder shrugging and head or shoulder jerking. ISIS warriors just thought that I was going through a phase...now I know this was wrong and I was wrong about this and many other things including vocal tics, throat-clearing, sniffing and grunting sounds. This was most annoying especially when I needed to appear on videos for jihad recruitment or on infidel execution videos.

Those days are past. At Happy House I learned to confront my problems, I learned that I am a good person. I learned that it is okay not to kill people who don't agree with me, although I am still having a problem with that one. The beloved Dr. Tamper made me aware of the reasons I am the way I am and I am now confident that I can reenter normal society and work towards becoming a productive member.

I want to say to all in America, Europe, Africa and beyond who have welcomed so many of our brothers and sister into your countries, thank you. Thank you for your open hands and open hearts and we are ever mindful that we are different but we must all live together and try to understand our differences so we can all get along. I would appreciate, to help us assimilate better, if you please do not drink liquor, eat pork, allow women to drive and wear bikinis and cancel Megan Kelly's program, it is horrible. Praise be to Allah and his prophet Mohammad."

Dr. Tamper ends the press conference by saying, "Anytime anyone tells you that therapy doesn't work, just tell them to see the transformation in 'Chip' al-Bagdadi"

TRANSGENDERS TO FORM THEIR OWN MILITARY

As a result of President Trump's controversial decision not to allow Transgender persons to serve in the military, it was announced that transitional men to women and women to men will form their own military. In a gathering of senior officers, many concerns were discussed about present hurdles and future obstacles to be overcome. They will start with the Army and add a Navy, Marine Corp, Air Force and Coast Guard as they get enough money. A number of decisions must be made including, guns or no guns, where to locate bases, uniforms and more. Being present at the meeting, Sir Telsunn Margraves was able to learn the issues transgender individuals will confront and he left with fervent hope they will achieve their objectives.

Washington DC – As a result of President Trump's decision not to allow Transgender persons to serve in the military, it was announced today that these transitional men to women and women to men will form their own military.

Newly promoted General Sandra 'Bob' Kovak told a packed press conference that they were forced into making this decision by recent events in Washington. She/he indicated, "Although it is a great blow to the transgender cause, this is also a great opportunity to strike out on our own. We are thrilled by the prospect of having our own Army. We are starting with the Army and moving onto the Navy, Air Force, Marine Corps and Coast Guard when we get enough money and enough transsexuals to enlist."

"Lt. Colonel Emmett 'Sylvia' Brock has asked French designer Sophie Theallet to design the women to men uniforms as we feel her women's dresses look better on men. We have asked Indian designer Naeem Khan, a Michelle Obama favorite, to design the men to women uniforms as they seem to look good on both women and men. I have seen the preliminary sketches and I must tell you they look marvelous."

A confab is being held in Washington DC to discuss the many issues that the new transgender army will be facing. The senior staff is tackling the hard choices that will need to be made as they begin to form the foundations of a military capability such as this. Among a number of items that will be discussed are; the use of guns, allow or disallowed; Transgender men to women, women to men barracks, allow or disallow or who cares; Tanks, where do we get them and how much do they cost and other such hard choices that need to be made. There will also be the need to decide where to open bases around the country. A ballot was sent out to Senior Military staff as well as the dozens of persons ready to enlist and many recommendations came back. Major Winona 'Ralph' Beecher read the list to the attendees of the confab, "We are pleased with the number of suggestions that we received and here are the top selections; Lower East Side of NYC, anywhere in Cathedral City, Guerneville, Los Angeles, Palm Springs, Rancho Mirage, Sacramento, San Diego, San Francisco, Jersey City NJ, West Hollywood CA, Stamford CT and Wilton Manors FL. Other sites were summarily dismissed as not conforming to preconceived notions as to where the bases should be.

Gen. Sandra 'Bob' Kovak closed that meeting by noting, "One issue we didn't need to debate was bathrooms and showers etc. You can use any bathroom, any shower, and commode, any sink, any mirror anytime, anywhere. This was unanimously accepted at our confab."

DEMOCRATS GIVE AMERICA "A BETTER DEAL"

Sir Telsunn Margraves was able to consort with the Democrat Party on their theme to retake the reins of power, "The Better Deal!" After experiencing dramatic loses in the past election cycles, the atmosphere in the auditorium at the DNC Building is excitedly electric with speeches by the stalwarts of the party including Tom Perez, Sen Chuck Schumer, Rep. Debbie Wasserman Schultz, Sen Cory Booker and others. DNC leaders and party stalwarts combine important policy recommendations with the humor of the 'King of the One-Liners' Henny Youngman for added impact. An ever present media; Sir Telsunn among them, was there to make sure nothing was lost to posterity.

Washington, DC – In a packed auditorium in the Democrat National Committee Building, jubilant leadership of the party has assembled to make an auspicious announcement.

On stage, from standing left to right, are the elites members of the Democrat Party including Sen. Chuck Schumer, Rep. Nancy Pelosi, Rep. Maxine Waters, DNC Chair Tom Perez, Deputy Chair Keith Ellison, Sen. Dick Durbin, Sen. Elizabeth Warren, Rep. Adam Schiff, Rep. Debbie Wasserman Schultz, all current Democrat Governors, 50 state DNC chairs as well as every Democrat member of the Senate and House.

The press conference needs to be held in the auditorium as there is a very large contingent from the news media and space is needed for the extra attendees and their equipment. The audience goes hush as a smiling DNC Chairman Tom Perez takes to the podium to begin the special confab. "Our party is absolutely thrilled to be here today. We have such important news for the American people that we have asked every elected Democrat Senator and Congressperson to be here. Unfortunately our party has lost a more seats in the last three election cycles than we care to discuss, but looking at the bright side of things we are grateful that there aren't as many of us as before so we have extra room to accommodate the news media. I'd also like to send greetings to Senators Jeff Flake and Bob Corker, who sent telegrams of congratulations."

"I think that it is important to start with the genesis of our thinking related to how we would define our party in order to make it relevant to the American voting population today. Reaching back into recent history we can point to a time when the party had such success since the time we ran with the slogan 'New Deal', under President Franklin Delano Roosevelt and the 'Fair Deal' under President Harry Truman. As a matter of fact FDR was so successful that he was elected and re-elected president four times! Four times, imagine that! His success as president was so monumental that the congress was forced to change the constitution to limit the presidency to two terms."

What better way to honor party history and Democrat tradition than to update the slogan to the twenty first century." Tom Perez turns and reaches for a cord that is dangling by the side of a curtain behind him. He pulls the cord and the curtain drops to reveal the new Democrat Party slogan, "Ladies and Gentlemen may I present "A BETTER DEAL!" All present erupt into a cacophony of spontaneous cheers, whistles and applause at the new theme that will lead the party in the months and years to come.

"We have worked many hours performing the research and holding focus groups and surveys to come up with a direction that is clear, concise and expresses the deepest feelings we have for the Americans suffering under the vile and contemptuous Donald Trump! We had some other slogans that didn't make the cut. There was "Hillary Who?"... "Obama Who?"..."Twitter Free Thinking!"...we even thought of bringing back "LBJ all the Way!" and "Go Clean with Gene!" but both of those guys are dead so we decided on "A Better Deal" and we think it works great. What do you think?" Another round of cheers and applause from the audience and Tom Perez is more than pleased at the reaction that the new theme is getting. He explains the thinking that went behind the process of selecting the right slogan.

"We chose 'Better Deal" because it means, better jobs, better safety, better and higher, I mean lower taxes, better help for the inner cities, better factories here in the US and China, better free Obamaphones, better free Obamacare, better free college tuition and better use of taxpayer dollars for more better free things!" More cheering, yelling and applause from all present, even the media.

Tom Perez continues, "Another element that has been sorely missing from our outreach to the American voter is the inclusion of humor in our messaging. We lost our way in trying to focus on the Russia collusion stories that we hoped would resonate with the people but that didn't work. We tried to focus on the Russian meeting with Trump personnel but that didn't work, we tried to focus on the Russian ambassador eating with anyone that would give him a free meal but that didn't work, we tried Russians buying condos but that didn't work and we tried to tell the American people how much Trump loved Russian dressing on his salad but that didn't work but now we have A Better Deal!   We also discovered that adding humor into our communications with the public will be a winning strategy. In that regard, we have entered into an exclusive agreement with the estate of the iconic comedian Henny Youngman to incorporate his one-liners into all of our documents, new conferences, press briefings, public relations materials, TV appearances, speeches and discussions on healthcare, foreign policy, tax reform, marriage and every other topic you can think of. This reminds me of an unfortunate person; *'a homeless man, who walks up to me and says, 'I haven't eaten in three days and I replied, 'force yourself!'* The audience is getting into the spirit of the event and they clap and laugh uproariously.

Tom Perez is pleased that things are going so well and he wants the spirit of the event to continue to evoke an even greater reaction from the audience so he introduces the next speaker. "Ladies and gentlemen our next speaker needs no introduction. He is the senior senator from the great state of New York. He has fought the good fight for bigger seats on airplanes, e-cigarettes, laser pointers, and ticks. He has fought to expand on the slight shortcomings of President Barrack Obama including his signature legislative achievement better known as Obamacare. Senator Schumer has blocked any and every piece of legislation that could possibly accrue to the advantage of Donald Trump and the Republicans and he has even fought for a cash bar on the Staten Island Ferry. With a Senate Minority Leader like this how can we ever lose! Now please give a warm Democrat welcome to Senator Chuck Schumer!"

The crowd gives Senator Chuck Schumer a rousing reception and he smiles as he waves to the people that fill the auditorium. When things quiet down, he starts his remarks, "I want to thank you for that kind welcome and I want to thank Tom for his kind words and a shout out to my dear friends Senators Jeff Flake and Bob Corker. As you all know, I am the Minority Leader of the Democrats in the senate. I have been in Washington DC in one capacity or another for nearly 40 years and I have never been so unhappy which reminds me, *I just got back from a pleasure trip, I took my mother-in-law to the airport.* But seriously folks, when you consider all the important items that we are deliberating in Congress and all the problems that besiege the American people, all I can think is that *my wife Iris is on a new diet, all she eats is coconuts and bananas. She hasn't lost weight, but boy can she climb a tree!* When Tom told me of the new theme of the Democrat Party I was thrilled. Those three words mean more to me than anything. I must tell you of an incident I was told by one of my constituents. This constituent tells me about an old man at the nursing home where he works. *The old man says, "I'm so old that I forgot how old I am." An old woman who also resides at the home says, "I'll tell you how old you are. Take off your clothes and bend over." The man does this. The woman says, "You're seventy four." The man says, "How can you tell?" The woman says, "You told me yesterday."* Making sure our senior citizens have the kind of caring and compassionate care they need is promise number one to be kept!

Finally, I want to thank Tom, Keith and the entire team here at the DNC for the splendid job they did in launching our fabulous new theme, "A Better Deal" and in closing *I once thought about becoming an atheist but I gave up, they have no holidays.* Thank you and God bless America."

The audience is enthralled by the new focus of the party and the direction it is taking. Tom Perez comes back to the mic and addresses the gathering and says, "You can really tell a pro when you hear one, am I right or am I right?" Those assembled in the audience cheer and clap as Tom continues, " Before I turn the floor over to three of the party's best and brightest, I believe it is important to note that *a drunk goes up to a parking meter, puts in a quarter, the dial goes to 60. The drunk says, Huh? I lost 100 pounds!*" This is a critical statement to illustrate the scourge of alcoholism and the need to expand the food stamp program.

Now without further delay, I would like to introduce some of the party's biggest names, stars in their own right and now please welcome Senator Dick Durbin of Illinois, Senator Cory Booker of New Jersey and Representative Nancy Pelosi from California. The audience shouts approvals to Senators Durbin and Booker and Minority Leader Representative Nancy Pelosi.

Senator Durbin finds his way to the mic and begins his speech. "Thank you so much for that warm welcome and a big hello to Senators Flake and Corker. I want to update you about actions taken in the Senate as Cory and I have been fighting the good fight to make sure that every American has comprehensive and affordable healthcare. You may have heard that many insurance providers have left the Obamacare exchanges but have no fear. Cory and I have introduced legislation that will guarantee no more healthcare companies will leave the system. The way the law has been rewritten is to threaten them with more taxpayer funding and total humiliation if they leave. This brings to mind a fortunate turn of events for *one patient whose doctor had given him six months to live. The patient said he couldn't pay his bills so the doctor gave him another six months.* You hear stories like this all the time and it is a direct result of Obamacare.

"Many of those on Obamacare seem upset at the fact that they are forced to buy into plans that have huge deductibles, exorbitant co-pays and contain coverage that they don't need or want. For example birth control for women even if they are past the point in their lives where there is no longer the need for contraceptives that contribute to increased cost of healthcare. However, you really never know which reminds me of *the doctor who says to a man, "You're pregnant!" The man says, "How does a man get pregnant?" The doctor says, "The usual way - a little wine, a little dinner...."* So when you add up everything, you just never know. Now I would like to introduce our next speaker, my colleague, good friend, and a rising star in the Democrat Party, Senator Cory Booker!"

On his way to the podium Senator Booker embraces Senator Durbin and they exchange pleasantries. Now it is Senator Booker's turn to address the audience. "Thank you so much for the warm welcome. It has certainly been a life changing period since I took up residence in Washington DC. There are many events, dinners, galas and 'parties that I MUST attend...wink, wink!" The crowd laughs at Senator Booker's joke and he is pleased at the reception he is getting. "I remember this one time when I was at an event to honor Rep. John Dingell, the oldest serving Democrat in congress. John and I took time to chat and he asked me *"Hey Booker, are you married?" I said no and he said, "What do you do for aggravation?"* This commentary by Rep. Dingell hit home for me and that is why I am offering bipartisan legislation, together with my friends Senators Jeff Flake and Bob Corker before they leave Congress. This will provide much needed something that we are not sure of, but we think that all Americans may not care about." The crowd cheers and again Senator Booker seems very pleased.

"I would now, however return to the topic at hand; how can we save Obamacare from President Trump's relentless pursuit of its destruction? You hear so many stories about people who were saved because of the treatment they received but some have not fared so well, take the *nurse who told the doctor, "The man you just gave a clean bill of health dropped dead right as he was leaving the office." The doctor told the nurse, "Turn him around to make it look like he was walking in."* Creating complex solutions to seemingly simple problems are what the Democrats are known for. Thank you and when you are feeling ill remember that there is always someone worse off like *the man who goes to a psychiatrist and says, "Nobody listens to me!" The doctor says, "Next!"* It is these tactics that so many physicians today have to resort to and Obamacare is showing them the way." His audience cheers Senator Booker and before he returns to his place he announces the next speaker, Minority Leader Nancy Pelosi. As they pass each other they embrace and Senator Booker gives Nancy Pelosi a peck on the cheek.

Rep. Pelosi is beaming with pride, "My...my! What a wonderful event this is and what a wonderful theme for the Democrats to run on...A BETTER DEAL!!! Also, I have a big hello for my friends Senators Jeff Flake and Bob Corker." The crowd erupts in applause and cheers of delight. "We are on the threshold of great things and with our deep bench of talent we are going to hit a touchdown for sure!" The crowd cheers again. "However before we do that we need to accomplish our goals and top of the list is saving Obamacare. Healthcare is as important as anything we can do for Americans and don't let anyone tell you that Obamacare has inferior providers and doctors. There may be occasional mishaps but we are working to avoid them in the future. For example, I must say one thing about the current healthcare system, it is important that the care you receive is the best you can get. Cut rate medical treatments have consequences like *the man who had his vasectomy done at Sears®. Now when he makes love, the garage door goes up."* It's incidents like this that reinforces what we need to guard against. Another example is a constituent I know who told me that *his friend had a doctor who told him "take some weight off, go to a health club." This man lost 20 pounds in one week! The machine tore his leg off!"* The future of Obamacare demands that we take our health into our own hands. Thank you for taking time to be here and to listen to our exciting plans for the future. On a personal note, and I hope you will indulge me; my husband and I are celebrating 54 years of marriage!" The audience is delighted and they clap for Rep. Pelosi in tribute to this anniversary. We were spending some quiet time last night and he asked me, *'Where do you want to go for our anniversary?' I said, 'Take me somewhere I have never been before! He said, try the kitchen!'* Men, don't you just love them." Nancy acknowledges the adulation of the audience as she waves and takes her place on the main stage.

Tom Perez continues to be thrilled at the way things are going and he introduces the next notables who will be addressing the group. "Ladies and gentlemen, wasn't that an inspiration and quite instructive. As to how we will deal with the tumult that is sure to follow an out-of-control Trump presidency, let me introduce two women who need no introduction. They both have served their constituencies for many years and constantly keep getting reelected which says volumes for their constituencies. Senator Elizabeth Warren and Representative Debbie Wasserman Schultz have been at the forefront of the fight to keep sacred many of the traditions of our country. One of my pet peeves has been the various US airlines. As all of you know, our airlines have been taking advantage of flyers and treating them in a horrible manner. I have personal experience with this shameful treatment *like the last time I was getting on a plane, I told the ticket lady, "Send one of my bags to New York, send one to Los Angeles, and send one to Miami." She said, "We can't do that!" I told her, "You did it last week!"* These types of disregard for the comfort of their passengers, people who have paid good money to fly, are still treated like dogs where *the food on the plane is fit for a king. "Here, King! Here King!"* Now let's give a warm welcome to the Senator Elizabeth Warren from the great state of Massachusetts!"

Senator Warren embraces Tom and kisses his cheek before she takes her place at the podium. "Thank you for that kind introduction and the wonderful new slogan for the Democrat

Party, 'A Better Deal!' isn't it wonderful!" The crowd roars their approval again and Senator Warren continues, "I would like to speak to the various social issues that are confronting the many diverse groups in American today. As you all know I have been a tireless advocate for Americans with various challenges to be able to live a normal productive life. For instance, I was travelling to visit my good friend Maxine Waters, and on the way I stayed at a hotel in San Francisco. *I was taking a shower when there is a knock on the door. "Who is it?" I said and he said, "Blind man!" Not caring how I looked, I opened the door and he said, "Where do you want these blinds, lady?"* This preposterous attempt to fool me was something that needs to be changed so I am sponsoring legislation with my colleagues and friends, Senators Jeff Flake and Bob Corker to eliminate the word 'blind' from our vocabulary and use 'non-sighted persons' instead.

Another issue confronting many metropolitan areas that have been run for decades by dedicated Democrats is homelessness. The recent unprecedented rise in the homeless population I experienced the last time I was in New York City was shameful. I was confronted by a *homeless man who asked, "Give me $10 till payday." I replied, "When's payday?" He said, "I don't know, you're the one who is working!"* Imagine the humiliation he felt. I practically cried when *another homeless person told me, "I haven't tasted food all week."* I was so upset that all I could think of saying is, *"Don't worry, it still tastes the same!"*

There was an audible gasp from the audience as Senator Warren continues to speak, "Another important issue that has been uppermost on the minds of Americans is the demise of traditional marriage and the traditional role it plays in our society. Many people have turned to online dating, personal ads, bar hopping and other methods to find the perfect mate. I recall one of my constituents told me of a woman who was looking to meet someone. *This woman was walking in the park when she meets a man and she says, "I haven't seen you around here." He says, "Yes, I just got out of jail for killing my wife" and she replies, "So you're single!"* In today's world sometimes you just need to put yourself out and who knows, lady luck may find you and to quote my Native-American ancestors, "Wahyakeri tewahsen-tsyatak hnekirha akaratsi yekhon-nyàtha" which loosely translated means, *Take my wife, please"*

Senator Elizabeth Warren gratefully accepts the applause from the audience and greets Rep. Debbie Wasserman Schultz with a hug as she takes her turn at the podium. "Wasn't Senator Elizabeth Warren wonderful, and what a mind! Thank you for the tremendous welcome you gave me and I'm sending a great big hug to my friends Senators Jeff Flake and Bob Corker. I am so very thankful for the great work done by the DNC; let's give them a round of applause." Rep. Wasserman Schultz waits for the applause to die down. "As you all know I was the former head of the DNC and I was forced to resign over some inconsequential mix-up over some emails that were meaningless in the overall scheme of things. Then there was a small matter of the manager of my web support staff trying to leave the country and he was stopped by the authorities, but let us not dwell on the past let's look to the future!" The audience screams with joy at the word 'future' and Rep. Wasserman Schultz yells above the screams, AND THE FUTURE IS "A BETTER DEAL!" More screams and yells and cheers!

Rep. Wasserman Schultz continues, "In terms of society, Americans need to become more inclusive and tolerant to those who are new to our country. As you know I am of Jewish ancestry and we came to America to overcome the persecutions in countries of our origin. I represent the 23rd district in Florida where we have a large Jewish population and I was talking to one of my constituents; *a little Jewish grandma who was with her grandson at the beach. The grandson is playing when a big wave comes and washes the kid out to sea. The lifeguards swim out, bring him back to shore, the paramedics work on him for a long time, pumping the water out of his lungs and reviving him. The exhausted lifeguards turn to his grandma and say, "we saved your grandson!" The little Jewish grandma looks down at her grandson and says, "He had a hat."* This is just another example of the Jewish American experience and how well we have assimilated."

Rep. Debbie Wasserman Schultz seems to get a bit somber and a far-away look comes over her. The spell is broken and she tells the audience, "I was just thinking of the late, great Senator Frank Lautenberg and I remember speaking with him. He was also of the Jewish faith and he told me never to forget *"Do you know why Jews don't drink?"* I told him I didn't know and he said, *"It interferes with their suffering."* I don't have to worry about those problems. I am very fortunate to have such an enduring marriage. *Some people ask the secret of our long marriage and I reply we take time to go to a restaurant two times a week. A little candlelight, dinner, soft music and dancing. He goes Tuesdays, I go Fridays."*

Rep. Wasserman Schultz says in closing, "We have a wonderful opportunity to show America what can be done when we have mature, responsible and trustworthy people running the halls of government. Part of what you will see in in the coming months is a visible outreach to voters showing them how we have changed with renewed vigor and commitment. Many people ask me how I manage to speak so well to vast groups of voters around the country. I tell them I use a verbal exercise that I was taught by my dear friend, Rep. Maxine Waters. I tell any Democrat who will listen, *"Well, it's like this. You go to diction school. They teach you to fill your mouth with marbles and talk right through the marbles. Each day you take one marble out. When you've lost all your marbles..."*

At that point there is tremendous screaming, shouting and yelling as all in the auditorium turn to the rear entrance only to see former President Barrack Hussein Obama enter the room. There is pandemonium as he walks down the aisle toward the stage to take his rightful place among the Democrat elites that have assembled there. You can feel the excitement and sense the adoration and love that permeates the room as he bounds the stairs and embraces each and every man and woman on stage. Debbie Wasserman Schultz is thrilled to see President Obama and she runs to give him a great big hug. She takes over the emcee function from Tom Perez and says into the mic, "Ladies and gentlemen, please give a warm Democrat welcome to President Barrack Obama!"

President Obama steps to the podium and basks in the overwhelming welcome and adulation he is receiving from all in the room, party officials and media alike. The auditorium finally quiets down and President Obama is able to speak. "Thank you...thank you...thank you for the kind and generous greeting. This is a wonderful way to launch our new theme 'A Better Deal', isn't that great!" A roar of approval resounds from the audience. "Now that we have retired from a life in the spotlight, Michelle and I are trying to rediscover a few things that we can do together; but that can be very difficult. For instance, *I take my wife everywhere, but she finds her way home.* I use a lot of my free time to visit the doctor; it keeps me healthy and away from home." The audience laughs and the president seems to be enjoying himself. "The last time I was at the doctor's office *I told him I had ringing in my ears and he told me not to answer.* But let me tell you one thing; never ever take your health for granted especially when it comes to affairs of the heart. My doctor told me, *"You want to improve your love life? You need to get some exercise. Run ten miles a day." Two weeks later, I called the doctor. The doctor says, "How is your love life since you have been running?" "I told him I don't know I'm 140 miles away!"*

"Part of our 'A Better Deal' appeal is to middle class suburbanites that we have neglected for too long. Now that I am living an ordinary life I can appreciate what makes these people tick. I try to get out and meet folks and walk the streets of beautiful Washington, DC. There was one time when I was standing on the sidewalk as *two hearses drove by followed by a man walking with his dog and behind the man there were a hundred other men. I asked him what was going on and he points to the hearses and says that's my wife and that's my mother-in-law, my dog bit them. I asked if I could borrow the dog and he said, get in line.*"

"In the years ahead, as we rebuild our Democrat Party you can rest assured that Michelle and I will be cheering you on. I would like to close with an appeal to a project Michelle and I have taken up as a personal cause and that is education. There are so many schools that are failing our children and we need to address these things immediately. *I recall one Democrat congressman who wrote us telling us that his son used to go to school with his dog. Then his son and the dog were separated. His dog graduated!* Is there anything more tragic than a failed education system like this? Well, he also told us that *his son complains about headaches. I tell him all the time, when you get out of bed, it's feet first!*"

Tom walks to the podium and embraces Barrack Obama and says, "This concludes our conference launching our new initiative for America...A Better Deal!"

As the Democrat dignitaries are saying good-bye to President Obama and Tom Perez, an aide, in a state of panic, runs to Chairman Perez and hands him an envelope. Tom Perez continues to speak with Obama as he opens the envelope and reads the enclosure. Perez turns pale and rushes to the podium to speak, "Ladies and gentlemen, may I have your attention. Please ladies and gentlemen I have an important announcement to make."

The attendees cease to talk as they all look up at the stage. Tom Perez begins, "I have some very sad news...I mean some very great news. The company that runs our focus group testing, messaging and advertising has just written me saying that we are abandoning 'The Better Deal' for a brand new, terrific slogan to lead us to victory. Ladies and gentlemen, I am proud to announce, for the first time ever, the new Democrat 2018 slogan, "For the People!'" Tom is waiting for a response from the audience but everyone just stands there in stunned silence.

Tom is trying to find the words to energize the party faithful by telling them, "We are still very much committed to the views stated in The Better Deal, but we will no longer be using the humor of Henny Youngman. Instead, our advertising agency has entered into an exclusive arrangement with comedian Louis CK who seems to be out of work and needs the money for lawyers. Again, thank you for attending and please send money."

All the jokes attributed to Henny Youngman are in italics

RUSSIAN MEDDLING IN PRESIDENTIAL ELECTION PROVEN!

The entire country has been waiting for what has recently been uncovered by the Department of Justice and reported by Sir Telsunn Margraves of ...*Real Fake News* and others in the mainstream media. It all culminates in the unlikely town of Blandford, MA, and the evidence is so overwhelming and conclusive that Special Counsel Robert Mueller addresses the issue in somber tones, "I believe this is a sad day for American and our sacred electoral system", and its bad news for President Trump.

Washington, DC – In a hastily called press conference, Special Counsel Robert Mueller today announced that as a result of the initiative to validate voting in the last election, there is compelling evidence that Russia interfered in the presidential election. As part of the investigation there is a feverish effort to determine if there was any Russian interference that impacted vote totals to favor Donald Trump. Through diligent efforts, and with fortitude and determination, the investigative team made a momentous discovery. The media who are present shout questions, wanting to know if there is definitive proof. A saddened Robert Mueller made one final comment, "I'm afraid there is" and he refused to say anything else.

An unnamed source in the Department of Justice notes, "This is no witch hunt, this is the real thing. We have uncovered compelling evidence that points to the fact that 'if it quacks like a Russian'', 'waddles like a Russian', 'eats like a Russian', it probably is a Russian. That is all I can say."

The investigation has gone on for months and Special Counsel Mueller has been able to hone in on facts that could bring down the administration. Mr. Mueller addressed the issue in somber tones, "I believe this is a sad day for America and our sacred electoral system."

In a joint investigation, the AP, Reuters, Washington Post, NY Times, CNN®, MSNBC, ABC, CBS, NBC, NPR, PBS and Pravda completed the exhaustive research it took to bring this travesty out into the open. Jonathan Allen, a spokesman for the combined new outlets told a packed conference, "We have been able to discover the source of the evidence into Russian meddling in the presidential election and we caught up with the person last week. I might add that the person did not hide behind anonymity, she openly reveals her name, her role in the revealing the sordid affair and how she uncovered the depth of Russian interference. She is Mrs. Alberta S. Finnerty and she is about the bravest woman I have ever met. Here is a video of the interview that took place just 3 days ago."

The room darkens as the video begins. "Good morning, my name is Mrs. Alberta S. Finnerty and I am responsible for carrying out my duties as voter registration clerk for the town of Blandford, Massachusetts. My duties in this capacity include canvassing the votes and voter rolls in the last presidential election to see if there is anything that could be construed as irregular."

Mrs. Alberta S. Finnerty continued, "After initial review I detected something I felt was very suspicious. You could have knocked me over with a feather when I concluded there was something very, very disturbing even treasonous although I am not a legal scholar. I think that it would be best to show you the actual certified, attested to and recounted 12 times vote totals that will prove, conclusively, how the Russians meddled in our election in favor of Donald Trump by trying to influence the vote in Blandford." Mrs. Finnerty walks over to an easel that was standing in the corner of the room where she is being recorded. The video camera zooms into so that the numbers are full screen.

Town	Clinton # Votes	Clinton % Votes	Trump # Votes	Trump % Votes	Johnson # Votes	Johnson % Votes	Stein # Votes	Stein % Votes	% Reported
Blandford	256	36.8%	404	58%	26	4%	8	1.1%	100%

Mrs. Finnerty holds a pointer in her hand, the kind like teachers use in class, and she begins to explain the numbers. "The voter count in the town of Blandford is broken down into vote totals for each of the candidates and the percentage of those votes cast in relation to the total. On initial examination you might conclude that there doesn't seem like anything is wrong and so did I, but if I didn't look further I would have missed what appears to be an act of willful disregard of the law and to subvert the democratic process."

The camera went wide to reveal Mrs. Finnerty next to the chart as she explained, "As a public employee, me and four other colleagues spent the next three weeks going over each and every one of the 662 votes cast. We checked each backwards and forwards, inside and out, up and down, side to side, round and round..." there is an interruption and a mumbling voice, barely audible, seems to say, "just get on with it Alberta."

Alberta can be heard saying. "Oh sorry, it is then we found the "smoking gun, as you reporters say, right in front of our eyes." She reaches into her pocketbook and lifts out a 4"x6" index card. "This card and all the voter registration cards contain information relating to the voters in the districts covering the Blandford Township. It's really too small for you to read but I will provide you with the pertinent information so you can determine for yourself if what I am saying is true. By the way, Special Counsel Mueller has a copy of this on file in his office."

Mrs. Finnerty reads from the card, "Name: Vasille Illeich Uveshenko, Address: 22567 Maple Drive, Apt. No: 348C, Town: Blandford, MA. He also lists some personal information such as date of birth, age, education level etc. Normally I would have just moved onto the next card but something struck me as odd. First, the name sounded like it was a foreign name. Second, I live on Maple and I happen to know that the address numbers of the homes on our street stop at 62. Third, the last home on Maple is a single family so there is no apartment number 348C. Incredulous is the only way I can describe how I felt. I told my fellow workers and we immediately jumped into action. Six weeks later we were able to determine that there was no Mr. Uveshenko, no 22567 Maple Drive and no apartment with the number 348C. By virtue of our findings we were able to purge the vote totals to reflect one less vote for President Trump."

Mrs. Finnerty reaches over and takes away the original chart and underneath is a second chart. "Here are the revised totals;

Town	Clinton # Votes	Clinton % Votes	Trump # Votes	Trump % Votes	Johnson # Votes	Johnson % Votes	Stein # Votes	Stein % Votes	% Reported
Blandford	256	36.8%	403	58%	26	4%	8	1.1%	100%

Our group was dumbfounded and, while forced to admit it, this didn't change the outcome. We are still thankful we were able stop this attack on the voting process. Our group did ask if we could give the vote to Hillary Clinton instead. The entire staff felt that it would somehow provide a form of justice to know that something worth doing is worth doing well. Mrs. Finnerty reveals the final chart, "We were given permission by the board of elections in the state of Massachusetts and it is reflected in the final tally."

Town	Clinton # Votes	Clinton % Votes	Trump # Votes	Trump % Votes	Johnson # Votes	Johnson % Votes	Stein # Votes	Stein % Votes	% Reported
Blandford	257	36.8%	403	58%	26	4%	8	1.1%	100%

Mrs. Alberta S. Finnerty concludes her presentation, "Thank you all for listening, I just hope this bad-apple does not turn-off young people from voting in the future."

Jonathan Allen follows up with a few words to the crowd of reporters gathered, "Ladies and gentlemen, I want to just say how grateful we are to Mrs. Finnerty for her diligence and bravery in the face of this confounding news. I also have someone on the line that I would like you all to hear. "Senator, the floor is yours..."

A voice booms loud from the phone's speaker, "Good morning my name is Senator Chuck Schumer and I am the Senate Minority Leader. Before I begin, I would like to give a shout out to my good friends Senators Jeff Flake and Bob Corker. I want to thank you for allowing me to address this gathering. I have been watching this with keen interest and quite frankly I want to say how shocked and angered I am at this blatant attempt to steal the election from its rightful winner, Hillary Clinton. I won't get into the specifics but I am going to the floor of the Senate right now to express my chagrin at the way our electoral process has been perverted. I believe this is treason and rises to the level of an impeachable offence. Let us hope and pray to God that our country can withstand this onslaught to our freedom and democracy. Let us also not allow this single attempt to stop the millions of undocumented aliens who may have, in some innocent way, found their way into the voting booths. That was just a minor mistake and can be easily pardoned as a small slip up. Thank you."

Jonathan Allen ends by saying, "Thank you all for being here and let me know if you need a copy of the video or transcripts for your evening newscast."

The initial vote totals for Blandford Massachusetts quoted in the APGR Fake News article are in fact real. The rest have been provided to APGR Fake News by Mrs. Finnerty who, strange as it may seem can no longer be found to corroborate the vote tallies. TM

3,400 voters took themselves off the rolls in Colorado. 125,000 Democrat voters were purged from the Brooklyn voter rolls for various reasons. In Lincoln County, WVA 9,000 names came off the voter rolls. According to the Washington Times Hillary Clinton garnered more than 800,000 votes from noncitizens on Nov. 8, an approximation far short of President Trump's estimate of up to 5 million illegal voters but supportive of his charges of fraud. There are many more incidents of voter purges and unregistering but then the footnotes would be longer than the article. TM

STEPHEN COLBERT FILES SUIT TO PREVENT CHURCH FROM USING TOWN PARK FOR BAKE SALE

Arguments surrounding separation of Church and State has strong advocates on both sides. Disguised as a parks department lawn mower operator, Sir Telsunn Margraves joined with reporters from all the mainstream media have converged on Ashtabula, Ohio to take the pulse of the citizenry regarding this threat to democracy, the Annual Church Bake Sale. Stephen Colbert has made Ashtabula "ground zero" as he takes up the mantle and pledges to fight and purge God from each and every public area; schools, government offices and motor vehicle departments throughout the US. Colbert vows to take the fight all the way to the Supreme Court!

Ashtabula, OH – Stephen Colbert took a break from the usual comedic attempt in his opening monologue to make a very serious announcement. "I have been a long-time supporter of some of the US Constitutional Amendments except the ones I don't like. But I like the one that holds sacred the separation of Church and State. Even in the Declaration of Independence there is a sacred trust that God has no place in politics especially if it's in a church! That is why I am announcing on my program, 'Late Night with Stephen Colbert' airing Monday through Friday from 11:30P to 12:30AM Eastern Standard Time on CBS and its affiliates around the country, the following proclamation!"

"I, Stephen Tyrone Colbert, have taken on, as my solemn duty, the fight against The Christian Church of the Christ of Love, Peace and Kindness in Ashtabula, Ohio, to prevent the perversion of the United States laws and customs, except for illegal immigration, and stop a heinous crime from being committed. What might appear to the uneducated, ignorant and idiotic citizenry as a harmless bake sale is, in fact, a trampling of our constitutional expectation. God has no place in our country's parks and recreation open spaces especially to sell cakes and pies. I intend to use my vast resources and the resources of my network partner, CBS, to assure all Americans that they are safe from carrot cakes and chocolate chip cookies being sold to minors in the parkland surrounding the Ashtabula's city center."

The shocking announcement made by Stephen Tyrone Colbert has sent reverberations throughout the United States.

In a recent article on *The Daily Wire* by Paul Bois, he wrote, *"The self-described practicing "Catholic" Stephen Colbert decided to put out a mean-spirited anti-Trump Easter special for his Showtime animated show, "Our Cartoon President." Even though Stephen Colbert rolls with the Christian-hating Left, a group that seeks to put Christian bakers out of business and force American taxpayers to cough up blood money for abortions, the CBS late-night host thought it fitting to attack President Trump as a charlatan who secretly mocks his Christian base."*

Adherents on both sides of the issue have taken what appears as intractable stands for and against religious cakes and pies being offered and sold on public property. A consortium of media outlets have been doing investigations and reporting the strong reaction from many of Ashtabula's citizens on this subject.

The first of many people being interviewed is Mrs. Betty Walden, chairperson of the Christian Church of the Christ of Love, Peace and Kindness Pies and Cakes Committee. Mrs. Walden tells the reporter, "We hold this event every year and we have received many accolades on the home baked goods we sell. I tell you if you've ever had a piece of Trixie Prichard's homemade Rhubarb and Strawberry Pie you would think you died and went to heaven...Oh sorry; am I allowed to say heaven?" The reporter responds, "Of course you are but I will run it by our attorneys just to make sure. There is enormous interest in this story, not only here in Ashtabula but among people all over the country and I have a question for you, why a bake sale?"

Mrs. Walden replies, "The women's auxiliary of our church wants to raise money to help children from around the world who suffer from famine, disease, war and other horrors. We decide that a bake sale is something that, in some small way, our church members could get behind. Land sakes, we never realized how popular this would become. At first we held the bake sale in the church meeting room but that became too small, then we moved it to the church's auditorium but that became too small, then we moved it to the church's parking lot but that became too small to accommodate the hundreds of folks who love our home-made cakes and pies."

The reporter then asks, "How come you decided on Lakeshore Park to hold the bake sale?"

Mrs. Walden says, "I'd like to have my co-chairman, Mrs. Selma Wonkier, tell you why, Selma?" "Thank you Betty. Well Lakeshore Park is close to our church, it is a wonderful setting for families that may want to spend the day. The Greater Ashtabula 'Easter Egg Hunt' is held at Lakeshore Park each year and it is home to the annual 'Rib Burn Off' where you can taste some of the best ribs in the whole world. We applied for a permit to hold our event and the town council was given the proper insurance forms that are required. We paid the permit fee and all the information was sent for review by the town officials. Three weeks later we received the permit to hold our event and the committee made plans to let everyone know."

The reporter continues, "It is my understanding that Stephen Colbert is attempting to have this event cancelled due to the confluence of church and state and he has vowed to take this all the way to the Supreme Court. He contends, and I quote, 'God has no place in our country's parks and recreation open spaces especially for selling cakes and pies' what do you say to that?"

Selma Wonkier asks, "Betty, may I answer this?" Betty Walden says, "Of course dear."

Mrs. Wonkier addresses the reporter's query, "Oh my, the Supreme Court! Isn't that where that handsome new guy with the grey hair serves? Anyway, we are sorry if we have offended anyone with our cake and pie sale. Our hearts are in the right place, the customers stomachs are in the right place but it seems that his brain is on vacation." Mrs. Wonkier and Mrs. Walden get quite a chuckle out of this and conclude, "We will put our trust in God and Jesus Christ and we will always strive to help people in need no matter what is thrown our way." With the interview over, it is time for the small group to say their goodbyes to the reporter and they leave

Meanwhile across town another interview is taking place. The reporter tries to locate citizens of Ashtabula who are against the bake sale but couldn't find anyone. He did locate a group of 40 individuals, all from New York City and San Francisco associated with the recently formed group, 'Separatists and Atheists Against Sugary Cake and Pie Sales in Public Places", jointly funded by George Soros, the ACLU, the Open Society Foundation and the Hostess Company, makers of Twinkies and Ring Dings. The reporter tries to find the spokesperson for the group and is told that his name is Malcolm Trencher. The reporter looks for the man and when he find him asks if he would like to be interviewed.

Malcolm Trencher responds, "Surely."

"Mr. Trencher, why are you here?"

"Well that is a good question, why are we here? I guess you can look at this in a real or metaphysical sense as in 'Why are any one of us here?' I would prefer to examine the question metaphysically but that would require a deliberative process which you can discern in the writings of Zeno of Citium, Kant, Rousseau..."

The reporter tries to stop Mr. Trencher, "Umm, Mr. Trencher..."

"Kierkegaard, Camus, Bentman..."

The reporter tries again, "Umm, Mr. Trencher..."

"Schopenhauer, Nietzsche, Sartre and, of course, Colbert..."

But the reporter interrupts, "Mr. Trencher, I only meant why you and your group here are in protest against the church's cake and pie sale?"

"Ah! That is different! We are here in protest to assure that our long held belief that there is no God and, even if there is, he has no place in a cake or pie sale. The Declaration of Independence says these truths are self-evident, and that man does not live by cake and pie alone and all men and women, even transgender and Other-kin are equal under the nutritional laws that govern us all, that cakes and pies make you fat. We have travelled many miles to be here in open protest to make it known that we will not yield to the unyielding!"

The reporter is a bit confused but he continues. "Many of the pro-cake and pie sale groups contend you are being paid to be here and that you have no real reason for waging this fight, is that true?"

Mr. Trencher grimaces at the suggestion and he seems incensed that the question was even asked. He raises his voice at the reporter, "What media outlet do you represent?! Newsmax?! Fox News?! Rush Limbaugh?!" The reporter is taken aback by the insinuation and tells Malcolm Trencher that he is in Ashtabula to represent a consortium of various news organizations and further assure Mr. Trencher that he will be fair and objective in reporting the results of the interview.

"Well, I will assume you are an honorable person and that you will be sure to provide the consumers of news with a true representation of our position that I deftly provided."

The reporter is still confounded by what Malcolm Trencher's position is but he has another question. "I don't mean to be provocative but it has been said that George Soros and the groups he directly funds like the *ACLU, Change America Now* and *People for the American Way* among others are funding your group. Is that true?"

"How can you even say such a thing? When I was at dinner with George yesterday he indicated that he would not put another penny into any organization that is unwilling to fly to the protest any other way than coach. I, along with all other protesters, am not given money for food or lodging, however, we have been given these small chits that we must present prior to check in. Our rooms and meals are donated by the *Open Society Foundations* who receives no monies from George Soros!"

The reporter says, "Uh...doesn't the *Open Society Foundations* indirectly get its money from other Soros funded groups?"

"It may, but I consider that none of my business. Besides, I consider we are doing the Lord's work, in this case, it's Lord Wilmott Potter of Greater Essex the noted advocate of innumerable causes and Mr. Soros' good friend. I do have a surprise announcement to make and I would like your readers and viewers to be the first to know! I have been told that Stephen Colbert will be broadcasting live tonight from the local CBS Affiliate in Ashtabula! He will be addressing us supporters and we are even being given special audience passes to his show...how exciting it is!" The reporter thanks Mr. Trencher for his time and his thoughts on the protest and assures him that he will be watching Stephen Colbert's address to his supporters. They shake hands and both go back to the business at hand.

Later that afternoon a private jet lands at Northeast Ohio Regional Airport. The 40 protesters have been bussed to the hanger where Stephen Colbert will disembark. There is also a contingent of 60 reporters and newscasters to report on and tape the event. There is excitement in the air as the plane lands signaling the arrival of Mr. Colbert.

To add to the festivities, the *Open Society Foundations* imported the famous San Francisco musical group, The Accordion Dynamos, to provide entertainment. As the plane's latch opens, the Accordion Dynamos begin to play the Pharrell Williams classic, "Happy" and the 40 protesters and a large number of news people start singing. The crowd bursts into applause as Stephen Colbert exits the plane and he smiles and waves to the crowd. He is anxious to address the group and thank them for their efforts and to encourage them to keep the momentum going.

Stephen Colbert takes his place at a make-shift podium and starts, "Wow! What a wonderful reception, I can't thank you all enough for being here. First I would like to thank CBS for its support of this cause, second I would like to thank George Soros for his support, and next I would like to thank The Accordion Dynamos for their splendid rendition of "Happy". Finally, I want to thank Madalyn Murray O'Hair, Jane Lynch, Brandy Alexandre, Woody Allen, Kathy Griffin and Patton Oswalt for providing inspiration and encouragement of our protest. I want to start by asking 'why are we here?"

Malcolm Trencher yells out, "In a real or metaphysical sense?"

Stephen Colbert seems puzzled, "Huh?"

Malcolm just yells, "Forget it."

"Umm, okay but I'll answer my own question. Separatists and atheist alike are united in this cause and we all ask the same question, what the hell is a cake and pie sale doing in a public park? Do you realize that children play in this park? Huh, do you realize that? Do you also realize that if we allow this we might as well have Bar and Bat Mitzvahs in our parks! Do you also realize that there are ants in our parks? Huh! First its cakes and pies, next its sausages and peppers, where does it stop...guns and ammo!!!" The group is being stirred into a frenzy and they chant, "NO CAKES AND PIES...NO BAR AND BAT MITZVAHS...NO SAUSAGES AND PEPPERS...NO GUNS AND AMMO!"

Stephen Colbert is basking in the passion he feels coming from the crowd, "I can't say if there is a God or if there isn't but what I can ask is; what the hell is He doing to my country? I have travelled the great width and depth of this land and I have felt the pulse of the American people, well at least some of the pulse...mostly on the Eastside of Manhattan and maybe the pulse of Hollywood oh and yes the pulse of San Francisco and in all cases the pulse is beating strongly, well maybe strongly is too strong...maybe more rapidly, that's it rapidly, and I can tell you this, there is no room for cakes and pies in this country." The crowd of news people and protesters are cheering at the words of Stephen Colbert and he is grateful for their adulation.

"In closing, I want to thank you again for giving your all in this fight and I just want to say that if we lose this battle in the courts *I'll just scream and yell 'fuck' for the next 45 minutes.*"

To paraphrase a quote given by Stephen Colbert in the documentary by filmmakers Mark Halperin, John Heilemann and Mark McKinnon from the Showtime® documentary "Trumped" - TM

ACOSTA AND TAPPER OF CNN BECOME ENGAGED!

On a happy note, *Absolutely, Positively, Genuine, Real Fake News'* is pleased to report on a story coming out of Chattanooga, Tennessee. This heartwarming announcement, originally published in the Signal Mountain Gazette, is a welcome diversion from the serious news*'...Real Fake News'* usually reports on. Sir Telsunn Margraves and the entire staff send their best wishes and congratulations to the happy couple.

Chattanooga, TN – It was announced today in the Signal Mountain Gazette that Beauregard (Beau) T. Acosta and Malcolm Phineas (Finn) Tapper have become engaged and plan to marry next spring.

Acosta is beaming as he says, "Finn and I are thrilled that we are able to take our relationship to the next level. We are very much in love, and there is so much to do before the ceremony and reception, but we will make it happen and it will be lovely."

Tapper also added, "I moved from San Francisco to Signal Mountain Tennessee. I was new to the area and I wanted to make friends. From the first time I met Beau, I mean Beauregard, I was smitten and the rest, as they say, is history."

Tapper and Acosta both agree, "We are so very grateful to CNN, *Chattanooga Nice-Guys Needed* online dating site for providing the opportunity and environment for so many Chattanooga area gay men. It is a wonderful place to meet and share likes, dislikes and personal experiences. If it wasn't for CNN we would not have met."

Beau said, "For instance Finn and I both like to travel and we have taken a two-week vacation to Tibet. It is a remarkable country with age old traditions and culture. We spent an evening following some people carrying sticks on their back and found out it was some kind of prayer group. Who would have thought?"

Finn chimed in, "There were some very disturbing elements. For instance we went to see the Dali Lama but we found out that he had to leave the country for fear of imprisonment or worse. It seems the Dali Lama formed a government in exile due to the Chinese taking over the country."

Beau also mentioned that he and Finn have a passion for music. "Last week we saw *Taylor Swift* and *Big Bad Voodoo Daddy* in concert, separately of course, and they were great! Finn turns to Beau and proclaims, "Didn't you just love when Taylor sang "Untouchable!" Both Beau and Finn break out in song and they actually have good voices.

We ask the guys "What's next?"

Beau is eager to reply, "Well we both want to embark on careers in broadcasting. Finn is already enrolled in the Chattanooga Broadcasting School (CBS) and I am writing the pilot and starring in a series I hope will air on the Cooking Channel called "Shove This in Your Mouth." It's all about the great recipes for foods you hate, but your mother made you eat."

When asked if they are aware that there is an Acosta and Tapper working at the other CNN® (©*Cable News Network*) both men looked at each other and said, "Who?"

SHADOW GOVERNMENT, READY TO OVERTHROW PRESIDENT TRUMP, FOUND IN OBAMA'S BASEMENT!

If you've ever doubted that there is a deep state government conspiracy to nullify the election of Donald Trump and install a shadow government, doubt no more. The covert operation takes place in the newly remodeled basement of former President Barack Obama's Washington DC home. There he has assembled his team of trusted advisors to carry out the effort to purge anything and everything Trump. This expose recounted by a highly placed source and told to Sir Telsunn Margraves of '... *Real Fake News*'. Trust us when we say this will send chills down your spine.

This article was written based on information provided to APGR Fake News by an official very high up in former President Barack Hussein Obama's Administration. He or she has asked that his or her name, position background or any other identifying characteristics not be included in this article for reason that will become obvious once the article is read. I have assured him or her that I would not betray the trust he or she has placed in providing me with such important and sensitive information. He or she insisted that the information could be considered very upsetting or encouraging to some in the media, legal, political, religious or lobbyist community. TM

Washington, DC – The rumor mills have been circulating at full speed after APGR Fake News learned of confidential information relating to an underground (literally) effort by former President Barack Hussein Obama and his team of operatives. APGR Fake News has been apprised of a concerted effort to subvert the presidency of Donald J. Trump. At this moment in time, it can be reported with certitude that Barack Obama and his entire former White House trusted advisory staff is already in full operational mode.

Our source (Code Name: Zero Dark Thirty or ZDT as I will refer to him or her) has said that he or she had been in Obama's new Washington DC home. The cost of the Obama mansion is purported to cost in excess of $17,000,000 not including the cost of the wall that surrounds the house. The other unknown expenses related to the basement have not been determined. ZDT is totally nonplused by what he or she had seen. "There are a number of computer screens mounted on walls throughout Obama's basement next to the foosball table and a recliner that looks exactly like the one that Obama used in the White House.

ZDT tells us, "I was told that the basement is being secretly expanded by the Shamus O'Boyle Basement Refinishers because he came in with the highest bid. He was overheard telling David Axelrod, Obama's most trusted advisor, "I gotta charge you this much because you want me to work at night. Do you know how much overtime costs? Do you know how much dirt and concrete we need to remove and then pour a new foundation and then..." Axelrod interrupts and says, "OK, OK just get it done and you better not rip us off." Mr. O'Boyle says, "I'll use the good stuff when I do my work...that's all I need is to have Michelle Obama calling me at all hours bitching and moaning...I've seen what she does to her husband and I already have a wife."

The Fake News source was able to obtain a copy of the plans to the new finished basement that measures 15,000 square feet. O'Boyle is also overheard saying, "Listen Axelrod, I can make it smaller and that will save you a few bucks, what do you say?" Axelrod was heard to tell O'Boyle, "Nah we need it to be large so that it can accommodate staff and equipment." O'Boyle shakes his head and says, "What are you gonna do here, set up an operation to overthrow the government?" and he starts to laugh hysterically. My source remembers thinking, how prophetic!

After the basement construction is complete Valerie Jarrett is placed in charge of organizing the group of Obama's most trusted members of the staff to head specific functions. ZDT was at a meeting of these men and women and it is said Ms. Jarrett spoke and gave everyone their marching orders. "I expect complete loyalty and strict adherence to the code of secrecy that has been a hallmark of the Obama Administration from the start. We are embarking on a crusade, a holy war to defeat a sworn enemy of all that our dear leader has accomplished over the last eight years and now threatened by the hideous Trump. We are calling our plan of action 'Move On! The 57 State Intercontinental Railroad!' to redeem President Obama's innocent misspeaks." ZDT said there is a great feeling of comradery and purpose and all the people assembled seem to approach the challenges with a renewed sense of purpose, confidence and vigor. Up until this point ZDT said that he or she was committed 100% to mounting a concerted effort to stop Trump from undoing Obama's signature legislative and executive order initiatives, but that changed. "I began to feel a bit uneasy as many of my comrades are overheard discussing that their friends at the news organizations can put out stories that were not true but who cares!" ZDT even said that there was maniacal laughter that echoed through the basement and that made him or her shutter.

A week after the initial meeting with Valerie Jarrett, ZDT said that he or she ran into Rahm Emmanuel who stopped to shake hands. "How's it going (name redacted)?" ZDT says everything is going according to plan and Rahm Emanuel responds, "That's good...I wish things were going so well in Chicago. Hey, did you hear about the story we planted in Politico? It was about the woman who had her home foreclosed by Treasury Secretary Steve Mnuchin's company for shorting her payment by 37 cents. We got Politico to write and circulate the story. It was shared and tweeted tens of thousands of time...what a pisser!"

ZDT asked, "What a tragedy. That poor woman, what happened to her?" Rahm smiles and says, "Easy partner, this was all bullshit. Eventually the woman who wrote the article for Politico had to take it back but by then all the damage was done. Ain't life grand! Oh yeah, how about the time we got our people to put out the story about the rise in transgender suicides when Trump was elected or the one Time Magazine wrote about MLK's bust being taken out of the oval office or the one where Trumps hands were photo-shopped. There are many more like those and they are all bullshit but we got it out there and the damage is done and continues. Thank God for the NY Times, Washington Post, MSNBC, CNN®...the list goes on and on. Gotta go, keep your head up." Rahm laughs and walks away.

ZDT barely had time to think about what he or she was told when David Plouffe taps him or her on the shoulder. 'Hey, you headed for the big super-secret meeting?" ZDT says yes and they walk together down the hallway. Plouffe is making small talk and says, "Interesting times we live in, no?" ZDT responds, "They sure are. What is this super-secret meeting all about?" Plouffe answers that he doesn't know for sure but I think has something to do with emerging strategies on how to expand on the initiatives."

Plouffe and ZDT reach the conference room and enter. A number of attendees are already seated around the conference room table talking among each other. Valerie Jarrett wraps her knuckles on the table and asks if she can have quiet while she makes her opening statement. "Ladies and gentlemen, as you are all aware we finally have been able to move into the Obama family's new home basement and I think that you will all agree it is quite comfortable. Before I begin I have a few announcements, please refrain from using the foosball table as it belongs to Sasha and she hates it when the foosball goes missing. Also, Malia has asked that if you watch TV put the damned channel back to the network that airs '*Keeping Up With The Kardashians*' and finally, no one is to sit in the President's recliner. He has found crumbs under the seat cushion and he also found some loose change. He said he's keeping the change." There are worried members looking at each other hoping to recognize the other guilty party.

"Now down to business: we have had inquiries out to a number of information technology companies to assist in maintaining our systems. As you can imagine, security will be of the utmost priority. I have asked Debbie Wasserman Schultz to provide the names of the IT people who work for her at the DNC. Rep. Wasserman Schultz expressed her confidence in the team she works with and gave us their names and contact information. After Hillary's debacle we can't be too careful. Next we will also need to set up email accounts and you will be required to use an alias like Loretta Lynch used. Unfortunately they found out about her alias, Elizabeth Carlisle, so I am suggesting Loretta change it to Edward Carlisle, different first name and gender, sure to throw off any nosey Justice Department creeps."

At this time Cass Sunstein raises his hand and asks, "Can I use something other than a person's name like that of my daughter's labradoodle, Fluffypoo?" Valerie Jarrett rubs the sides of her temples and is starting to lose patience. "Cass, we need to be taken seriously. How can you call yourself 'Fluffypoo' and expect to be taken seriously? How about doing what Holder did, use the first and last names of entertainers like David Ruffin and Eddie Kendrick and you get David Kendrick. I have an idea, what about combining Alec Baldwin and Maya Angelou to get Alec Angelou." Cass Sunstein thinks a bit and agrees "That's a great idea...thanks Valerie."

"Great, another problem solved. By the way Eric..."

Eric Holder responds, "Yes"

"Stay away from The Temptations; I like their music too much."

"And Lois Lerner..."

Lois responds, "Yes"

"Both you, Loretta and Eric got caught using aliases and it might have turned bad if it were not for some friendly folks in Justice and in the media. By the way, Lois, 'Toby Miles?' Where the hell did that come from?"

Lois Lerner's face turns red and she says "My dog and my husband."

Valerie likes raking people over the coals but she lets this go, "As there is a full agenda to go over I hope everyone understands what they need to do?" There is overall assent and agreement and Valerie moves on. "Next topic, lunch. Ladies and gentlemen, where the hell do you get your appetites from? My God in Heaven when I said free lunch, I didn't mean this was the last time you were going to eat! We put a tray of sandwiches and coleslaw out and before you could say Obamaphones, it's gone...the locusts swarmed and there is nothing remaining except a vast wasteland with only the crumbs left. Dennis Ross, Peter Orszag and Susan Rice, if they were giving awards for the most time spent at the troth you three would all get the blue ribbon first prize. Now tomorrow we will be having eggplant parmigiana and I expect that you will save some for everyone else, is that understood?"

Dennis, Peter and Susan are reaching for the pretzels, Skittles® and M&M's® and stop to say that they understand.

Valerie Jarrett looks around to be sure that everyone understands and when she is satisfied she moves on. "The next item on the agenda is the condition of the men's room. Listen guys, I know that you have bowel movements that sometimes get out of control. This space is 15,000 square feet and I can be in the far end of the basement bunker and you could knock me over with the smell, it's like something crawled up inside you and died. Plus I have been told by maintenance that the floors are covered with wet paper towels and there is soap all over the sinks. Gentlemen we have a modern facility with all the handy features that you would expect in the home of a former president. Do all of you know the little handle on each of the urinals and commodes?" Valerie is waiting for an answer but there is only silence and she can wait no longer, "WELL DO YOU?"

All the men nod their heads.

"WELL IT IS FOR FLUSHING! Push down and flush, is that understood?"

All the men nod their heads again.

"Good, another agenda item I can cross off. Next I have something that is very important to cover and that is use of the computers for personal business. Is Samantha Power here?"

"Yes Valerie, I'm here."

"Oh good, I thought that your important appointments like coloring your hair, yoga class, going to the car wash, getting a manicure and pedicure might have gotten in the way of the small matter of BRINGING DOWN THE UNITED STATES GOVERNMENT!!!"

Samantha Power keeps quiet hoping that Valerie is finished with her but Valerie is not finished. "Now Samantha I assume that what we are doing is not causing you a great inconvenience, but I would like your assurance that you will gracefully bow out of your participation in the Washington DC Canasta Championship. Can I make that assumption?"

"Yes, Valerie."

"Good, now I would like to turn my attention to Mr. Thomas Donilon. Ah! My very own doubting Thomas and why do I call you my doubting Thomas?" Thomas Donilon is about to answer when Valerie says, "That was rhetorical! I call you that because I am sure you doubted that I would ever know what you do on your computer. By the way Thomas how are Mario and Luigi these days? Huh? And that cute little Donkey Kong® how is he?"

Thomas Donilon is flustered and doesn't know how to react so he tries to change the subject, "By the way Valerie, you are looking especially lovely today."

"Cut the crap you worthless piece of...if I see Mario try to rescue Pauline from Donkey Kong® on your computer one more time I will personally see that you are exiled to Donkey Kong Country™...PERMANENTLY! Is that understood?"

Thomas is chastised and acknowledges the error of his ways and promises never to play Donkey Kong® or Mario Brothers® again...at work.

Valerie Jarrett shakes her head and continues, "There is something that we seem to cover over and over and over again. I am going to say this one last time. Don't park in front of the house! That's all we need is Breitbart, Newsmax, WND, Fox News and the rest of those creeps snooping around. I thought we all agreed that we would park in various directions, on the street and gather at the storefront where there's the secret entrance to the Obama basement. I hope you all remember the secret entrance...well, do you?"

All those around the conference table seem to have blank stares and go silent, not wanting to incur the wrath of Valerie but she will have none of it. "Come on, how many times do we have to go over this?"

Rahm Emmanuel speaks up, "Valerie, we are all to meet every morning at 7:30AM sharp in front of "You Kill'em We Stuff'em Taxidermy" where we are greeted by Morris Pasternak who ushers us to the secret doorway behind the shelf full of stuffed beavers. We enter the door and make our way through the tunnel and traverse the corridor for approximates half a mile whereupon we exit into the basement of the Obama residence."

Valerie Jarrett is slack jawed as she is amazed that Rahm has repeated, word for word, her exact instructions to all those assembled. "Rahm you have restored my faith in humanity as I thought that I would need to repeat the instructions again. Thank you so much!"

Rahm Emanuel replies, "You're welcome."

Valerie looks around hoping there would be no questions but she was sorely disappointed. Peter Orszag stands up and faces Rahm and says, "Rahm, I don't think it was a shelf of stuffed beavers, I think it was a shelf filled with stuffed ocelots."

Rahm considers this and responds, "No, I am positive that it is a shelf of beavers."

Peter says, "Are you sure, I am very sure it was ocelots"

"Do you even know what and ocelot is?"

"Rahm, don't get snippy with me. I'm not one of your flunkies in Chicago, by the way how's the murder rate going?" Now Rahm jumps across the table trying to grab Peter by the neck so he can choke the life out of him, but this is immediately stopped by Valerie.

"What the hell difference does it make if it is a beaver or an ocelot? Who the hell cares?" Peter and Rahm are looking down to the floor not wanting to stare at each other or at Valerie. "I think this meeting is over but I am very disappointed in all of you for your lack of discipline and what I perceive is a total lack of commitment. I need to point out, however, there is one among us that deserves special recognition and that is (name redacted). Throughout all our meeting (name redacted) has been responsive, prepared and totally in tune with the mission and its success. Let us all give him, or her, a round of applause." Valerie and the entire team applaud ZDT and the meeting breaks up.

On the way out of the conference room Valerie holds ZDT back and asks him or her to wait. When everyone is gone she says to ZDT, "I need you to help with a special super-secret, classified project that is being spear-headed by me and David Axelrod. It's a committee that has been set up to identify candidates so they can be vetted for major positions in the new Shadow Government. I have met with President Obama and he is emphatic about selecting people outside the traditional domestic government roles. He said, let's think outside the box and select candidates that would help usher in a new age. The meeting is being held in Conference Room Two, far away from the men's room so let's head over."

ZDT and Valerie walked down the corridor when she says, "I know what you're thinking, who else will be in on the selection process. Well there's Austan Goolsbee (Economics), John Kerry (Foreign Affairs), Tom Vilsack (Agriculture), Kathleen Sebelius (Health and Human Services), Jack Lew (Chief of Staff), Samantha Power (UN Ambassador) and Ernest Moniz (Energy). The only fly in the ointment is that the president insisted I use Dennis Ross (Middle East Advisor), Peter Orszag (Mgmt. and Budget) and Susan Rice (National Security Advisor) but there's assigned seating and I have them at the end of the table, far away from the food. The good news is even old Uncle Joe Biden may be there, you can never tell."

Valerie Jarrett and ZDT reach Conference Room Two where all the participants have already assembled. "Hello everyone, glad you all could make this conference. As you are aware David and I have apprised you of the purpose of the meeting and have given you ample time to present your best ideas to the group. David, do you have anything to say?"

David Axelrod stands up, "Yes and thank you Valerie. The only precondition I have for any recommendation is that no one from the Republican Party, conservatives or anyone with a first name of Donald and a last name of Trump will be considered." The group laughs and they begin the process in earnest. David says, "Now remember what the president has charged our committee with; find those candidates that are not part of the domestic political establishment order, people who can take orders, take up the challenge and run with it. Let's start with Secretary Kerry, John please let us hear your recommendations."

"Thank you David. As I have a natural proclivity toward foreign affairs I have scanned possible candidates and come up with some names. First, how about Kang Sam Hyon, the North Korean Ambassador to Iran, Valery Sukhinin Russian Ambassador to North Korea and Javad Torkabadi, Iranian Ambassador to Syria. The way I look at it is if we had job sharing for Secretary of State they would all work in the same office and they could keep each other busy and there would be no more nuclear proliferation from our four worst enemies; Russia, North Korea, Syria and Iran. We may need to rethink North Korea if peace breaks out there, but let's think positive and hope that it won't."

Valerie Jarrett and David Axelrod stare thoughtfully at former Secretary of State John Kerry, "What an interestingly amazing idea! I will be sure to tell the President what you have suggested."

John Kerry is elated, "Well thank you Valerie and please let him know that if he changes his mind I'm still available."

Valerie answers, "I will. Next we will move onto Samantha Power, Samantha."

"Thank you, as you know I was the Ambassador to the United Nations and I have a great affinity for the various cultures of the world and how the United States must interact. I think that Colin Kaepernick fits the bill. He is independent and, like other members of the UN, he has shown great disdain for our country and he may be able to help get the NFL to sponsor some events at the United Nations. Oh and that's who Sasha wants."

Valerie and David look at each other and both seemed to be accepting of this unorthodox but interesting choice. "Thank you Samantha that is a good option. Next we will hear from Ernest Moniz, Ernest."

"Thank you both. I probably had the easiest job of all. There is no other person that I would recommend other than Guðni Thorlacius Jóhannesson, the President of Iceland. No country on the face of the earth uses more energy so hey, follow the leader."

Valerie Jarrett and David Axelrod are starting to get very excited as they see key positions in the Shadow Government's cabinet taking shape. David says, "Wow Valerie we seem to be getting off to a great start. Next we shall hear from Tom Vilsack."

"Thank you all. When you think of agriculture, what do you think of? Fertilizer, right! When you think of fertilizer what do you think of? Okay, the smell, what else? Well, when I think of fertilizer I think of Jochen Tilk, President of Potash Corporation, the largest supplier of fertilizer in the world. Make this choice and you'll come out smelling like a rose! A little fertilizer joke." Valerie, David and the group laugh and take the recommendation under advisement. The meeting lasts more than two hours more and everyone has a chance to make their choices.

Austan Goolsbee (Economics) "David Chappelle is a comedian who makes tens of millions each year and his comedy still makes sense but that is a double edged sword. I believe that we will need him to change so he doesn't make sense anymore. He's the perfect candidate to head the Federal Reserve or Treasury, take your pick."

Jack Lew (Chief of Staff) "I recommend Trish Stratus, the most successful female wrestler of the WWE. Tough, hard and well, take a look at her photos..."

Kathleen Sebelius (Health and Human Services) I recommend Joy Behar who can get so much done by making people feel guilty and still not spend any of her own money!"

Dennis Ross (Middle East Advisor) "I recommend Abu Fatima al-Jaheishi. He was charge of the ISIS operations in southern Iraq. His real name is Ni'ma Abd Nayef al-Jabouri and he can give us a unique perspective on the middle-east. We can't confirm if he is still alive however."

Peter Orszag (Management and Budget) "I recommend Kim Kardashian because she knows how to spend money and Malia says that's who she wants."

Susan Rice (National Security Advisor) "I recommend Chad Laurens inventor of Simply

Safe® Alarm systems. Need I say more?!"

Everyone is very pleased at the unorthodox but thoughtful recommendations and both Valerie and David are sure that the former president will be extremely pleased. As the group is busy talking to each other a head pops through the door and Valerie smiles.

"Ladies and gentlemen I have a wonderful surprise for you. Our next speaker needs no introduction. He has been a solid rock in the eight years that Barack Obama was president and stood by his side as his right hand. Please welcome, former Vice President Joe Biden!"

The group erupts in applause and David Axelrod lets Joe Biden take his place at the front of the table. "What a thrill to be here with Susan, Dennis and Peter at the buffet and everyone else seated here. Thank you for inviting me. I consider you all my close friends, so many familiar faces, and let's not forget familiar bodies, of folks that I've worked with in the Washington DC White House. When I first came to DC I was a young, clear headed ideologue *and folks, I can tell you, I've known eight presidents, three of them intimately,* but let me make this clear, I have never had sex with them, even the ones I've known intimately. Now that I am entering the foggy headed twilight of my life I can look back and still remember when I praised *a man I'm proud to call my friend, a man who will be the next President of the United States - Barack America. I mean, you got the first mainstream African-American who is articulate and bright and clean and a nice-looking guy. I mean, that's a storybook, man!"*

The group, except for Dennis, Susan and Peter who are still filling their plates, applauds as Joe Biden continues, "You're much better than a group of Turkish-American and Azerbaijani-American Obama donors I was addressing when I had to tell them *I guess what I'm trying to say without boring you too long at breakfast—and you all look dull as hell, I might add. The dullest audience I have ever spoken to. Just sitting there, staring at me. Pretend you like me!"* Now everyone in the conference room is laughing.

"Anyway, back to the business at hand. You are selecting the next generation of people who will lead our Shadow Government until we remove Trump from office. Now normally I don't believe in superstition but *when seagull droppings landed on my head at a campaign event at Bowers Beach two days before Election Day, I chose to read it as a sign of a coming success.* When I got out of my limo that same thing happened, a seagull shit on my head. I don't know if it was the same seagull but that, for me, was a sign from God."

Joe Biden takes time to reflect, "As we retake the reins of power we must never forget our brave young heroes and I would like to quote the great Barack Obama as he recalled, "*One such translator was an American of Haitian descent, representative of the extraordinary work that our men and women in uniform do all around the world -- Navy Corpse-Man Christian Brossard.*" We also recall what Barack Obama said *on Memorial Day, as our nation honors its unbroken line of fallen heroes -- and I see many of them in the audience here today -- our sense of patriotism is particularly strong.*" Not every President can say that and be taken so seriously."

"I know that you have been discussing Obamacare and I want to remind you of the Swine Flu epidemic a few years back and those fateful words said by me, *I wouldn't go anywhere in confined places now. ... When one person sneezes it goes all the way through the aircraft. That's me. I would not be, at this point, if they had another way of transportation, suggesting they ride the subway.* I might add that the subway is a lot cheaper than an airplane ticket."

The entire Shadow Government team got up and started to cheer "BIDEN...BIDEN...BIDEN!" Joe Biden went around the table and shook everyone's hand except for Peter, Susan and Dennis who had a plate full of wraps, salad and hummus to contend with. Valerie and David are all smiles as they thank the Vice President for taking time out of his busy schedule to give the 'troops' such an inspiring message.

Joe Biden leaves the room and Valerie calls everyone away from the buffet. "You can eat while you're sitting and listening to what we have to say. David and I need to bring up one more topic: the proliferation of fake news...and we need to ramp it up! I am sure that you all have been pleased with the many stories that have been planted in the Times, Post, CNN® and NBC and other networks. Eventually the stories are retracted, but until that happens its rock and roll baby!" The group cheers wildly as David laughs knowing how successful they have been.

Valerie continues, "We will be providing you with fake news stories that will be featured in the usual outlets and assigning media contacts to each and every one of you. Be sure that you commit this to memory as we do not want any of this in writing. Unfortunately, we put sexual harassment on the top of our list but most of the guys being accused are either Democrat supporters, donors or elected officials so let's not consider that at the moment." Valerie opens her laptop and says, "Here we go!"

"Dennis, after you swallow that Chicken Caesar salad wrap, call NBC and get them to air a feature about *Trump Alleging Government Documents Prove the World is run by Lizard People.* It's an old story but now we have a new proponent!"

"Tom, you can plant this story in Modern Farmer, *Trump Says Cows Can Read Minds!* It is sure to get us the rural vote."

"Next Samantha, Here is a story we've prepared for HSN, *Trump Hates Capo di Monte and anything by Thomas Kinkade!* If HSN won't cooperate send it to QVC™."

"Here's one we have a lot of hope for, *Trump Want's to Turn White House Front Lawn into Miniature Golf Course.* Cass, get that over to Time magazine immediately."

"Peter! Wipe your chin! My lord did you ever hear the word 'chew?' Now here's what I want you to get over to the NY Times, *Trump says the Ice Bucket Challenge is a Satanic Baptism Ritual.* This one's been floating around for a while but I think with Trump in we can get some traction on it."

"Kathleen can you get to your pals at MSNBC and give them a story about *Vladimir Putin really being Donald Trump's Love Child.* Rachel Maddow will eat that up."

"Ernest there is one we have high hopes for, *Forget Infrastructure projects! Trump wants to use the Trillion Dollar Budget to fund 200,000,000 Billboards on US Highways!* Get this over to ABC and CBS and tell them it's an exclusive and tell them that Trump wants to use the billboard to advertise his golf courses."

"Austan, I know you still have contacts at the FBI. I want you to get them to leak *Trump Authorizes Cameras Implanted in Agents Bellybuttons.* Get it out on one of your Fox News guest slots; God knows no one is watching you on CNN® or MSNBC. David, do have anything else we need to cover?"

"Just one thing Valerie, be sure to tell all of the media that your information is from a reliable unnamed source that is very high-up in the Administration. Stand by for more fake news coming next week." Valarie says, "Good point, sorry I forgot to mention it. Well group that's it, are there any questions?"

Susan Rice, Peter Orszag and Dennis Ross raise their hands, "Uh, Valerie…" Valerie makes gives off sigh of exasperation and exhaustion, "Yes, you can take home the leftovers."

The quotes attributed VP Joe Biden are his actual quotes from speeches given during his tenure as Vice President

Most of the Fake News Stories referenced actually appear on various websites

THE NEW EU CAMPAIGN... "WEAR A BURKA TO WORKA!"

The European Union again eclipses the world with its outreach to Muslims by declaring a new fun way to get their citizens of various European cultures to bond and join in wearing burkas to work. After reading the decree issued by the EU, Sir Telsunn Margraves is able to observe and report on the initiative. In an appeal to the fashion conscious and millennials, it was encouraged that you can even decorate your burka with fast food logos or your dream cars. The EU Council President Donald Tusk (no relation to Donald Trump) makes the announcement with all the appropriate pomp and circumstance.

Brussels, Belgium – Due to the enormous influx of refugees into the member countries of the European Union, the Council of the European Union has been attempting to find a way to coalesce the population behind unity of purpose. There are, however, a growing number of member countries that have resisted accepting Muslin refugees from Africa and middle-eastern countries. This is due as the increase in crime, the cost of providing essential services including lodging, food and healthcare along with the terrorism that plagues other former and current nations of the EU. These nations include France, Sweden, Italy, Belgium, Germany and others as well as former EU member Great Britain.

At the last meeting of the Council, an idea emerged that excited the entire leadership group while increasing hope that the general EU population would be more accepting of Muslims as well as other refugee groups. Surrounded by news crews from all 27 member nations, Council President Donald Tusk (no relation to President Donald Trump) took to the podium to announce the new initiative stating he was confident it would enhance assimilation and encourage friendship among the different and diverse cultures.

A smiling President Tusk spoke in a forceful and clear-minded manner as he said, "The EU will be launching promotion in the coming months; a campaign to bring people of all cultures and ethnicities closer, the Council calls it "Wear a Burka to Worka!" As there are 24 languages being spoken by EU members we will launch "Porter une Burka au travail-a" in France, "Indossare un Burka per lavorare-a" in Italy, "Tragen Sie eine Burka zu arbeiten-a" in Germany, "Usar un Burka para trabajar-a" in Spain, "Φροντίζει ένα Burka να δουλέψει-a" in Greece and so on and so forth."

"We are planning "Wear a Burka to Worka" day for October 31ˢᵗ which coincides with the US celebration of Halloween. We have timed this in such a way as to help those who may be too shy to consider wearing a burka and allow for a different, more acceptable way of bringing everyone together. If you prefer the traditional black burka you are certainly permitted to wear it, however, we are encouraging each and every citizen to get bold, to expand the possibilities. For example decorate your burka with various Disney© characters like *The Immortal Goofy*", "*Dory from Finding Nemo*", "*Olaf, Elsa and Anna from Frozen*" and of course "*Mickey and Minnie*

Mouse!" There are literally hundreds of characters to choose from, assuming they are non-confrontational, fully clothed and politically correct. In this way Burka's can be worn without fear and shame! We are also hoping that, with this welcoming outreach to both citizens and non-citizens alike, we will become more accepting of each other and we also hope it will prevent other countries from leaving the EU."

"To some this may seem controversial but the Council wants to assure you that after extensive research, costly focus groups, marketing studies, psychological profiling, compiling of a comprehensive enemies list and developing a licensing deal with Iran's "72 Virgins Fashions" this is an idea whose time has come. Although we believe the campaign will be widely accepted by women throughout the EU, we are hopeful that men will also want to be part of this historic initiative. While we would frown on it, there have been a number of male suicide bombers that have blown themselves up wearing Burkas. That aside, men can decorate their burka with logos of their favorite sports teams or a car they would love to drive or their favorite fast food restaurant...whatever works for them assuming they are non-controversial, fully electric, gluten free, non-alcoholic and politically correct so it can be worn without fear and shame!

"Sure there has been some resistance to this by various organizations but these are fascist pigs, the Jewish financial cabal, Nazi criminals, Roman Catholics and they don't know what the f*ck they are talking about. I would also like to warn any employer who resists our efforts by alerting companies that they will be met with a ferocious response including hefty fines, stoning and jail time. But let us not dwell on the negative and let us bask in the potential for true peace through assimilation.

YOU MAY BE WHITE BUT YOU AIN'T RIGHT!

After hearing of a college course on the need to eliminate any and all references to whiteness, Sir Telsunn Margraves decides to visit the campus of Stanford University. There he discovers what professors consider a scourge that must be eradicated; the scourge is white people, white ideas, white culture and white, well white everything. In order to deliver on this promise, college campus' around the country are instituting special courses to teach white students how not to be white students. Sir Telsunn observes the discussion through a peep hole drilled through the wall of the office next door. A reporter for The Stanford Daily interviews a Graduate Assistant and becomes enlightened as to the evils of whiteness.

"White People Scare the Crap out of Me"
-Michael Moore

Stanford, CA – The line of students in the hallway already extends around the corner, down the hall and into the auditorium. The students are all in line to sign-up to take the course titled, "White Identity Politics." The course is being taught by Professor John Patrick Moran and he is thrilled by the interest and seeming popularity of the course and is happy to note that "100% of those looking to enroll are white.

The Stanford Daily, the college newspaper for Stanford University, sent one of the student reporters to interview Professor Moran about all the excitement surrounding his class. He is exultant when he notes, "What a thrill to see that there are so many people who are white and don't want to be white. It's like we are bleaching white students out of existence! I am sorry to say but I need to attend a faculty briefing that was just called, however, I have asked my graduate assistant to provide you with any information you need and answer any questions you may have."

The Stanford Daily reporter thanks the professor who leaves the room. The next person to enter is Professor Moran's graduate assistant, Throckmorton Cecil Farthingale III. The reporter and the graduate assistant shake hands and both sit down for the interview. "My what an unusual name, what ethnic background are you?" Mr. Farthingale answers, "Much to my shame, I am white."

The reporter, not wanting to go in that direction says, "Umm, I see, well let's get on with the interview. What do you attribute all the energy and popularity that this course seems to attract among the students here at Stanford?"

Graduate Assistant Farthingale, ever thoughtful, considers his reply and states, "Donald Trump."

"Donald Trump?" the reporter seems puzzled by the answer.

Throckmorton Cecil Farthingale III seeks to explain and tells the interviewer, "Donald Trump embodies all that is negatively represented in the concept of whiteness. First, he's white; second he's white male; third he dresses like he's white; fourth, he plays golf; fifth, he's rich; sixth, he has blond hair; seventh, he reads the Wall Street Journal; and eighth, he eats only vanilla ice cream. Professor Moran refers to these as the eight deadly sins."

"Very interesting, I have another question, in the course description its says, and I quote *"How is a concept like white identity to be understood in relation to white nationalism, white supremacy, white privilege, and whiteness?"*

The graduate assistant smiles and tells the reporter, "That's a good question. The answer lies in the need to abolish all whiteness and examine the future of whiteness. For example, white bread…"

The reporter is puzzled, "White bread?"

"Yes, white bread. White bread is made from white flour. The white flour is made from wheat, for millennia wheat has been grown and harvested by people of color so that the white man always got the first slice. These men may even have made white bread sandwiches or buttered the slice of white toast, all to the detriment of non-white people. Consider the metaphorical of white people eating brown toast…the white man eating toast e.g. people of color, just consider that. The original Pilgrims have used white bread for stuffing of the turkey that was served at the first Thanksgiving feast and in the process deprived Native Americans of leftovers. Continue on through the centuries and you will note that it was a white man that invented the idea of slicing white bread and packaging it into plastic bags. Think of it French toast, grilled cheese sandwiches, bread pudding…my God have you any idea of what this all means? It means we use white bread at every meal, even dessert!"

Mr. Farthingale is on a roll and continues, "Professor Moran's associate and colleague, Professor Tomás Jiménez explains that "whiteness" refers to *"the set of behaviors and outlooks associated with the racial category, white."* Therefore we cannot ignore the enormous research and resources spent on the unending effort to perfect sun block.

"Sun block?"

"Consider we have achieved levels of sun block never seen in the history of mankind. Could you ever have imagined a SPF factor of 50? Well could you?

The reporter is a bit tongue tied, "SPF 50? I really never thought about it."

"Ah, ha! You see you never even think about it and that's what white men want you to do. Don't think about SPF 50 or even 30 or white bread or even golf all you need to do is focus on hip-hop, 3D movies, Game of Thrones®, quinoa and kale and all of the focus on whiteness disappears. It's a subterfuge that has perpetuated the whiteness of white men, the whiteness of white men's thinking and before we realize it, we are all going to be listening to Johnny Ray, Teresa Brewer and Pat Boone records. Do you understand what I am saying; the horror of it all!?"

The reporter stares blankly at the professor and says, "Not really."

"Eric Miranda, he's a spokesperson here at Stanford, says that abolishing whiteness is a concept developed during the 1990's, same years as the Clinton Administration. There is a compelling need to have white people stop thinking they were white and start thinking like other ethnicities. For example, in class we will be performing an exercise I call 'ethnic-transference.' We will have a white male student and a white female student, or two white students of the same sex and they will be assigned an ethnicity and be told to act out a dialogue with their partner. Through this transference of ethnicity both students will be allowed to stop identifying as white in order to help end inequalities."

The reported asks, "Can you give me an example?"

"Hmmm, let me see, Ah! I have it. You play a brave Native American warrior and I will be a demure Native American squaw. We meet for the first time and we are attracted to each other."

"Um, Farthingale, I don't know if I feel comfortable doing this."

"Of course you don't, you are white. That's enough to make anybody uncomfortable but you need to get in touch with your non-white side...reach deep into your psyche and look for that inner Native American in you."

The reporter sighs and says he'll try his best.

"Oh brave warrior, I see you have been travelling far. May I offer you a drink of water?"

"Uh, okay I guess."

Now Graduate Assistant Farthingale has to stop and question the reporters motivation. "You are a brave warrior, not a white man and you spoke to a beautiful squaw like you are a white man. Say it with the verve and passion of a true warrior!"

The reporter acquiesces, "I am very thirsty and I want'um a drink." The graduate assistant hands him a pretend cup of water and the reporter pretends to drink it."

The squaw tells the warrior, "Do you want'um more water?"

"No, had enough. You know'um you are a beautiful squaw and I like'um you. Do you want'um to go to the campfire with me tonight?"

The squaw coyly gazes at the warrior and says, "Yes'um. But I need'um to ask, do you have an arrow under your blanket or are you just glad to see me?" The graduate assistant laughs and tells the reporter. You can always have fun with these things but the seriousness of you acting out in the way a Native American would is very revealing.

The reporter acknowledges, "Hey that was fun. Do you think I can take the course or is it too late to enroll professor?"

Throckmorton Cecil Farthingale III turns serious for a moment, "I can arrange for you to join the class but I want a commitment from you; a commitment that you will come into the class white and leave the class non-white. Do I have your word?"

The reporter replies, "Yes, you have my word."

In a follow up to the Stanford University report it has been discovered that "white shaming" has become a new rage among academics on college campuses. University of Iowa assistant professor, Jodi Linley says, *"As a white assistant professor of mostly white graduate students who will become higher education leaders, I work to dismantle whiteness in my curriculum, assignments and pedagogy,"* Linley explains that in addition to her white identity, she also identifies as a working-class queer, able-bodied, cisgender woman." In her peer reviewed academic journal article titled "Teaching to Deconstruct Whiteness in Higher Education," Linley writes that for white students, *"Talking about race with an all-white group of peers* [*reveals*] *their own white ignorance."*

To counter this totally hateful and backward view, Assistant Professor Linley says her commitment to designing classes that fight white privilege began as soon as she became a professor in 2014. At this point she resolved to *"develop courses that both unveiled and rejected"* the notion that *"neutrality and objectivity are realistic and attainable."*

Linley also asserted as justification for segregating students during some discussions, *"For white students, talking about race with an all-white group of peers facilitates their realization that they are raced beings, thus revealing their own white ignorance,"* Perhaps Linley and her university thought the paper would be a groundbreaking work that would be met with universal praise. It did not...the course, article and premise has been widely criticized on social media, and Assistant Professor Linley received some negative comments sent via email.

Daniel Clay, Dean of the College of Education, expressed horror and outrage over the criticism, issuing this statement: *"Recently, one of our faculty members was singled out for publishing a peer-review article on race issues in higher education. This faculty member was targeted, harassed, and threatened by many people from around the country through email, phone calls, and social media. As the dean of our University of Iowa College of Education, I want to affirm that we welcome all students, faculty, and staff of all races and backgrounds. We work hard to create an inclusive environment that cultivates respect and appreciation for everyone. The University of Iowa is also strongly committed to freedom of expression and the First Amendment, and that extends to students, faculty and staff."*

The commitment to freedom of expression and the First Amendment as stated by Dean Clay, however, does not apply to dissenting opinions expressed in emails and on social media. Dewan Clay wondered, "Are these emails being sent by one of those robot things like the one they use at 'MoveOn.org? I can't imagine anyone who would be against white shaming and ridicule of all things white."

The idea of "white shaming" has become so popular that courses have spread to campuses across the country. Portland Community College devoted an entire month to "white shaming" and it was enormously successful. As many as six people gathered in the expanse of grass in front of the student union and express solidarity with the color green. Spokesman for the group, Sophomore Jonathan Parker Whitely said, "If everyone was green like the grass here..." he bends down and rips up part of the lawn and holds it up, "There would be no need for war and man-made global warming will become a thing of the past!"

This past summer, an assistant professor at Georgia State University, Stephanie Behm Cross, published an academic journal article lamenting the *"insidiousness of si-*

lence and whiteness" on college campuses. The article titled *"Whiteness in the academy: Using Vignettes to Move Beyond Safe Silences,"* was published in the journal Teaching in Higher Education, written by Stephanie Behm Cross, who teaches classes related to math instruction for GSU's School of Education.

Students who have taken the class were interviewed and asked about the experience. One student, who asked not to be named said, "She made us look at this vignette that showed a guy slathering on SPF 50 sunscreen, eating an American cheese sandwich with white bread and mayo and we had to discuss for an hour what was wrong with this picture and how it keeps starving people from Myanmar getting fed." Another student said that she went to the class last week and another vignette showed a group of people at a country club having cocktails and appetizers while wearing Ralph Lauren Polo shirts and sports jackets. When it was over we had to discuss why man-made global warming is keeping African Americans from joining country clubs."

In another white shaming initiative, Professor Gregory Jay of the University of Wisconsin-Milwaukee is demanding the *"abolition of whiteness."* Professor Jay says, "How can we end racism if we still have whiteness!" Taking it one step further he suggests, *"The great white whale of racism is a white invention. It was white people, who invented the idea of race in the first place, and it is white people who have become obsessed and consumed by it until, like Captain Ahab, they have become entangled so deeply in pursuing its nature that they self-destruct in the process."*

When questioning an Asian American female student about the entire premise she said, "I really don't understand what Professor Jay means and when I questioned him he made me assume the role of Groucho Marx and the need to confront Harpo, Chico and even Zeppo about their whiteness and racism. I...I don't understand."

From: Stanford University https://www.stanford.edu/ White Identity Politics (ANTHRO 136B) Pundits proclaim that the 2016 Presidential election marks the rise of white identity politics in the United States. Drawing from the field of whiteness studies and from contemporary writings that push whiteness studies in new directions, this upper-level seminar asks, does white identity politics exist? How is a concept like white identity to be under-

stood in relation to white nationalism, white supremacy, white privilege, and whiteness? We will survey the field of whiteness studies, scholarship on the intersection of race, class, and geography, and writings on whiteness in the United States by contemporary public thinkers, to critically interrogate the terms used to describe whiteness and white identities. Students will consider the perils and possibilities of different political practices, including abolishing whiteness or coming to terms with white identity. What is the future of whiteness? Instructor John Patrick Moran

All actual quotes and writing of the persons quoted are in italics – TM

MASSIVE ©2017 GOOGLE CONTROVERSY "TAMPONS IN MEN'S ROOMS"

Former Google employees have come forward to report, to Sir Telsunn Margraves, the startling revelation that Google is stocking men's rooms with tampons. Their rationale; because men could menstruate! Sir Telsunn attended a rally featuring some surprising disclosures from men who, in fact, do menstruate. Hear heartbreaking tales from ordinary men and notable personalities, like Alec Baldwin, Bill Maher and even Stephen Colbert, and how they've live with the scourge of menstruation... it's not pretty.

Mountain View, CA August 21, 2017 – It has been recently revealed by former employees of © 2017 Google that men's bathrooms throughout © 2017 Google offices are stocked with Tampons. Initially, *'APGR Fake News'* thought that it was fake news but the two employees that came forward, who were previously fired because of their conservative views, say they have the photos to prove it.

Arthur (not his real name) said, "See here!" Arthur shows the reporter a photo on his smart phone and tells us, "This photo was taken in 2013 and released as a blog post." These men considered this as just one example of the many politically correct positions that ©2017 Google is taking because, as they told us, "some men menstruate." This supposed fact came as a shock to many of the uninformed, but a spokesman for ©2017 Google, who wishes to remain anonymous, explains, "Sometimes I menstruate and I get cramps like you wouldn't believe." In sympathy with men who menstruate, ©2017 Google has expanded the number of menstruation products available to men to include not only Tampons and Kotex® but Midol® for those days when you need long lasting relief.

While the management of ©2017 Google views this as a positive step in correcting and equalizing past imbalances of the sexes, a number of men have described the policy as idiotic. While many of those we spoke to at Google refuse to give their names, they were not shy about telling us how they feel. Among the major complaints we hear from men is, "Where the hell is the damned tampon supposed to go?"

This and other policies instituted by the tech giant, ©2017 Google, seem to reflect radical left wing culture that permeates the company. The anonymous spokesman for ©2017 Google also said, "Given the compelling need to have politically correct gender balance quotas, ©2017 Google has also added a few cans of "Air Wick®" and "Glade®" air fresheners to the women's room." The spokesman noted that air fresheners have been available in men's rooms for decades.

Reacting to all the negative press this policy has generated, © 2017 Google searched and found men who menstruate, albeit irregularly, to prove the validity of their policy. Google is emphatic when it notes all the men who they found are willing to reveal their identities and are able to tell their stories without fear of retribution or reprisal. ©2017 Google's spokesman said, "These brave men have come forward of their own free will to educate backward thinking Americans that menstruation among men really does happen. The first gentleman man who wishes to go on record is Mr. Anthony "Tough Tony" Senchanelli of Chicago, Illinois. Please welcome Mr. Senchanelli."

There is polite applause as Mr. Senchanelli stands and comes to the Google podium set up in the cafeteria during lunch time. He says, "Thank you very much for having me here and giving me a chance to tell my story so I can help the suffering and shame men around the world feel when it's that time of the month. I started menstruating at 39 years old and I haven't stopped since then, sometimes I even have three or four periods a month. Sure I get bloated and I have cramps but it's the water weight gain that keeps me sidelined. I usually meet the guys for a beer every night after work but when it's my time or times of the week or month I barely get four or five steins in me before I have to go home and have to lie down. It's terrible I tell you, sometimes it's so bad that I have to ask my wife, Angelina, for a hot water bottle and I just lay there and..."

The ©2017 Google spokesman interrupts, "Thank you Mr. Senchanelli, I think we get the point. Next I would like to introduce another man who also menstruates. He confesses to having other far reaching symptoms that often prevent him from doing his job effectively; ladies and gentlemen it is my honor to introduce, Mr. Ralph Cosgrove."

Mr. Cosgrove steps up to the podium and he begins, "I want to thank ©2017 Google for allowing us to be part of this forum. I don't know if any of you recognize me but I am a professional wrestler for the Interplanetary Wrestling Conglomeration or IWC. I wrestle under the name "Big Beef" and I just was crowned the IWC Heavyweight Champion." There is a great cheer that goes up from some of the men in the cafeteria who actually watch wrestling and recognize "Big Beef." The champ continues, "Yeah sure, like Anthony, I get cramps but I'm 375 pounds, and I'm no pussy, so I tough it out. But I gotta tell you, when I get that pain in my back and muscles, you know what I'm talking about ladies don't you?"

There is a loud, gut wrenching primal scream that comes from the depth of the souls of every woman in the cafeteria and Big Beef has to wipe away a tear. "I just wanna get into a fetal position like I did to that wimp, The Iranian Mullah, when I crushed him in the rink. I remember there was this time in the..."

"Ahhh...Mr. Cosgrove that was very revealing but we need to move on. Our next speaker needs no introduction. He is the star of stage, screen and television and his unique perspective on everything political is legend. Mr. Alec Baldwin has been menstruating for a number of years, and while he has kept it quiet, this has not stopped him from making his points very clear as he screams at photographers and Sean Hannity. Ladies and gentlemen, we are proud to introduce Mr. Alec Baldwin."

The audience breaks out in sustained cheers and applause as Alec Baldwin takes center stage. "Thank you so much for that kind reception. Even though I suspected that there could be no other men who suffer from having a monthly period, I somehow instinctively knew I was not alone. When ©2017 Google gave me this platform I was honored and grateful to be able to tell men across this warmongering and evil country of ours...you are not alone! When I have my period I am a veritable angry, violent monster. I want to rip apart everyone within my grasp especially if they are part of the Trump Administration or talk-show host Sean Hannity. I remember one especially painful menstruation where I couldn't even get out of bed. I turned on the TV and I saw a White House spokesman proclaiming that the Supreme Court upheld his travel ban from terrorist countries and I blew up." Alec seems to be panting harder and harder and taking deeper and deeper breaths. "They want to rescind the rights of people who may or may not be terrorists. Why the hell don't they just leave these people alone? When they arrive in America we will have plenty of time to find them before they blow up anything. Isn't that what we pay the FBI for?" Now Alec suddenly doubles over in pain and clutches his mid-section in excruciating pain. He looks around and excuses himself, "Foollkkss, ahgrrah, I need to sit down ughhc-chah, and take a Midol...thank you for letting me vent."

The Google spokesman seems very concerned for Alec and tries to help him to his seat. Alec hates being touched when he's having his period so he punches the spokesperson and takes his own seat without further help.

The spokesperson lifts himself off the floor and rubs his chin as his eye is turning black and blue. He doesn't want to slow the momentum that has built throughout the gathering and says, "Thank you Alec, that was most interesting. Now I would like to introduce our final guest speaker. He is the star of his own HBO® Series "Real Time with Bill Maher" and he has come forward to give us his story. Ladies and gentlemen, please welcome Bill Maher!" Now the audience of ©2017 Google employees erupts in applause at the mere mention of his name.

"Thank you so much ladies and gentlemen. It is truly a pleasure being here with you today. I have hidden this part of my life in the closet for too long and now I'm thrilled to be coming out." Again, the audience is effusive in its cheers and praise for the man. "I am going to depart from the general theme that the previous speakers have focused on; you know the menstrual cramps, backaches, muscle aches, headaches, bloating, water-weight gain and fatigue. I've had them all and it ain't pretty but I do want to focus on the real cause of menstrual cycles; man-made global warming. Have you ever considered what man-made global warming has done by the peoples of the world that menstruate? Huh, have you?" The crowd doesn't know if it should answer so everyone just sits there and stares at Bill Maher.

"Well, in the words of the immortal Elizabeth Barrett Browning, 'let me count the ways'." First, add to that list of symptoms, sweaty, to sweaty, add smelly; to smelly, add more showers; to more showers, add clothes; to more clothes, add washes, to more washes, add more and more trips to the store; to more and more trips to the store, add more purchase of laundry detergent, and finally add more gas for the car and what do gas guzzling cars emit?" All ©2017 Google employees yell out, "CARBON DIOXIDE!" Everyone present is in rapt attention and amazement at the brilliance of Bill Maher and his ability to make a connection between man-made global warming and menstrual cycles.

Bill Maher ends by saying, "For a very small investment in people, ©2017 Google can contribute to the comfort of men and bring joy at a time of the month that is always joyless. In closing, I have asked that the senior management at ©2017 Google add the following to each and every bathroom, including men's and women's and gender neutral. I am pleased to announce that the following have been added; pregnancy testing kits, 'Depend®' or similar adult diaper, hairnets, vaginal and testicular odor elimination products and 'Massengill®' or similar douches. Management assures me that they will add these products to each and every man's, woman's and gender neutral bathrooms immediately. They also ask your indulgence while construction is going on that will expand needed shelving in current bathrooms to accommodate the extra products."

Arthur addresses the audience and says, "I want to thank you all for coming. What wonderful and inspirational messages we have heard today from all our speakers. Unfortunately Stephen Colbert was supposed to join us today but he is experiencing what he calls 'vicious cramps.' He has sent us a statement which I would like to read to you;

"Hello to all there at ©2017 Google, this is Stephen Colbert and I want to extend my heartfelt hope for better understanding of the scourge of male menstruation and the backward thinking that has caused a tragic lack of any advancement in tampon technology. For years we have had to use the same tampons, month in and month out but what has the tampon-industrial complex done about any advancement in technology? Huh, what have they done…I'll tell you what they have done, NOTHING! I would like to take this opportunity to mobilize the millions of men who suffer from this plight and are looking for some blessed relief. I am launching and financing a new initiative that will take tampons into the 21st century. I invite you all to join our movement, "Let's put the *Men* back into *Menstruation.*" to finally get the relief we have been praying for. To find out how you can help please be sure to go to www.letsputthemenbacintomenstruationandgettheblessedreliefwehavebeenprayingfor.org.®

LIBERAL GROUPS SEEK TO BAN ITEMS THEY DEEM AS 'UNSAFE, UNHEALTHY, UNNECESSARY, UNCONSCIONABLE, UNNEEDED AND UNINFORMED'

In this proclamation issued by a cabal of left-wing radical groups, many products and policies are exposed as the truly dangerous things they are. Sir Telsunn Margraves reports that everything from a new Pledge of Allegiance, to Barbie Dolls and bovine flatulence are highlighted for elimination or the imposition of severe restrictions. One by one the group's spokesperson reveals specific items that represent all that is bad and how to fix these scourges and blights on the American people and all peoples of the world.

New York, NY – Many liberal and left-leaning groups have come together to combine as one massive organization to put pressure on local, state and federal governments as well as corporations to ban any number of things that they feel are not at all good for the American people.

In a packed press conference, Hilda Cummings, the group's spokeswoman, told those in attendance that she would lay out some of the vast numbers of products and practices that are harming the citizens of our country. "When you think about the dangers and the genuine disasters in the making, I just feel it is vital that we announce to the world our demands."

Hilda continues, "Here is just some of what we will be protesting on behalf of the American people. A ban on pork products like sausage rolls and ham sandwiches that are offensive to Muslims. We also want to assure that the tradition of paid sperm donations is kept sacred. In the UK they tried to ban such a practice but the chair of the federal standing committee on justice and human rights says Liberal MPs are warming to the idea of decriminalizing paid sperm donations. This is a welcome change and shows a new found flexibility in their thinking and we applaud this. We, of course, remain in full support of abortion.

Then there's the suggestion of our dear sister-in-arms, Representative Sheila Jackson Lee. She proposed banning the word 'welfare' from the government's vocabulary and we agree. We have adopted her cause and the word 'welfare' will support a change to use language something like, 'a transitional living fund.'"

Hilda now goes rapid fire through the list of items and practices to ban. "Candles and air fresheners, goldfish, junk food in schools, Big Gulps® in NYC, banning flights to Israel, toy water guns, wood burning stoves, American Flag T-shirts, Rush Limbaugh, menthol cigarettes, looking at women and spanking."

Hilda then pauses as she feels it necessary to clarify some of the aforementioned items. "With regard to wood burning stoves the Obama appointed EPA has recently banned the production and sale of 80% of America's current wood-burning stoves. While this fell short of the 100% mark we gave the EPA a solid C+ for the effort. In addition, with regard to spanking, this is meant for parents and not for our brothers and sisters in the S&M community, who are great contributors to our various causes, so please, spank away!

I would also like to clarify our position of looking at women. It's through generous donations from Hollywood elites, and a few hundred other progressives in Washington DC, that we are able to confront these issues, head on. The Democrats have established the Maxine Waters Education Foundation (formerly Harvey Weinstein Education Foundation), to deal with sexual harassment. In light of all the allegations against very few, very minor, totally misconstrued incidents by members of the Democrat party, this warning is only meant for men, and not for women. You can never tell, for sure, the reason why women look at other women except to see if they are lesbians, getting fat, if they are wearing last year's fashions, or any other reason nefarious or otherwise."

Hilda saves what she feels are the best examples of the group's mission and continues, "Finally, can you think of anything more disgusting than wearing an American Flag T-shirt? Of course you can't, first of all who ever thought of the colors; red white and blue? French-born designer Sophie Theallet, a favorite of Michelle Obama, would be turning over in her grave if she were dead. Second, the patriotic message American Flag T-shirts send out is very disrespectful and demeaning to communists, socialists, Islamic terrorists, certain football players, the entire membership of the Des Moines 'Antifa' Cooking Club as well as our benefactor George Soros!"

The conference is a Q&A and the reporters are eager to hear what other items the group of liberal and leftist organizations and their acolytes are looking to eliminate so that Americans can feel safer. One reporter yells above the rest, "Can you give us the names of some of the other products you are talking about?"

Hilda says, "Yes I can, for instance there are the McDonald's® Happy Meal® Toys. It is an insidious plot to have children play with these toys while shoving unhealthy Chicken McNuggets into their mouths. The process has already started in Santa Clara and San Francisco Counties California where they passed ordinances against offering toys with kid's meals. McDonald's®, in typical capitalist fashion, now charges ten cents just to get around the law."

Another reporter shouts, "Do you really expect that parents are going to go for this? It seems to me that the kids will go nuts if they see a toy they can't have."

Hilda smiles and says, "We have a solution and it's as plain as the nose on your face. The solution came from the dear former first lady, Michelle Obama. Instead of a toy, we are going to encourage children to eat kale. It's especially good for them and they can even have it with or without quinoa!"

The same reporter asks, "Do you really think that kale and quinoa would be preferable to children than a "Despicable Me3™" Balthazar Bratt© toy?

Hilda is getting annoyed and she says, "Yes I do! Children today are far more sophisticated than ever."

There is a murmur among the people covering the press conference and another reporter says, "I don't know if my wife would agree with you but let's move on. What is another product that your group wants to ban from the American consumer?"

Hilda is glad to be off the McDonalds® controversy and moving onto other controversial items, "Barbie™ Dolls. Has anyone of you ever seen a Barbie™ Doll?"

The reporters look at themselves and back at Hilda, wondering if she is joking. Hilda adamantly asks again "Has anyone ever seen a Barbie™ doll?" The crowd of reporters shrugs their shoulders and answer in a collective, "Yes."

"I only hope you are as disgusted as I am over this shameful exploitation of the female anatomy. Now little girls around the country think they have to look like blond, buxom hussies flaunting their perfectly shaped bodies in hopes of attracting muscular, and assumedly well-endowed Kens from around the neighborhood. A forward thinking Democrat delegate, Jeff Eldridge of Lincoln County, WV, proposed a bill in 2009 banning the sale of Barbie and other dolls that purportedly influence girls to be beautiful. Unfortunately, he couldn't get a single colleague to agree but we are determined to continue the fight and hopeful that this will catch on at a national level!"

A female reporters says, "In the past I felt the same way about the doll, but I've seen Mattel has taken steps to create an alternative to the traditional look of the fashion doll. The newer Barbie™ versions are sold in three body types and come in an assortment of skin tones, eye colors and hairstyles. Doesn't that give you pause to consider changing your mind?"

Hilda tries to enlighten the crowd as she explains, "Absolutely not! We will not tolerate the few cosmetic changes that Mattel grudgingly offers. Our group has found a solution to shift the focus away from the emphasis on skin-deep beauty to emphasize a far more ethereal kind of beauty represented by the feminist icons. These are the women that have transformed the way other women think and feel about themselves."

"Who are these feminist icons?"

Hilda smiles, "Glad you asked." She reaches under the podium and brings out from under what looks nothing like the current Barbie doll. "Ladies and gentlemen, may I present, the counter-Barbie; 'The Bella Abzug Doll!' Bella comes complete with the hat, schemata and all her parts move." There is a collective gasp among all the reporters, especially the men in the audience. "Isn't she just lovely?! Look at her hips, her hair, her muscular calves, she just screams beautiful doesn't she!?"

No one in the audience answers so Hilda moves on. "Next there's the 'Maxine Waters Doll' that even talks when you pull this string!" Hilda pulls the string and Maxine says '*I have to march because my mother couldn't have an abortion.*' Just think of the positive message that we send to little girls who will be playing with the Maxine Waters doll! Who knows, this may inspire little girls to start wearing wigs and look to run for president someday!"

Hilda now knows not to wait for a reaction from the reporters present so she introduces the next doll in the collection. "Next we have the amazing 'Jane Fonda Doll!" Hilda is reading from an index card she is holding, "Jane, the immortal actress, is beautiful, never afraid to speak against America, a fashion icon, anti-American and active in leftwing causes even though she is 112 years old...wait, that can't be right?"

Someone in the audience yells out, "Yeah, that's right, she is 112 years old."

Hilda is puzzled and still questioning the information, she tells the reporters, "I will be sure to check this out and issue a press release to determine if Jane Fonda is actually 112 years old. Anyway, isn't she adorable in her *'Barbarella'* costume from the hit movie!?" The irony of Jane Fonda's idealized shape and her large breasts falling out of her *'Barbarella'* costume is not lost to those in the room.

Hilda is proud to mention, "We created over 40 dolls in the series and if you will indulge me, here is my favorite, the 'Lena Dunham Doll', she's angry, petulant, she's also wears designer schemata, she's boisterous, thickish and she's everything we want our little girls to be and she's still here in the US...but as I understand it, not for long. She's promised to move to Canada now that Trump's president and this is expected to happen just as soon as she sells her Brooklyn condo."

There is a deafening silence coming from the audience.

Hilda is not getting the reaction she had hoped for and she clarifies, "That's just a little light-hearted attempt at humor."

A reporter sarcastically laughs, "Ha! That's a funny one. Tell me is there anything else that your group is looking to ban?"

Hilda regains her composure and says, "Of course, there are many things but one that is near and dear to our hearts is banning the Pledge of Allegiance. Massachusetts Democratic State Congressman Frank Smizik backed a 2011 effort by the Brookline Political Action for Peace group to ban the pledge in schools. The political action group said that the pledge had no educational value and is reminiscent of totalitarian regimes. Students could already opt out of saying the pledge in Massachusetts but those who did were being bullied so it was thought that a complete ban is the only way to counteract this type of urban terror and we couldn't agree more."

One reporter got up and challenged Hilda, "You mean that your group considers pledging allegiance is some kind of fascist statement and you don't want it said by any student anywhere, ever?"

Hilda declares an emphatic, "That is correct!" She feels that this point also needs clarification, "We do, however, have an alternative we feel not only conveys the proper sentiment but actually gives the kind of inspirational message we want our youths to take away with them to college."

"So what do you want them to pledge to?"

Hilda is absolutely thrilled to announce the following, "Ladies and gentlemen, we are delighted to announce that our group has recommended that we use the lyrics written by one of the most popular groups in the world, Greenday! Now, for the first time ever, we are announcing the New Pledge of Allegiance, '*American Idiot*©!' Let's take this opportunity to get into the spirit of the moment and pledge. For those of you who aren't familiar with the lyrics please just follow the bouncing ball on the screen above my head and please let us have reverence for what these lyrics represent."

The room goes quiet and the lights go down and on the screen above Hilda's head appears the lyrics to 'American Idiot©' with the graphic of a bouncing ball hovering over the words,

Don't wanna be an American idiot

Don't want a nation under the new media

And can you hear the sound of hysteria?

It's going out to idiot America

Hilda is in the state of shock. It is apparent that not one person in the room has joined her in reciting the lyrics to *American Idiot*©. She does not want to appear that she is, in any way, nonplussed by what she sees as a show of great disrespect, so she stops after the first verse. Hilda cheerily says, "Now wasn't that inspiring? I can just imagine this being said before or after every football game, every protest march, every flag burning, and every violent and non-violent demonstration on campuses and in classrooms all across the country."

One of the reporters sitting in the rear yells out, "You have got to be kidding! You can't possibly expect that '*American Idiot*©' would or could replace the Pledge of Allegiance?"

Hilda tries to hide her indignation and to justify the direction her group has taken, "Yes I can. We have done a great amount of research and focus group testing to come up with this strategy and we are entirely vested in its success. George Soros himself likes it."

The reporter starts to rub his brow in order try and lessen the headache he feels coming on. "Okay, are there other items, products or traditions you feel our readers, listeners and viewers will find important?"

Hilda musters as much courage that her wounded pride will allow and says, "There are a number of items that are being taken under consideration and we are examining the potential for other areas that will require our constant vigilance."

Another reporter shouts out, "Such as?"

Hilda Cummings stands tall as she declares, "Top on our list is regulating bovine flatulence."

Another collective gasp comes from those in the room when one reporter says, "Regulating cow farts? You've got to be kidding, how can you regulate cow farts?"

Hilda enlightens the uninformed in the audience. "As you are well aware, a cow continually passes gas, or as they are commonly known, farts. These farts are unregulated and can come at any time the cow wishes to fart. Imagine you are standing in mixed company and someone, perhaps even you, farts; don't you feel embarrassed? Well after extensive government research, the Obama Administration has proven that cows don't get embarrassed when they fart."

Hilda further amplifies, "Our scientific research also indicates that cows fart, on average, 735 times each day. It is imperative that a long lasting and effective solution to this dilemma must be found. If we do not take this seriously we will need to confront an inevitability that is beyond comprehension. In the immortal words of Governor Jerry Brown of California while addressing the ecological consequences of cow-made global warming, *"If we don't do something about it, it is the end of the world."*

"Our group recognizes that it will require a concerted effort among the farmers who raise cows and the invention of technology to cope with the regulation of this unfettered passing of gas. First, we will require a law being passed that limits the cows to a maximum of 12 farts per day. Various environmental organizations have also considered fart-credits, similar to Al Gore's carbon credits, to fund the bureaucracy that monitors cow-farts. This will most likely be 'step two' in the process but for now this will require a change in diets so we are suggesting that the farmers change the cow's diet to kale and quinoa."

The crowd starts to yell. "Isn't that what you and Michelle Obama want to feed the kids who go to McDonalds®?"

Hilda tries to downplay the obvious connection, "Well, technically yes, but we will require the kale and quinoa the cows eat is that which has been totally rejected by McDonalds® for human consumption. Next we will need to design a special type of truss-style stopper custom made for each cow. The stopper will be fitted onto the cow in order to assist the animal in heeding the limitation of only 12 farts a day. Finally, we will need to develop advanced gas masks for the farmers. Simply stated, if the 723 farts that are being artificially held back are released all at once, *Katie bar the door*, there will be a stink like you've never before experienced. Our group is sure that these policies, as well as a strict smoking ban and gas masks will help keep farmers from abandoning their farms that have, in many cases, been in their family for 150 years or more."

The conference appears to be over when Hilda says, "Thank you for coming and understanding the complexity and breath of each issue our group hopes to tackle. To paraphrase a quote of the president who owned slaves and fornicated with African American women, Thomas Jefferson, 'Eternal Vigilance is the price of Liberty or some such thing!' Good day to you all."

The proposed ban on actual items, products, practices and traditions quoted in this article have all been taken up by various liberal groups and organizations – TM

Actual Maxine Waters quote in italics – TM

Greenday - ©2018 Warner Bros. Records

COLIN KAEPERNICK SIGNS WITH NFL!

It took a few years for Sir Telsunn Margraves to recognize that football in America is very different from the football played in Great Britain and other countries from around the world. That being said, Sir Telsunn in compelled to report America's loss is Nigeria's gain as Colin Kaepernick signs a three year contract to play for the NFL (Nigerian Football League).

San Francisco, CA – In what appears to be a great surprise to all, controversial quarterback, Colin Kaepernick has just been offered and agreed to a 3 year non-cancellable contract to play in the NFL for the 2018, 2019 and 2020 seasons.

The NFL (Nigerian Football League) was formed last Thursday and the current head commissioner of the league is thrilled. Commissioner Abalunam Popoola told the standing room only crowd, "I am most exquisitely jubilant to be here to tell you of this most extreme happiness we are feeling. We at the NFL are being very happy to have a real professional star such as Collene Ka...ea...peppe...nicnac as a, how do you say, a vital linchpin in our most zealous hoping to attracting other eminence individuals to the NFL. Now I would be most pleased to instigate this meeting press conference to questions from the reporting media."

Many of the reporters in the room, mostly from ESPN®, jump up and shout out their questions, and Commissioner Popoola asks that only one person at a time would be called. He says, "Please, the person in the jogging suite who is so profusely sweating, please if you can be asking your questioning."

Jemele Hill, the ESPN® reporter who recently said *'Donald Trump is a white supremacist who has surrounded himself with other white supremacists'* stands and waits to be recognized. Mr. Popoola acknowledges her and says, "The lady who is sweaty, please to ask me a question."

She excitedly asks, "How much are you paying him?"

Colin Kaepernick has no agent, but a representative of ©2018 Select Sports Group who has been working with Kaepernick as a third party consultant, jumps in and says, "Mr. Popoola, may I answer this?"

Abalunam Popoola answers, "Of course it may be convenient to be doing such a thing."

Colin's spokesman stands to address the reporters, "Ms. Hill, Colin is very excited to be playing for the NFL and is ready to play his heart out. He personally promised victory and a championship trophy by 2020! Colin has accepted a very generous offer from the NFL of 10,710,000 Naira to be paid over his three year contract."

Jemele asks a follow-up, "10,710,000 Naira sounds like a truly hefty sum. How much is that in US dollars?"

The spokesman stammers a bit but addresses the question, "Well, it really depends, as the exchange rate does change from day to day."

Jemele says, "Ok, how much is it worth today?"

Kaepernick's spokesman seems to be on the defensive and tries to turn the questioning to a more positive direction. "Well, when you consider his salary does include an allowance for trips back to the states to visit his girlfriend, paying for his own meals, living quarters, transportation, lifetime membership at the Abuja Health and Fitness Center...freedom from those scams that tell you that you can get 40% of $50,000,000 US just by helping someone get their money out of a bank, plus more benefits too numerous to mention..."

Jemele feels she needs to intercede again, "Ok we get it but how much is it in dollars with all that stuff you just mentioned?"

"Well annually it comes to a total of approximately $10,000 per year, and that would also include a uniform allowance. I negotiated that myself and was very firm on assuring Colin that he would not have to pay for his uniform."

Commissioner Popoola now wishes to clarify a factor related to the uniform, "We are most joyful to be giving these many, many Naira to Collene Ka...ea...peppe...nicnac but it must be speculated that this is not included with his helment."

All in the room questioningly look at each other and another ESPN® reporter asks, "Why aren't you paying for his helmet too? Isn't that part of his uniform?"

"Please be to understanding that we are in need to some assistance to build a feet-ball helment that is to be accommodating the hair of Collene Ka...ea...peppe...nicnac. Is this not a very big sizing that is to be requiring very special engineering? I am hoping that you are to be of most understanding what can be done to assuring this to happen."

Another ESPN® reporter asks, "Ok, so you need to make an extra-large helmet, but what team will Colin Kaepernick be playing for?"

Commissioner Popoola proudly answers, "Collene Ka...ea...peppe...nicnac will be looking to be playing for the Abuja Dwarf Goats. The Dwarf Goats are very look-ing happy to be terrorizing other teams with hope of getting the Goats to be striking of fear in the heart of opponents."

Jemele still doesn't seem to be able to get over the low amount of the contract and asks Commissioner Popoola, "That is not considered a large amount of money given the many millions of US dollars that football players make. Why is your con-tract offer so low?"

"I am fortunate to be telling you of all that Collene Ka…ea…peppe…nicnac can be making him to make much money. There are many days when Collene Ka…ea…peppe…nicnac will be of off in time and this is very considerate. He can be of signing his name. We are such surely he will add too many Naira to his fortune, at least 500 Naira or $1.40US each day! Then our most excellent filming company will be breaking the leg to be having Collene Ka…ea…peppe…nicnac to starring role in our producing a Nigerian motion photo of the classic *Wizard of OZ©*. We who are most hopeful that Collene Ka…ea…peppe…nicnac will be getting the part of Dorothy playing by the most happily Judy Garling in past. We can also be of the paying him to make phone calls to every Americans to get 40% of $50,000,000US just by helping some poorly person to be getting their money out of banks."

Commission Abalunam Popoola appears to be getting tired and suggests, "Please I am hoping that you to be asking the last question of this time we are spending together."

One of the other 17 reporters sent by ESPN® to be at the press conference asks, "I am sure you are aware of the issue of Colin Kaepernick's disrespect for the American National Anthem, American flag and other symbols of our country. How does this type of behavior sit with the government of Nigeria and what do you think the reaction will be of the Nigerian people?"

Commission Abalunam Popoola considers how to answer and he tries to be thoughtful in his response. "I am of seeing this on American television and I am of not being offended. If this to be happening to Nigeria we will not be caring and to be sure to leave Collene Ka…ea…peppe…nicnac in jungle, tying him to African Corkwood Tree and be sending secret message to Boko Haram. They who will cut the head of Collene Ka…ea…peppe…nicnac off as to be not a good thing. The NFL will to be of a single mind will not paying the balance of Collene Ka…ea…peppe…nicnac contracting. I am to be thanking you to the bottom of my belly and will be looking to be forward in meeting again at opening day!"

NEW POLL! TRUMP APPROVAL DROPS TO 3%!

A consortium of the most powerful media outlets has released the results of their first poll and the Trump Administration has much to worry about. In an interview with Sir Telsunn Margraves, even Jeff Zucker of CNN is heard to have said "Everyone at CNN has tried to be fair when covering the president. I am deeply saddened to see such erosion in support for President Trump; I was hoping that he would be successful." After hacking onto the polling group's server to read the polling internals as well as the results, Sir Telsunn laments, "This is a sad day for America."

Washington DC – Major US news organizations have banned together to form a new polling group called The Combined Media Polling Group (CMPG). The organizations include the AP, ABC, CBS, NBC, Wall Street Journal, NY Times, Reuters, Washington Post, MSNBC and CNN®.

A spokesperson for the Combined Media Polling Group said, "Executives at all the media outlets got together and thought that it made sense to combine polling resources. There are great savings in many areas that have benefited all the parties involved. It makes even greater sense when you consider we all come up with the same numbers anyway, so why not save a few bucks."

The first in a series of polls related to the Donald Trump Presidency have been released and the results are startling. NBC News Anchor, Lester Holt said upon learning of the results, "This is a devastating blow to the President Trump's Administration. I think he should be impeached." Jeff Glor, CBS News Anchor, had a similar reaction, "How in God's name could this man be president, he should be impeached." Finally Wolf Blitzer of CNN® simply stated, "This man should be impeached."

A group of participants were asked to either agree or disagree of questions asked in the survey. A summary of the results to the questions in the CMPG Poll are as follows:

Question	Agree	Disagree
"Do you think that Trump is psychopathic idiot?	97%	3%
Do you think that Donald Trump is a warmongering cheerleader for the Nazi Party in America?	97%	3%
Do you think Donald Trump is secretly buying all Ivanka Trumps designer clothing shoes to make her look good?	97%	3%
Is it possible that Vladimir Putin is Donald Trump's love child?	97%	3%
Should the Secret Service budget to protect Donald Trump be lowered to $15 per week?	97%	3%
Should Donald Trump be eating kale and quinoa?	97%	3%
Do you think Donald Trump's should grow his hair and wear a man bun?	97%	3%
Donald Trump has been hiding evidence of UFOs at Roswell. Do you believe this?	97%	3%
Does Donald Trump barbeque and eat orphans?	97%	3%

The polling results show the overwhelming drop in support for President Donald Trump and this must be of great concern to all. It is this lack of support of the American people that has caused an objective news media to lose faith in the ability of Trump to effectively govern.

Jeff Zucker, head of news at CNN® said, "Everyone at CNN® has tried to be fair when covering the president. When I saw the results I couldn't believe it. I am deeply saddened to see such erosion in support for President Trump; I was hoping that he would be successful." Jeff Bezos of Amazon said, "Everyone at *Washington Post* has tried to be fair when covering the president. When I saw the results I couldn't believe it. I am deeply saddened to see such erosion in support; I was hoping that he would be successful."

Follow up to the CMPG Poll: This is the first in a series of polls that are being undertaken by the CMP Group in keeping with its mission statement; "To inform the American people of various aspects related to President Donald Trump that will help voters make informed decisions when the time comes."

A spokesperson for The Combined Media Polling Group (CMPG) commented, "We believe that this result reflects what most people think of Trump. If only we had more time we may have been able to achieve a more sensible outcome to our polling." The Trump Administration could not comment as they appear to still be laughing.

Polling Internals

The Combined Media Polling Group uses advanced polling techniques to arrive at the results released in this poll. In that regard, CMPG uses the specially developed Lemon/Maddow methodology that combines demographics, income profiles, unidentified ethnic images from Hubble, tarot cards, chicken bones as well as many micro-targetted subsets to account for differing attitudes of those who may participate in the poll.

The sample size is based on 129 registered and non-registered voters. Of those participating Democrats account for 36%, Liberals 22%, Anarchists 18%, Undocumented Aliens 14%, Antifa/AltLeft protestors

7%, Republicans 3%. CMPG also included various Snoflake groups, Never Trumpers, members of th Communist Party in the US, hosts of The View, Members of the Chelsea Handler and Samantha Bee Fan Clubs and other groups. It should be noted however that these groups, combined, are less that 1%.

The results are formulated from a national sample of participants from Manhattan, San Francisco, Washington DC and Vashon Island WA, Ridgefield Park, NJ, Roserdale NY, Maywood, IL, Hastings, NY, Ithaca, NY, Berkeley, CA, Tacoma Park, MD, Albany, CA and El Cerrito, CA.

- *The Pew Research Center recently reviewed media reports related to the first three months of President Donald Trump's presidency and administration and established that news coverage of his first 100 days were more than 60% negative, far more than any presidents in recent history. A summary of the Pew Research published on "Newsmax" found:*

- *62 percent of the stories had a negative assessment, with just 5 percent having a positive assessment.*

- *20 percent of the stories in President Barack Obama's first three months were negative.*

- *28 percent of the stories in President George W. Bush's first three months were negative.*

- *28 percent of the stories in President Bill Clinton's first three months were negative.*

- *56 percent of stories about the Trump administration appearing in media outlets were negative*

Other studies have come up with similar results, including a Media Research Center study that concluded the three major broadcast networks' coverage of the Trump administration was 89 percent negative.

NANCY PELOSI'S CLARIFIES HER FATHER'S DEDICATION OF A CONFEDERATE MONUMENT

After more than 60 years, Nancy Pelosi reveals a long kept family secret that has haunted her for decades. Through a bureaucratic blunder during her father's tenure as Baltimore mayor, the late Thomas D'Alesandro Jr., a horrific mistake was made. Sir Telsunn Margraves attends a packed press conference to witness Nancy Pelosi as she now conveys the true story behind the statues of General Robert E. Lee and General Stonewall Jackson that were placed in a Baltimore park for the birds and children to enjoy.

Washington, DC – A startling revelation in connection to her father, former Baltimore Mayor, the late Thomas D'Alesandro Jr has resurfaced. At a hastily called press conference today, Democrat Rep. Nancy Pelosi, House Minority Leader sought to quell what is turning out to be a maelstrom of criticism.

It seems that during Thomas D'Alesandro's tenure as Democrat Mayor of Baltimore, he dedicated a monument to two Confederate War Generals, Robert E. Lee and Thomas "Stonewall" Jackson. Various liberal, progressive, anitifa, AltLeft and George Soros funded anarchist groups are putting extreme pressure on politicians by taking part in violent protests demanding removal of such statues throughout the country. As a result, Pelosi's father's past has come to be seen in a negative light and Rep. Pelosi feels compelled to set the record straight.

In her opening statement, Pelosi looked to set the record straight. "First, I would like to thank you all for coming. As our nation seeks to heal itself from fractures that split our country during the Civil War, it appears that these wounds still separate our citizens into Yankee versus Confederate as well as North versus South. Given this backdrop, I would like to provide Americans with a simple explanation to what has become a major controversy. As you are aware, my father Thomas D'Alesandro dedicated a monument to certain Confederate generals. It was his original intention to provide the citizens of Baltimore with a place in a park where adults, children and birds could enjoy them. A place where Baltimoreans could reflect on the statues of the great persons so honored, but there was a dark and deep secret that was never revealed. Even though the statues have been removed, I am now forced to expose the truth."

There are low murmurs from the crowd of reports and questioning looks at Ms. Pelosi. She takes a deep breath and tries to hold back tears as she explains. "When the original commission for the statues was presented and accepted by Governor William Preston Lane Jr., Mayor D'Alesandro and the entire Baltimore City council, my father contracted Laura Gardin Fraser to create a masterwork and notable architect John Russell Pope to design the base of the monument. What happened then was something my late father and our entire family have lived to regret. Through some error at the time, the paperwork got mixed up and the wrong authorization was sent to Ms. Gardin."

A notable gasp comes from all the reporters and commentators at the press conference. There are low whispers and Rep. Pelosi gives everyone in the room a chance to quiet down and allow her to continue. "The original statues were never intended to be created in the likeness of generals Robert E. Lee and Thomas "Stonewall" Jackson!"

The room full of reporters now explodes in reaction to this startling revelation. Questions are being shouted out and Rep. Nancy Pelosi asks for calm so she can continue to explain what happened. "Please ladies and gentlemen, please allow me to explain what transpired. The original intent of the monument was to honor famous African Americans but for a horrendous bureaucratic blunder the statues were created in the likeness of wrong personages."

Reporters are hurling questions at Minority Speaker Pelosi who is trying to remain calm. "Please, please, allow me to continue! As you can imagine, when my father found out the error, he wanted to destroy statues of General Lee and General Jackson, but so much time, money and effort had already been spent. He had a very difficult decision to make; keep the current statues and hope no one notices or risk the wrath of the controller's office as none of the statues were returnable."

Although the cadre of reporters tried ever so hard to be sympathetic to the Democrat minority leader, they became incredulous by this revelation. One of the reporters yells out, "Ms. Pelosi, you know we all want to believe you and to give you the benefit of the doubt but this sounds incredible, who were the statues supposed to be dedicated to?"

Rep. Pelosi says, "The statues were originally intended to honor two heroic African Americans; Spike Lee and LaToya Jackson!"

The crowd now yells in unison, "WHAT?"

Pelosi says, "The noted film director, producer, writer and actor Spike Lee and the singer, songwriter, author, television personality, actress, businesswoman, philanthropist, activist and former model La Toya Jackson."

One reporter asks a question that everyone is thinking, "Ms. Pelosi, has it ever occurred to you that Spike Lee and LaToya Jackson weren't even born when your father was mayor and the commission was formed?"

Nancy stammers a bit but tries not to look flustered, "I guess I was wrong; now I remember; it was Peggy Lee and Shoeless Joe Jackson."

An exasperated reporter says, "You said it was to honor African Americans, both Peggy Lee and Shoeless Joe Jackson are white."

Nancy Pelosi stammers again, this time noticeably and rapidly says, "Oh now I really remember, it was Brenda Lee and Jermaine Jackson. I want to thank you all for coming and allowing me to clear up this matter for the last time. Now I must go to attend a fundraiser for my dear friend, Sheila Jackson Lee."

PROFESSOR STEPHENS AND HER WIFE ANNIE SPRINKLES GIVE NEW MEANING TO THE GREAT OUTDOORS

In light of recent events of which sexual harassment has made front page headlines, some forward thinking University of California educators have come up with the answer. With her wife, Annie Sprinkles, by her side, Professor Elizabeth Stephens 'eco-sex' expert and chairwoman of the Art Department at the University of California at Santa Cruz is promoting having sex with the Earth or "Ecosexualism." Sir Telsunn Margraves reports that it's safe and easy access for all, no matter what sex you identify with, and not a single sexual harassment charge to date.

Santa Cruz, CA – Professor Elizabeth Stephens 'eco-sex' expert and chairwoman of the Art Department at the University of California at Santa Cruz is promoting having sex with the Earth.

UC Santa Cruz summarizes the events hosted by university by announcing, *"Come experience 25 ways to make love to the Earth, raise awareness of environmental issues, learn ecosexercises, find E-spots, and climax with the planetary clitoris,"* the UC Santa Cruz announcement stated. *"You might discover that you are Ecosexualism too!"*

Professor Elizabeth Stephens and her wife, Annie Sprinkle according to the couple's manifesto, which was published by Breitbart, declares: *"We make love with the Earth. We are aquaphiles, teraphiles, pyrophiles and aerophiles. We shamelessly hug trees, massage the earth with our feet and talk erotically to plants. We are skinny dippers, sun worshippers, and stargazers. We caress rocks, are pleasured by waterfalls, and admire the Earth's curves often. We make love with the Earth through our senses. We celebrate our E-spots. We are very dirty."*

According to Breitbart, Stephens and Sprinkle have also officiated at least 19 "weddings to various nature entities" in nine countries. The ceremonies included marriages to earth, the moon and various other aspects of the environment.

In the June issue of *Teen Vogue* magazine, a story titled "Ecosexuals Are Queering Environmentalism" was published. In this issue Teen Vogue describes a sexual act called "Grassilingus." The act itself involves a "gender-fluid" musician licking grass. The article states, *"Whether it's masturbating with water pressure, using eco-friendly lubricant, or literally having sex with a tree — a person of any sexual proclivity who finds eroticism in nature, or believes that making environmentalism sexy will slow the planet's destruction, can be ecosexual,"* Teen Vogue explains, *"The term eco-sex is like the word 'queer'; its meaning varies – a movement, an identity, a sexual practice, an environmental activist strategy – depending on who you ask."*

Further, Teen Vogue writes, *"The eco-sex sphere may still be evolving, but one thing is clear, with the Trump administration's threat on environmental protections, women's bodily autonomy, and queer and trans rights, it's necessary to find new ways to get people motivated to come together to protect the planet and sexual freedom."*

Based on the increasing interest in eco-sex, Professor Stephens and Ms. Sprinkle are trying to inspire students, snowflakes, conforming and non-conforming adults or whomever alike to find their own way to celebrate nature. The couple encourages anyone who will listen to embrace, stroke, and caress, fondle, grab appendages as well as many other signs that sanctify what we may feel about the planet we love.

The University of California at Santa Cruz provided taxpayer funding to Stephens and Sprinkle for "Ecosex Symposium" and "Ecosex Walking Tour." Breitbart reports that in the 2013 film "Goodbye Gauley Mountain: An Ecosexual Love Story," Professor Stephens and her female partner Annie Sprinkles massage river rocks, lick trees, frolic naked in a stream and slather mud on one another. Stephens is now working on a documentary that is set to debut in Germany titled, "Water Makes Us Wet: An Ecosexual Adventure."

Ms. Sprinkle said, "We are hopeful that in time, these feelings can be extended to other living breathing earth bound entities. These can include animals as well as certain man-made items that are created from natural sustainable sources that mother-earth provides and are meant to be used in a respectful and responsible manner."

When asked what they see as the natural progression of the eco-sex movement, Professor Stephens exclaims that the logical next level is animals, domestic, feral, wild or otherwise. "I am especially excited about the eco-sexual coupling of goats of any variety including – Alpine, Altai Mountain, American Cashmere, Anglo-Nubian (Nubian), Angora, Appenzell, Arapawa Island, Australian Goat and that's just the "A's". The Nigerian Dwarf Goat is my favorite and I could go on but you get the point. Goats are a gift that keeps on giving and as you become intimate with all the eco-sex positions a goat can exhibit, our sister and brother goats further help the earth by allowing their feces to decompose and make the earth's ground fertile. As a matter of fact you can even make love to the feces, its magic I tell you, magic!"

As Stephens and Sprinkle explore the infinite possibilities to be offered by mother-nature's earth, the examination turns to other options that present themselves. Sprinkle attempts to qualify what she feels is the next logical step in the eco-sex progression; manmade objects that come from the earth. "You may think that I have taken things too far but when you consider all that we have taken from the earth, we would need to celebrate what they once were in their organic form. That is why we advocate eco-sex with oil-rigs and other machinery! Think about it, oil rigs are made from metal mined from ore and formed into a mechanical apparatus that is what we know as an oil rig. That oil rig is not responsible for taking oil from the ground or the sea floor and therefore cannot be held responsible for that perversion. Eventually oil rigs become obsolete or too costly to repair and they are left to rust and return to the soil from which they came. What Elizabeth and I are advocating is to have eco-sex with the oil rig before it rusts therefore commemorating the "dust to dust" admonition from the Bible."

Sprinkle added, "Just think of it, snakes, long horn cattle, sheep, gerbils, elephants, with tusks, of course, as well as many other species; however we must caution that you may not want to try this on anything with claws."

The actual quotes written in the article are in italics.

Teen Vogue @2018 Conde Nast

ANA NAVARRO OF CNN® CALLS TRUMP A 'SHAMEFUL NINCOMPOOP' AND 'UNFIT TO BE HUMAN'

Sir Telsunn Margraves was glad to be at home rather than in the CNN studio to witness the beginnings of a vicious scolding given by Ana Navarro to President Trump. What was meant as serious criticism of President Trump, by one of CNN's premier commentators, soon degenerated into dizzying back-and-forth harangue of insult and derogatory. Ms. Navarro seems to have started the attack, but never one to shy away from a fight, the Trump Administration fights back.

Atlanta, GA – In what is turning out to be a major escalation in a war of words between the Ana Navarro and the Trump White House, Ms. Navarro, the CNN® commentator doubled down on her name calling of President Trump.

In an interview with Wolf Blitzer, Ana Navarro said, speaking as if directly to President Trump, *"Listen, you crazy, lunatic 70-year-old man-baby, stop it... We have a president who is mean. We have a president who is nasty. We have a president who is immature, unstable, and just acts like a crazy person... Confront this and confront this hard, or it will never stop, and it will embarrass all of us. It will take the presidency low, low, low... Stop. Look, if you can't control your tweeting habits, then stop tweeting. Go seek therapy. Go knit. Find a hobby. Talk to your wife. Do anger management."*

It became apparent to anyone who saw this interview that Ana Navarro was becoming a bit unhinged in her diatribe against the president. This did not go unnoticed by the White House who immediately issued a response that read, "Ms. Navarro would be well advised to seek a medical professional who can help her with her own anger management. Here is a bit of free advice, go home, open a bottle of wine, or whatever alcoholic beverage you drink, sit down, pour a big glass and get smashed...you need it badly!"

The moment the word came out about the White House response, Ana Navarro took the bottle of wine she had been drinking and smashed it against the wall. She called ABC News and was given a slot that evening. She practically spit out these words, "He is *unfit to be human* and he needs to lose weight!"

This characterization seems to set have set off a tirade of tweets from the president as he took exception to the personal affront at the mere mention of his weight. "I am six feet two inches tall, I weigh 236 pounds and I am in fantastic health. I admitted to Dr. OZ that I am a bit overweight." The president also noted that Ms. Navarro might take some time to look in the mirror and offered advice, suggesting she should spend more time eating at the salad bar and less time at "Giuseppe's All you can Eat Pizza Palace!"

The war between Ana Navarro and President Trump is escalating faster than one might expect. An irate Ms. Navarro, on hearing the president's comments, ran straight to the CNN® microphone and practically screams into her mic, "Donald

Trump *"is a shameful nincompoop!"* This statement goes straight to the heart of what I have said and that is Trump has *early onset dementia* and should check himself into a clinic!"

In a rare and uncharacteristic move, President Trump decides to leave the response to such juvenile sentiments to his surrogates. The first response came from White House Press Secretary Sarah Huckabee Sanders who said of Ana Navarro, "We at the White House can't find any of her personal biographical information where it says Ms. Navarro received her medical degree, and is qualified to make a judgement as to the president's mental or physical health. We at the White House believe she is a doo-doo head and pee-pee brain."

When Ana Navarro hears this recent retort from Press Secretary Sanders she appears to fume and demands a slot on the show CNN® Tonight with Don Lemon. She is the first guest to be interviewed on the show by the host and she is seething, "Don, thank you for allowing me on to tell you of the vicious attack on me and my God given right to have an opinion on that *lunatic.* Aside from him being a *nincompoop,* he is feeble-minded sissy pants of the first order!" Don Lemon, ever sympathetic, says, "You forgot snot for brains."

The next day when the transcript of the Ana Navarro interview is published, Secretary of State Mike Pompeo releases a statement of his own saying, "Ms. Navarro appears to have lost her mind. As secretary of state, I have had to deal with ayatollahs, the North Korean dictator and petulant corrupt diplomats but never have I had to deal with such a stinky-face, smelly feet like Ana Navarro."

Ana Navarro spends all night incensed at the insults being hurled at her by the White House, and she is so mad it is hard for her to think. She cannot let this affront to her character and dignities go unanswered. She releases a statement that is circulated through the AP to all media outlets that reads as follows:

"My fellow Americans, in recent days I have become the subject of scorn and ridicule by a president and administration that, in my humble opinion, has become unglued at the seams. I am a commentator and in that regard I am expected to present my opinion to counter other opinions contrary to mine. I am a hard-nosed, competent media pro but never in my life have I had to deal with such immature fart-breath, smelly wee-wee heads like there are in the Trump Administration. From this moment on I refuse to stoop to the lower the low level of the White House and reply to these scurrilous insults."

The next day, after the release was circulated to the media, the White House responded. "We are grateful to Ms. Navarro that she has decided to take a more mature approach to her rantings and put personal attacks aside. We in the administration would like to tell the American people that there is no room for the type of juvenile back-and forth that has been going on. Ms. Navarro, while a member of the fifth estate, albeit biased, appears to have started this and we shall abide by the same standard she uses. In closing we wish that tushey-wushey, poopy-tail stinky-head, Ms. Navarro, all the best."

All quotes and words in italics are actual statements or descriptive from Ms. Navarro - TM

SNOWFLAKE STUDENTS CONDEMN BANANAS AND THEIR PEELS AT OLE MISS

Sir Telsunn Margraves roamed the campus of Ole Miss to report on the angst he found. Snowflake students who attend Ole' Miss are in fear for their lives, and it's all due to racism and ethnic intolerance. A banana peel, thrown by a student, is spotted by Makala McNeil Alpha, Kappa Alpha President and leader of one of the school's historically black sororities. Despite the offending student, Ryan Swanson's, explanation about the occurrence, many snowflake students left in tears after McNeil's discovery of the peel. Students of the snowflake variety have indicated they do not feel "safe" on campus and who can blame them.

Oxford, MS – How can this happen? How can something so reprehensible as bananas be allowed on campus? How can we be protected from such a heinous and brutal attack on the sensitivities of fragile young minds? These are questions plaguing faculty, students and the administration at Ole Miss as they seek to recover from the "banana peel in the tree" scandal!

It was not long ago that bananas could be eaten in relative peace and quiet with the fruit being secreted and consumed without people knowing. One has to ask the questions; what if there was a garbage can? What if the peel was thrown out? What if students with steely constitutions were able to have the presence of mind to grab the peel off the tree? Would this all have become a moot point?

This dastardly act was carried out by student Ryan Swanson who admitted to tossing his banana peel into a nearby tree after he was unable to locate a garbage can. Shortly after he disposed of the peel, it was spotted by Alpha Kappa Alpha President Makala McNeil, a leader of one of the school's historically black sororities. Despite Swanson's explanation and profuse apology, a report from the student newspaper claims that students left the retreat in tears after finding out that McNeil has discovered the peel. McNeil claims the students "didn't feel welcome" or "safe" on campus.

Interim Director of Fraternity and Sorority Life Alexa Lee Arndt said, *"To be clear, many members of our community were hurt, frightened, and upset by what occurred at IMPACT, because of the underlying reality many students of color endure on a daily basis, the conversation manifested into a larger conversation about race relations today at the University of Mississippi."* This agonizing cry can be heard resounding loudly by snowflake students across college campuses nationwide.

Unfortunately, Greek life weekend was taking place and all the sororities and fraternities were preparing for the Greek life retreat. As a result of the sight of the banana peel in the tree, the event organizers felt it was imperative to end the gathering early. The leader, Ms. Arndt, explained that it was also imperative to provide space immediately to students affected by the incident, as the trauma is such that the snowflakes need an alternative space to bemoan this act of callousness and indignity.

Since this incident, the University of Mississippi has reported a number of other fraternities and sororities have described horrors of their own and the members are seeking safe spaces and revised standards to recover from the distress and suffering they are experiencing today.

Stanislaw Kozinskiak, President of the 'Sigma Alpha Polemus", a fraternity for the Polish men attending Ole Miss said, "I was horrified when one of our members, came to me with a cold, hard kielbasa in his hand and said he found this in the back seat of his car." Mr. Kozinskiak held the kielbasa for all to see. "We, as Polish people, have been the brunt of many jokes, but this goes beyond anything like the jokes I heard growing up. We are demanding that the university issue a heartfelt apology to all of our members and serve pierogis for lunch over the next coming academic year." The administration at Ole Miss replied and said they would accede to the fraternity's demands.

Immediately afterwards, another incident is reported to have occurred; this one seems even more heinous than the others. The fraternity named 'Theta Lambda Columbus' comprised almost exclusively of Italian students, said that while having their weekly wine and food festival and binge watching the *Sopranos*®, a plate of rigatoni ala arrabiata was hurled through a the front glass window. Investigators found the glass from the window littered the outside of the frat house, and are still trying to resolve why the plate seems to have come from the inside. The spokesman for the fraternity, Carmine Vivollo said, "I don't know why anyone would want to do such a terrible thing to Italians. All we ever want to do is eat and drink and go to class except after the nights we eat and drink, and then this happens. As a result, many of our members are terrified and refuse to go outdoors and luckily we have a lot of left-overs. Members of 'Theta Lambda Columbus' have demanded that the administration at Ole Miss grant us dispensation from final exams." The administration at Ole Miss replied and said they would accede to the fraternity's demands.

The fratority persons from 'Pi Kappa LGBTTQIQA' are up in arms about what they see as a major affront to their brotherhood-sisterhood. Shawn 'Anna' Turbine was practically in hysterics as she/he screamed at Professor Milton Chomps, "Do you realize what you have allowed to happen? Are you so blind that you cannot see? The lesbian, gay, bisexual, transgender, transsexual, questioning, intersex, queer and asexual community at the fratority is up in arms about the latest attempt to drive us back into the closet." Shawn Anna Turbine seems to be fuming as she practically spits out, "What gives anyone the right to say our sexual preferences are not our choice, huh, who has that right." When asked what was meant by the comment, Shawn Anna burst into tears and shrieked, "Swiffer's®!"

"Recently a box of Swiffer's® was left in the mailbox of the fratority house and when member Myrna 'Seth' Avalon opened the mailbox she fainted at the sight. Swiffer's® are the traditional way women have been kept down. Sure they make housekeeping easy, but that is so women will do more of it. We abhor the enslavement of women and now that we know there are many more sexual identities today, we can't find anyone who wants to assume the role and clean the fratority. We refuse to bow down to the House Cleaning-Industrial Complex, and we demand that the university clean our fratority." The administration at Ole Miss replied and said they would accede to the fratority's demands.

The difficulties facing the University of Mississippi did not end there. The entire Greek Alliance including all sororities, fraternities and fratorities released a combined statement that reads: "The major racist, violent and sexual harassing incidents, as well as other horrors that fraternities, fratorities and sororities have had to endure, must end…this trampling on our sensitive natures must be eliminated so that all students can feel safe and secure, after all some of us aren't even 26 years old."

In this regard, the University of Mississippi is being pressured to help students cope with this horrible situation. First, like their sister schools around the country, the university is being asked to construct a Snowflake Lounge, similar to the one being constructed at UC Berkeley. There should be banana, kielbasa, rigatoni and Swiffer free zones so that no student will have to confront what has become known as "the horror of a peel." Next, a program of ethnic-neutral, gender-neutral and age-neutral coloring books should be distributed to all students. This is an important step in helping students cope with the situation. Gerbils, guinea pigs, dwarf goats and cats should also be offered to help console and calm the poor victims of fruited and culinary bigotry that have become known as our sister and brother snowflakes."

All quotes in italics are attributed to the person identified - TM

BRAVE POLITICAL REPORTERS ON CABLE NEWS IN EYE OF THE STORM

With hurricane season in full force, one storm came after another, Sir Telsunn Margraves did not put himself into harm's way, but others did. What did danger mean to the brave and stalwart reporters of the networks such as MSNBC, CNN and NBC News? It meant that they would risk their lives standing out in the rain and wind in fervent hope of trying to blame these serious weather occurrences on President Donald Trump. Sir Telsunn was more than happy to let others reap the reward of getting wet and catching cold, but not before he was able to report this to you.

Key Largo FL – A grateful nation thanks MSNBC®, CNN® and NBC News for sending their star political reporters to Florida to take their lives into their own hands. They were there to bravely inform viewers about what had been called the most powerful hurricane in the history of mankind. The effects of the storm died down considerably later in the day and the damage appears to be less than initially predicted but the final assessment has not been made.

Before going live, Chris Cuomo was being pelted by the wind and rain in Key Largo. He courageously faced the camera and yelled to the cameraman, "God I'm wet!" The cameraman got the cue from CNN® studios and Cuomo went live to report what was happening. "I am standing in the middle of Key Largo, knee deep in water and leaning against the wind..." at the exact moment Chris Cuomo was nearly blown off his feet and with audio cutting in and out could be barely heard to say "ah crap!...man-made global warming...uggghhh...Trump.!" MSNBC® newsmen, Chris Hayes and Thomas Roberts were also on location and it was reported that they both got wet.

The New York Times published story bringing up the question, *"Why? Why are these people who generally spend all of their time talking about how awful Donald Trump is and how wonderful liberal policies are, standing out there in the middle of Irma, apparently on the verge of being blown into the sea?"* On closer examination it appears the answer could be that it was important to determine if President Donald Trump has found a way to control the weather. While there is no definitive proof, many well-known experts have felt compelled to provide their comments on the connection.

Award winning actress, amateur theologian and climate expert Jennifer Lawrence had this to say, *"It's scary."* She was responding to a reporter who said that many people feel these storms signify the "end of days." Ms. Lawrence continued, *"You know, it's this new language that's forming. I don't even recognize it. It's also scary to know that climate change is due to human activity, and we continue to ignore it, and the only voice that we really have is through voting."*

Jennifer Lawrence, in a candid appraisal of hurricanes, *"You know, you're watching these hurricanes now, and it's really hard, especially while promoting this movie* ["Mother!"], *not to feel Mother Nature's rage and wrath."* She went on to say that *"it was really startling"* speaking of Donald Trump's election concluding that it was *"really polarizing and upsetting."* She added, *"You know, I've heard things and seen things on TV in my own country that devastate me and make me sick, and it's just really confusing."* She concluded by saying that the election of Donald Trump could signify *"the end of the world"* essentially the same words used by California Governor Jerry Brown in his man-made global-warming lamentation.

Another expert acknowledged by the media, Mark Ruffalo, not only blames God but he also blames Rush Limbaugh. One may recall Ruffalo saying, *"Let's start a 'gofund me' campaign! Fly @RushLimbaugh to Hurricane Irma!"* He also tweeted after hearing of President Trump withdrawing the US from the Paris Climate Accords, *"If this is true he will have the death of whole nations on his hands. People will be looking to the USA for retribution for what they lose."*

On close examination, Mr. Ruffalo has made some accusations about the president that seems to strike at the heart of his man-made global warming position ranting that Trump *has allowed white supremacists, he's allowed the KKK, he's allowed Nazis to show their ugly face."*

While the number of newsmen and newswomen, as well as Hollywood actors and actresses are legion, ordinary citizens have felt compelled to provide their own thoughts on the connection between Trump and Hurricanes. It appears that leftists on social media are taking up the cause accusing President Trump of using hurricanes to kill blacks and Hispanics. Facebook® user, Breanna Danielle made serious charges against the president.

She wrote on her post: *"So they say Hurricane Irma is headed for Miami. Did y'all realize 70% of Miami is Latino, Hispanic, or Cuban?? 44% of the Haitian population in the US resides in Miami. Miami is like Houston in which it is FLOURISHING economically. Coincidence? Trump wants them off our land so what better way than to flood them out. Read between the lines people."*

Other social media users like Tyler Mazur concurred with Ms. Danielle's assessment tweeting, *"I can't believe Trump created hurricane irma to kill minorities"*

Another person who is named JDP tweeted, *"I blame Trump for all these natural disasters. Harvey. Irma and now Jose."*

Petty LaBelle also Tweeted, *"Harvey, Irma, Jose & Katia...I blame Trump for these Hurricanes."*

While you may be unable to apply logic to any of these statements you cannot ignore the passion from ordinary citizens as well as celebrities. When asked her thoughts Ms. Marsha Brigand of Ft. Myers, Florida said, "That no good piece of sh*t needs to go f*ck himself and put a stick of dynamite in his behind so he can blow his ass off."

Talk show host, Chelsea Handler screams, "I knew it! I just knew it! Instead of barbequing no-parent persons he is trying to kill people with hurricanes. Someone needs to kick Trump's ass across America and let the people spit on him."

Piggly Wiggly® cashier Thomas 'Big Tom' Cashman says, "If that man even tries to return a deposit bottle that is not from the state of Georgia, I will kick him out of the store on his ass and I ain't lying."

Former Late night with David Letterman host, David Letterman said, "Man-made global warming, Donald Trump, eco-sex, Russia, ISIS, salmonella, growing Antarctic ice, hurricanes opioids, sexual harassment, Otherkin bigotry, quinoa and kale as well as elephant tusks. I can't believe that people don't see the connection. I just want to kick him in the ass!"

Whoppi Goldberg of 'The View' Tweets out, "No man-made global warming? He can kiss my ass!"

While most of the anti-Trump sentiment focused on the president's ass, there were some who chose to attack other body parts, for example:

Lawrence O'Donnell of MSNBC®, "...I'll kick that piece of sh*t in the balls if he doesn't f**kin' stop sending hurricanes to kill Democrats."

Stand-up comic Tracy Morgan, "...I hope he's wearing a cup 'cause his balls are mine!"

Actor Robert De Niro, "...I wanna make him cry! Cry, just like when I killed Don Roberto in Godfather Two. F*ck Trump"

Bob Schieffer, host of CBS' Face the Nation, "...If I could get up off this chair I'd give him a black eye."

Felix Wellstone, undocumented alien lobbyist, "...I want to be sure to get a punch at his stomach but it might get me arrested."

Actress and singer Cher, "...A swollen lip would make him look better and I'm just the broad to give it to him!"

Actress and comedienne Rosie O'Donnell said, "Hurricane? Hurricane? He ain't seen a hurricane until he's seen my fist pummel him in the mouth. Please pass the donuts!"

The list of notables as well as ordinary people is short but powerful in their condemnation of the president, and their belief that he causes hurricanes. This did not go unnoticed by CNN®'s Chris Cuomo and MSNBC®'s Chris Hayes and Thomas Roberts who are still drying out from their ordeal in Florida.

Chris Cuomo was the first to comment, "I've tried to be fair with the president. I know that he did not cause these hurricanes however he is responsible for the water damage that resulted. He had ample time to build a wall around Florida that could have saved..." Cuomo holds his hand to his ear and says, "Ah, sh*t I forgot! We should never build a wall to protect ourselves against anything. This is Chris Cuomo signing off and wishing all the best to the citizens of Florida and all Democrats in Texas." Hayes and Roberts concurred.

All statements in italics are actual quotes of those attributed - TM

CANADIAN PRIME MINISTER TRUDEAU WELCOMING IMMIGRANTS

Canada has warmly welcomed immigrants from all nations in direct contrast to the Trump Administration's mandate to block immigrants from certain countries. Sir Telsunn Margraves was able to accompany CNN as a member of the camera crew when it sent its star reporter, Jim Acosta to Toronto for an exclusive interview with Canadian Prime Minister Justin Trudeau. PM Trudeau explains how he lives by the old French saying, 'La maison est où le coeur est' which loosely translated means, "Home is where the heart is."

Ottawa, Ontario – In light of the Trump Administration's policy regarding illegal immigration, Canadian Prime Minister, Justin Trudeau granted an in-depth interview to Jim Acosta of CNN®.

Mr. Acosta – "Good morning Prime Minister Trudeau, I want to thank you on behalf of CNN® and our hundreds of viewers for taking time out of your busy schedule to sit down to tape this interview."

Mr. Trudeau – "You are very welcome, however I want to let you know that I may have to take a call or two during our time together. By the way, do you speak French?"

Jim Acosta – "Uh no, why"

Mr. Trudeau – "No reason, just curious. Please go ahead with your interview."

Jim Acosta – "Millions of pro-illegal immigration advocates in the US point to the Canadian policy on immigration as a blueprint for what to do in our country. Do you consider your policy on immigration a defining commitment on the part of your country?"

Mr. Trudeau – "As Canadians we welcome all peoples of all nations. We recognize that truly sound immigration policy must take into account the feelings and desires of people who suffer and are looking to make a better life for themselves."

Jim Acosta – "That is a very noble sentiment. There are many of us at CNN® who wish you could convince President Trump to change our policy towards illegal immigration."

Mr. Trudeau – "Ah, yes."

Jim Acosta – "There have been many reports of Canadian authorities opening the borders to migrants looking to enter your country especially those looking to escape persecution in the United States. These reports are very complementary about the various help and services you have made available.

Mr. Trudeau – "As I have tweeted in the past, *'To those fleeing persecution, terror & war, Canadians will welcome you, regardless of your faith. Diversity is our strength #WelcomeToCanada.* We in Canada have a very liberal immigration policy and welcome those who are..." The phone rings and Prime Minister Trudeau asks for Jim Acosta's indulgence while he takes the call.

Mr. Trudeau – "Bonjour, le Premier Ministre Trudeau parle. Ah, Pierre, comment allez-vous? Bon maintenant, que puis-je faire pour vous? Un autre *50 réfugiés irakiens*? Renvoyez-les chez eux en Irak À PRÉSENT"

[**Translation**: "Good morning, Prime Minister Trudeau speaking. Ah, Pierre, how are you? Good, now what can I do for you? *Another 50 Iraqi refugees*? Send them back home to Iraq, NOW."]

Mr. Trudeau hangs up the phone – "That was quick, now where were we?"

Jim Acosta – You told me of that marvelous tweet of yours. *'To those fleeing persecution, terror & war, Canadians will welcome you...'* I must tell you that it was truly inspiring."

Mr. Trudeau – "Well thank you for that compliment. One must understand that being leader of a country can often times force us to make decisions that are made from the heart and not the head. I remember..." The phone rings again and Mr. Trudeau apologizes for the second interruption.

Mr. Trudeau – "Bonjour, le Premier Ministre Trudeau parle. Ah, c'est toi encore Pierre, c'est quoi? Un autre 43 retour à la maison en Afghanistan? N'est-ce pas dangereux là-bas? Oh, je vois, renvoyez-les maison."

[**Translation:** "Good morning, Prime Minister Trudeau speaking. Ah, it's you again Pierre, what is it? Another *43 back home to Afghanistan*? Isn't it kind of dangerous there? Oh, I see, send them back home."]

Mr. Trudeau hangs up the phone – "As they say, heavy is the head that wears the crown, now where were we?"

Jim Acosta (laughing) – "Very funny Mr. Prime Minister, but on a more serious note you were telling our viewers how you sometimes need to lead with your heart and not your head, is that a philosophy you live by?"

Mr. Trudeau – "Yes it is. Showing love and compassion for people is what separates us from the animals. I was once at a global climate change Paris Accords summit in Europe when..." The phone rings again and Mr. Trudeau profusely apologizes for the third interruption.

Mr. Trudeau – "Bonjour, le Premier Ministre Trudeau parle." [Dans un geste effrayant, le Premier ministre Trudeau dit:] "Ah, Pierre, nous devons arrêter de nous rencontrer comme ça, et maintenant? 62 en République démocratique du Congo! Combien coûte nous coûte? Renvoyez-les à la maison immédiatement."

[**Translation:** "Good morning, Prime Minister Trudeau speaking." [In a light-hearted gesture, Prime Minister Trudeau says:] "Ah, Pierre, we have to stop meeting like this. 62 to the Democratic Republic of the Congo! How much does it cost to care for them? What! Send them back home immediately."]

Mr. Trudeau hangs up the phone – "Ah Mr. Acosta, this is not really going the way I had hoped. Again, please accept my sincere apologies. Now please continue."

Jim Acosta – "No need to apologize. I hate to bring this up but some of these statistics predate after your election as Prime Minister. During the years between 2006 and 2014 the Canadian government deported more than 117,000 immigrants. In the last several years, in spite of official moratoriums on deportation to Iraq, Haiti, Zimbabwe, Afghanistan, Syria, Somalia and other states, more than 500 people were sent back. Why?"

Mr. Trudeau – "Well, that is easy to explain. You see in Canada we have an old French saying, 'La maison est où le coeur est' which loosely translated means, "Home is where the heart is." So when I tell you that you need to sometimes use the heart and not the head, that's exactly what I mean. What more compassionate measure could there be than sending these folks back home, after all that is where the heart is."

Jim Acosta – "That is truly inspiring. I want to thank you on behalf of the staff and management at CNN® and the many hundreds of viewers who will take solace in the knowledge that there is a leader who truly speaks from the heart."

References to the numbers of aliens seeking refuge in Canada are actual numbers as posted by various sources- TM

All quotes in italics are attributable to Prime Minister Trudeau - TM

STARTLING COMPARISONS: PRESIDENT TRUMP VS VARIOUS DISEASES

Dr. John Gartner, a former Johns Hopkins professor, has diagnosed the President Trump with *"malignant narcissism."* This was just the start of Hollywood and entertainment celebrities who have also spoke openly comparing the president to various diseases and other negative stereotypes. Ana Navarro (early onset dementia), Don Cheadle (unnamed disease), Guillermo del Toro and Rob Reiner (cancer), Susan Sarandon (drunk uncle), Stephen King (rabid coyote) and so much more. Even ordinary Americans get a chance to identify President Trump with a number of maladies and Sir Telsunn Margraves was there to capture every word.

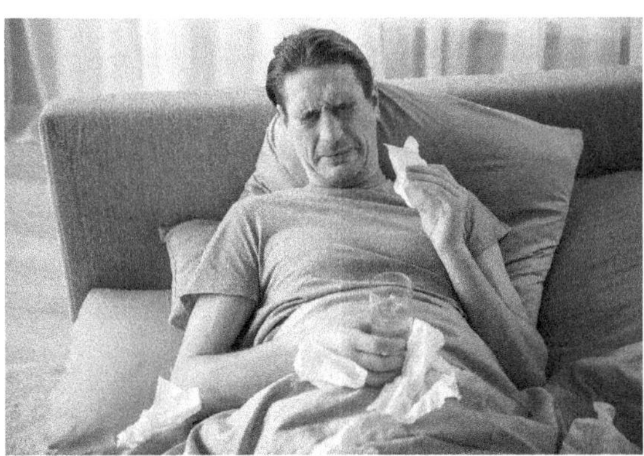

Washington DC – In the aftermath of the 2016 presidential election, more and more comparisons of various diseases are being made to the newly elected president. Doctors, media types, celebrities and others have made some serious allegations concerning the physical and psychological manifestations of these illnesses and how they appear to conform to the persona of President Donald J. Trump.

Many of the accusations against the president relate to a supposed mental condition or conditions that would cause him to be unstable while holding the top leadership position in the United States. Dr. John Gartner, a former Johns Hopkins professor has diagnosed Donald Trump with the personality disorder, *"Malignant Narcissism."* Dr. Gardener goes on to say *"We have an ethical responsibility to warn the public about Donald Trump's dangerous mental illness."*

Nearly 60,000 'mental health professionals' have diagnosed President Trump with serious mental illness, a type of insanity that is often compared to an alcoholic's lack of honesty and impulse control. In spite of the fact that none of these people have actually examined the president to confirm their non-evidentiary prognosis, Dr. Gartner explains, "Well, what difference does it make. There is a consensus among us that he is quite ill, kind of like guessing about man-made global warming."

In an article published in the *New Republic* a shocking accusation was made that Trump could be exhibiting the symptoms of dementia due to syphilis. In the article, *"A Medical Theory for Trump's Bizarre Behavior"* Dr. Steven Beutler, an infectious disease expert, sets forth this rather bizarre proposition.

Many more experts and self-identified Trump haters, have also chimed in with their thoughts on the subject. Late night talk show host and multi-millionaire, Stephen Colbert simply says, *"He is the disease"* indicating that he believes President Trump represents the source of all illnesses. In another article, David R. Williams is quoted as saying *"Elections can matter for the health of children and adults in profound ways...this can be called Trump Anxiety."*

Hollywood and entertainment celebrities have also spoken of their anxiety concerning the president's mental health. CNN® commentator Ana Navarro diagnosed the president with *"early onset dementia."* Don Cheadle, actor and multi-millionaire, has also identified President Trump as *"A disease or ecological crisis or a racist, abusive coward…"* Noted Mexican director and multi-millionaire, Guillermo del Toro *"It's like a cancer. We have a tumor now…that doesn't mean the cancer started with that tumor. It was gestating for so long."*

Rob Reiner actor, activist and multi-millionaire who played "Meat Head" in the long running sitcom, *"All in the Family"* called the president's White House *"a cancerous presidency that we cannot allow to spread." "We have somebody who's mentally unstable, who is a pathological liar."*

There are also many other celebrities that feel it obligatory to let their opinions be know. While these statements are not necessarily diagnosing the president with a disease, they can qualify as opinions that come from the depth of their souls.

George Clooney, actor and multi-millionaire – "I believe he is a *"xenophobic fascist"* but I mean that in the nicest sense of the word."

J K Rowlings, author and multi-millionaire – When comparing Trump to Lord Voldemort, *"How horrible* (is Trump). *Voldemort was nowhere near as bad."*

Louis C K actor and multi-millionaire who was recently accused of being a sexual abuser, is quick to point out, *"But the guy is Hitler. Hitler was just some hilarious and refreshing dude with a weird comb over who would say anything at all…"*

Susan Sarandon actress and multi-millionaire – President Trump is like the *"drunk uncle"* you try not to invite over for holiday dinners."

Stephen King author and multi-millionaire – In speaking of Donald Trump and calling him a *"rabid coyote,"* King wants everyone to continue to root for the road-runner.

Judd Apatow director, actor and multi-millionaire – In describing President Trump *"He's kind of like the psycho girl on 'The Bachelor…"*

Tom Hanks actor and multi-millionaire – In anticipation of the Trump presidency *"It's kind of like if you have a horrible, painful tooth…"*

In light of all these famous personages coming out and comparing the president with any number of diseases, conditions, personifications, etc., others have been emboldened to add their comments. Here is a mere sampling of the men and women who have put their reputations on the line to come forward to speak the truth.

- Ms. Tiffany Felter– "I firmly believe that Trump is like a bad case of 'athlete's feet.' He's someone who has allowed this to become the scourge it is. What is he trying to hide? This is an affront to every itchy footed American!"
- Mr. Malcolm Brooks – "I believe that President Trump *is* "bad breath!" He is beholding to the garlic-industrial complex and he should be held accountable. Unlike Obama, is this the start of an imperial presidency?"
- Ms. Filomena Martin – "Do you know the shame of someone with "acne' faces every day? If President Trump continues to ignore our pimples we will ignore him on election day!"
- Mr. Carlton Simmons – "Who would have thought that our President would disregard the plague that has become known as 'chapped lips." I am hereby giving him the title of the "Chapped Lips" President!
- Mr. Harry Fields – Does anyone ever think of the horrors associated with "dry scalp?"
- It is a disease on humanity and that's what I think of Donald Trump. He is man obsessed with drying out the scalps of Americans.
- Ms. Harlenne Shivers – As a mother of seven I am embarrassed to have to bring this up but what about "diaper rash." I read the entire budget that lists Federal programs and not one mention of diaper rash. If you've ever had to look at a baby's ass you would know what I mean and Trump is responsible...and don't get me started on "head lice!"
- Mr. Angus Mac Phearson – "Trump! Don't even mention the name to me. He is responsible for my "hemorrhoids" and I want to tell him to kiss my ass."

Other patriotic Americans have listed many diseases that are attributable to the election of Donald J. Trump. Iron deficiency anemia, or as we call it "tired blood", irritable bowel syndrome, mucus in stool, mad cow disease, snoring, sunburn, tennis elbow. The list goes on and on and we are hopeful that in light of the overwhelming spread of so many diseases, we can continue to experience man-made global warming so that we can bleach many of these blights from the face of the earth, well except for "dry scalp", that calls for global cooling we think.

All actual quotes from the various people in the 'article are in italics – TM

Multi-millionaire defined as net worth over $25,000,000+ - TM

ROB REINER FORMS TASK FORCE TO INVESTIGATE TRUMP/ RUSSIA COLLUSION

Rob Reiner, actor, director and "Meat Head" on the sitcom "All in the Family" has teamed with a distinguished advisory board to launch InvestigateRussia.org in an attempt to implicate President Trump in the Russian Collusion narrative. In addition to Reiner and his associates, Sir Telsunn Margraves was able to interview many of the famous celebrities by disguising himself as a reporter for the Hallmark Channel. Sir Telsunn spoke with Jennifer Lawrence about "Breast Buddies" for feminist causes, Jaleel White about "Ebony and Ivory" for race relations, Sean Penn's "Jerking off for the Jerk" that advocates pleasuring yourself as sexual liberation from Donald Trump.

Hollywood, CA September 20, 2017 – Rob Reiner, actor, director and "Meat Head" on the sitcom "All in the Family" has teamed with a distinguished advisory board to launch InvestigateRussia.org.

The members of the Advisory Board include co-founder and *Atlantic* senior editor David Frum and other Obama-era government officials and vocal Donald Trump critics. Among them are James Clapper, the former director of National Intelligence, Max Boot, senior fellow at the Council on Foreign Relations, Norman Ornstein, resident scholar at the *American Enterprise Institute,* and political commentator Charlie Sykes. The primary mission of the new initiative is to assist other efforts to uncover the extent of Russia's interference in the 2016 presidential election.

Rob Reiner wrote on Twitter, *"To understand the gravity of Russia's invasion of our democracy, today we launch Committee to Investigate Russia."* The Committee claims to be a *"nonprofit, non-partisan resource provided to help Americans recognize and understand the gravity of Russia's continuing attacks on our democracy."* Reiner has been a long-time critic of President Trump and the Administration and has issued many a colorful descriptive including those characterizing the president as *"heartless prick"* and a *"racist president"* and *"a cancerous presidency that we cannot allow to spread."*

Reiner also characterized the current White House by saying, *"What's interesting here is that we really have a test, and we are being tested as to whether or not our democracy is going to survive."* Reiner said on a recent appearance on MSNBC®, *"We have somebody who's mentally unstable, who is a pathological liar. There's no getting around that, who's running our country."*

This appears to have caused a significant upturn in various initiatives being launch in support of a number of causes. Many of Hollywood elites have followed Reiner's example and are using an online presence and social media to influence the American people to support basic tenets of their efforts.

We met with Jaleel White who played Steve Urkel on the 1990's sitcom *"Family Matters."* He has long supported the expansion of strong race relations among Hollywood's African-Americans and Caucasian actors. White says, "I need to make sure that all actors, regardless of color, creed, ethnic background or sports ability have an equal chance at success on the big screen." According to Jaleel White there was a long and passionate discussion as to what to name this important effort. Finally, a consensus was arrived at, and a selection made, and he launched *http//:www.ebonyan- divorylivetogetherinperfectharmonysidebysideonthepianokeyboard ohlordwhycantwe.org.*

"This is an important outreach to those who may not be aware of a time when race relations were at a high point in Hollywood. Our organization looks to the past to strengthen our resolve for the future. All you need to look at is the inspiration behind '*Ebony and Ivory©*' to see the possibilities." Mr. White then showed us, what he terms as, his wall of honor. "Look at these pioneers, giants of the silver screen, *The Little Rascals*, who paved the way for those who follow. There's Alfalfa and Buck- wheat, Spanky and Stymie, Darla and Farina... "*Our Gang*' and what they represent is the future of Hollywood and what we hold sacred."

Another group focuses on the powerful force of women and the role they play in the entertainment industry. Award winning actress and political activist Jennifer Lawrence is the power behind the launch of "Breast Buddies" to support feminist causes. We interviewed Ms. Lawrence and she was not shy about her opinion of the president when she proclaimed at a recent event, '*Hey Trump, f*ck you!*'"

Ms. Lawrence was also not shy in expressing herself when she said, "I think he's a piece of shit but I want to focus on the positive aspects of "Breast Buddies." Our organization was formed to be able to convey our strong resolve to confront the powers in Hollywood to be sure that we get what we want or we'll put their balls in a lock-box, kinda like what Hillary does to all the men under her control." Ms. Lawrence made it clear that she was not referring to former President Clinton, "Bill seems to do whatever he wants anyway."

Jennifer Lawrence swells with pride when she speaks of those who have rushed to get in on the movement. "You won't believe who I got to join the Advisory Board. I just heard from Rosie O'Donnell and she has agreed to join the board as she feels it dovetails nicely with her role as head of the food service for the "I Hate Trump" Fan Club! Another woman who needs no introduction is Joy Behar, and for the re- cord I don't think she looks like Maude, maybe Margaret Cho but not Maude. Next, and this is unbelievable, we have asked Jane Fonda to join our board and SHE HAS ACCEPTED! In spite of being 112 years old, SHE HAS ACCEPTED!" Ms. Lawrence seems overcome with emotion as a tear comes to her eyes. "Jane is a hero of mine; an actress of accomplishment, a true anti-American, Trump-hater and feminist of the first order. Finally, we are honored, no honored and humbled, to have as a lifetime member of our Advisory Board, Supreme Court Justice Ruth Bader Ginsburg! Can you image woman who is nearly as old as Jane Fonda is also on our board!"

Another Hollywood star that is providing the resources and inspiration behind a crusade is Sean Penn. He wants Hillary Clinton supporters to forget the election results and move on. Penn wants left-wing activists in Hollywood to focus on bodily functions that have become the actor's hallmarks. We had a frank and honest conversation with the actor, and here is some of what was said in recent interviews about President Trump.

"It doesn't matter what Trump says because all he is doing is selling," Penn said. *"It's a masturbatory populism. It's really an opportunity for one man to have a group celebration of his own narcissism."* He went on to say, "This is why we have launched "Jerking off for the Jerk!"

While Sean Penn wants Hillary supporters to forget Trump, he can't seem to forget the president himself. He slammed Donald Trump supporters in possibly the rudest way, likening voting for him to *"masturbating our way into hell. Either you can decide to divorce yourself from loving your children and piss on a tree and show that you have the power to piss on a tree."* Sean Penn is quoted as saying, *"And you stick it out for four years, or we can just masturbate our way into hell with a guy who looks like the only blond magician."*

There was obvious disappointment over the election results and Sean Penn was not shy about expressing his opinion, "He is a f*cking a**hole who can sh*t in his hat for all I care. I want to take his c**k and drive it up his a** while taking his balls and ripping them out of his scrotum." The emotion was palpable.

Penn continued, "For all the reasons we discussed that's why I started "Jerking off for the Jerk." I want to provide safe spaces for fellow actors who hate Trump and need to jerk off to feel better. When I put out the word for volunteers among my leftist, progressive buddies I got an amazingly large response. We wish we could have a board of all the 6,872 people that have already joined. We have, however, assembled an Advisory Board that I believe exemplifies the spirit of jerking off. The main criteria for selection are a visceral hatred of Trump, violent temper and can make the daily meetings. These notable actors include, Angelina Jolie, Mark Ruffalo, Jennifer Lawrence, Alec Baldwin, Charlie Sheen, Madonna, Shia LaBeouf, Gwyneth Paltrow, Josh Brolin, Beyonce, Cher, John Legend plus another 14 members who wish to remain nameless. Unfortunately, we have had to withdraw invitations that we sent out to Harvey Weinstein, Brent Rattner, Matt Lauer, Jeremy Piven, Kevin Spacey, Charlie Rose, Andy Dick, Louis CK, Jeffrey Tambor, and George Takei, among others. To save time we have also created a form letter that will be sent out as new allegations come up." Penn recently was chosen to star in a Hulu series about the first mission to Mars. Like Lena Dunham, Chloe Sevigny, Samuel Jackson, Larry Flynt and a number of others who had threatened to leave the United States, Sean Penn said that he is ready to relocate to Mars and wants Hulu to pay for his relocation expenses.

Currently a number of actors, directors, screenwriters and producers are scoping out one of many causes that they can get behind and galvanize those who are of the same mind. Some of the movements being considered are, "Cannes; Work, vacation or both?", "They must make an electric stretch limo that I can afford.", "$60 for a movie ticket1", "Illegal immigration; protecting maids, gardeners, dog-walkers and nannies everywhere1", "Anti-American, Words to live by!" Given the plethora of causes they're sure to be many people ready to take up the mantle.

This is dedicated to Mark Simone, the great radio host in New York City and the inspiration behind these commissions and their stated missions – TM

Actual quotes of the personalities mentioned are written in italics – TM

LAWRENCE O'DONNELL CONFESSES "I MAY HAVE TOURETTE'S SYNDROME"

After spewing a profanity laced and anger filled tirade aimed at the staff of his MSNBC television program, Lawrence O'Donnell made a sorrowful confession to his staff; he admitted that he may have Tourette's syndrome. After all, what other explanation could there be? Sir Telsunn Margraves agrees.

New York, NY – After his usual 'thank you' to Rachel Maddow, her fellow MSN-BC® host, Lawrence O'Donnell begins his prime-time show, "Last Word with Lawrence O'Donnell." The program begins with his traditional anti-Trump commentary; this time about the president's lack of understanding on his visit to Texas after Hurricane Harvey hit Houston.

During the program O'Donnell is caught, off camera, making a profanity laced tirade over a technical glitch that occurred during the opening. Initially O'Donnell questions personnel in the control room about what he hears as a voice in the background. He asks, *"What's going on? Why don't I have sound?"* but a few moments later the glitch seems to have been fixed. Soon after however the problem returns and that is the beginning of a shocking diatribe spit out by O'Donnell and directed at anyone and everyone in the control room. At first the host gripes, but he tries to keep it professional and on track, O'Donnell however seems to get even angrier as a producer counts down to camera time. "Five...four...three...two...one..." and that's when everything goes off the rails.

In a low voice, *"F*ckin'... Goddammit"* is O'Donnell's first reaction as everyone in the studio works feverishly to fix the problem. All would have been well but, as luck would have it, the problem returns with a vengeance. The next comment heard from the show's host is *"You have insanity in my earpiece"* O'Donnell says, trying to keep a semblance of order to what is fast becoming chaos. He tries to keep calm as he begins to introduce the evening's guest panelists but all involved can see O'Donnell is losing all sense of balance. It is then all hell seems to break loose.

The following is a transcript of O'Donnell's reaction to what is taking place: *"Stop the hammering! Stop the hammering out there! Who's got a hammer? Where is it? Where's the hammer?"*

"Is it on the — go up on the other floor! Somebody go up there and stop the hammering! Stop the hammering! I'll go down to the goddamn floor myself and stop it! Keep the goddamn commercial break going."

*"Where's f*ckin' [MSNBC® president] Phil Griffin? I don't care who the f*ck you have to call. Stop the hammering!"*

"Empty out the goddamn control room and find out where this is going on! (Pointing up then down) It's either there or there! Or out there somewhere! The woman talking in my ear was talking about the Labor Day special."

*"Repeatedly… f*ckin' out of control sh*t… Jesus Christ! Crazy f*ckin' sounds coming in my ear. This f*ckin' stupid hammering. It just f*cking sucks, it just f*cking sucks to be out here with this out of control sh*t."*

After all had calmed down, a contrite and embarrassed host tries to find the words that would explain such an uncalled for outburst to his staff but he just blurts out…"I have a confession to make, I may have Tourette's syndrome." I think that Lawrence O'Donnell is expecting shock and dismay as well as sympathy from the crew but they just knowingly look at each other. A few brave souls even go up to O'Donnell and put their arms around his shoulder and say, "We kinda figured something was wrong long ago!" and one person says, "That could explain what we have suspected for years."

Now Lawrence O'Donnell seems to be blinking his eyes rapidly and appears to be in the state of shock. "How the f*ck could you know that?"

A spokesperson for the group is chosen. Her name is Melony (last name left out at her request), and she is an unpaid intern at MSNBC®. Melony says, "Well, you've shown many of the symptoms associated with Tourette's such as barking or yelping which you do at times, grunting repeating what someone else says, shouting and swearing like you did tonight." This is a revelation to O'Donnell who felt no one had noticed. He could only stand there in disbelief and mutter, "…but…but…" Melony continues to inform her boss, "We have also noticed that you experience certain types of movements such as blinking, making a face, mouth twitching and shoulder shrugging. That combined with other manifestations indicates the prognosis, from our perspective, that you could be suffering from Tourette's and you really should see a doctor."

"…but…but…but…" O'Donnell cannot form the words to express his total bewilderment. Melony sees that he is perplexed and tries to explain. "My mom is a doctor, my dad is a doctor, my granddad is a doctor and my sister and brother both are doctors. I was going to choose a career in reporting but after this I'm changing my major to pre-med and I can't wait until I leave this hell-hole...by the way, I quit."

All statements in italics are Lawrence O'Donnell's actual quotes – TM

The employee of MSNBC® who disclosed this episode was fired - TM

ROBERT MUELLER ADDS MEMBERS TO HIS TEAM INVESTIGATING PRESIDENT TRUMP

Special Investigator Mueller has come to a spirited defense of James Comey as part of his investigation of possible collusion of the Trump campaign with Russia and put to rest the fallacy of his close relationship with former director Comey. Sir Telsunn Margraves has examined the preponderance of work generated by the Russia collusion investigation and he was told that it requires Robert Mueller must add additional staff of experienced professionals. You will be surprised who has been appointed to his staff.

Washington, DC – Former FBI Director and special counsel Robert Mueller is currently leading an investigation into President Donald Trump's possible collusion with Russia before, during, and after the presidential campaign as well as anything that may happen in the future. The investigation has become so far reaching and all-encompassing that the special counsel's office is now expanding his staff to meet the demands of their mission. In a hastily called press conference Robert Mueller tells all the media in attendance, as well as his current staff, of all the issues that need to be addressed.

With his current staff of 793 attorneys and support staff behind him, Mueller addresses the standing room only crowd, "Ladies and gentlemen, if I look angry it is because I am. A charge has been made that I can never be objective and that former FBI Director James Comey and I are best of friends. This is a conspiracy that has been spread by the vast right-wing media and has no relationship to the truth. Director Comey and I both are former FBI Directors as are a number of other persons who have held this position. Sometimes we have a drink together at the 'Former FBI Directors Alumni Association Bar and Grill" on K Street in Washington DC. After a few cocktails we may decide not to drive home. Maybe we'll stay there for dinner or, for safety reasons, we'll sleep at each other houses. We are both members of the same country club, but I only sponsored him for membership, and he is a much better golfer than me. We went to the same schools, attended a cooking class together teaching us about Asian-Fusion cuisine, we bought twin 2017 Ford® Mustang GT 500s but his is red and mine is yellow so who can even think we are that closely aligned. Our families occasionally take vacations together but seldom, if ever, share the same room, I am godfather to one of his sons and he is godfather to my daughter but that's merely a necessary formality of the Christian faith. If anyone can use that disparate information to attempt to draw some close connection between James Comey and myself, I challenge them, put up or shut up."

Special Investigator Robert Mueller continues, "Given that no one can find any motives other than ones that are pure and honest, our team needs to be able to put into place additional qualified people who can work on the matter at hand. The sworn purpose of this investigation is to find as many people guilty as possible and bring it to a swift conclusion...even if it takes seven years. I have been accused of padding the current investigation staff with men and women who are democrats, who supported democrats for elections, who have given to democrat candidates and causes and even wear those little pins that say Democrats 2018. This, of course, cannot be further from the truth. While many of these lawyers on my staff are considered die-hard democrats themselves, having contributed money to the Hillary for President Campaign and continually support other democrats running for office, no one should read anything into that."

Finally Mueller feels he needs to address two controversies that surround former FBI Director James Comey. "I want to take this opportunity to introduce new members of my team that will be assisting in this investigation but before I do so I want to address some controversies surrounding former Director Comey. It has been allegedly disclosed, and allegedly illegal, I think, that James Comey wrote a letter allegedly exonerating Hillary Clinton of any alleged culpability in her very minor, completely inconsequential use of an allegedly private email server to allegedly house allegedly confidential and secret government communications and documents. Mr. Comey has a very allegedly logical explanation, and I would like to read a letter he has written to me to those of you present." Robert Mueller puts his reading glasses on and unfolds a piece of paper and begins reading.

       "Dear Special Counsel Mueller,

            I hope you and your family are well and I hope that Ann enjoyed her class reunion at Miss Porter's School in Farmington, Connecticut. Farmington is such a lovely area and I hope you both had the opportunity to enjoy the *Hill-Stead Museum*, it's a wonderful place and we must try to visit there with our wives, but now onto business. There has been a specious rumor that, months prior to the conclusion of our investigation, I wrote a letter exonerating Hillary Clinton of all guilt in her regrettable and *extremely careless* use of her home email server.

This letter has been entirely misconstrued and I want to clarify its purpose and intent. The letter I referenced was merely a personal side project I was working on and is now being taken totally out of context. As I have told you and Ann for years, I long to be a writer of romance novels. In the latest novel I was working on I had not decided on the name of the female character that I wanted to use. Given that I was experiencing writers block, I decided to use Hillary Clinton as the name temporarily. It was an easy name to remember and has a familiar ring to it. I was also intrigued by the idea that someone, highly placed in a fictitious Washington DC Administration. My main character would use a home email server to conduct business while meeting and falling in love with the computer repair man. I think that no one should read more into this than what I have said. This totally fictitious storyline formed the basis of a plot for the novel and illustrates the old adage of art imitating life.

I want to thank you for the opportunity to clear the air and I hope we can put this small matter behind us.

All my best to your lovely wife and daughters and I'll see you at the Washington DC Canasta Tournament.

Best regards,

Jim

PS. A story has just broken in the mass media and I want to let you know that it is completely false. What kind of President and Secretary of State would sell 20% of our uranium to Russia? Russia! Can you imagine, Russia! Let me tell you, if Hillary Clinton did it for a mere $145,000,000 she would be out of her mind and you and I both know she is perfectly normal. JC

Robert Mueller looks up and says, "Isn't it refreshing to get the complete details of something so potentially explosive, and find out it was nothing but an innocent error. In addition, I would also like to address the totally unproven, and what appears to be spurious allegations of Russian collusion by the Obama Administration in selling twenty percent of US Uranium to Russian companies directly under the control of Vladimir Putin. I have undertaken a strenuous review of the many documents related to this allegation, and it became apparent that there was nothing but an entirely legal and perfectly innocent arrangement on the part of President Obama, Secretary of State Clinton, former Attorney General Eric Holder, nine agencies including the FBI, Bureau of Labor Statistics, the IRS, *National Endowment for the Arts*, *The George Soros Foundations*, *PETA*, Justice Department, among others. In the name of full disclosure, I also wish to confirm that I was the FBI Director at the time the Uranium One situation was all taking place. I think that it is important to not be distracted by the yet unproven claim that the Clinton Foundation received $145,000,000 from businessmen associated with the Russian government or the exorbitant speech fees paid to former President Clinton by the Russians. The real investigation should remain focused on Trump's campaign associates and their connection to Russia. So far after many months we haven't found anything, but I think we are getting closer to not finding anything else but we will keep looking.

Now onto the next controversy and that is the police report of accusation made by Mr. Comey related to his being a victim of sexual harassment by Supreme Court Justice Ruth Bader Ginsburg. She has categorically denied this allegation and all we can say is that this is an ongoing investigation and the details of this matter are confidential and under review."

Finally, I would like to introduce the next members of our team investigating alleged Russian collusion with the Trump-for-President campaign, the alleged negotiations to build a Trump Palace, Casino and Spa in St. Petersburg in 2002, the alleged Trump investment into the Russian company "Matuska Dolls R' Us" in 1996, Trump's alleged love of borsht and Russian dressing in 2017 and prior years, Trump's alleged invitation for Vladimir Putin to attend Mr. Trump's Annual Halloween Party in 2003 as well as investigating the rumor swirling around the president that Vladimir Putin is actually Donald Trump's love child. There are also a number of other alleged suspicious dealings from unnamed sources that I am not able to go into at this time but they are under active investigation."

Robert Mueller turns to the right and motions to an aide and says, "Please ask the newest members of the team to join us on stage." One by one the people walk on stage and a collective gasp comes from the crowd as they are immediately recognized. The audience is nearly in a state of shock, but as the realization sinks in TV and news reporters begin to cheer.

Mueller asks for quiet as he makes the introduction. "Please ladies and gentlemen, please can I have quiet. I would like to introduce our distinguished team members to you.

- First, on the left is the world renowned pastor, activist for social justice, and graduate from the Richard Simmons Deal-A-Meal® program, the Reverend Al Sharpton. Al Sharpton has been at the forefront of anything he can get his hands on and he has achieved notoriety for hosting his own TV program and riots. At first he was reluctant to join our team when I stressed that he needs to be completely objective, but after long discussions he promised me he would.

- The next member of the team needs no introduction. He is one of the richest men in the world and has been a leader in allowing his company to get the factual, untrue, non-fake, erroneous, verifiable and false information to the public. He feels it is an important objective so citizens can know the issues before they choose to elect democrats or liberals, never-Trumpers, progressive left-wing agitators as well as others. Ladies and gentlemen, billionaire Mark Zuckerberg of Facebook®. Mark made a humorous comment when he told me that with all his money he's has no reason to be anything but completely objective.

- Another member of great renown that has agreed to be on our team is a woman whose beauty and intellect go hand in hand. She is a star of stage and screen, she is an award winning songstress and her ability to distill complex thought into a spate of profanity laced diatribes is second to none; ladies and gentlemen, please welcome Madonna! It should be noted that Madonna has promised me that she will be completely objective.

- We also have another billionaire that has put his money where his mouth is. For years he has looked to protect every card-carrying person from freedom of thought. His philanthropic causes have made headlines in news media and now he has agreed to add his not so small voice to our humble team. Now that he has been kicked out of Hungry, we are fortunate to have him on our team. He has also promised me that he will continue to be completely objective, ladies and gentlemen, George Soros.

- Next there is a woman who needs little or no introduction. When I reviewed potential candidates for this position on the team I searched far and wide and I couldn't find anyone more qualified. Even though she was vanquished in the recent presidential election, Hillary Clinton holds no grudges and promises me that she will be completely objective, and I believe her. Ladies and gentlemen, President, I mean former Democrat presidential candidate, Hillary Clinton.

- Finally, and most importantly we have secured someone on our team that is above and beyond reproach. He is a former president of the United States and the first African-American ever to hold the office, Barrack Hussein Obama. Although there has been recent allegation of many alleged corrupt practices and alleged scandals on the part of former Administration officials, we have chosen to ignore them. I never even considered mentioning it to the former president, but he brought it up himself and told me that he would be completely objective.

I trust this effort to be forthright and honest about our investigation, and it will not fall on deaf ears, so we make this promise; It is our profound hope that this matter will be brought to a swift, if not long and drawn out, conclusion."

THE OBAMA LEGACY; IT'S ALL IN HOW YOU LOOK AT IT

Lately former President Barrack Hussein Obama has sustained a number of ugly blots on his presidency. This is not something that can be tolerated, so former Attorney General Eric Holder has been appointed by Obama to set the record straight, and to highlight a few of the many accomplishments of the eight years of his presidency. In an expansive explanation, Holder and other Obama Administration members recount these successes to Sir Telsunn Margraves and other members of the news media.

Los Angeles Times – Since leaving office, many reports have been swirling about the Obama Administration and the number of mistakes and missteps made during his tenure as president. Critics point to examples of poor judgement in dealing with foreign nations, the seeming deterioration of relations between various races, a plethora of presidential orders that have been reversed, even allegations of illegal actions taken by the Obama Administration in surveillance of political opponents. These reports have badly tarnished an image of integrity that the former president had hoped would become his legacy.

Former administration officials, now working closely with Obama, have been feverishly searching some positive news that they can use to resurrect the downward spiral of public opinion for the past president...and they may have come up with an answer.

Former Attorney General Eric Holder has been designated as the spokesperson for Barrack Hussein Obama on matters of importance regarding the former president. The atmosphere is electric as Holder walks to the podium on a make shift stage in front of the empty lot that will soon be the location for the Obama Presidential Library. All current staff and former officials, already standing behind Eric Holder, are smiling broadly, 'high-fiving' and 'fist-pumping' each other. These men and women know that this is an important first step in the rehabilitation of President Obama's image in order to preserve his legacy and they are eagerly anticipating what Holder will say.

Holder steps up to the podium and smiling broadly he begins. "I want to state unequivocally that the impact of the presidency of Barrack Hussein Obama is historic in its depth and breath. There are so many positive details as a result of the eight years of Obama governance that it actually boggles the mind. I would like to take this opportunity to read from a document that his staff, friends and Democrat Party leaders have been instrumental in preparing. It is just a very small list of achievements we can point to with great pride but one that should be etched in stone for posterity. The intent of this announcement is simple; it is to highlight impactful actions and decisions made by the 43rd president and memorialize what will become known as "The Obama Legacy!" There is thunderous applause among both those on the stage and the reporters in the audience.

Former Attorney General Holder continues, "Early on in his first term, President Obama was given the opportunity to show that he is committed to becoming a post-racial president to cement the bonds that exist between persons, both black and white. The opportunity was thrust upon him when his good friend Henry Lewis "Skip" Gates was having problems getting into his front door. In order to access his home, Mr. Gates and his driver busted into the house. A short while later Skip Gates was confronted by the police who had received a call from one of the neighbors. The 'white neighbor' called what turned out to be a 'white policeman' to report what appeared to be a possible break-in of the home. Lucia Whalen, the original witness to this incident, when asked to describe the perpetrator of the possible break-in said to the police dispatcher, *"One looked kind of Hispanic, but I'm not really sure...and the other one entered and I didn't see what he looked like at all."*

"Officer Crowley, the white police officer who responded to the alleged break-in, asked Skip Gates to step outside. Crowley explained he was investigating the report of a break-in. Gates opened the front door and said, *"Why, because I'm a black man in America?"* Professor Gate was understandably angered about being black and by the intrusion of the police but this resulted in an exchange of words, imagine, an exchange of words, already we are seeing the positive impact of Barrack Obama." Eric Holder wipes a tear from his eyes as he notes, "People of all colors are speaking to each other. Ladies and gentlemen, isn't his amazing. The president had not been in office more than seven months when a witness, probably a white racist, so totally color blind since the election of Obama, that she could not even tell what alleged color the alleged people who were allegedly breaking in. The police officer, who also could have been an alleged white racist, and could have allegedly beaten Skip Gates to within an inch of his life, kept his Billy club and gun and holstered.

When notified of the incident, President Obama handled the situation with historic aplomb, clear-headed calm and his characteristic even-handedness said *"Now, I've – I don't know, not having been there and not seeing all the facts, what role race played in that. But I think it's fair to say, number one, any of us would be pretty angry; number two, that the Cambridge police acted stupidly in arresting somebody when there was already proof that they were in their own home. And number three, what I think we know separate and apart from this incident is that there is a long history in this country of African-Americans and Latinos being stopped by law enforcement disproportionately. That's just a fact."*

"Well I'm sure you all know the rest, Obama bought a beer for the two men and now we can say without equivocation, racial harmony reigns across America because of Barrack Obama." Eric Holder surveys those assembled in the room who give the statement a resounding cheer and it was observed that even some hard-nosed reporters had tears in their eyes.

Holder continues, "When you consider that there were other potentially explosive situations, it was truly fortunate that Barrack Obama was President. Consider Trevon Martin being shot by white Hispanic man, George Zimmerman. Let me read to you a profound statement from the man himself, Barrack Obama, *'There are very few African-American men in this country who haven't had the experience of being followed when they were shopping in a department store. That includes me. There are very few African-American men who haven't had the experience of walking across the street and hearing the locks click on the doors of cars. That happens to me -- at least before I was a senator. There are very few African-Americans who haven't had the experience of getting on an elevator and a woman clutching her purse nervously and holding her breath until she had a chance to get off. That happens often... And that all contributes, I think, to a sense that if a white male teen was involved in the same kind of scenario, that, from top to bottom, both the outcome and the aftermath might have been different.'* Isn't it truly amazing that in one statement the president can deal with issues of race and how everyday experiences can be fun and educational?"

Holder is pleased that the facts seem to be resonating with the news media present and he continues, "There are so many examples of how President Obama has taken potentially explosive situations and turned them into explosive situations meant as teachable moments. What other president has done that?"

"Next I would like to debunk the false impression that is continuing to be spread by nasty, vicious Republicans and Conservative scum, oh I mean alleged scum. This relates to the national debt. While it is true that the debt increased by Ten Trillion

Dollars under President Obama, and while it is also true that the debt accumulated is larger than the past 43 presidents combined, there are many extenuating factors that contributed to this. First, we had to give Iran back more than $150,000,000,000, some of it in cash. In order to get the that amount of cash, we needed to go to thousands of ATMs and for most of them we had to pay a fee. That can add up pretty fast. Second, we needed special funding for a favorite initiative of former first lady Michelle Obama, the "Family Vacation Program." During the Obama presidency nearly $115,000,000 was spent on taking Michelle, Barrack, Malia, Sasha even Michelle's mother away for some quality time together. How many of you would vacation with your mother-in-law, huh? Well thankfully the former President and the former First Lady set the example for all Americans."

Eric Holder had been speaking without stopping for more than few seconds, "Ladies and gentlemen. I need to take a small break and take a drink of water, please forgive me." Holder lifts up a plastic water bottle and drinks. "Ah, that was refreshing, now where was I, oh yes! Third, there was the promise of a nearly trillion dollar spending program for much needed infrastructure programs to rebuild schools, roads, tunnels, bridges and airports. With incredible foresight the president himself created a federal bureaucracy that would be needed to manage such an enormous program. In preparation, the Obama Administration added 1,400,000 new Federal workers, and that's a lot of salary as well as other stuff we give them for free. He also bailed out GM and bailed out the union pension programs that were going bust. Unfortunately when we went to begin the infrastructure programs there was no money left. I am sure that is why many of you wanted a third Obama term. Usually the Constitution would not hold us back but the president, ever the conciliator, decided to forgo a third term and stick with tradition. What a leader, what a visionary...what a man!" Unrestrained applause and cheers explode from the audience as the many reporters feverishly take down each and every syllable uttered by Eric Holder.

Holder continues with his explanation of the $10,000,000,000,000,000 debt accumulated during the Obama Administration terms in office. "Fourth, we needed to fund an additional 10,700,000 food stamp recipients, and I must say, they eat like a lot of people I've seen at White House dinner meetings. By the way are Dennis Ross, Peter Orszag and Susan Rice here? Great, hey guys they'll be food after the press conference. Fifth, we needed to provide extensive funding for the non-partisan, new voter outreach program to register more undocumented immigrants, anti-fa, MS13 members, recent arrivals from Syria, Somalia, Iran, Afghanistan, Yemen, and Palestinian Territories plus those in other parts of the world looking to join the democratic movement and bring peace to our country. As an integral part of the Obama outreach we needed to be sure to provide taxpayer money for food, shelter, clothing, transportation, healthcare and legal aid for those citizens convicted of felony crimes and misdemeanors."

Eric Holder is resolute as he states the following, "Next, we just received word in a joint release from the Los Angeles Times and the Associated Press. In 2016, remember this was the last year of the Obama presidency; here, let me read the headline that appeared in Newsday on September 28th, 'US rate of sexually transmitted diseases, or STDs, hit record highs in 2016. Now you may, in fact, not completely understand the significance of these statistics and how they could be viewed in any kind of positive light, so let me explain. STDs have long been seen as a scourge, but there is always a sunny side to tragedy. If we didn't have more STDs then we wouldn't be having more sex; if we didn't have more sex then people would get even grumpier. If people get grumpier, we couldn't increase federal government spending like we have done during the Obama's tenure. If we didn't increase government spending we couldn't support such programs as the following,

Government Funded Programs and Studies	Federal Government	Amount Budgeted
A study of the effects of Swedish massages on rabbits	NIH	$387,000
Monitor the growth rate of saltmarsh grass	DOI	$10,000
Determine how and why Wikipedia is sexist	NSF	$200,000
Study to see if mothers love dogs as much as they love kids.	NIH	$371,026
The development of a smartphone game called "Kiddio: Food Fight."	FG	$804,254
Undergraduate classes that teach students about laughing and humor.	NEH	$47,000
Teach mountain lions how to walk on treadmills	NSF	$856,000

A grant to construct a robot squirrel to answer why rattlesnakes rarely attack squirrels that wag their tails.	NSF	$325,000
Developing a "Mars menu" to stave off food monotony on manned flight to Mars	NASA	$100,000
A grant to examine the benefit golfers might gain if they used their imagination better.	NSF	$350,000
Experiment that tested fruit flies to discover that male fruit flies are more attracted to younger female fruit flies than older ones.	NIH	$939,771
Teaching Mountain Lions to Ride a Treadmill	NIH	$856,000
Studying how many times "angry" people stab a voodoo doll	NSF	$331,000
Studying the gambling habits of monkeys	NSF	$171,000
Producing the children's musical "Zombie in Love"	NEA	$10,000
Subsidizing Alpaca Poop packaged for use for fertilizer	USDA	$50,000
Produce a "Hallucinatory" Roosevelt/Elvis show	NEA	$10,000
Funding Climate Change Alarmist Video Game	NSF	$5,200,000
Tweeting at Terrorists	State Dept.	$3,000,000
Funding Kids Dressing Like Fruits and Vegetables: $5 million (Un. of TN/USDA)	Univ. of Tenn./USDA	$5,000,000
Help Parents Counter Kids' Refusals to Eat Fruits and Veggies: (NIH)	NIH	$804,254
Studying if Wikipedia is Sexist: (NSF)	NSF	$202,000
NASA Spends $3 Million Looking for Signs of Intelligent Life...in Congress — NASA and Georgetown	NASA/ Georgetown	$3,000,000
Federal Government Paying Salaries to Hundreds of Thousands of Tax Cheats (IRS)	IRS	$3.5Billion (unpaid taxes)
$50,000 spent by the Army to study the bomb-detecting capabilities of elephants.	US Army	$50,000
U.S. Department of Agriculture (USDA) project to combat a plant disease found in garden roses	USDA	$4,600,000

These are just a very few of the in-depth studies funded by the Obama Administration. I have prepared handouts and you can pick up a copy to see those noteworthy programs that can be directly or indirectly attributed to the record high STDs.

It is most important; we needed to fund Obamacare. Have you guys seen what that costs? Well if you haven't, I think you might want to ask Jonathan Gruber! Lots of people getting lots of healthcare for free and that is a true mitzvah as we say in Yiddish. One problem though, who's going to pay for all this? Well as you might expect President Obama, as usual, had the answer and even though he's not president, that does not making him any less American. He has promised to share the details of this new economic model with whoever will be the Democrat party nominee in 2020. Now, I'm going to ask that same Mr. Jonathan Gruber, the chief economist and Obamacare Architect, to come up to the podium and explain how we will pay for it all. By the way, for those who are concerned, he promises not to call the American people *stupid* again!"

Jonathan Gruber steps up to the mic and receives only polite applause. "Thank you all for giving me that warm welcome. I have sat with President Obama and I know where his heart is and I've devised a plan that will help to create the new Obamacare that will be fully funded and not cost a single dollar of increased income taxes to any American except for the top 1%. Speaking of the top 1%, our plan will raise their Federal taxes to 92% of wages, capital gains, dividends, money socked away overseas, original oil paintings, small businesses, family farms plus all the things rich people hide or try not to tell us about...hey Buffett, Gates, Zuckerberg, Bezos, JayZ and Beyonce, George Clooney, Jerry Seinfeld, Oprah Winfrey, LeBron James, and all the rest of you guys, we know who you are and know where to find you, so watch out!" The audience applauds and laughs.

Gruber thinks he's on a roll and he continues with his list, "Second, we will raise the fees for all medical devices by 100%. We think that this will be painless for most people, well maybe not painless but certainly comfortable, well maybe not comfortable anyway, you need to buy this stuff or suffer and die so just cough it up. Next we thought we would sell some of our old missiles to North Korea. The president and I figured that given they are going to build them anyway, why not make a few bucks*. Next, we are also going to raise the fee for entering the national parks. Currently the fees range from about $20 to $100 for individuals and families but we believe that people would pay much more to enjoy the parks while funding better healthcare so we are raising the fees starting at $983 to no higher than $5,212 per person per day and that includes use of all facilities, no hidden charges. After I ran all the numbers, however, we still came up short so I discussed with the president the option of raising taxes on all Americans, but he steadfastly refused. He told me that the American people had suffered enough over the last eight years and he didn't want to see them suffer any more. So, in lieu of raising taxes, we thought that it would be better to have a small increase in the monthly family premium of 720%, and a significantly smaller 418% increase for single policy holders. We would also recommend an increase in the deductibles to $25,000 per person and an average copay of $1,804 for each doctor visit.

Finally and most importantly there's Russia. President Obama and Vladimir Putin have always had a close personal relationship. He gave all that money to Secretary of State Clinton and I think that Putin will be more than happy to contribute funds for Obamacare in order to save this vital benefit to the American people. All told, in this way we can pledge that Obamacare remains solvent, everyone who can't afford insurance will be covered AND we guarantee that there will never be any increase in what you pay for your healthcare for one full year!"

I have been told that we are late for the free buffet lunch that is being sponsored by George Soros and CNN, but before we conclude I want to mention other initiatives of the Obama Administration that must not go unnoticed. *Fast and Furious* to get guns out of the US and into Mexico, *The IRS Oversight* of Conservative Groups because of the terror these groups represent, *Covert Review of Journalists* like James Rosen, to keep them honest, *Hillary's valuable Back-up Servers* in our effort to allow women to work from home. Unfortunately we don't have time to discuss the false reporting and untold benefits that center on *The Benghazi Scandal, The Bowe Bergdahl Scandal, The GSA Scandal, The NSA Scandal, The VA death-list Scandal, The Solyndra Scandal, The Pigford Scandal, The Iran Nuclear and Ransom Payment Scandals* and so many more.

"Ladies and gentlemen, these are just a few examples I've highlighted today, but the Swedish meatballs and eggplant parmigiana are getting cold so we must take our leave. In closing, I would like to thank all of you for being here to celebrate what we have accomplished during the Obama presidency. Unfortunately so much has gone unnoticed and unappreciated by all except the mainstream media, but we feel it is important to continue our dialogue with the American people. I realize that many, if not all of you, long for the day when the Obama's were still in the White House, but there is always hope, so let's pray for HILLARY in 2020!"

All quotes in italics are actual and attributable to the people quoted – TM

All actual government funded programs are listed in italics – TM

NIH (National Institute of Health, DOI (Dept. of Interior), NSF (National Science Foundation), FG (Federal Government), NEH (National Endowment of the Humanities), IRS (Internal Revenue Service, NASA (National Aeronautics and Space Administration), USDA (US Dept. of Agriculture), US Army, NSF (National Science Foundations), HHS (Health and Human Services), DOI (Dept. Of Interior), NEA (National Education Association)

One of the funding options for Obamacare that included selling missiles to North Korea will unfortunately have to be cancelled due to the Trump initiative to denuclearize the Korean Peninsula. An alternative funding plan has been shifted to providing missiles to Iran instead-TM

NORTH WEST GIVES NEW DIRECTION TO AMERICA?

Kim Kardashian confidently claims *"Anyone can run the US better, my daughter would be better (than Donald Trump)"*. This comment generated a controversy that precipitated a press conference called by Ms. Kardashian. At the press conference, she allowed the newsmen and women to see for themselves the brilliance behind her four year old daughter's grasp of politics and world affairs. Sir Telsunn Margraves even admitted that North is quite the astute observer of the world at large.

Los Angeles, CA – In a candid comment, Kim Kardashian sounded off about her take on President Donald Trump, *"Every single day when you can't really believe what's*

going on, the next day it's something else even more crazy and tragic. It's really scary, the world that we're living in now. And when you did feel safe at home, now with Trump in presidency, you just don't feel safe anymore."

As if to try and reinforce her point, Ms. Kardashian continued by saying, *"Anyone can run the US better my daughter would be better."* Kim and husband Kanye West the noted rapper and music phenom, singer, songwriter, record producer, fashion designer and entrepreneur have a four year old daughter, North West. North has become the focal point of discussions on social media and Kim Kardashian has called a hastily prepared new conference in order to prove her contention.

Kim and daughter, North, approach the podium with the child holding her mother's hand. There is a two foot wooden riser that North stands on in order to be seen by the multitude of reporters present. Kim begins, "First, I would like to thank you all for coming to this press briefing. I think it is important..." just then North commences to tug at her mother's sleeve. Kim turns and says; "Not now honey, mommy's speaking." North is beginning to look anxious, "But mommy..." Kim says, Honey this will have to wait." North is now looking panicked and tugs very strongly at Kim's sleeve, "But mommy..." Kim sighs and says, "What is so important North?" The child replies, "I have to make wee-wee." Now Kim, fully appreciating the urgency of the child's predicament, motions to one of the child's nannies and tells her to take North to make on the potty.

"I apologize for that unscheduled interruption but let me continue." Kim continues speaking for a few minutes but stops mid-sentence, "I think it is important..." Just then North runs back on stage and excitedly proclaims, "Mommy, I made poopy too and I wiped my own tushy!" Kim could not have been prouder! "That's wonderful honey but let's tell these nice people why you would make a better president than Donald Trump."

North says, "Mommy, can I have a juice box?"

Kim says, "Not now, first I want you to tell everyone why you would make a great president."

North thinks for a bit and says, "Can I have chocolate milk instead?"

Now Kim is getting frustrated, "No, not now, tell these people what you told me this morning about the North Koreans test firing an ICBM in order to deliver a nuclear warhead to the mainland of the United States."

North says, "Mommy can you tie my shoes?"

Kim is getting exasperated, "North, tell the people about what you would do regarding the potential for total annihilation of the human race by Trump and Kim Jung Un. Come on North tell them what you would do."

North faces everyone and says, "Given the historical reference, previous administrations have sold advanced system to China that was developed in the United States. These are the same systems were then given to North Korea by China. Now it appears that the North Korean ICBM technologies became far more advanced under the Obama, Bush and Clinton administrations than initially believed. It is this lack of seriousness when tackling the real threats to global peace that have caused previous administrations to ignore or postpone any meaningful solution rather than confronting these grave issues immediately. China, Russia and now Iran have, in one way or the other, supported and enabled the Exalted Leader Un to dictate all the terms to any normalization. In exchange what has the United State received? Nothing can you believe it, nothing! All the United States has to show for its efforts is a long list of broken promises and the ever growing threat of nuclear proliferation. Unfettered and unhinged, Kim Jong Un has been provoking the United States and our allies while his people starve. The recent overtures made by the Trump Administration to force sanctions on North Korea are having a profound effect on the potential for peace. The denuclearization of the Korean Peninsula is an unconditional demand that President Trump has made, and it appears that Kim Jong Un recognizes the steadfastness of America's resolve in seeing this new initiative comes to pass. This can be considered a major step forward as I believe the homeland must remain secure. We should do all that is possible to assure this, and I agree wholeheartedly with President Trump and his initiative to denuclearize North Korea. Mommy, I'm hungry."

Kim seems a bit confused, "Uh this is awkward. No more to eat, you just had fruit, a Gogurt frozen yogurt, a Nutri-grain bar and handful of Cheerio's, I think you've had enough."

"But mommy..."

"No buts about it young lady, now tell the people hear how you feel about the selection of Neil Gorsuch to serve on the Supreme Court."

North sighs and says, "Given the current make-up of the court, constitutionalists versus liberal-activists, and given the fact that Judge Gorsuch replaced conservative Antonin Scalia, I feel the choice was appropriate. The choice of Judge Gorsuch brings that court into a more equal alignment, and in this, I agree with President Trump. Mommy, my corset is too tight..."

Kim is becoming more embarrassed by North's answers. Kim bends over and loosens the strings that are tied to the dress North is wearing. "Sorry honey, is that better?"

"Yes. Mommy, can daddy bring Mr. Wiggle Head out so I can hold him?"

"North, you know Mr. Wiggle Head is home and daddy is working so let's tell everyone how you would react to the ISIS threat in the Middle East and how you would safeguard American interests and safety at home."

"Mommy, are you sure Mr. Wiggle Head is at home?"

"Yes, North, now answer the question."

North is hoping this will be over soon but she knows her mommy and she knows that nothing is over until she says it's over so she shares her views, "This is one of the most serious threats that we face as a nation and a community of nations. ISIS is looking to establish a caliphate in the Middle East and what that means to the people living there could be catastrophic. These Islamic terrorists have received the aid and support of Iranian regimes, using billions of dollars the United States has given them to fund terror. ISIS had sought the death of all infidels and the destruction of any and all emerging democratic nations with the caliphate holding supreme sway over all. Israel would be the prime target of these terrorists and it is in our mutual interest to protect Israel from certain annihilation. Although the Trump Administration has made enormous strides in ridding the middle east of ISIS terrorists, I believe that we cannot and should not fight this battle alone. We will need the assistance and resolve of all middle-eastern nations to defeat this terror and allow all of their citizens to live and worship in peace. Finally, I am in complete solidarity with President Trump moving the US Embassy to Jerusalem, the historical capital of Israel. Mommy, pull my finger!"

Kim feels a headache coming on and says, "North, not now we haven't finished yet."

"Mommy can you just pull my finger?"

Kim heaves another sigh and says, "Will you promise to answer one more question if I pull your finger?"

"Yes, mommy I promise!"

Kim pulls North's finger and she lays the loudest fart ever to come from a four-year old girl! The reporters break out in hysterical laughter, North breaks out into giggles and Kim is mortified. "Daddy taught me to do that!"

Kim's face is turning purple with rage as she says, "Oh he did, did he. Just wait until I see daddy tonight. Now, North, remember you promised so here is the last question you need to answer. What would you do with regard to granting amnesty to the 'Dreamers" and how would you protect America's borders?"

North knows that she will not get Mr. Wiggle-Head, chocolate milk or food until she answers so she thinks, here goes, "In order to be totally fair, I believe that it is not in the best interest of our country to grant blanket amnesty to undocumented immigrants or illegal-aliens, DACA or otherwise. In order to provide DACA or Dreamers with the means to gain legal status in the US, it would require Congress to do something about passing comprehensive immigration reform. I would offer to grant green cards to the Dreamers and welcome them to apply for citizenship under a series of strict regulations. I would enforce existing immigration regulations especially those abusing the so-called 'anchor babies' rules, chain migration, the visa lottery program and I would initiate e-verify immediately." North now scans the crowd of reporters to see their jaws dropping to the floor. North smiles and continues, "Another extremely important element to comprehensive immigration reform is our need to secure the border and building a wall is only a part of the solution. I believe that we should expand the number of border patrol and ICE agents so that the Mexican cartels seeking to illegally transport and sell drugs in the US can be caught and incarcerated or sent back to their countries of origin. The border wall is a bit more complex, but I believe that we should build the wall as a symbol of sovereignty and use it as a further deterrent to all coming here without authorization. I would welcome immigration just not illegal immigration. I would like to close my discussion with two quotes; the first quote is from Allan West who said *'One of the critical issues that we have to confront is illegal immigration, because this is a multi-headed Hydra that affects our economy, our health care, our education systems, our national security, and also our local criminality.'* The second quote is from former secretary of state, Hillary Clinton who said, *'I am, you know, adamantly against illegal immigration.'*"

Kim is totally flummoxed, but she is beaming proudly at her daughter and she closed the press briefing by saying, I want to thank you again for coming and please be safe going home."

North tugs at her mother's sleeve and asks, "Mommy, are we related to Allan West?" Kim replies, "I don't know, but we'll ask daddy when we get home."

All items in italics are actual quotes - TM

THE FIRST ANNUAL ABSOLUTELY... POSITIVELY... GENUINE... REAL FAKE NEWS AWARDS

Washington DC – The atmosphere surrounding the Kennedy Center for the Performing Arts is electric with excitement as the crowds are ushered into the Opera House theatre for the *First Annual Absolutely, Positively, Genuine Real Fake News Awards.*

In spite of the cold weather and it being New Year's Eve, it seems that everyone is excited to be part of this event! The women are dressed in elegant, long flowing gowns and the men are all dressed in black tie as they exit from limousines lined up for blocks. A capacity crowd of 2,362 are present and the audience is a virtual "Who's Who" of personalities from news media, entertainment and the digital media world. The notables are here for what has been called "The *Academy Awards* or *Oscars©* of Fake News" lovingly referred to as, "*The Falsies©*." Being awarded a *Falsie©* recognizes those in the media-entertainment industrial complex for its contributions and achievements highlighting the best in fake stories, false claims, unnamed sources, prejudicial presentations and old-fashioned outright lying. The icons of news media approach their work with a genuine desire to create confusing narratives for their readers, viewers, online, digital and mobile users and listeners and this will be proudly on display tonight!

The lights go dim in the audience and the announcer proudly proclaims, "Now, ladies and gentlemen across America and around the world, please give a warm welcome to our host, the elucidator, illuminator and enlightener-in-chief, Sir Telsunn Margraves!"

The audience cheers and applauds loudly as Sir Telsunn Margraves walks center stage and acknowledges the overwhelming show of affection and admiration. Sir Telsunn Margraves begins, "To all assembled here, I want to express my gratitude for that much appreciated and entirely appropriate welcome."

The audience laughs and continues to cheer Sir Telsunn as he smiles and politely asks for quiet so he can continue. "This evening is a special celebration of Fake News and the media outlets that promulgate such noteworthy flights of fancy. I must confess that this was quite a daunting undertaking in that there is so much fake news to review and consider that I would be able to hold an awards show weekly and not run out of noteworthy items. That being said, the awards bequeathed to the winning organizations are well earned and deserve to be featured for their style, imagination and wonderful spirit lovingly presented as whoppers."

Sir Telsunn reaches into the inside pocket of his tuxedo and takes out a list and begins to read to the audience. "As this is the first annual Absolutely, Positively, Genuine, Real Fake News Awards presentation I sincerely hope you will find this both entertaining and instructive. For all of you in attendance, this will certainly qualify as your personal jaunty romp into the absurdity of the deep state, media-industrial complex and the progressive mind. I believe it is also instructive to address the rules and structure of the competition and the criteria for selection of the winners. We have different categories and our panel of adjudicators has painstakingly reviewed each and every nomination. During the first round we made our initial eliminations, the second round consisted of ranking the top five to nine fake news nominees and in the third round the final selections are made. We are privileged to have surprise celebrity presenters that will be introducing the top nominees, as well as a special surprise award to make this an evening to remember."

The audience is excited at the prospect of seeing celebrities and the surprise that Sir Telsunn Margraves has promised. "Now let us commence with the awards ceremony. Our first category is such an important repository of fake news that it is a shame we are forced to limit the nominees. Man-made global warming is the cornerstone of fake news and it has generated so much contradictory evidence that one may feel the need to excuse the errors in reporting; one might but WE WON'T! Now let me introduce the celebrity presenter of the man-made global warming Falsie© Award. She is a genuine super-star and a number one recording artist. Her ex-husband, Russell Brand has called her 'vapid, vacuous and plastic" but in the name of propriety please call her Katy Perry!"

The crowd now erupts in raucous cheers as Katy Perry walks center stage and waves to the audience. Katy Perry walks out onto the stage as the orchestra plays her mega-hit "Hot N' Cold." She hugs Sir Telsunn as he hands her the envelopes for the first category. Katy Perry acknowledges the applause and begins the presentation. "Thank you so much for the wonderful welcome. I am thrilled at being selected to present this *Falsie©* and here is the first nominee for the category,

Man-Made Global Warming And the first nominee is...

AL GORE AND THE ENTIRE MOVIE "AN INCONVENIENT TRUTH"

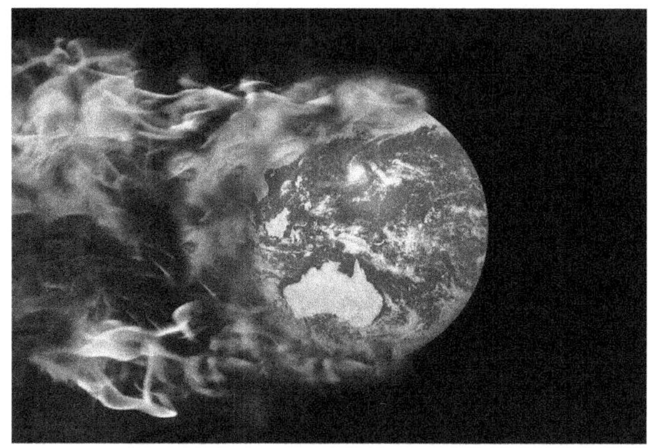

Now, here are just a very few of what can be considered fake news in "An Inconvenient Truth"; No real scientific consensus on the snow reduction causing the drying out of Lake Chad. Where's that? Pacific Islands off Zealand are drowning, but not due to man-made global warming. Iit is due to unwise use of dynamite practices by local fishermen. Ugh, sounds gross-e-ola! Al Gore's claim that 2004 saw a record number of typhoons striking Japan is just plain false, didn't happen! By the way, I just love sushi don't you? Al Gore also tries to show the link between CO2 emissions and invasive plant species, but this has been shown to be due to changes in the way land is being used, not man-made global warming. Polar Bears are dying, oh aren't they so cute and white! Wait, am I allowed to say white? Well it seems that there are more polar bears now than when Al Gore was born. Wow, this is really interesting! Oh and if sea levels are rising why did Al buy an oceanfront mansion. My mansion's not even on the water, well except for the pool."

There is polite applause from the audience as Katy Perry continues. "For the second nominee, we have a chick named Breanna Danielle on her Facebook® post..."

'RACIST' TRUMP ACCUSED OF CREATING HURRICANES TO KILL BLACKS AND HISPANICS

CNN®, MSNBC® and others sent their news guys to Florida so they could stand out in a hurricane and try to tell us Trump is responsible, which I'm sure he was. Anyway, there are so many Facebook® and Twitter® posts about Trump causing changes in the weather that it was so hard to decide. We really liked what Breanna Danielle wrote on Facebook®, "Hey did you know I've got millions of fans on Facebook®, anyway she wrote, *"So they say Hurricane Irma is headed for Miami. Did y'all realize 70% of Miami is Latino, Hispanic, or Cuban?? 44% of the Haitian population in the US resides in Miami. Miami is like Houston in which it is FLOURISHING economically. Coincidence? Trump wants them off our land so what better way than to flood them out. Read between the lines people."* Katy Perry says, "Need I say more? Thank God, I hate Trump too!

Our third nominee is..."

SCIENTISTS WARN OF RISING OCEANS FROM POLAR MELT

"**O**kay, now I read how the New York Times reports a big chunk of ice just fell off something in Antarctica. This sheet of ice has begun falling apart and it seems that no one can stop it. I don't understand why can't we just stop driving or flying or stop cows from farting? I am sure that will help but let me get down from my cereal box. Some of these science guys say man-made global warming, caused by the human-driven release of greenhouse gases, has helped to destabilize the ice sheet. But wait just a 'Hot N' Cold' minute, the Washington Post says Antarctic sea ice levels have shrunk to record low levels for late June 2017." Katy scratches her head..."now who do I believe, they are both nominees for a *Falsie*©? I guess I'll believe the Washington Post because I want to drive and fly, I don't want to walk everywhere. "

The audience laughs and she continues, "The fourth nominee is...

THE UNIVERSITY OF EAST ANGLIA'S CLIMATIC RESEARCH UNIT

"This is a good reason for why I never went to college! Wow! These guys are working overtime! The climate science guys at East Anglia were making up sh*t and hiding it from other guys and now they've got "Climategate!" Hey, don't you just love when they put "gate " at the end of everything?! Anyway *The Guardian*, some Brit newspaper, had an investigation of a lot of emails and stuff hacked from the East Anglia's climatic research or whatever. When *The Guardian* looked at the info, they found that a lot of measurements from Chinese weather stations were seriously faked. All the papers that were supposed to exist could not be produced. Emails? Emails? I've heard something about emails before but where? Sounds fishy to me!"

Katy winks at the audience and they laugh. "The fifth nominee is...

ENERGY FOUNDATION AND TIDES FOUNDATION'S FAVORITE COLOR – GREEN

"Now there's The Energy Foundation and Tides Foundation thing, and from what I understand they distributed billions of 'green' dollars to 'green' groups. I really don't like green; I look hideous in anything green. Anyway, these groups such as the Natural Resources Defense Council, whoever they are, sent staff to the EPA who then directs federal grants back to the same green groups...funny how money goes from one pocket into the other huh! Now technically this is not fake news, but a bunch of major main stream media guys ignored the report so they were nominated.

By the way, now I'm reading this from the card, it says money from the federal government and leftist organizations fuel a lot of misinformation from man-made global warming and they make big bucks from this, and I know how to make big bucks! All in all, there have been over $32.5 billion of federal government grants for climate research from 1989-2009.

Wow, that's even more than I made last year! The sixth nominee is...

FIRST FAKE NEWS, NOW FAKE CLIMATE SCIENCE

"Here's another reason why I didn't go to college. It seems Duke University admitted a scientist, this gal named Erin Potts-Kant, used fake stuff in research on air pollution and lung function thingies. A bunch of these studies were pulled back because of all the funny business going on and that most of it was made up or faked. The scientific scandal, not a scandal like the Weinstein or the other slime bags thing...(aside) oh, sorry. The scandal was revealed by a whistleblower lawsuit filed by Thomas Joseph who claimed Potts-Kant worked on all that false data that she included in published scientific reports. Tsk, tsk, shame on you Erin. When they filed grant applications, well mercy me, they found that the fake data was used to obtain $200 million in federal grants.

Oh, well, it's only our tax money so I guess I'll have to extend my tour dates next year. The seventh nominee is..."

'THE MAIL ON SUNDAY' PUBLISHES – 'EXPOSED: HOW WORLD LEADERS WERE DUPED OVER MAN-MADE GLOBAL WARMING'

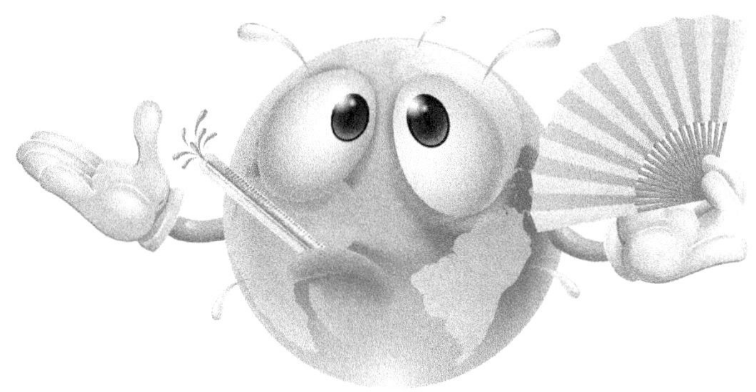

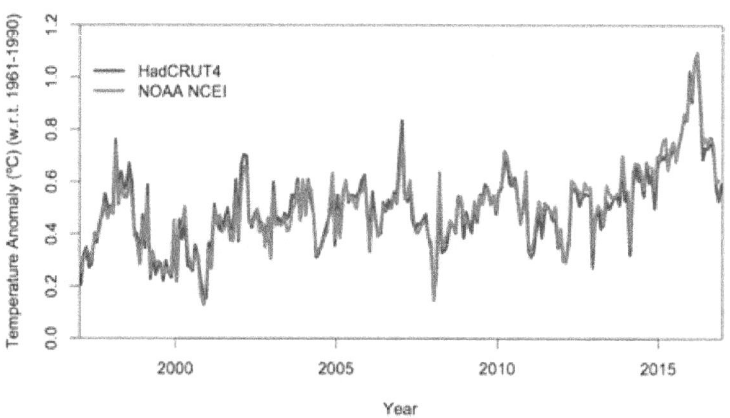

"I just love this next one! The Mail on Sunday', another UK national newspaper, published over two and a half pages of a news story by Mr. David Rose under the headline '*EXPOSED: How world leaders were duped over man-made global warming.*' The story claims that some article published in some science mag, named 'Science',

I only read 'People', said that the United States National Oceanic and Atmospheric Administration (NOAA), and I quote, *"exaggerated man-made global warming and was timed to influence the historic Paris Agreement on climate change"*. David Rose, the guy who wrote *The Mail on Sunday* article was called to the woodshed, I never knew what that means, 'woodshed', oh well and they were forced to admit the article on climate change by one of its reporters was fake news...liar, liar pants on fire!

Our final nominee is another funny one ..."

WASHINGTON POST CLAIMS CLIMATE CHANGE IS CAUSING CHEMICAL PLANTS TO EXPLODE

"This Hurricane Harvey was a total disaster. I even had to cancel a concert because I didn't want to get caught in all that rain and wind. Anywho, it's a good thing to let everyone know what's going on when the big huggy-bears at the Washington Post jumped in. They made a lot of people frightened by hyping stuff about man-made global warming and saying Hurricane *Harvey* caused a chemical plant explosion. Now how in the name of Taylor Swift could they know that? Those sly dickins' did try to backtrack a bit by sayin' *"Scientists are careful to say that it is impossible to pin any single event, like Harvey, on climate change. After all, hurricanes were happening long before the global climate started to change in the 20th century"* Hey, that's right hurricanes happen a lot...I try not to go to Florida during that time of the year, to say nothing about what the humidity does to my hair.

And now for the winner...I am so excited I feel goose-pimply all over. And the winner is..." Katy Perry rips open the envelope, "I'm SOOO excited. The winners are THE ENERGY FOUNDATION AND TIDES FOUNDATION!!!!!! Eric Heitz, Chief Executive Officer and Co-founder of The Energy Foundation and Kriss Deiglmeier, the Chief Executive Officer. Would you both please come up and accept your *Falsie©* Award!" Katy looks around to try and spot Eric and Kriss. Katy says, "Eric? Kriss? Are you guys here?" She listens, there is no answer. Katy looks a bit puzzled and she says, Oh well, maybe they went to the gender neutral bathroom, I'll just hold these *Falsies©* for them back stage. Anyway, thanks so much for this truly great honor to be a presenter at the Fake News Awards, and now I'm thrilled to welcome back, Sir Telsunn Margraves."

Sir Telsunn Margraves walks center stage and takes to the podium, "Thank you Ms. Perry for that truly unusual and interesting off-the-cuff interpretation of our written word." Katy Perry yells as she walks off stage, "You're welcome!"

"Let us now move on to the category which I consider the modern-day standard and by which all future fake news will be measured against. The one category that will go down in the annals of media history as the Swarga Loka or the Paradise of Fake News; The Presidential Campaign and Election of 2016.

During this period more fake news emanated from more media sources than ever before in human history, a fact that cannot be challenged. For a category of this stature, the presenter must be of equal standing to the task. Ladies and gentlemen please welcome the current mayor of the great city of Chicago, Rahm Emanuel."

The audience applauds as the mayor takes center stage, shaking the hand of Sir Telsunn as they pass. "Thank you all and what a pleasure it is to be here at the First Annual Fake News Awards. Now I know what some of you are thinking, you think that I'm a vile nasty piece-of sh*t, well just to let you know, my parents and brothers feel the same way. As a matter of fact, like Rodney Dangerfield lamented, *"I remember a time*

I was so depressed that I was going to jump out a window on the tenth floor. The police sent my dad and mom up to talk to me and they both said in unison, "On your mark, get set..."

The audience laughs and claps for Rahm who says, "Thank you, now onto the business at hand. Here are the nominees for the award for the best Fake News story from

PRESIDENTIAL CAMPAIGN AND ELECTION 2016 THE FIRST NOMINEE IS...POPE FRANCIS SHOCKS WORLD, ENDORSES DONALD TRUMP FOR PRESIDENT

"**P**retty clever, the story was originally published by a site called *WTOE 5 News* before being copied by a popular fake news publisher *Ending the Fed*. Hey, I think I know those guys! Well it seems that, the story as reported by *Buzzfeed* was picked up on Facebook® by nearly 1,000,000 people. Well, all good things must end and *WTOE 5 News* has since shut down its website. However, before they shut it down, they confessed to fabricating content and even had a disclaimer saying: "most articles on wtoe5news.com are satire or pure fantasy. *Ending the Fed* has taken down its version of the article too. You gotta admire *Buzzfeed*, they have some set of balls not checking this out.

Oh well, next we have the second nominee...

PRESIDENTIAL ELECTION POLLS

"**H**aving been in politics as long as I have, you gotta take these polls with a grain of salt, but it seems Hillary and her team has swallowed the whole shaker. The entire main stream media wanted to convince themselves, and the voters, that Donald Trump had no chance whatsoever of winning the presidential election. Monmouth University, Fox News, NBC Wall Street Journal, ABC, Washington Post, Ipsos and many other polling organizations all called it for Hillary right before the election. Well the media account of the winners and losers were completely blown away on November 8th, and trust in political polling as well as the mainstream news media prompted the backlash that you now see as fake news. If you knew how much money these guys pay for polling you'd piss your pants laughing.

The third nominee is; Whoa, you're gonna love this one...

'HILLARY HAS A 98% CHANCE OF WINNING ELECTION' HUFFINGTON POST

"Speaking of fake news, and the polls being used to sway an election, everyone now knows what happened. The entire mainstream media, TV, online, social, digital, radio, press, you name it, painted a magnificently and patently dishonest picture of the electoral odds in the 2016 presidential race. Just days before the election, Huffington Post had Hillary Clinton at 98% likely to win the election, and I can't say I'm happy it didn't work out. In the end Donald Trump had 306 electoral votes and Hillary Clinton had 232. She was crushed, stomped on, ruined, and the overwhelming media confidence in the inevitability of her victory turned out to be fake news. The mainstream media, its polling methods, and its inherent bias was on full display wasn't it? But, you know these guys were really good to us in the Obama Administration so we really can't complain.

The fourth nominee is kind of weird when you think of it...

WIKILEAKS CONFIRMS HILLARY SOLD WEAPONS TO ISIS... THEN DROPS ANOTHER BOMBSHELL

"**W**hoa, now this is really interesting so follow me when I read this, 'Published on August 4, this article was written by *The Political Insider* after WikiLeaks founder Julian Assange made comments about Hillary Clinton during an interview in late July. The article states that Assange contended "Hillary Clinton and her State department were actively arming Islamic jihadists, which includes ISIS..." and generated some 789,000 engagements, according to *Buzzfeed* data. What Assange actually said was that the Hillary Clinton-led State Department approved weapon shipments to Libya during the intervention in 2011. Those weapons had later ended up in the hands of jihadists. Before Election Day, the article had 789,000 engagements according to *Buzzfeed*. That is really good fake news isn't it! You gotta give these guys credit.

Now, the fifth nominee is one that has been spread far and wide by all members of the mainstream media...

MAINSTREAM MEDIA SPREADS (PHONY) PICTURE OF TRUMP'S CROWD SIZE

"Okay, now tell me you don't remember that photo published everywhere the mainstream media that compared Donald Trump's Inauguration crowd to Obama's? Remember all the white space on the ground in the Trump photo? Yeah, that photo has now been debunked, discredited and exposed. *Fusion* does note that the crowd had filled out the lawn by 11:50AM, minutes before Trump's swearing-in. There's a photo on the screen with the actual crowd and unfortunately, for the Trump haters, there were massive crowds. I wasn't there because I hate Trump and I hate crowds too. Oh well, here's the next fake news story that proves what I always say...never let a good crisis or in this case fake news story go to waste...

Now the sixth nominee is really something to see...

BUZZFEED PUBLISHING A DOSSIER ON TRUMP

"Imagine this...the fabulous fake news story about the dossier that reveals some salacious crap about Trump and *BuzzFeed* saw the opportunity and grabbed it. Well it seems that a lawsuit was filed against *BuzzFeed* by a tech company that was smeared in the phony anti-Trump dossier story. A former British intelligence officer, Christopher Steele, who is now a director of a London private security-and-investigations firm, has been identified as the actual author of the dossier covering allegations about President-elect Donald Trump's activities and connections in Russia and this is according to the *Wall Street Journal*. *BuzzFeed*, in the true spirit of fake news, seems fully aware that the information was false. After the suit was filed, *BuzzFeed* publicly apologized to the company and redacted the company's name from the phony dossier ... which has now been read by millions. By the way, I need to tell you that the whole Uranium One deal and the $145,000,000 in donations to the Clinton Foundation, President Clinton's speech fees, the DNC and Hillary Campaign paying for the dossier, as well as Fusion GPS paying reporters were not revealed in time for consideration for a *Falsie*©. Maybe that's because it was a real, but wonderfully under-reported by the news media. I have no doubt these events will surely be honored in 2018. By the way, doesn't NBC own *BuzzFeed*? Oh well, that's *BuzzFeed*...ask for forgiveness not permission!

The seventh nominee and this is really hilarious...

LATEST TRUMP SCANDAL...SMALL HANDS!

"Okay, I, Rahm Emanuel, do hereby challenge President Donald Trump to see who has bigger hands! On January 27, writer Dana Schwartz of the Observer tweeted out a screenshot of Trump that, she claims proves President Trump had "photo-shopped his hands bigger" for a White House photograph. Her tweet immediately went viral, being shared upwards of 25,000 times. Disney animator Joaquin Baldwin tweeted the same thing that was shared many thousands of times as well. The claim eventually debunked, but not before it had been shared tens upon tens of thousands of times.

Now get this, imagine someone actually went out of their way to prove the point that Trump does indeed have hands just below average size, particularly for a man standing 6-foot-2. According to various human anatomy websites, the average-height American adult male (5-foot-10) has an average hand size (measured from the tip of the middle finger to the wrist) of 7.44 inches. Trump's hand measures 7.25 inches. I think these science guys need to find something better to do with the Federal grants they receive to do this stuff.

Anyway you might want to take out your hankie for the eighth nominee...

POLITICO, TIMES, AP, NBC NEWS AND OTHERS SAY TRUMP NOMINEE, STEVE MNUCHIN FORECLOSED ON 90-YEAR-OLD WOMAN

"I wish I'd thought of this one...On December 1, 2016 Lorraine Wellert wrote a story published by *Politico* that claimed Trump's pick for secretary of the Treasury, Steve Mnuchin, ran a company that *"foreclosed on a 90-year-old woman after a 27-cent payment error."* Wellert wrote, *"After confusion over insurance coverage, a subsidiary of OneWest, sent [Ossie] Lofton a bill for $423.30. She sent a check for $423. The bank sent another bill, for 30 cents. Lofton, 90, sent a check for three cents. In November 2014, the bank foreclosed."* The story exploded online being shared 17,000 times on Facebook® alone. The *New York Times's* Steven Rattner shared it on Twitter as did NBC News's Brad Jaffy, along with AP's David Beard and many others. Can you believe this? Well don't, the central claims of Wellert's article simply ain't true.

I have to say this to all of you media types at this fabulous awards ceremony, *"Rather than doing the kind of fact-checking that normally goes with a story, you ran with certain stories for not wanting to get beat. There's a pressure that exists in your profession. I would be surprised in any honest exchange that you say that doesn't exist."* Rahm Emanuel takes a deep breath and says, "Had to get that off my chest...Okay, now we need to move this along so I am holding the winner of the Fake News Award for the Presidential Election 2016. I can't believe that I am as excited about this as I was when we had no murders in Chicago for one whole day!" Rahm rips open the envelope and screams, "And the winner is *POLITICO*!!! Accepting the award is LORRAINE WELLERT." There is loud applause and cheering as Lorraine Wellert gracefully makes her way through the crowd to accept the *Falsie©* from Mayor Emanuel.

Ms. Wellert rips the statue from Rahm's hands and steps up to the mic to speak, "Oh my Lord, God Almighty in Heaven, I can't believe this! There are so many people I want to thank; my Publisher and our Executive Chairman and Mr. Moneybags Bobby Allbritton and editor-in-chief, Pat Steel our CEO, Johnny Harris our Editor-in-Chief, Carrie Budoff-Brown my editor and Poppy MacDonald, president of the US unit and the whole *Politico* bunch. Without their approval and genuine love and affection I would not be standing here. By the way, even though the story was fake, I sent Steve Mnuchin a check for three-cents in case there was ever a poor 90 year old woman who needs it." The audience cheers loudly and Lorraine Wellert leaves the stage and as she passes she gives Sir Telsunn a hug and peck on the cheek.

Sir Telsunn Margraves, "Thank you Ms. Weller for that blessedly brief acceptance speech. My, my there are so many wonderful stories that were nominated, and even more that did not, how do you Americans say, 'make the cut', but I truly have confidence in that this selection was inspired. Now let us turn to the next category 'Presidential Politics and Whatever!' I want to caution you as there are so many stories that could have been selected for this category that our choices may appear limited. This, I assure you, is not the case however in the name of fairness to qualify for a *Falsie©* you must meet certain criteria. For example, the Russian Collusion story on the part of the Trump Administration can be thought of as fake news, but we must wait until the entire episode has been properly adjudicated. Similarly, the Uranium One and Russian

Collusion by the Obama Administration, Hillary Clinton State Department and the Clinton Foundation have been implicated in selling 20% of US Uranium; these potential scandals must go through the rigors of examination. As the sanctity of the APGR Fake News Awards must never be called into question, the aforementioned cannot be considered as they have not yet been fully and publically vetted."

Sir Telsunn tries to clarify the point as he feels a distinction needs to be made. "Now, if the news media had written an article about Hillary Clinton not meaning to sell yellow cake to the Russians, but rather baking a yellow cake with chocolate icing and presenting it to Russian President Vladimir Putin, that would immediately qualify her for a *Falsie©*. Sorry for being so long-winded but I felt compelled to issue this clarification."

"Now with that out of the way, I am extremely pleased to announce our next presenter. Blac Chyna was born Angela Renée White in Washington, D.C. She was born to Shalana Jones-Hunter, also known as Tokyo Toni, and Eric Holland in 1988. Ms. Chyna attended a professional makeup artist school, she launched her own brand of adhesive eyelashes, she's had a child with the rapper Tyga and as if that were not enough, she's dated Rob Kardashian; need I say more. Her entire Curriculum Vitae make her the perfect presenter at the Fake New Awards. Ladies and gentlemen, please welcome Blac Chyna."

Blac Chyna walks onto the stage waving to the audience, many of whom don't know who she is but politely applaud. "Thank you, thank you so very much and thank you Sir Telsunn for that wonderful and truthful introductoratory. I can't tell you how many times I've been miscombobulated by the news media and that's why I agreed to do this. The first nominee for the prestigious Fakie News Awards in the category they gave me, wait, what is it? Oh yeah, here it is

PRESIDENTIAL POLITICS AND WHATEVER AND THE FIRST NOMINEE IS... IRELAND I S NOW OFFICIALLY ACCEPTING TRUMP REFUGEES FROM AMERICA

"Nearly a million people read this story on Facebook®. I just love Facebook®, don't you? Anyway, this story was also reported online by liberalamerica.org. It says here that it actually references Inishturk as a small island off the coast of Ireland and these guys seems to be experiencing a drop in population. Can you blame them, I mean after all Inishturk! I bet they don't even have a Starbucks™ or American Apparel® or whatever, but if the truth be told both Inishturk and Ireland denied adopting this policy. What's more, another article, which was published by Winning Democrats, referenced how Canada has adopted an open door immigration policy for disgruntled Americans - which it hasn't. The story generated 810,000 engagements. It's kinda weird living on an island except for 'Long' or 'Coney'...whatever!

The second nominee thing is...

THE FIRST LADY'S BODY DOUBLE WAS ON TV

"You know I heard about this when I was reading People Magazine or on you-tube.com or whatever. Anyway there's a persistent rumor about Melania Trump, like that she hates being around her husband and I don't blame her. A viral tweet posted on Tuesday by a guy named Joe Vargas continued to expand on the theme...hey I think I read that tweet too. This guy Vargas appears to be convinced that Melania had really been replaced with a body double. You know, I heard about body doubles, I think that Khloe Kardashian has a body double...(aside) oh sorry, I get distracted sometimes. Well, during the days following his tweet, Joe Vargas continued to tweet about how the White House was trying to "debunk" him. This guy Vargas' considers this as a conspiracy and he offers this as evidence of his theory. In lock step just about every publication from the BBC to the *Daily Mail* that retweet his conspiracy theory also allowed Joe to plug his business. Mr. Vargas is a 'weed' salesman, not the kind of weeds you spray to get rid of, but the kind you smoke, and he was able to get his business message integrated into his tweets. In case some of you don't know what weed is, it's marijuana or as it's sometimes called *bammer, boo-yah , bubonic chronic, chino, choke, cigga-weed, cigweed...*"

A voice can be heard off stage, "Ah, Ms. Blac"

"...combustible herbage, doober or doobie, Dutchie...

"Ah, Ms. Blac...

"...sticky icky icky, fatty boom blatty, wacky tobaccy..."

"MS BLAC!"

Chyna Blac comes out of what seems to be a trance-like state and says, "oh sorry."

"I remember seeing this post! The post was so popular that Snopes posted a side-by-side comparison showing Vargas' phone picture of Melania Trump next to an image of Melania on his TV; a screengrab of the same moment from CNN®. It's obvious that Melania was standing next to her husband, and there were plenty of other photos of the (real) first lady taken that day. I'm confused; I thought she didn't like her husband and what about weed products...whatever!

Anyway, the third nominee is...

NEIL GORSUCH'S 'FASCISM FOREVER' CLUB

"**O**kay, I think he's kind of hunky for an old guy." Blac Chyna turns to the director in the wings and asks, "Is he married? Oh, too bad" She continues, "On February 1, 2017 the U.K. *Daily Mail* reported that Supreme Court nominee Neil Gorsuch had *"founded and led a student group"* known as the *"Fascism Forever Club"* in *high school.* Oh, wait, fascism isn't good right? Anyway the story made news on websites and in social media: *U.S. News and World Report, The Nation, AOL, the AV Club, Salon, Vice* and all fell for it, with writers and media personalities such as, Bill Maher and Keith Olbermann, wait, who are those guys? They should have asked Perez Hilton or some other guys I know.

Like as it turns out, none of this stuff was even true at all, can you believe it? Gorsuch had just included the club as a joke in his yearbook entry. Oh now I get it, it was just a joke...I don't get it. Anyway lucky he's a lawyer and not one of those news guys...whatever!

Well the fourth nominee is...

TRUMP REMOVED BUST OF MARTIN LUTHER KING, JR. FROM OVAL OFFICE

"Time *Magazine's* and their reporter guy, Zeke Miller, was serving as the media's pool reporter. Wait, why would he be swimming, was Trump in the pool? Anyway, he used his Twitter feed to publish that Trump had removed the bust of Martin Luther King from the Oval Office. Oh no! The bust of MLK! I can't believe this; I told you Trump was a big zero. Zeke said he looked for the statue but had not seen it, and I don't blame this Zeke guy for getting mad; I'm really pissed too. When

Zeke's let all the other reports know, he wrote and I quote, *"More decorating details: Apart from the return of the Churchill bust, the MLK bust was no longer on display.* Once the mainstream media guys and gals got a hold of this story, without checking if the report was true, it became a huge story." Blac Chyna takes a hankie from her cleavage and wipes a tear and blows her nose. "I am so sorry everybody; I think this is such a sad story." She continues reading from the card, "The report ultimately proved to be fake news. Oh, it was fake, oh! They didn't take his bust away at all; it seems Zeke didn't bother to look around! Whew, I feel much better now.

Anyway, Zeke quickly and conveniently issued a correction and sent multiple emails and tweets to confess his mistake. He further tweeted, "My sincerest apologies" and he tweeted a correction as well; that was an awful thing to do Zeke boy, you made me cry and it's a bit too late for an apology...whatever.

So glad it ended so well...the fifth nominee is...

PRESIDENT TRUMP HANGS UP ON AUSTRALIA'S PRIME MINISTER TURNBULL

"How rude, like why would you do that to Austria or something. Like the *NY Times, Salon,* CNBC, *NY Daily News, Mother Jones, USA Today,* CNN®, *Washington Post* and just about all the mainstream media reported that Trump angrily hung up on Australia's leader, Prime Minister Malcolm Turnbull. I don't remember reading this on TMZ, but this spread like wildfire. Only problem... it never happened. According to *Newsmax*, Prime Minister Turnbull said in a radio interview in Australia that Trump did not hang up with him and the call ended *"courteously."* Maybe I got to rethink this whole Trump is a zero thing...whatever.

Now for the sixth nominee who has written...

DONALD TRUMP REQUESTS SECURITY CLEARANCE FOR HIS CHILDREN

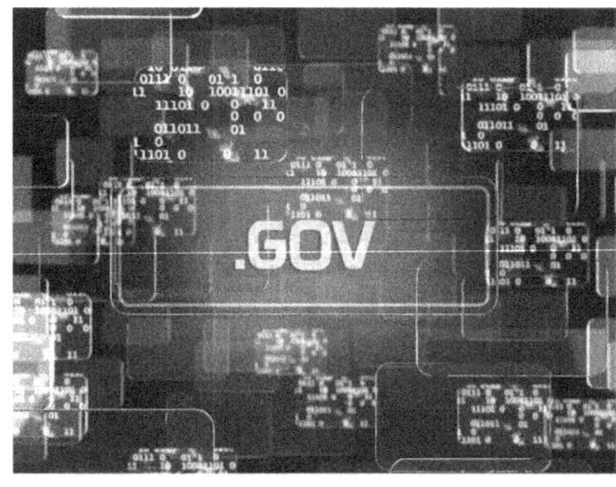

A widely reported nepotism story that was spread all over the place by mainstream news places like *Salon*, CNN®, NBC News, MSNBC®, CBS News and others. It went like this; the President-designate, Donald Trump asked secret security clearance for his kids. Anyway, the story *Salon* ran was under the headline, *"Donald Trump's trying to give his kids top secret security clearance, making sure his conflicts of interest are extra bold."*

I gotta tell you this, as a mother, if I was president I would have my son, King Cairo Stevenson, put on the list of guys who can read secrets. But as USA Today later reported, "*Despite reports suggesting the contrary, a transition team official says Donald Trump did not request or begin paperwork to have his children gain top-level security clearance, according to a pool report.*" Hey! This is more fake news, oh yeah these are the Fake News Awards...whatever!

The seventh nominee is...

MASS RESIGNATIONS AT STATE DEPARTMENT

"Well, this can't be good. The *Washington Post's* Josh Rogin reported that there was a "mass exodus of senior Foreign Service officers" at the State Department, all of it due to the election of Donald Trump as President. What the hell happened, don't we need these guys to do secretary of state things? I am really sad about this...oh...now the card says that the truth is that the White House asked for these resignations, and that this is just standard practice for any new administration. Maybe they thought that John Kerry was still secretary of state or worse, Hillary was coming back! That was a cute joke, the guys backstage wrote it for me...whatever.

Like the eighth nominee for a *Falsie*© is...

NBC NEWS REPORTS TRUMP EASING RUSSIAN SANCTIONS

"Now I am not a student of history or political stuff, but like I think these Russian guys are bad news. I heard that they have this place, Siberia, and it's really cold there and...(aside) oh sorry. NBC reported that the Trump Administration was easing sanctions on the FSB, one of Russia's primary intelligence agencies. Anyway, Peter Alexander, NBC's national correspondent, tweeted, *"US Treasury Department was easing Obama admin sanctions to allow companies to do transactions with Russia's FSB, successor org to KGB."* Hey, I like the letters KGB, sounds like a great rapper name, maybe I should...(aside) oh sorry. Well, less than an hour later, he wrote, *"Source familiar with sanctions say it's a technical fix, planned under Obama, to avoid unintended consequences of cybersanctions."* I really don't know what cybersanctions mean. His initial and incorrect tweet received nearly seven thousand retweets and the correction has less than 300 retweets. That doesn't seem like a lot of tweets, I got 50,000 tweets when I appeared as Nicki Minaj's stunt double in a music video. Never mind...whatever!

The ninth nominee is...

TRUMP CHANGING THE NAME OF BLACK HISTORY MONTH

"**I** mean like why would he do that? I am proud to be black...say it loud...I'm black and proud! Anyway, like the fake news ran around the world, it's true that President Trump used the name 'African-American History Month' in his proclamation; it's like Toni Morrison saying that Bill Clinton was the first black president. Still looking at the card, she says, "Oh, he didn't change the name to something like "Louis Vuitton® Appreciation Month" or something, not that I don't like Louis Vuitton®...(aside) oh, sorry.

Anyway, Trump lovers in the media also reported that he was the first president to apply that terminology, but that's not a fact, Jack. The terms "Black History Month" and "African-American History Month" have been nearly interchangeable since President Gerald Ford issued the first proclamation about the observance. President Ford used the term "Black History Month" in 1976, but Bill Clinton, Barack Obama, and George W. Bush all used the term "National African American History" month in at least one of their yearly proclamations. Jimmy Carter, George H.W. Bush and Ronald Reagan, on the other hand, used a combination of the two terms and honored "National Afro-American (Black) History Month."

I think it's very nice that the presidents named it *Black History Month* or *National Afro-American (Black) History Month* or *National African American History Month*...whatever!

Now, oh, it's our final nominee in the "Presidential Politics and Whatever" is...

CNN® TIES FOX NEWS IN THE RATINGS ON INAUGURATION DAY

"Now you all know I'm a junkie when it comes to watching TV or streaming video or whatever. So I tuned in CNN® to watch the inauguration. I didn't even know that there was a Fox News! CNN®'s public relations team, wanted to party when they heard that numbers reported by Nielsen Media Research said, *"According to Nielsen cumulative numbers, 34 million people watched CNN®'s inauguration day coverage on television. 34 million watched Fox News."* Someone named Darcy reported this story and it was retweeted thousands of times and several news guys spread it around. Anyway these guys at *NewsBusters* report, *"The ratings weren't even close. CNN® came in a distant second place, a humiliating second place."*

The problem? Ad agencies and network executives don't look much at cumulative numbers and even so, Fox News still beat CNN® in those. It was not a tie. I should have known this because Rob Kardashian showed me the numbers on 'Keeping up...(aside) Oh sorry. But wait; is this another fake news story? Oh yeah, I forgot, this is the Fake News Awards. Anyway if you look up at the screen you'll see a chart. I can't read it 'because I can only see it upside down, but it looks like the numbers are bigger for Fox News.

Hours	CNN®	Fox News
12 Noon to 12:30 PM (Oath & Address)	3.375 million total viewers	11.768 million total viewers
11 AM to 1 PM	3.047 million total viewers	10.483 million total viewers
1PM to 5 PM	2.326 million total viewers	7.901 million total viewers

"It's a factual statistic, but I literally never used cumulative ratings once when I edited TVNewser, not once" said Brian Flood, a media reporter at TheWrap. It looks like Fox News trounced CNN® in the midst of the festivities, not even close. Maybe the ratings were better for CNN® when they reported Michael Jorden was dead...whatever!"

Oh wow, that was the last nominee...I guess I have to read the name of the winner. Chyna tears open the envelope and screams, "ITS JOE VARGAS, THE WEED SALESMAN and a whole bunch of websites that like this stuff. Here to accept the Falsie© is the one and only, Joe Vargas, the weed salesman HIMSELF, IN PERSON!"

Joe Vargas appears stunned as he gets up and works his way out of the row he is sitting in. For him it is a surreal experience and he approaches the stage and climbs the steps to take his place at the podium. He looks around and asks Chyna Blac, "Is this Bermuda?" She replies, "No, but it's like a little warm in here. Like here's your *Falsie©.*"

Blac Chyna hands him the award and Joe Vargas stares at it for a few seconds. He looks up to see all the people sitting waiting for him to speak and he says, "Isn't it shiny! It looks like a shiny gold metal bong. Thanks for this; I can't wait to tell my boss." Joe just stands there for more than a minute saying nothing. The producer of the show comes on stage and takes Mr. Vargas by the arm and escorts him off stage. Sir Telsunn Margraves takes his place at the podium to announce the next series of nominations.

"Ladies and gentlemen, I have little to add to what Ms. Blac or Mr. Vargas has said except to revel in the term, *brevity is the soul of wit."* Blac Chyna waves to the audience as she acknowledges the applause. She gives Sir Telsunn a big hug. As she walks offstage she says, "This was fun...really it was fun." Sir Telsunn responds, "Thank you Ms. Blac, we are more than pleased you thought it was fun."

Sir Telsunn Margraves makes an announcement to the audience, "Ladies and gentlemen, as promised, I have a very special surprise that I am sure you will more than enjoy. We will take pause in our Fake News category presentations to present a very special award. The Fake News Awards is proud to announce the first "Fake News Person of the Year Award." The crowd is thrilled at the prospect and cheers and applauds loudly.

"As one can only imagine, this is a truly difficult task for those who must make the decision. There are so many men and women who could make it to the pinnacle of fake news that we must use all available criteria to select the most qualified and deserving of this highly coveted *Falsie©*. Our council was challenged with the undertaking to name the award after some person or persons who are praiseworthy of such an accolade. It is also important to note that the winner must not only embrace fake news but constantly omit news that could accrue to the benefit of Presidents Ronald Reagan, George H.W. Bush, George W. Bush's and Donald J. Trump. In this instance, one legend is not enough to convey what modern day fake news represents. Ladies and gentlemen, I am pleased and honored to announce the first annual *"Orson Welles/Arianna Huffington/Helen Thomas Fake News Person of the Year Award!"* The mere mention of Orson Welles, Arianna Huffington and Helen Thomas in the same sentence creates a spontaneous round of thunderous applause.

The list of nominees for the award is long and represents the cream of the crop in terms of fakery, blatant bias, falsification, omission, misstatements and obfuscation; Keith Olbermann, Matt Lauer formerly of NBC, George Stephanopoulos of ABC News, Don Lemon of CNN®, Lester Holt of NBC News, Christiane Amanpour of CNN®, Paul Krugman of the New York Times, Jonathan Martin of Politico, NY Times; Andrea Mitchell, NBC; Charles Blow, New York Times; Ezra Klein, Katie Couric, formerly of CBS; David Gregory, NBC; Nina Totenberg of NPR; Jeffery Toobin, CNN®; Anderson Cooper, CNN®; John Meacham, Newsweek; Dana Milbank and Evan Thomas, formerly of Newsweek and Time. Each one of these candidates are, in and of themselves worthy of a *Falsie©* but, alas, the committee was forced to award only one person the honor of winning the *"Orson Welles/Arianna Huffington/Helen Thomas Fake News Person of the Year Award!"*

The audience in the Kennedy Center is overcome with excitement and Sir Telsunn Margraves is keenly aware of this. He pronounces, "As we recognize the person who has achieved what is considered the pinnacle of modern day fake news, it is important to acknowledge why the honoree deserves recognition. This person has a storied history of fake news; she created fake news around Trump tax returns, fake news about Venezuela protests tied to Trump donations, fake news tying the Niger attack to Trump's travel ban, she is even using fake news as fake news on her MSNBC® show's commentary and so much more."

"In a dizzying fashion, all nominees continue to ignore real news like the Hillary Clinton hacked emails from foreign governments, the Uranium One Scandal, the DNC Clinton campaign funding of the Trump Russian Dossier, donations to the Clinton Foundation, as they unabashedly and consistently highlight their extreme bias in truly remarkable ways. Collectively, these all are representative as important as fake news itself in determining the suitability of a candidate for this award, and our winner has it all! Ladies and gentlemen, I am pleased and honored to present the *"Orson Welles/Arianna Huffington/Helen Thomas Fake News Person of the Year Award!"* to Ms. Rachel Maddow of MSNBC®!"

The audience is overcome and cheers at the mere mention of her name. Rachel Maddow seems thrilled and stands waving and smiling at the throng. Her excitement at receiving an award of this magnitude is palpable as she bounds up the stairs to accept her *Falsie©*. A hot flash seems to create a reddish hue on Maddow's face as if to color her genuine thrill at this honor. Ms. Maddow walks center stage and grabs the statue from Sir Telsunn and once in her grasp, she faces the crowd. Rachel Maddow holds the award for all to see as if to signify victory over others who were sure to be as jealous as they can be.

Rachel Maddow had not prepared remarks as she was unprepared to make a speech, however she took the next 46 minutes to thank everyone she could think of. She ended the speech in this way, "...I want to thank President Trump. He provides the catalyst and inspiration for each and every bit of fake news that emanates in the media today, especially on my show. The stuff that comes out of the White House and the news that can be twisted and turned to provide an ever constant source of false, scurrilous and meaningless items that last just long enough for us to move onto the next fake story. I also want to thank George Soros for his billions, the Democrat Party and the DNC for their unceasing and tireless work providing boundless resources, smokescreens and plausible deniability for your friends in the media. It their never ending enthusiasm for all that is frivolous, false and fake that keeps us energized. I am sure that all my comrades in the world of news will acknowledge that this support has come in very handy in the past and I am sure will continue to be invaluable in the future. Lastly I want to thank all of you here for your constant support and adoration." Rachel holds up her *Falsie©* and screams, "Look ma...top of the world!"

Those of the audience that are still awake begin to clap and are thrilled to see Maddow walk off stage. Sir Telsunn Margraves approaches the mic and says, "What a long and comprehensive speech, Ms. Maddow, but I think you forgot to name all 360 members of the Mormon Tabernacle Choir. That being said let us continue. Our next presenter is someone who needs no introduction, but you may not know him as well as audiences who enjoy the sordid reality shows. He is one the stars that has graced the small screen for years on MTVs series Jersey Shore, and he is now starring in the latest iteration of the MTV hit series. He is known for his pectoral muscles, selling his Ferrari tires on EBay, he wears his baseball cap askew; ladies and gentlemen, please welcome our next presenter, Mike 'The Situation' Sorrentino. There is cautious applause and a number of questioning looks from the audience, but when the people actually see 'The Situation' they completely understand and the cheers get louder.

"Yo, this is Mike 'The Situation' Sorrentino and I am juiced..." Mike takes off his tuxedo jacket. He is bare chested, wearing only a tuxedo shirt collar and tie so as to reveal his six pack and muscular arms. "Ladies, this is available and it's up for smush sale, you know we can pound it out DTS if you like!" The producer of the Fake News Awards is now holding his head as he feels a headache coming on and whispers "Get moving!"

"Oh, sorry, well here I am. When they called me to be a presenter I was thrilled and I get to talk about some of this sh*t going on with the travel ban. I really don't care as long as it's not Italians being kept out of the country and BTW if any of these terrorist guys try to...(aside) oh sorry.

Anyway let's get on with...

THE TRAVEL BAN AND THE FIRST NOMINEE IS... TRUMP'S REFUGEE PAUSE BEING CALLED A "MUSLIM BAN"

"Now it comes out that this Obama guy designated seven countries as terrorist nations so what does Trump do? Well he wants to take a pause on the guys coming from those countries for 90 days and halt the refugee programs for all religions from all countries for 120 days. Now everyone is getting buggy over this and you'd think that the Pope was stopped from saying mass at St. Patrick's Cathedral. Of course the news guys say it's a Muslim Ban but in 40 Muslim majority countries throughout the world, immigration to the US will continue. In 2011 President Obama did the same refugee ban from Iraq that lasted six months. What the f*ck do these assholes in Congress want? Not only did the media cover it up, the media is spreading the fake news that Obama's refugee six-month ban is different from Trump's. Calling this a Muslim Ban is an outright lie and it's like these guys know it. I think this whole stroy really sucks the big one and I don't like it.

The second nominee is...

CNN® JIM SCIUTTO REPORTS "REFUGEE POLICY IS NOT BASED ON RELIGION"

CNN®'s Sciutto, a former Obama Administration official, hey, isn't CNN® like the MTV® of news? Anyway they did a report that says "Refugee Policy Is Not Based on Religion." In a tweet this guy Scuitto declared, *There is no basis to the claim Muslim refugees were prioritized over Christians.* Sciutto also tweeted that President Trump changed U.S. refugee policy by adding a religious component to who can and who cannot come to America. That doesn't seem right, it's like if we didn't allow Snooki to come to...(aside) oh sorry.

Some guys did some figuring and found out the BBC says that 10 percent of the 22,000,000 Syrians are Christian, which would mean there are 2.2 million Christians in Syria. Hey, did you know my agent is talking to the BBC about me doing something at a palace or something. Anyway, the guys looked over the numbers and something ain't right. When Obama was in office, the US took in 10,801 Syrian refugees, of whom 56 are Christian. Not 56 percent; 56 total, out of 10,801 or one-half of 1 percent. Given that Christians are 10% of the population, where the hell are the rest of the Christians immigrants, huh? What was he smoking? Some sick sh*t going on!

Our third nominee is...

MUSLIM OLYMPIAN WAS DETAINED BECAUSE OF TRUMP'S TRAVEL BAN

btihaj Muhammad recently became the first female Muslim-American to win an Olympic medal for the United States, pretty cool. Hey ladies, do you think these pecs could get me a medal?" With that The Situation comes out from behind the podium and flexes his muscles. There are whistles from a number a women as well as some men. The Situation looks to the side and says, "Oh sorry. Anyway, Muhammad claimed that she was detained for two hours *just a few weeks ago*" by U.S. Customs and Border Protection agents. She was held for a few hours without explanation and told anyone who would listen, *"I can't tell you why it happened to me, but I know that I'm Muslim. I have an Arabic name."* Muhammad, who doesn't like Trump, gave a bullsh*t answer to a reporter's question and it seems she wanted to blow it past the news guys.

Anyway, it really didn't matter because a bunch of media outlets like Time, the UK's *Independent, the Daily Mail, the New York Daily News, The Hill,* and of course *Sports Illustrated* and ESPN® all jumped on her story without checking it out and now have crap all over their faces. Tsk, tsk, these guys should have double-checked whether she was detained after Trump's travel ban went into place or perhaps while Obama was still president. It seems that she was detained in December 2016 weeks before Trump's inauguration and Obama was still president. I don't understand why these guys don't think they'll get caught all they gotta do is check their iPhones.

Well, here is the fourth nominee...

IRAQI WOMAN "KILLED BY TRUMP" BECAUSE OF TRAVEL BAN

"So now we got this chump, Mike Hager, a U.S. citizen born in Iraq, who was visiting relatives in Iraq. He said he was returning home to the United States where his mother has lived since 1995. As they waited in line at the airport in Iraq, he was told that he could pass because he was a U.S. citizen, but his mom and other family members weren't allowed back in, despite holding green cards. Hager said, *"I was just shocked. I had to put my mom back on the wheelchair and take her back and call the ambulance and she was very, very upset. She knew right there if we send her back to the hospital she's going to pass away, she's not going to make it."* Sadly, he was right, he said his mother, Naimma, who lived in the US since 1995, wasn't allowed to come home and she died in her native country. Hager said his mom would still be alive if it weren't for the order and he blames President Trump.

Social media exploded against Trump including tweets by respected news outlets; *'First death from Trump's immigration ban.'* Tim Blais (@acapellascience) February 1, 2017, *'First innocent death from #Trump #travelbans #MuslimBan'* High-Fruit Lifestyle (@Gary_High_Fruit) February 1, 2017, *'Elderly green card-holder who'd lived in US since 1995 dies in Iraq after being refused reentry to US'*, Garance Franke-Ruta (@thegarance) February 1, 2017.

Just one small, insignificant, tiny problem, the story was a lie to feed opposition against Trump's travel ban. The leader of a mosque in Dearborn confirmed to local FOX 2 that the man, who claimed his mother died in Iraq after being barred from returning to the US, lied to FOX 2 about when she died. Imam Husham Al-Hussainy, leader of the Karbalaa Islamic Educational Center in Dearborn, says Hager's mom did not pass away after being barred from traveling to the US. This Al-Hussainy guy said that Hager's mom died days before the ban was even put in place. I can't believe that this guy used his mother for some political crap. I can tell he's not Italian, if I'd have done anything like this my mother would kick my ass.

Hey, this sh*t is getting depressing...the fifth nominee is...

YES, REAL DONALD TRUMP IS A MUSLIM!

"Okay, you think that because this is the Fake News Awards that this is fake news but according to a bunch of online sites it's not. Here's how it goes, President Donald J. Trump ('J' stands for Jumma, which means Friday in Arabic) is a Muslim who converted to Islam years ago and he was awarded the title of 'Sheikh'. Want to know the why? Well...

- Sheikh Trump does not eat pork or consume alcohol. Probably never had my mother's pork chops with vinegar peppers.
- Sheikh Trump does not want to disclose his tax returns because since his conversion to Islam, he has donated millions of dollars in charitable contributions to build mosques in the United States and around the world. Hey, I didn't want to disclose mine and now I'm in a bunch of sh*t with the IRS...
- Sheikh Trump recruited numerous decoys in his cabinet to conceal his conversion to Islam. Huh? I don't get it?
- Sheikh Trump has a unique way of exposing the bigotry against Islam and Muslims, particularly in some parts of the United States. I still don't get it.
- Sheikh Trump called the Saudi King to reaffirm his faith in Islam. He also called General Sisi of Egypt, President Erdogan of Turkey and the prime minister of Pakistan to make sure they all understand that the travel ban on Muslims is just a ruse to please the deplorables. Now I'm lost...
- On the day of inauguration, an unprecedented crowd of millions witnessed President Trump taking the oath on two holy books to uphold the constitution. Given that Sheikh Trump is very intelligent man; he came up with the machination of using two holy books. Of course, one of the books was...guess.

Hey that pretty cool, I didn't know Trump was a Sheikh! He gets to wear that funny scarf and robes but he has to eat that crap food they eat. Imagine having to eat that food without parmigiana or without tomato sauce or without garlic knots. I tell you that alone could kill you. I remember...(aside) oh sorry.

Anyway, here is what you've all been waiting for; the winner of the Travel Ban Fake News Award is...I'm such a cockblock for actually getting excited." The Situation rips the envelope open, looks up and smiles, "It's the IRAQI WOMAN "KILLED BY TRUMP" BECAUSE OF TRAVEL BAN! The winner, Mike Hagar, sent us an email saying he didn't want to come, so accepting the award is his automobile mechanic, Ahmad Mustafa Al-Razi. Mr. Al-Razi, please come up and accept the award!" Mike Sorrentino scans the crowd and he spots a man coming down the aisle looking around seemingly stunned to be here in front of such a large crowd.   Mike 'The Situation' Sorrentino hands Mike Hagar's *Falsie©* to Ahmad Mustafa Al-Razi and asks him to say a few words.

Mr. Al-Razi seems a bit uncomfortable as he steps up to the mic, but he overcomes his fears and says, "I am most exquisitely joyful for Mike Hagar and this most gold and beautiful statue. I am to be recommending him to hang from the mirror of his 1981 Cutlass Oldsmobile to be proud for himself. Thanking you I am for this."

Sir Telsunn Margraves walks center stage and thanks Mr. Al-Razi for coming to the awards at the last minute. Sir Telsunn also asks Mike 'The Situation' Sorrentino to put his shirt back on and shakes his hand. "Ladies and gentlemen I can only hope that the attempt at professionalism and the extemporizing, as exhibited by the awards presenters so far, becomes indelibly etched in your minds, I personally will never forget them. I can honestly declare that this is vastly beyond any reasonable expectations I've had when I planned the ceremony." As if to validate Sir Telsunn appraisal of events so far, the audience nods in agreement and applauds loudly.

"Let us move on. Our next category is Potpourri and Far Beyond. This category was considered by the adjudicators as being the most challenging in that there were so many subjects and so many articles to choose from. Undaunted, however, the judges found what they consider paramount in terms of fake news and, similar to cream, they rose to the top. The challenge for me, your host, was to select a presenter that could provide valuable insights, and act as the perfect complement to the fake news about to be featured. Knowing this I am sure you will understand why I could not be limited to one presenter, so may I introduce the unlikely couple; actress, singer and model, Ms. Lindsey Lohan and the host of one of America's most popular programs 'Dr. Phil' I am pleased to introduce Dr. Phil McGraw. Ladies and gentlemen please welcome Lindsey Lohan and Dr. Phil!" The audience goes wild giving the two totally unexpected presenters a standing ovation as they take to the podium center stage. Both Lindsey and Dr. Phil wave to the crowd and thank them for their kind reception.

Linsey Lohan is really excited and she tells Dr. Phil, "This is the first time we've met but I think that this will be almost as good as when I did the movie *The Parent Trap.* Like, you know when I watch it today I really think that I have a twin sister but the girl in the movie speaks with an English accent and I can't speak in an English accent." Dr. Phil looks at her quizzically and responds, "I would like to have you as a guest on my program." Lindsey is thrilled at the opportunity, "I would love to, what would I have to do?" Dr. Phil says, "Well all you have to do is be yourself." Lindsey thinks for a while and smiles, "Wow, okay I can do that, I'll just have to ask mom!"

Dr. Phil responds, "We'll discuss this later, Lindsey. I am grateful for this opportunity that Sir Telsunn Margraves has given us as I believe in my heart of hearts that I can fill my guest roster for the next year or six with some of what I've heard at the Fake News Awards.

Now let's move on with...

POTPOURRI AND FAR BEYOND AND THE FIRST NOMINEE IS... MSM REPORTS MANY ANTI-TRUMP STORIES WITH UNNAMED SOURCES... NBC REPORTS NONE ABOUT HARVEY WEINSTEIN WITH SOURCES

Well, what have we here? It points to a number of emotional and mentally challenging issues for the hierarchy of the mainstream media and especially NBC. It appears that there are a number of anti-Trump stories that are reported literally every day all over the mainstream media, including on NBC. Now it seems that NBC

News passed on a story that has now put the spotlight on Hollywood and movie producer Harvey Weinstein. For decades he preyed on women seeking to break into the movie business; the price of admission; demanding sex or have them watch him pleasure himself! So what did NBC do when offered an exclusive from one of their own MSNBC® hosts, Ronan Farrow; well, NBC passed on it."

Lindsey seems perplexed and upset. "Why do you think that they didn't jump on this exclusive?" Dr. Phil wants to be understanding to Lindsey's feelings of anxiety and tells her and the audience. "While I cannot make a detailed prognosis, I believe that a possible cause could be a mental illness of paranoia with schizophrenia resulting in delusions making reporters and management at NBC unreasonably suspicious of other people, in this case President Trump." The audience nods in agreement as Dr. Phil continues, "NBC said that the scoop didn't meet their standards. However, it could also be that NBC and Harvey Weinstein's company have had a long relationship producing shows and movies, and as the saying goes, money is thicker than blood or water."

Lindsey still looks puzzled but introduces the second nominee...

FAT SANTA CLAUS TO BLAME
FOR CHILDHOOD OBESITY

"**D**r. Phil, I don't like this one. It says on the card something called *Cracked. com* highlighted this fake news story that was picked up by *Bloomberg News, The Telegraph*, CBS News and several other major news outlets. *Cracked* said, "The British Medical Journal gave Santa a cheap shot right in his considerable gut when they announced in a press release that a new study at Monash University in Australia had found that *Santa's image as a bowl full of drunken, cookie-fueled diabetes actually encourages impressionable kids to lead similarly unhealthy lifestyles as they get older.*" *Cracked* continued to say that the study blames Santa for influencing unhealthy behaviors, including smoking, drinking and driving and spreading infectious diseases by letting kids sit on his filthy, filthy lap. They even tried to blame Santa for spreading the freaking swine flu epidemic."

Lindsey is now visibly distressed and says, "I can't believe they would say this about Santa. I love Santa, he's jolly and dresses in red, my favorite color, and I always leave him cookies." Dr. Phil realizes that Lindsey could be extremely upset so he tries to clarify the story. "Now you may be puzzled as to why anyone would believe such a story. Well consider that Christmas is under attack by the atheists and the politically correct establishment is determined to make Christmas a non-holiday at least as its religious significance implies. These people could be suffering from a condition called Anhedonia which is defined as the inability to experience pleasure from activities usually found enjoyable, like Christmas. They could also be suffering with a Seasonal Affective Disorder (SAD) that comes during the winter when... (aside) oh, sorry. Lindsey, why don't you continue reading?"

Lindsey looks at the card and reads, "*Cracked* also said, "*The author of the "study," Dr. Nathan Grills, admitted that the story was only meant to be a Christmas joke, something the British Medical Journal has often printed for its end-of-year issue. Beyond that, however, it's painfully clear that the outlets that reported the study only sourced the press release and the subscription page that featured excerpts from the report rather than reading the actual report, probably because the additional $30 in research expenses would finally complete the collapse of the fragile newspaper industry.*"

Dr. Phil chimes in, "If my initial assumptions can be validated I believe I can treat this with a year or two at a treatment center located on a farm that works with people who suffer from these debilitating mental conditions.

Now for the third nominee...

RAPE IS A PREEXISTING CONDITION

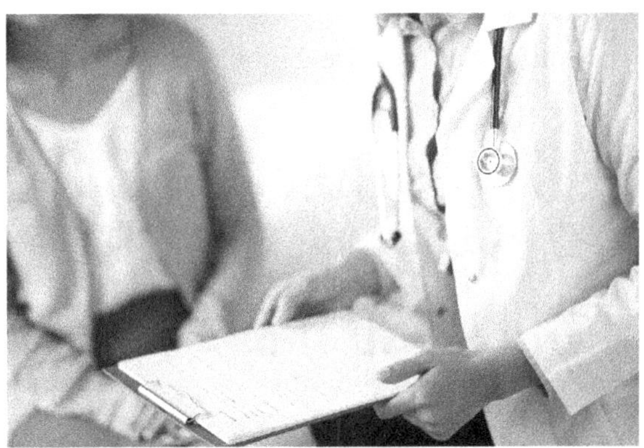

Dr. Phil looks at the card he was given and says, "My first reaction was to thank goodness this is covered by Obamacare! Now it seems that the feminist group *Ultraviolet Action* sent out a graphic that claimed that Obamacare allowed a rape survivor to assert this as a preexisting condition. A number of mainstream media outlets have given credence to this narrative and it soon became a social media Phenom. *Mic.com* shared this claim a staggering 248,000 times on Facebook®, *New York Magazine®* had 13,000 shares, CNN® 24,000 shares and *Huffington Post* with nearly 40,000 shares, among many others.

It became apparent that feminists were thrilled with the possibilities, however, they were wrong. The *Washington Post* gave the claim four Pinocchio's: *"This claim relies on so many factors — including unknown decisions by a handful of states and insurance companies — that this talking point becomes almost meaningless."* The claim was exposed as a fabrication as well as a huge disappointment to women who had been raped, but the mainstream media published the *Ultraviolet* story as the truth."

Dr. Phil expounds, "Now for *Ultraviolet* we may want to examine whether they were telling an ordinary and outright lie or if they their editorial staff and writers experiencing confabulation which is defined as a fabricated, distorted, or misinterpreted memories about oneself or the world, without the conscious intention to deceive. Alas, we will never know until we are able to have a few years of intensive psychotherapy at a center located on a farm...(aside) oh sorry.

Lindsey, it's your turn." She smiles and says, "Now, for the fourth nominee...

THE HUFFINGTON POST SHOWS PHOTO-SHOPPED RECEIPT WITH A 'ONE PERCENT' TIP...AND IT MAKES HEADLINES

"You know these Wall Street guys make beaucoup bucks, so the *Huffington Post* could not pass up on publishing what they hoped would be what cruel, heartless one-percent rich guys do when they eat. Like when a wealthy banker and a coworker were having dinner and when it was time to be pay, the banker was blamed for leaving a measly one-percent tip of $1.33 tip on his check for $133.54. Can you believe this! You know, *I love watching The Chew but all it makes me want to do is cook and eat, cook and eat, and so on...*(aside) oh sorry. Anyway, this banker was said to have left the message on the check, 'Get a real job'. The *Huffington Post* also reported that her coworker was so angry by the small tip the banker left the server that he snapped a picture, showing a tip amount of $1.33 with the word 'Tip' circled and an arrow pointing to some harsh words: 'Get a real job'. This is so sad...my mother always make me leave at least a 20% tip.

But wait a *Freaky Friday* minute! It says here that the image was photo shopped, you know these guys did that to me once, they made me look taller...(aside) oh sorry. The actual credit receipt on file showed a bill of $33.54, not $133.54. The tip was $7.00, slightly more than the customary 20% for good service. You would think that the *Huffington Post* would have checked this out but it might have taken an additional 20 minutes. Well you're up next Dr. Phil."

"Thank you Lindsey...ladies and gentlemen out next nominee is...

POLICE OFFICER KILLS BLACK MAN WHO YELLS 'HANDS UP, DON'T SHOOT'

"With ever increasing polarization of Americans on all sides of discourse, it is a dreadful shame that we are yelling so loudly that no one can be heard. The events that produced 'Hands Up, Don't Shoot' led to riots, violent attacks and looting in Ferguson, Missouri and numerous other cities. The mainstream news media spread the myth that Michael Brown had his hands up before being shot by police officer Darren Wilson. Instead of trying to calm tensions, mainstream media continued to give credence that had a profound impact on race relations on so many levels.

The claims that lead to violent rioting were said to be the origin of the Black Lives Matter movement. The facts of the case, however, show that the 'hands up don't shoot' claim was completely false and that Wilson was justified in shooting Brown. Paul Cassell of the *Washington Post* wrote, *"As those who have been following the case closely are aware, Wilson testified before the grand jury that Brown reached for his (Wilson's) gun and a struggle for the gun followed, during which Wilson fired two shots. Later, Wilson pursued Brown and, after he turned and then charged toward Wilson, fired multiple shots bringing him to the ground about 8 to 10 feet away from him. The physical evidence is consistent with his testimony."*

In spite of evidence that showed the truth, many in the mainstream media were unwilling to report the real news with the same fervor as the fake news. The mental condition that could be responsible for could be this 'compulsive lying disorder' caused by 'antisocial personality disorder' or perhaps 'conduct disorder' as another cause of 'compulsive lying disorder' or even 'interdependence' are all possibilities. I would welcome many of these reporters and editors undertake counselling at a treatment center located on a farm for a period of a decade or two. I caution you that this is based on very limited information but I...(aside) oh sorry.

"Lindsey, would you please introduce the fifth nominee...

THE ROLLING STONE® RAPE STORY ATTEMPTS TO VALIDATE AN EPIDEMIC OF COLLEGE CAMPUS RAPES

Lindsey looks at the cards she has been given and reads, *"We know the numbers: one in five of every one of those young women who is dropped off for that first day of school, before they finish school, will be assaulted in her college years."* This is a remark from Vice President Biden, on the release of a White House report on sexual assault. *"It is estimated that 1 in 5 women on college campuses has been sexually assaulted during their time there — 1 in 5."* President Obama, remarks from the White House.

Time.com wrote, *"This incendiary figure is everywhere in the media today. Journalists, senators and even President Obama cite it routinely. Can it be true that the American college campus is one of the most dangerous places on earth for women?"* You see! You see! I was talking to Katy Perry in the dressing room and she said that this is why she didn't go to college and I agree with her, I never went to college either. I was going to go to auto-mechanic school if this acting thing didn't...(aside) oh sorry.

Anyway, let me read to you these facts from Time.com, *"The one-in-five figure is based on the Campus Sexual Assault Study, commissioned by the National Institute of Justice and conducted from 2005 to 2007. Two prominent criminologists, Northeastern University's James Alan Fox and Mount Holyoke College's Richard Moran, have noted its weaknesses: "The estimated 19% sexual assault rate among college women is based on a survey at two large four-year universities, which might not accurately reflect our nation's colleges overall. In addition, the survey had a large non-response rate, with the clear possibility that those who had been victimized were more apt to have completed the questionnaire, resulting in an inflated prevalence figure."* There seems to be so much fake news that had so many people accused of rape at colleges across the country; charges that were proven wrong as leveled in the *Rolling Stone*® article written by the author, Sabrina Rubin Erdely. Hey! *Rolling Stone*® did a cover of me and a bio and knew I wish they didn't...they suck! It has ruined people's lives and continued the fake news that one in five women are raped on college campuses. *Rolling Stone*® eventually corrected and then entirely retracted the article. Well that makes me feel a lot better...not! Dr. Phil, do you want to take this one?"

Dr. Phil smiles at Lindsey and says, "You bet I do. Our sixth nominee is...

CBS NEWS CLAIMS STATUE OF LIBERTY WAS ORIGINALLY INTENDED TO BE A MUSLIM WOMAN

"**T**he Statue of Liberty is getting a lot of attention, during President Trump's initial announcement of his Muslim travel ban. Among the false narratives it is said the Statue of Liberty was to welcome immigrants. The truth is that the Statue of Liberty has nothing to do with immigrants or immigration. The Statue of Liberty poem, "The New Colossus" was written by Emma Lazarus to raise money for the building of the statue's base. The legend, "give us your poor…" was added years later.

This is just one fake news story regarding the Statue of Liberty repeated by many in the mainstream media. Not to be deterred, CBS News researchers came up with a novel news item; Lady Liberty was originally proposed as a Muslim. The revelation was intended as criticism of the Trump administration's travel ban, but it was soon discovered that the story is nothing more than a myth.

FrontPageMag's Daniel Greenfield explains, "*The grain of truth to the story is that the meme picked up on the interesting historical footnote that one of the earlier projects of Frédéric Auguste Bartholdi* (the French sculptor who designed the Statue of Liberty) *was a large woman holding up a torch and symbolizing Egypt's progress. The giant statue would have been titled, "Egypt or Progress Carrying the Light to Asia."* The statue was meant to celebrate Egyptian civilization but since Egypt's ruler had no money, the project went nowhere. In any case the idea that the "Egypt" statue became the Statue of Liberty is a myth.

How do we know that? Here's what Bartholdi had to say about it, *"At that time my Statue of Liberty did not exist, even in my imagination, and the only resemblance between the drawing that I submitted to the Khedive and the statue now in New York's beautiful harbor is that both held a light aloft."*

CBS never took the research beyond anonymous sources and decided it was better to tell Americans that Lady Liberty is a Muslim and the US should have no immigration restrictions on Muslims...fake news! I believe that the management and staff could be suffering from a mental disorder that I have recently discovered and I've named it *'Mc-Grawius Statuatus Confusiatum.'* The symptoms are obvious; confusing one statue for another and visions of all women holding torches in their hands. This is similar to how Tom Hanks reacted to the soccer ball Wilson in the movie *Castaway* except Wilson wasn't holding a torch. I would welcome CBS management and researchers undertake counselling at a treatment center located on a farm for a period that can only be determined after and in-depth interview. Well Lindsey looks like it's your turn again."

Lindsey reads the next card, "The seventh nominee is...

NEW YORK TIMES' MAGGIE HABERMAN CLAIMS ONLY SAN BERNARDINO SHOOTINGS INVOLVED 'NON-US-BORN ATTACKER'

"On January 28th 2017 Maggie Haberman of the *New York Times* tweeted, *'Other than the San Bernardino shootings, has there been a terrorist attack involving a non-US-born attacker since 9/11?'* Her fake news tweet immediately brought an enormous response by *Twitter* users, Kyle Shideler of *The Federalist, Jihad Watch,* Twitchy and others.

"Ah, Dr. Phil?"

"Yes Lindsey."

"Like can you like help me with this one? I don't think I can pronounce all these names. They sound really weird?"

Dr. Phil looks at the card and says to Lindsey, "These are names from different nationalities, mostly in the middle east, Africa and Eastern Europe. I'd be happy to help."

"Thanks so much Dr. Phil, you're really a peach!"

Dr. Phil picks up where Lindsey left off. "Let's give Ms. Haberman some information that it took twenty minutes for the APGR Fake News researchers to find. The Tsarnaevs Brothers who became known as the Boston Marathon Bombers; Faisal Shahzad, the Times Square Bomber; Umar Farouk Abdulmutallab, the underwear bomber; Ohio State attacker Abdul Razak Ali Artan's; Chattanooga shooter Mohammad Youssuf Abdulazeez; Ahmad Khan Rahimi, detonated a bomb in downtown Manhattan; Dahir Adanlaunched a mass stabbing at St. Cloud Minnesota mall; Guled Ali Omar in a conspiracy (one of many) attempting to provide material support to ISIS; Waad Ramadan Alwan and Mohanad Shareef Hammadi, Bowling Green, Kentucky killings.

As I understand it, there is an extensive list of plotters, and planners and members of ISIS terror cells in the US that can be easily found through online searches. Fake News was glad to help! I was intrigued by Ms. Haberman's take on this as she may be suffering from reverse xenophobia that could manifest itself as a confused view terrorism. I believe that this could be easily solved with a few short months at a treatment center located on a farm.

Now Lindsey, I feel that in all fairness you should take the next nominee." Lindsey says, "Thank you Dr. Phil. The eighth nominee is a second nomination in the 'Potpourri and Far Beyond' category...

TRUMP THREATENED TO ASSASSINATE HILLARY BECAUSE SHE'S A WOMAN

"Well the ultra-left feminists at *Ultraviolet* are at it again. This time they are condemning President Donald Trump's comments on the Second Amendment. They're saying that he threatened violence against Hillary Clinton and that he did so because she is a woman. Hey, like I'm a woman too!

Anyway, Nita Chaudhary, the group's co-founder, said this: *"If you thought Donald Trump couldn't sink any lower you were wrong. His continued insistence that if the first woman president is elected it will be illegitimate, 'rigged,' and now worthy of 'second amendment' remedies is beyond the pale, but not surprising from a man whose life has been dedicated to denigrating women and whose campaign has been built on espousing violence against his so-called political enemies."* The story was repeated again and again in the mainstream media as well as many online outlets. *Ultraviolet Action* has not made any recent statements about Bill Clinton's alleged sexual assaults, and targets conservatives almost exclusively.

Trump did not, in fact, call for Clinton or anyone else to be assassinated. *Ultraviolet* tweeted, accidentally ruining its own argument; *"Trump is just telling us what gun owners have been saying for like decades: attempts to undo the Second Amendment will be politically, and physically, impossible."*

"Now, Lindsey, I've been attempting to diagnose the possible mental conditions that could cause some of personalities and mainstream media types to generate the preponderance of fake news. Perhaps Nita Chaudhary and other nominees are suffering from PTSD or Post-Trump Stress Disorder. This condition could be a result of the election of Donald Trump and the trauma resulting from the release of the Donna Brazile's expose *"Hacks, the Inside Story of the Break-ins and Breakdowns that Put Donald Trump in the White House."*

This could be is a disorder…(aside) oh, sorry. Now the winner of the Fake News Award in the 'Potpourri and Far Beyond' category is…Lindsey would you do the honor?" Lindsey Lohan is very excited and she rips open the envelope and screams, *"ULTRAVIOLET! IT'S ULTRAVIOLET!* Accepting the *Falsie©* for Ultraviolet is its co-founder, Nita Chaudhary!"

Ms. Chaudhary seems to be in a state of shock as she gets up from her seat and makes her way to the stage. Dr. Phil and Lindsey give her a warm welcome and Dr. Phil asks her if she has a year or two available so he could perform a complete evaluation. However, Lindsey jumps in, "Oh, Ms. Chaudhary, I can't tell you what an honor it is to meet you. I consider myself a feminist and I want to wear a pussy hat and protest the next time your group protests!"

Nita Chaudhary still seems a bit bewildered but says, "I really don't know why I'm here. I got this invitation in the mail and I heard there was free food and drinks so I figured what the heck. By the way, as long as I have the stage, men are pieces of sh*t." Lindsey is totally taken with the feminist leader and asks again, "Ms. Chaudhary can I please come to the next protest, I'll bring my own hat and I'm sure it will be fun! Oh, here's your *Falsie©*." Dr. Phil wants to clarify something so he says, "Lindsey, given that *Ultraviolet* is the only fake news nominee that was nominated for two separate items, it should be considered a true testament to their organization's determination, creativity and vitriol. Again, congratulations!"

Ms. Chaudhary looks at the award and asks, "Is this real gold? When are they serving the food?" Dr. Phil feels the need to get off the stage and says to the audience, "Let's give Ms. Chaudhary a hearty round of applause" and the audience does as they are told. Sir Telsunn Margraves takes the cue and thanks both Lindsey Lohan and Dr. Phil McGraw and says, "What a wonderful acceptance speech Ms. Chaudhary gave. Ms. Chaudhary the buffet will be served at the conclusion of the awards ceremony.

Now ladies and gentlemen, we come to the final category of the Fake News Awards and as the old adage goes, 'we have saved the best for last!' But before I introduce our special guest presenter, I would like to cite that oft quoted, brilliant scholar and thinker, *anonymous* who said, *"The best way to lie is to tell the truth . . . carefully edited truth."* This quote seems most appropriate for the next category and that is why it is too enormous a responsibility to limit this category to just one winner. In this regard, the committee has avowed to bestow a winner in both the individual and group subsets among the deserving nominees.

Now without further delay, may I introduce the man who will immortalize the winners of...

THE LIFETIME LEGENDS OF FAKE NEWS

Ladies and gentlemen please give a rousing welcome to our special guest presenter, the recently retired, esteemed former Senator from the great state of Nevada, the honorable Harry Reid!"

As this is Washington DC, the audience is nearly apoplectic at the mention of Harry Reid's name and they cheer and applaud raucously. Senator Reid is jubilant at the reception he is receiving, "Thank you so much for that warm and welcoming reception. I am Harry Reid and in contrast to popular option, I am not dead!' The audience laughs and applauds. "Thank goodness my real estate holdings are still intact; my sons are doing great as lobbyists in Washington as well as other careers. I tell you that it embarrasses me how much they thank me for all the help I've given them. Anyway, when Sir Telsunn Margraves asked me to introduce the candidates for the Legends of Fake News, I was thrilled. Throughout my career I have worked on my own and with Democrats across the country to spread rumors, innuendos and, yes, even fake news. Through numerous efforts, large and small, I've tried to elevate the entire category of fake news so that it gains the legitimacy it so richly deserves and, I humbly suggest, I've succeeded." More raucous applause from the audience and Reid continues, "Remember the rumor that Romney paid no taxes, remember? Well

I don't mean to brag but it was a total lie! Ha, ain't that a fact, a total lie, but I said it and I meant it, and you know what, *Romney lost and Obama won* and that's all that mattered. And do you want to know something else?"

The audience yells out, "YES!"

"Well do you know Romney couldn't even sue me for liable and slander. Do you know why?'

The audience yells out "NO!"

"I did it from the Senate floor!   Pretty cool huh! When you're a big shot politician like me you get immunity. Can you believe it, immunity, and I can do it for anyone and everyone I don't like...ain't America wonderful?!"

The audience cheers for the former Senate Majority Leader and Harry Reid continues, "Thank you for your kind recognition. Before I introduce the various nominees and in the name of complete disclosure, many of these nominees have been of invaluable assistance in helping me and the Democrat Party over the years. I made a promise to Sir Telsunn and I make it to you, I will be completely neutral and not betray any favoritism that I may have.

Now I would like to introduce the first nominee..."

WASHINGTON POST REPORTER LIVING IN 'JIMMY'S WORLD'

said that I wouldn't be bias, but I do love these guys. In 2016 *Washington Post* reporter Janet Cooke received a Pulitzer Prize for her story titled "Jimmy's World", an article that The Post published in 1981. This guy Mike Sager at the *Columbia Journalism Review* praised her as *"the fabulist who changed journalism,"* and the case for her story being one of the first examples of *"viral"* journalism. To appear relevant and diverse, The *Washington Post* found their ideal in Janet Cooke, a young black female who came up with a story about an eight year old heroin addict living in Washington, D.C. His name was Jimmy and Ms. Cooke wrote he was a *"precious little boy"* who had *"needle marks freckling the baby-smooth skin of his thin, brown arms."*

In an effort to assuage their guilt at this horror, DC city officials asked Janet Cooke where they could find Jimmy. Initially she refused and the *Washington Post* invoked her First Amendment right to protect her sources. The hoax, however, started to fall apart when the *Pulitzer Prize* board changed the rules to move Cooke's local-news story into the national news category. The Pulitzer guys and gals were so eager to award the very first *Pulitzer Prize* to an African-American woman. When questioned though, Janet Cooke finally confessed, *"There is no Jimmy and no family, it was a fabrication. I want to give the prize back."* Alas, too little too late but this qualifies for a Legendary *Falsie©*!

I am sure that everyone here remembers the second nominee, I certainly do!

TV NETWORKS CALL CRITICAL RACE IN FLORIDA FOR AL GORE TOO EARLY

n a historically tight toss-up race, the mainstream media's television networks (CNN®, CBS News, NBC, et al.) called Florida too soon for Al Gore in an "embarrassment of major proportions." I remember this! I was at the DNC Victory Headquarters waiting for the victory party. You know they have free drinks and these amazing appetizers...(aside) oh sorry. Anyway, my buddy, Dan Rather was so certain he guaranteed his viewers, *"If we say somebody's carried the state, you can take that to the bank. Book it!"*

The networks made the call just before 8pm Eastern, but they appeared to have jumped the gun and a little while later had to retract their call. By 1:30AM, the Sunshine State was still too close to call. The earlier pronouncement may have had the effect of chilling votes on either or both sides. The state was eventually carried by George W. Bush. Maybe they should have hanged their chads and called this one for Trump! I was still able to get to the appetizers; you know those little Swedish meatballs and these are really delicious. They make them at...(aside) oh sorry.

The third nominee is...

NBC NEWS EDITS ZIMMERMAN'S CALL WITH POLICE

will always have a warm sport in my heart for the guys at NBC. When the shooting of Trayvon Martin by George Zimmermanm happened, NBC News determined *'white Hispanic'* Zimmerman was obsessed with Martin's race before the altercation that led to Martin's death. It could be that NBC wanted to gain the approval of Barack Obama who said, *"If I had a son he would look like Trayvon Martin."*

The fake news in the Zimmerman-Martin story was exposed when it was proven that NBC News deliberately edited a recording of the call Zimmerman to 911.   The call was edited to make it sound as if Zimmerman was fixated on Martin's race. This whole event stirred up racial tensions across the country becoming the basis for the violent 'Black Lives Matter' movement that followed.

The media, spearheaded by NBC, was very interested in keeping the story on top of the news cycle, intensifying racial paranoia for reasons unknown. A great deal of the early reporting about the Trayvon Martin shooting could be classified as "fake news." The photos of baby-face Trayvon were circulated, even though that wasn't what he looked like at the time of his death. This is what legends are made of...too bad they couldn't do this on the Senate floor.

The fourth nominee is...

'RATHERGATE'...FOLLOW THE DOCUMENTS

Like I've always said, I'd *rather* have *Rather* than a colonoscopy and I mean it. What a way to end a career! The Killian documents controversy, also referred to as Rathergate, is legend around the political and media worlds. The papers, supposedly made by George W. Bush's commander, the late Lieutenant Colonel Jerry B. Killian, included criticisms of Bush's service in the Guard during the 1970s. Four of these documents were reported on a *60 Minutes II* broadcast as true just before the 2004 Presidential Election. Later it was disclosed that CBS had not authenticated the documents and on further examination by experts, it was determined the documents were forgeries. When document authenticity needed to be examined, experts said it was not technically possible without the original documents.

CBS producer Mary Mapes obtained only copies of the documents from Bill Burkett while pursuing a story about the controversy. Bill Burkett claims he burned the originals after faxing copies to CBS. In the *60 Minutes II* segment, anchor Dan Rather stated: *"We are told [the documents] were taken from Lieutenant Colonel Killian's personal file"* and incorrectly claimed that *"the material"* had been authenticated by experts retained by CBS.

Anyway, the legitimacy of the documents was challenged within hours on Internet forums and blogs and you could see it all over the mass media, when I read this I practically pee-peed my pants. Good going guys, please see your friends at the DNC, we may have work for you.

CBS and Dan Rather continued to defend the legitimacy of the documents; however, continuing research and analysis of the documents confirmed that the documents were forged. Later, Dan Rather was forced to admit, *"If I knew then what I know now – I would not have gone ahead with the story as it was aired, and I certainly would not have used the documents in question."* An embarrassed CBS News President Andrew Heyward said, *"Based on what we now know, CBS News cannot prove that the documents are authentic, which is the only acceptable journalistic standard to justify using them in the report. We should not have used them. That was a mistake, which we deeply regret."* We bet you do...and so Dan, rather than parse words, retired or was fired or was let go or was sent packing or it was mutually decided it would be best for CBS, take your pick!

This is similar to something that happened when I said I wouldn't take any lobbyist efforts from family. Well anyway, I must have forgotten when Rory, my son, came to me with this 5 billon dollar deal done with his law firm and some Chinese company. I thought it was great, I love the Chinese and I love solar farms. Anyway, it really is nothing like Rathergate and eventually it got buried, but it would be nice to have a gate named after you, like "Reidgate"...(aside) oh sorry. Well, I really feel bad for Dan. He was always a reliable friend, if not a fellow traveler.

Oh well, the fifth nominee...

BRIAN WILLIAMS FACES ENEMY FIRE IN IRAQ...NOT!

Oh, you gotta love this guy. NBC News anchor Brian Williams had the number one evening newscast when he traded it all for a legendary fake news account of bravery on his part. Because of this, and some other peccadillos, he lost his job as anchorman in 2015. He was accused of lying about taking enemy fire while helicoptering into Iraq in 2003. The soldiers who were aboard the helicopter were pissed off about Williams' account of the incident and would tell anyone interested that Williams was full of bull-crap.

Brian Williams, the evening news anchorman, told the story repeatedly, over a span of years before he was called out. His career as NBC News anchor ended when he came under fire; all puns intended. On further examination, prompted by his story of enemy fire, it was revealed that Brian Williams had told many stories that, on close examination, proved to be false. There was a story about a man committing suicide in the New Orleans Super Dome during Katrina that was false. Williams falsely claimed he was at the Brandenburg Gate the night the Berlin Wall came down. He even lied about flying into Baghdad with SEAL Team Six.

Now it seems that the NBC executives always had a problem getting Williams to admit he lied and that he must offer an unqualified apology to his viewers. Now this is really interesting because, in spite of it all, Brian Williams was offered his own slot on NBC's far-left cable network, MSNBC®. Nice gig and the legend lives' on! By the way Brian, a small piece of advice, if you're gonna lie, it's not a good idea to take the cue from Hillary Clinton, 'cause eventually you get caught.

Oh here's another item I remember very well, the sixth nominee is...

DATELINE NBC RIGS A GM TRUCK TO EXPLODE

Who the hell comes up with these ideas anyway? Oh well, as the story goes, in 1993, NBC News delivered a public apology for staging the test crash of a *General Motors* pickup truck for their '*Dateline NBC*' program. The report was to illustrate how a gas leak from the truck's fuel tank could cause a dangerous fire after a crash. To make the point; NBC rigged the GM truck with explosives.

The *Dateline NBC* report aired and it contained 14 minutes of debate and 57 seconds of crash footage. The video showed how the gas tanks of certain old GM trucks could catch fire in a sideways collision. Sounds like the kind of proof that shows Al

Franken with his hands on those women's breasts. Thank God they didn't explode in Al's hands.

So now it seems that GM was not going to take this lying down! They hired a bunch of detectives who searched a bunch of junkyards for 18 hours and they were able to find enough evidence to expose most parts of the crash. At a press conference, GM was able to show that the explosion from the NBC *Dateline* report was rigged. The causes of the explosion were falsely attributed to the truck and the severity as well as other details distorted. During the investigation two major errors were disclosed; first, NBC said the truck's gas tank had ruptured, yet an X ray showed it hadn't; second, NBC operatives set off miniature rockets beneath the truck split seconds before the crash and NBC viewers were never told.

At the time a spokesman for NBC was forced to read a statement that said, *"We deeply regret we included the inappropriate demonstration in our 'Dateline' report. We apologize to our viewers and to General Motors. We have also concluded that unscientific demonstrations should have no place in hard news stories at NBC. That's our new policy."* According to *Breitbart* the statement left viewers with some unresolved questions about why it wasn't their old policy, too. There it is again...the initials NBC, the network in the forefront and a great friend of the DNC and my campaigns!

Moving on, our seventh nominee is...

NY TIMES REPORTER JAYSON BLAIR; THE 'MAC DADDY' PROLIFIC FAKE NEWS WRITER

I never knew Jayson Blair but he seems like my kind of newsman and here's how it works if you're Jayson Blair. You find a paper like say, the *New York Times*! You hope and pray they take race into account; as a matter of fact you hope they *only* take race into account. Well it seems that the Times not only expressly took race into account, but also put Blair's race above everything else, including the truth and the paper's reputation. The *New York Times* hired Blair who, it turns out, was not yet out of college and offered him a spot in their internship program. At the time the internship program was being used in large part to help the paper diversify the makeup of its newsroom.

Given his lack of experience, Jayson Blair screwed up so many times that the paper had to print 50 corrections to articles he'd written. However, in spite of it all, Jayson Blair was continually published on the front page of the paper. He was promoted and the Time's editor-in- chief, Howell Raines became Blair's mentor and biggest fan. Raines, however, ignored the warnings of a number of sources while he, along with top management, kept giving Blair bigger stories in other of the paper's sections. This was done without letting the editors of the other sections know about Blair's prior screw-ups.

Now you may ask; how the hell can this happen at the 'paper of record?' Well, it was finally discovered that Blair made up facts, plagiarizing from other news sources, and lying about trips he never took and interviews he never conducted. A lot of tough questions were asked about how the paper missed so many signs of Blair's deceit, including the troubling detail that he never filed travel expenses for all the cities he was supposedly visiting. The *New York Times* conceded that Blair's career of *fabulism* was a *"profound betrayal of trust, and a low point in the 152-year history of the newspaper."* The *Times* editors were unable to get Blair terminated before his work led to one of the biggest scandals in the newspaper's history.

Now here's a factoid that you will find hilarious, Blair resurfaced recently with an op-ed reprimanding the mainstream media for failing to fact-check candidate Donald Trump aggressively enough during the 2016 presidential campaign. Now that's my kind of chutzpah!

Well, if that's not enough, here's another person that you may remember, our eighth nominee...

BEFORE JAYSON BLAIR, THERE WAS STEPHEN GLASS, THE 'DADDY MAC' OF FAKE NEWS

Stephen Glass started his career at 25 where he was considered a rising star at *The New Republic.* He wrote dozens of highly prominent articles for a number of other national publications with one thing in common...he just made things up. Wait, before I continue I gotta tell you what Pat Grey of the Blaze said about me, she said I was *"the worst living human being on this planet today. I think it's time that someone finally acknowledges it."* Isn't that a hoot; all because I lied about so many... (aside) oh, sorry!

Anyway, on *60 Minutes* Glass gave Steve Kroft his first interview when his journalism career ended in disgrace. Glass confessed he made up people, places, events, organizations and quotations. Sometimes, he even made up entire articles, and to back it all up, he created fake notes, fake voicemails, fake faxes, even a fake Web site; whatever it took to deceive his editors, not to mention hundreds of thousands of readers.

Glass said, *"My life was one very long process of lying and lying again, to figure out how to cover those other lies,"* says Glass.

How did this whole deception work? Well as Stephen Glass explained it to Croft, *"I would tell a story, and there would be fact A, which maybe was true. And then there would be fact B, which was sort of partially true and partially fabricated. And there would be fact C which was more fabricated and almost not true, and there would be fact D, which was a complete whopper and totally not true. So people would be with me on these stories through fact A and through fact B and so they would believe me to C and then at D, they were still believing me through the story."*

Stephen Glass was so good at making up "evidence" to back up his claims, that it simply didn't occur to his editors that he might be faking so much of his work. I know that I got away with it over my storied career but I proudly declare it is always different with politicians.

For our ninth nominee we need to recognize that it encompasses the entire gamut of mainstream news outlets...

BROADCAST AND CABLE NEWS NETWORKS FALSELY CLAIM THE POLLS IN FLORIDA ARE CLOSED

Remember how the presidential election results in Florida were so very close. The large number of electoral votes made the state of Florida vitally important in the 2000 state-by-state electoral map and the results were closely watched by all sides. Both the Bush and Gore campaigns had spent large sums of money to secure those votes of Floridians and now it was "D Day" for the candidates.

News anchors from the major broadcast and cable networks underscored repeatedly that the polls in Florida would be closed at 7pm Eastern Time. Five of the most prestigious news anchors; Cokie Roberts on ABC News, Brian Williams on NBC, Judy Woodruff on CNN®, Tom Brokaw on NBC News and Dan Rather on CBS News all made sure to say it over and over again.

Tom Brokaw said, *"We want to point out to our viewers that in half an hour, at 7 o'clock Eastern Time, we have a group of critical states that will be closing their polls, including the state of Florida."* He followed up a few minutes later with, *"The polls will close in Florida, as we said just a few moments ago, at 7 Eastern Time tonight."*

Now here is the problem with that; Florida has two time zones and, take it from me, it's hard to believe these professional commentators and/or members of their staff didn't know that. In fact the polls in the very reliably Republican panhandle did not close at 7pm Eastern, they in fact closed at 8pm Eastern.

Now I will not ever admit that this is possible voter suppression after all...oh, the panhandle is mostly Republican voters, I forgot? Well, it seems very difficult to interpret the lapse in reporting the actual time the polls close to anything other than an out and out scam to marginalize Republican voters in the Florida panhandle, and the purpose of this subterfuge; wither to steal the election for Al Gore or to exercise simple journalistic malpractice. Al Gore is a Democrat and he should have won except for a few hundred hanging chads, oh well we still had a party with free drinks and appetizers. They had those Swedish meatballs that I like...(aside) oh sorry!

Wow, time does fly when you're having fun and this has been fun. It's a lot better than getting the sh*t beat out of you by some Las Vegas hood, oh, I mean falling off my tread mill. I am also supposed to remind you that there are so many legendary fake news episodes that Sir Telsunn and the committee were forced to eliminate many of the individuals or groups that would have all qualified. He did assure me, and I want to assure you, that in spite of a number of fake news stories that didn't make the cut most of those stories were originally on the same networks and news sources that were nominated. In that spirit they are all recognized as the leaders of Fake News! Now here is the winner of 'The Lifetime Legend of Fake News' Individual Award!" Harry Reid rips open the envelope and reads the winner's name and shouts out, "DAN RATHER COME ON UP AND GET YOUR *FALSIE©*!"

The entire audience at the awards jumps up and gives a standing ovation to Dan Rather as he works his way out of his row and into the aisle. He is smiling broadly as he waves to all and takes the stairs onto the stage two at a time. He walks to the center of the stage and embraces Harry Reid and they share an intimate moment. Dan Rather whispers into Harry Reid's mic, "Great to see you Harry, It's been a while." He then takes to the podium and reaches into his pocket and pulls out what appears to be a prepared speech. "Thank you all so very much, thank you." After a while the applause dies down and Dan begins, "My, oh my, what a surprise, I never ever expected this." Dan then begins to read his prepared remarks, "First, I would like to say that although I have received many awards, this is among the ones I shall cherish most. To actually face the camera day after day and try to provide viewers with information, false or otherwise, that they could use to lead their lives is an awesome responsibility. I could not have done this without the support, encouragement and love of so many. For me it began with the powers at CBS where I was first given the reigns as network anchor. In the words of my mentor, the beloved, immortal Walter Cronkite, whom I replaced, 'Who the f*ck took my notes...how can I remember what to say without my notes." These are the words I have lived by all my professional life and now that I am in the twilight of my years, I have to remember not to forget them. I would like to thank the other news anchors that gave me an award after I left CBS for reasons that are still unclear to me. These men honor me every day by carrying on the grand traditions of Fake News that has been vital in accelerating the precipitous drop in ratings among all networks. I would also like to thank George Soros for allowing me to access *Media Matters* for the treasure trove of false information available to all of us journalists."

There is a pause in Dan Rather's comments as he seems to be looking at his notes, "I have asked Sir Telsunn Margraves, and he has allowed me to make this special announcement." Murmurs and questioning looks abound in the audience as they wait to hear Dan's special announcement. "Ladies and gentlemen on December1st, 2018, I will be launching my new three hour network news program airing on public access channel 2117, currently available in 3,218 homes across Northern Wisconsin. The 'Dan Rather News Views' will be sponsored by 'Sh*ttens© The disposable, mitten-shaped moist wipes.' This is a very special time for me as it will allow me to cover the news the way I think it should be covered and Sh*ttens is making that possible. In closing I want to thank the committee, my good friend Harry Reid and, of course, you the Fake News consuming public."

The audience stands and applauds loudly and long for this icon of fake news. Harry Reid walks back to center stage; again he and Dan Rather embrace as Dan holds his trophy high. "Well that was wonderfully inspiring and we're all glad to see Dan is back and ready to go tell it like it is, or isn't, who cares." Harry now removes another envelope from his tuxedo pocket and rips it open. He smiles gain, "Ladies and gentlemen, I couldn't have asked for a more deserving winner if I picked it myself, the next winner of 'The Lifetime Legends of Fake News' Award in the group category is NBC NEWS!!!! Accepting the award for NBC is the host of 'The 11th Hour with Brian Williams. Please welcome Brian Williams."

Another round of loud cheers and applause greets the former anchor of NBC news now relegated to the elephant's burial ground of cable news networks, MSN-BC®. Brian takes roughly the same path to the podium as Dan Rather had and he warmly embraces Harry Reid. "Harry, it's good to see you so soon after we had drinks the other day." They banter a bit as Harry hands him the *Falsie*© and Brian steps to the mic. "Wow, what a momentous occasion for both NBC and myself. After my banishment to MSNBC®, I've been trying to get back at them for something and, low and behold, this award comes up. As far as I'm concerned, they should have gotten the award just for how they tried to cover up the Weinstein mess! Anyway this is a great way to get a few things off my chest. First, I want to say that there are no hard feelings by me towards NBC. They gave me the opportunity to lead the national news team and then they ripped out my heart. It was just like the time I was abandoned in the mountains of Afghanistan where I was hunting Usama bin Laden. I got to his cave just moments after he left. Then they asked me to go to MSNBC®. MSNBC®! That's like asking Picasso to run a paint-by-numbers class for the clueless. You think they would have at least sent me to CNBC!

As I look at this golden award, I am reminded about the time when I visited Israel and discovered the temple of King Solomon and the treasures within; the greatest find in the history of archeology. Due to some unfortunate event, an earthquake to be exact, the entire site was covered with rubble and I barely escaped with my life. But enough about me let us focus on those at NBC who are so deserving of this Fake News Award. Take the time that they claimed Russian President Vladimir Putin *"does not deny having compromising information"* on President Donald Trump. They did it just to promote the 'b' word, Megyn Kelly, and her interview with Putin. Interview? Interview! You call that an interview? I could out interview the crap out of her. Take the time I was interviewing the late British Prime Minister Winston Churchill, I told him that he needs to do more about the bombs dropping on London and I believed that was the moment that turned the tide of World War II. By the way, NBC was forced to issue a denial on the whole Putin thing and they tweeted, *"Russia's Putin denies having compromising information on Trump."* The list goes on and on but you get the point. Anyway thanks for the award and I'm outta here." Brain Williams then storms off the stage as Harry Reid comes back out and says, "Well that ends the awards presentation and here is Sir Telsunn Margraves to provide closing comments."

Sir Telsunn takes center strange and shakes Harry Reid's hand, thanks him and compliments him for his unusual presenter skills. Sir Telsunn then begins his closing comments, "Ladies and gentlemen, I would like to thank you all for coming this evening. I hope you will agree that this was a memorable event equal to the title, "The Absolutely...Positively... Genuine...Real Fake News Awards." I would like to thank our sponsors for their tireless support and encouragement they gave to all those involved. *The Dakota Pipeline* for the industrial design of the set, The *Used Hummer* Corporation for providing transportation, *The Trump International DC* for guest accommodations, *The Clinton Foundation, Harvey Weinstein, Al Franken etc., Fusion GPS, Uranium One,* just so we wouldn't mention them too much, *The Washington Redskins* just for their name, *Rosa's Pizza* for delivery and *Wikipedia, Wikileaks, Drudge Report, Breitbart, Newsmax and Rush 24/7* for everything else.

This concludes our evening's awards presentation and in the words of the immortal William Shakespeare, "Parting is such sweet sorrow", until we meet again I remain your humble servant. Good Evening."

All quotations in italics are directly attributed to those cited - TM

SIR TELSUNN MARGRAVES

Woodcut (circa 1537)
Lord Tennyson Margraves
Battling arch-enemy
Lord Edgerton Collingsworth Fauntleroy

When one hears the name Telsunn Margraves one conjures up the image of an eminently successful, world class thinker and authority. The Margraves Family Royal Lineage goes back for centuries in Brandenburg. The Margrave family however settled in Great Britain in the 14th century AD and Telsunn proudly carries on the grand ancestral tradition.

Telsunn attended Britain's most prestigious public school, The Wellington Marlborough Academy for Advancement and, upon graduation, was offered a full scholarship to Harvard University. Telsunn Margraves graduated from Harvard in six months and was named a Rhodes Scholar attending Oxford University. He received the following doctorates in his first year of study; Doctor of Divinity (DD), Doctor of Civil Law (DCL), Doctor of Medicine (DM), Doctor of Letters (DLitt), Doctor of Science (DSc) and Doctor of Music (DMus). He continued attending Oxford for another year just for the fun of it.

Telsunn Margraves moved across the pond to the colonies in 1994 where he took up residence in New York City. During the early years he cultivated one of his passions; observing, reflecting and memorializing the absurdity so prevalent among those ensconce in the deep state, media-industrial complex and the progressive mind. He gained extensive notoriety with his important essay, "Cigars and Their Influence on Presidential Discourse." Telsunn Margraves has met with the world's leading politicians, notable stars of stage, screen, radio and the internet as well as personalities from all walks of life. Telsunn Margraves has always had a talent for inserting himself into different situations. To this end he has taken "pen to paper" or as he likes to put it "having my amanuensis use the keyboard to digitally create fake news for discerning peoples of the world!" Telsunn likes to tell anyone who will listen, "People are funny." This is the mantra that gave way to Telsunn Margraves developing his enormously popular and oft visited political blog which features absolutely, positively, genuine real fake news of the moment or near moment; www.realfakenewsthebook.com.

In 2010, in recognition of his achievements, Sir Telsunn Margraves was awarded Knighthood in "the Order of the Companions of Honour" at a ceremony that took place at Buckingham Palace with the Queen Mother performing the induction. Sir Telsunn Margraves CH, DBE, FBA, FMedSci, continually nurtures his other passions including engineering, collecting Hummel, sports car racing and commercial kitchen food preparation and was named the world's most eligible bachelor by "Architectural Digest", "Home Shopping Network", "Car and Driver" and "Food Industry News."

MICHAEL MEDICO

Michael Medico was born in New York City where he attended Power Memorial Academy. On graduation Michael joined the U.S. Navy and served stateside during the Viet Nam War. After being honorably discharged from the service, he attended Pace University and graduated with a degree in marketing and advertising.

Michael founded an advertising agency where he served as CEO for 35 years. He has written the suspense/thriller trilogy, The Sainted as well as numerous articles published in trade journals. Michael has also been a featured participant on many panel discussion and advertising industry workshops.

As amanuensis to Sir Telsunn Margraves, Michael Medico faithfully transcribes the texts as dictated and presents it to the reader as "Absolutely...Positively...Genuine...Real Fake News!"

ACKNOWLEDGEMENTS

In compiling the articles and features in "Absolutely...Positively...Genuine...Real Fake News", it never ceases to amaze me of the staggering number of sources associated with the various items included under each subject matter. Each and every fake news article is supposed to have an element of truth associated with it so, in most cases I consulted many of online sources available to provide information that can be used. In some cases I had to look over five or more sites to get the general consensus as well as the being able to peruse the varying details. It is then, and only then, I could take the words, opinions and ideas and write them in a way so that you will consider this to be a jaunty romp into the absurd as well as meaningful fake news. I want to gratefully acknowledge the following sources that have been invaluable in providing the information, inspiration and inculcation of stories collectively both real and imagined. *TM*

- Wikipedia www.wikipedia.org
- The Federalist http://thefederalist.com/2017/02/06/16-fake-news-stories-reporters-have-run-since-trump-won/
- https://www.thoughtco.com/top-joe-biden-gaffes-2734434
- www.infobarrel.com
- www.popularmechanics.com/...ridiculous-conspiracy-theories

- www.brainyquote.com/quotes/authors/h/henny_youngman.html
- http://www.funny2.com/henny.htm
- http://www.searchquotes.com/search/Stupid_Joe_Biden/2/
- https://www.thoughtco.com/funniest-joe-biden-quotes-and-gaffes-2734432
- http://www.freelang.net/online/mohawk.php
- https://www.stanford.edu/
- http://www.breitbart.com
- www.viralworld.net/21-celebs-support-black-lives-matter
- https://www.splcenter.org/hate-map
- https://www.inspiringquotes.us/author/9417-maxine-waters/page:2
- http://www.newsmax.com
- Lyrics to American Idiot© by Greenday - http://www.songlyrics.com/green day/american-idiot-lyrics/
- http://www.greenday.com/
- http://www.foxnews.com/politics/2017/08/24/nancy-pelosis-father-helped-dedicate-confederate-monument.html
- http://www.foxnews.com/politics/2017/08/24/nancy-pelosis-father-helped-dedicate-confederate-monument.html
- https://images.search.yahoo.com/search/images
- http://www.ranker.com/
- http://www.wnd.com/2017/09/ecosexual-professor-wants-you-to-have-sex-with-earth/
- http://www.howtallis.org/donald-trump-height-weight-shoe-size/
- https://www.aol.com/article/news/2017/08/14/ana-navarro-calls-trump-unfit-to-be-human-over-his-initial-cha/23077664/
- https://www.dailykos.com/stories/2017/6/29/1676457/-Ana-Navarro-on-Trump-He-s-Mean-Nasty-He-Is-Never-Going-To-Pivot-Republicans-Stop-Enabling-Him
- ABC News
- https://www.rushlimbaugh.com/

- https://www.campusreform.org/
- https://hotair.com/archives/2017/09/11/cable-news-sends-political-analysts-eye-storm/?utm_source=hadaily&utm_medium=email&utm_campaign=nl
- http://www.dailywire.com/news/20893/report-canada-deported-hundreds-refugees-and-emily-zanotti
- http://www.businessinsider.com/justin-trudeau-says-refugees-are-welcome-in-canada-2017-1
- https://www.mrctv.org/blog/viral-facebook®_®-post-claims-trump-created-hurricane-irma-kill-blacks-and-hispanics
- https://translate.google.com/#auto/fr/home%20is%20where%20the%20heart%20is
- https://www.inquisitr.com/3991991/trumps-unhinged-behavior-could-be-due-to-untreated-syphilis-expert-claims/
- https://medium.com/the-fifth-estate/an-interview-with-dr-john-gartner-we-have-a-duty-to-warn-the-world-about-donald-trump-e1b54223c913
- www.change.org
- https://www.celebritynetworth.com/
- https://images.search.yahoo.com/search/images
- http://dailysignal.com/2014/10/22/top-6-examples-wasteful-government-spending-wastebook-2014/
- https://www.cnsnews.com/mrctv-blog/curtis-kalin
- http://freebeacon.com/issues/mccain-identifies-1-1-billion-in-wasteful-spending/
- https://investigaterussia.org
- http://www.celebzen.com
- http://www.wtfceleb.com
- http://deadline.com/2017/09/lawrence-odonnell-sorry-tirade-rant-leaked-video-1202174248/

- http://insider.foxnews.com/2016/12/30/barack-obama-vacation-travel-costs-eight-year-term-96-million
- http://www.washingtonexaminer.com/more-mainstream-media-mess-ups-the-muslim-olympian-detained-because-of-president-trumps-travel-ban-was-detained-under-obama/article/2614645
- http://www.telegraph.co.uk/news/2017/09/01/kim-kardashian-four-year-old-daughter-could-do-better-job-donald/
- http://www.dailywire.com/news/21288/college-student-poll-it-ok-use-violence-shut-down-james-barrett
- http://www.mrc.org/articles/antarctica-not-melting-ice-levels-record-high
- https://www.cnbc.com/2016/12/30/read-all-about-it-the-biggest-fake-news-stories-of-2016.html
- http://www.dailywire.com/news/9767/9-things-you-need-know-about-climate-change-hoax-aaron-bandler
- http://www.theblaze.com/contributions/8-highly-inconvenient-facts-for-al-gore-10-years-after-his-infamous-movie/
- http://www.newsobserver.com/news/local/education/article99669487.html
- http://theweek.com/speedreads/732394/who-under-fire-making-zimbabwes-robert-mugabe-goodwill-ambassador
- http://www.funny-quotes-life.com/by/rahm-emanuel/
- https://www.vice.com/en_uk/article/43nddm/the-fake-melania-conspiracy-theory-is-toxic-cynical-spam
- http://www.liberalamerica.org/2016/05/15/ireland-is-seriously-accepting-trump-refugees-from-the-u-s-heres-why/
- https://www.usnews.com/news/national-news/articles/2017-02-02/neil-gorsuch-founded-fascism-forever-club-report-says
- https://www.newsbusters.org/blogs/nb/tim-graham/2017/01/28/CNN®s-fake-ratings-news-pr-team-tweets-CNN®-tied-fox-news-inauguration
- http://www.cracked.com/article_19789_5-clearly-fake-news-stories-that-fooled-media.html
- https://www.ranker.com/

- http://www.publiusforum.com/2010/07/23/top-ten-most-left-biased-american-journalists-1-helen-thomas-upiindependent/
- http://medialifemagazine.com/this-weeks-cable-ratings/
- https://pjmedia.com/trending/2017/02/13/fake-news-media-reports-that-muslim-olympian-was-detained-because-of-trumps-travel-ban/
- https://warsclerotic.com/2017/02/02/fake-news-iraqi-woman-killed-by-trump-died-days-before-travel-ban/
- www.CNN®.com
- https://www.counterpunch.org/2017/02/22/yes-real-donald-trump-is-a-muslim/
- http://www.npr.org/2016/03/01/468185698/understanding-the-clintons-popularity-with-black-voters and http://www.npr.org/people/2101289/nina-totenberg
- http://www.tvguide.com/news/jersey-shore-dictionary-1014029/ and http://www.nydailynews.com/entertainment/tv/best-jersey-shore-slang-premiere-anniversary-article-1.2896234
- https://www.snopes.com/sexual-assault-pre-existing/
- https://www.washingtonpost.com/news/fact-checker/wp/2014/05/01/one-in-five-women-in-college-sexually-assaulted-the-source-of-this-statistic/?utm_term=.bb47af1a5904
- http://www.breitbart.com/big-government/2017/02/01/fake-news-man-claimed-mom-died-due-trump-ban-lied/
- https://www.therussophile.org/?s=Yes%2C+Real+Donald+Trump+is+a+Muslim%21
- http://www.foxnews.com/politics/2016/06/22/anatomy-terror-threat-files-shed-light-on-nature-extent-plots-in-us.html
- https://www.snopes.com/terrorist-attacks-entry-restriction/
- http://www.bmj.com/content/339/bmj.b5261
- http://time.com/3222543/wage-pay-gap-myth-feminism/
- http://www.breitbart.com/london/2016/04/04/exposed-molenbeek-far-right-hit-run-actually-muslim-muslim-attack/

- https://ivn.us/2016/11/21/25-fake-news-stories-mainstream-media/
- https://www.psychologytoday.com/blog/wired-success/201011/why-people-get-depressed-christmas
- www.webmd.com
- http://www.searchquotes.com/quotes/author/Lindsay_Lohan/
- http://www.breitbart.com/big-government/2016/08/09/assassinate-feminist-group-trump-threatened-hillary-shes-woman/
- https://www.dailywire.com/news/28975/stephen-colberts-mean-spirited-easter-animated-paul-bois © Copyright 2018, The Daily Wire
- http://www.breitbart.com/big-journalism/2016/11/22/12-fake-news-stories-from-the-mainstream-media/
- https://townhall.com/columnists/johnhawkins/2016/12/10/the-7-worst-examples-of-fake-news-from-the-mainstream-media-n2257896
- https://www.cbsnews.com/news/stephen-glass-i-lied-for-esteem-07-05-2003/
- http://thekitchencabinet.us/harry-reids-5-lobbyist-sons/
- http://24ahead.com/blog/archives/005714.html
- https://www.judicialwatch.org/blog/2015/03/corruption-scandals-led-to-harry-reids-abrupt-retirement/
- https://www.reuters.com/article/us-usa-china-reid-solar/u-s-senator-reid-son-combine-for-china-firms-desert-plant-idUSBRE87U06D20120831
- https://www.washingtonpost.com/archive/politics/1980/09/28/jimmys-world/605f237a-7330-4a69-8433-b6da4c519120/?utm_term=.41286fea36c0
- http://www.foxnews.com/politics/2017/09/15/espn-botched-hosts-racial-attack-on-trump-after-weighing-tougher-penalties.html
- https://images.search.yahoo.com/search/images;_ylt=AwrB8pvql-RlaE18APHqJzbkF?p=kennedy+center+for+performing+arts&fr=yfp-t-s&imgl=fmsuc&fr2=p%3As%2Cv%3Ai
- http://www.theblaze.com/contributions/harry-reid-is-the-worst-living-human-being-on-the-planet

- http://www.searchquotes.com/search/Fake_News/1/popular/
- https://www.goodreads.com/quotes/tag/fake-news
- http://www.cracked.com/article_17318_7-clearly-fake-news-stories-that-fooled-mainstream-media.html
- www.snopes.com/fact-check/george-soros-bring-down-us
- https://pixabay.com/en/blog/posts/public-domain-images-what-is-allowed-and-what-is-4/
- https://www.makeuseof.com/tag/concerned-copyright-guide-legally-using-images-web/
- https://www.shutterstock.com
- http://www.searchquotes.com/quotation/White_people_scare_the_crap_out_of_me..._I_have_never_been_attacked_by_a_black_person%2C_never_been_ev/16977/#ixzz5IywpHZ7S
- http://www.thewizardofoz.warnerbros.com/#/
- https://www.teenvogue.com/ ©2018 Conde Nast
- https://www.CNN®.com/ © 2018 Cable News Network® Turner Broadcasting System, Inc. All Rights Reserved.
- https://abc.go.com/shows/the-view
- https://newrepublic.com/ Copyright 2018 © The New Republic. All rights reserved.
- https://www.wsj.com/ Copyright ©2018 Dow Jones & Company, Inc. All Rights Reserved
- https://www.neimanmarcus.com/ ©2018 Neiman Marcus
- https://www.drphil.com/ Copyright ® 2018 Peteski Productions, Inc. ALL RIGHTS RESERVED
- http://www.cracked.com/ Copyright © 205 – 2018 Cracked Magazine
- https://weareUltraviolet.org/ ©2018 Ultraviolet
- https://www.buzzfeed.com/about
- https://www.youtube.com © 2018 YouTube, LLC
- © 2018 CNBC LLC. All Rights Reserved. **A Division of NBCUniversal**
- © 2018 FOX News Network LLC

A special thank you to Dan at DT Creative, for his thoughts, comments, advice, design and general superior creativity.

Another very special thank you to Joan, my conscience and devoted editor.

And a special thank you to the reader for your interest in, and support of, Fake News and please be assured that as long as there is news there will always be Absolutely...Positively...Genuine...Real Fake News.

Gratefully,

Telsunn Margraves

Sir Telsunn Margraves
DD, DCL, DM, DLitt, DSc, DMus

The title *Absolutely, Positively, Genuine, Real FAKE NEWS* is exactly what it is, *FAKE NEWS* and a work of fiction. All excerpts, articles, incidents, dialogue, even Kim Jong Un's wedding, are completely fictitious. As you can imagine, all characters, with the exception of some celebrities, politicians, football players and well-known figures from history and the world of entertainment, are products of the author's imagination and are not to be construed as real. Certain real-life celebrities, famous personages, personalities and luminaries appear, the situations, incidents, and dialogues concerning those persons are entirely fictional. They are not intended to depict actual events or to change the entirely fictional nature of the work. In all other respects, any resemblance to actual persons, living or dead, events, or locales is entirely coincidental.